LIBERATED

LIBERATED

ELLE CHARLES

LIBERATED

Copyright © Elle Charles 2015

Cover design by Rachelle Gould-Harris of Designs by Rachelle
https://www.designsbyrachelle.com

For all enquiries, please email: elle@ellecharles.com
www.ellecharles.com

ISBN: 978-1-69-716684-2

First publication: 14 August 2015

First Edition
Version 1.5
December 2019

Contents

Chapter 1

BROKEN.

THAT'S THE way my body feels. Broken beyond repair.

Pain.

That's what is currently consuming me. It's pain I can't even begin to describe – the breaking of my heart.

The motorway lights flash by outside. I can barely open my eyes in my semi-conscious condition, but still, they blind me intermittently; penetrating my minimal sight violently, as the car moves faster and faster into the unknown.

Every inch of my body feels battered and sore. Thinking back to what has happened, time is void; it could have been yesterday, it could have been last week. I don't know how fast time has passed by.

All I know is, I remember.

Invisible chains cut into my skin, and blood drips down my wrists. Inside my mind, I'm fighting against *him*, against death. Thrashing out as much as I can, yet bizarrely, he isn't stopping me. Maybe because he knows I can never win.

And therein lies the veracity; he's always held the power.

The truth is unimaginable, ripping through my body, punishing everything in its wake. Finally killing off the part of me that is still able to feel.

The car door slamming jolts my hearing, and heavy feet grow distant. Only the sounds of other vehicles, the laughs of children, and admonishment of parents, fill the emptiness. I sob uncontrollably, unsure if anyone can actually hear me, or if it's just a mental manifestation taking me back to the place I fear I'm sentenced to exist in until the end of my days.

Long minutes pass by until the door opens, and unexpectedly, a soft hand comes over my face.

"Sleep. I promise I'll take good care of you," Jeremy says soothingly. I shudder ominously - one might ask what his definition of good care is. Pushing the horrific thought aside, soft fabric is pulled over me. His hand grazes a fraction of exposed flesh, leaving an icy chill in its wake.

Yawning, a predictable tiredness ensues once more, but I know I

1

can't stay awake. My eyes flutter shut, and again, I'm back in the impenetrable darkness I know I shall never be able to escape from.

Waking slowly, the wipers squeak across the windscreen intermittently, working hard against the rain descending the heavens. I gaze up at the dusky street outside, not exactly sure where we are. My body wouldn't allow me to do anything other than sleep after we left the M25.

Turning to the front, I'm alone. Rubbing my eyes and looking around, Jeremy is nowhere in sight. Considering the events that have led us here, it is extremely fucking disturbing he can just leave me like this. Especially when I'm in no fit state to fight back - not that I ever could.

Dragging the cover aside, I stretch, wincing under the soreness of my skin as the tattered shirt and dried blood pull apart at my chest. Shuffling over the back seat and opening the door, a crack of thunder and lightning illuminates the horizon beautifully. Breathing in, that damp, distinctive smell penetrates my nostrils, while the rain continues to bounce off the pavements, soaking me through. I relish it, but a part of me shall never be clean.

"What the hell are you doing?"

Jeremy comes running towards me, already halfway out of his jacket. Placing it over my shoulders, he zips it up. I shake inconspicuously, unable to control the burn flaring up, as he holds me and moves to the car boot. Lifting out a few large bags, he lets me go, and guides us towards the building.

Stepping inside, the delightful aroma of bleach and disinfectant clears my foggy head instantly, while the three small flights of stairs are murder on my stiff, sore thighs.

Standing behind him, he unlocks a door and pushes it back. Passing me a holdall, I drag it since I'm unable to carry much more than my own body weight right now.

Abandoning it in the living room, I draw back the curtains. Insurmountable dusk seems to be the decoration of choice. Not that I'm bothered, because this bolthole will save whatever is still intact of my dignity and pride.

And my broken, bleeding heart.

"It's not much," Jeremy says behind me.

"Well, I wasn't expecting Buckingham Palace. Not even the Travelodge," I mutter under my breath. With a defeated sigh, he passes me my bag and a supermarket carrier.

"I stopped while you were asleep. I picked up some new clothes, a few toiletries, towels, and some items to clean up..." His eyes drop, and I instinctively touch my chest. The tenderness is brutal, punishing my resolve to stay strong.

Too late.

I drop my head; I don't want him to witness my decline. A part of me wants to wallow in solitary confinement, hiding away where I cannot be found.

"Look, get settled in. The bathroom and bedroom are through there," he says, jerking his chin. "I'll be back in a few hours. Stuff to do." Stroking my cheek tenderly, I pull back.

"Jeremy?"

"Make sure you lock the door and remove the key. I don't fancy sleeping in the car."

"Sorry?" I shake my head. He drops a phone on the sofa, and then he's gone.

Doing as requested and locking myself in, he's out of his goddamn mind if he thinks we're going to be playing house together.

No fucking way.

With a body that feels groggy and like lead, I pick up the towels and toiletries. Moving slowly down the landing, I pull the cord, illuminating the small bathroom. Like everything else I've seen so far, again it's also in need of cleaning.

Rinsing and running the bath, I carefully strip off the remnants of my torn clothing and stuff them into the carrier, ready to be incinerated at the first opportunity. Standing naked, brushing my teeth, I'm mesmerised by the painful truth that now partially covers my chest. Under the stark light, there is nowhere to hide. It looks like I have taken a red marker and drawn on myself. In time they will fade, but I will still feel them.

Sadly, feeling means I will also remember. And that is the one thing I know I can't make myself forget. This time, I need to remember, because remembering will ensure I survive.

Turning off the taps, I tentatively lower my foot in first. Bracing my hands on the sides, I sink deeper. The heat fires my skin as it passes over my thighs, covering my stomach. Hissing a little, I force myself to continue. The steam billows up, fogging the small room, and I come over lightheaded.

Lying back, needing to relax and momentarily forget, the hot water envelops my back, before lapping over my front. I cry out the instant the first scar is inadvertently cleaned. The raw sensation is indescribable. Searing pain culminates in the open wounds, and I yank out the plug and reach up to turn the shower on. The hollow sound of water draining, accompanied by the falling patter, does nothing to quell my tears. Hugging my knees, watching the water level drop, I shiver constantly.

Reaching over the bath, I fumble around for the shampoo and body wash on the floor. Inhaling deeply, I mentally disengage as my soapy hand reaches my chest. Holding in the gasp, the chemical irritates, but it's an unavoidable task. It's either suffer or become infected. I bid myself to tolerate it, because I've suffered far worse in the last forty-eight hours.

This is the lesser of two evils.

Getting to my feet, I wash carefully, ensuring I don't scratch or rub too hard on my new injuries. Everywhere else, however, is a different story, as I scrub as hard as I can, over my arms, my legs, between them. Ridding myself of the monstrous touch through saturation.

As I lather my hair and tip my head back, my memory is assaulted by all the times Sloan has held me. Pressing my forehead to the tiles, I really know how to destroy myself when I think I'm doing something for the best.

Turning around, I slide down and curl up. With my arms around my head, resting on my knees, the annihilation of my sanity begins. My cries fill the silence, partially concealed by the falling water pooling at my feet. Unable to control the pain consuming me, I don't try to fight it. Finally, I allow it to flow freely.

The sound of banging seeps into my psyche, while water floods my mouth and distorts my vision. Half-awake, I lift my head up. The shower is still running, warming me a little, and pruning my skin severely. I grip the sides the same moment someone comes rushing inside. The curtain is ripped back, and I stare as Jeremy quickly shuts off the water. He throws a couple of towels over me, covering the last shred of salvageable dignity I still have left.

Lifting me out, he wraps the fabric tight and sits us on the floor, soaking himself in the process. Cradling me in his arms, I shake incessantly, not from being cold, but because his skin is touching mine. He traces down the side of my face, slides back my wet hair, and wraps a towel around my head. No words are spoken as I reminisce on joyous days and joyless nights of late.

"Stay strong, Kara. He needs you," he whispers. "Don't give up."

"I can't, Jeremy. I have nothing left to give."

Resting my head on his shoulder, my flame finally dies out.

A slow throbbing bleeds through the haze lifting from my sub-conscience. Shuffling slightly, pain ripples through my core, intoxicating my nerve endings, and I flinch as the rough sheet rubs against my sore skin. I silently pray for the pain to subside and allow me an ounce of comfort. Rest evades me, but I know I can't sleep. Not because I have technically slept enough, but because when I do, I see evil.

Evil is real.

It has a face.

It has a name.

And its name is Deacon Black.

A lone tear falls, but I don't bother to wipe it away. It's already drying and staining my cheek - a reminder of how it came to be. In the muted light of the room, I'm taken back to the final torturous moments. Ones I desperately want to forget, but never will. I don't have the luxury of time or denial to help me through now. The truth is, my world is now a darker place than it was before. These last few days, the veil has finally been ripped from my eyes again.

Adjusting, Jeremy is slouched uncomfortably on the floor. His usually brooding features look pained. Even in his sleep he is suffering, praying for his precious redemption that he wants so badly.

The mattress springs creak under my movement. Gradually waking, his frown decreases. Drawing back, I can still identify the devastation he's hopelessly concealing. Stupidly, for a split second, I thought I could forget what had happened in that hate-filled place, but that can never be. Staring at the scar that now ruins his handsome looks, I know that my suffering is now his, just like it is Sloan's. He will share the pain with me forever. It's another strand of life's twisted rope that joins me to another in a way that is unimaginable.

"How are you feeling?"

My mouth is dry and scratchy, and my head is pounding. "Fine," I lie.

He rolls his eyes. "I'll get you some water."

Waiting for him to return, I lift up the thin sheet and glance down. As well as my chest and stomach, there are dark welts at the top of my legs. Lifting my arms to assist the blood flow, the old scar tissue over my wrists is now red again. This really isn't shocking; I knew when Deacon had me chained up I would receive further, permanent souvenirs.

Forcing myself upright, I yank the duvet over my scantily covered body. Clearly, Jeremy has cleaned me up. And judging by the smell of TCP emanating, he has also tendered my wounds. Not to mention, I'm just in my underwear, which means he has not only dressed me, but he's dried me, too.

Bizarrely, I'm not embarrassed that he's seen me naked, my only thought is that Sloan won't be happy if he ever finds out.

My heart beats unrelentingly until Jeremy strides back in and flicks on the lamp. The room brightens, and just like everywhere else, it's in serious need of scrubbing. Considering my susceptible injuries, I pray the sheets are clean. He puts down a pair of jogging pants and a long-sleeved t-shirt.

I reach for the water he has brought in, and swallow down as much as I can. My insides feel severely dehydrated, and the confirmation churns loudly in my stomach.

"Think you can manage something to eat?" he asks, and I nod, because I need something right now. He starts to reach over, but stops instantly when I shift back. The psychological discomfort of being touched is rearing its ugly head again. Watching his eyes downshift, I glance down my body.

He sighs, resigned. "Yes, Kara, I carried you from the bathroom. I dried you and dressed you. You're not the first woman I've seen naked." He smiles. It isn't salacious or untoward; it's one to break the tension between us.

"Sloan-"

"Will rip my heart out with a very blunt instrument. But I'm sure he would do far worse if I allowed you to freeze to death."

"I don't really remember much after you picked me out of the bath," I say honestly.

For the first time, I don't have to lie about not remembering. Although I know it's too early to believe that will last. He nods before reaching out for my hand again, and I acquiesce and allow him to touch me. The raw sensation burns, and I whimper when he tightens his hold. Flipping over my wrist, he studies the scars, both old and new, uncomfortably. He furrows his brows; a distinct concealment of an unknown truth. I can't bring myself to ask, and for once, I want to be left in the dark. Floundering, lost, never to be found.

"This might be too soon, but what you are planning to do?"

"Where are we?" I ask, feeling far too exposed. Picking up the t-shirt, he turns around.

"Yorkshire," he replies.

I swing my legs over the bed and pull on the jogging pants. "I'm decent," I confirm moments later. "Does Deacon have any connections here?"

He shakes his head. "Not that I'm aware of, but that's just speculation," he mumbles. "Regardless, we're too close to Manchester for comfort, though. Here, I had a friend sort you out some stuff. ID, documents, work history, things like that." I pick up the envelope he has dropped on the bed.

"Where are you staying?" I query, seeing his stocking feet.

His silence is deafening, then he opens his mouth. "I'll go make you some soup or something."

"I'm not hungry."

He gives me a glare that could slay me. He's well aware I'm being unduly rude in an attempt to get him to leave. I purposely look around the room, making a mental note of the things I will need to make this place liveable.

"I'm not gonna argue with you. I don't give a shit what you want, but I won't abandon you." I step after him. "Get settled in, I've got a couple of things to do. I'll be back tomorrow," he states firmly, walking towards the door.

"Don't bother," I say with a laugh, which dies the movement it leaves my lips. "I mean it."

"Kara…" His jaw hardens, and the fresh scar moves under his anger, revealing his infuriation at my insolence.

"What did you expect? That I would willingly live with the man who tied me down and let his best friend rape me?"

He snaps his head up in shock. "That's not fucking fair!"

"No, it really isn't. It isn't fair that I've spent nearly a decade terrified of living, because of a life I so desperately wanted to push back into the confines of hell. It also isn't fair that I finally had it all, and that bastard clawed it away from me again. You're completely right, Jeremy; it's not fucking fair!"

Moving towards the window, I stare out, running my finger down the glass.

"When you walk out of here, I want you to abandon me. I want you to forget that I ever existed and never look back. It's the only way."

A rustling behind me prompts me to turn. Coming face to face with him, only a few inches separate us.

"Fine, but hear this, you're not fifteen anymore, Kara. They can't take you into care now. You do what you have to, but you promise me something."

I sigh and shake my head. "I know what you want me to say, but I can't give you that."

"Tough shit, promise me."

The words float around my head. I need to say them in a way that will convince him of my sincerity. "I promise." I drop my eyes to the floor, because they will give me away if he looks into them and sees the truth.

His sarcastic snort fills the room. "You say it; you better fucking mean it. Say it, Kara!"

Raising my head defiantly, I look straight into his eyes. "I promise I'll return to him."

And eventually, I shall, because he is my true home.

Somewhat placated, whether he believes me or not, he quickly moves towards the door.

"There's money in the bag and the keys for the Golf outside. Make sure you keep that phone with you at all times, there might come a time when you need it; the car, too. Understand?" Tightening his hold on the architrave, he glares. "One last thing? Whether you like it or not, I'll be in your life until the day you die. I want redemption, and if that means I have to follow you to those pearly white fucking gates in years to come, then so be it."

The door slams shut, and I stare out the window. Eventually, he stalks across the street, climbs into his car, and finally drives away.

Watching the red lights disappear into the night, I realise this is my new reality, and I may never be free. Pressing my head to the glass, my tears fall steadily.

I was right; love does hurt.

Fact.

And my body of pain is once again proof of it.

Chapter 2

TAPPING MY PEN annoyingly, I stare at the time on the screen. It has been ten minutes since I was last shouted at. Or, as Sophie would put it, getting an absolute bollocking.

Waiting for the next irate caller, I glance over the floor. Resting my chin on my hand, I people-watch.

"Hey!" Melissa, a woman who I did my training with, flops down at the next desk in the empty pod of five. "I don't know what's worse, being screamed at or waiting to be screamed at."

I laugh, because if there is anything here that carries a certain element of surprise, it's that.

"I thought it was just me," I grumble, picking up a magazine.

From the corner of my eye, I can see her fidget; her intrigue growing. I know what's coming, and I sigh discreetly into the pages, as I try to concoct another amazing story. She thinks I'm a single girl living the Life of Riley. She couldn't be further from the truth if she tried.

As a young mother, she seems to want to live vicariously through everyone else. I can't imagine anyone wanting to do that with my life. She's nice enough, but after a while, it gets tired. *I* get tired of lying to someone who just wants to be my friend, but God knows friends aren't safe with me. And because of that, I now keep everyone at a distance.

"Good weekend?" she asks.

I stare at the page with disinterest. If she has picked up on my repulsion of chit-chat and contact in the time we have been working together, she hasn't voiced it.

"Yeah, it was great. Busy," I lie. "You?"

"Fabulous! Matt and I took Daniel to the farm. He loves the animals..." Her voice trails off, and I nod intermittently. I appreciate it's cruel, but honestly, after all these months, I'm jealous. Not of her, but the fact that someone cherishes her, the same way someone had once cherished me.

The way he may never will again.

"The phones are down but keep the noise to a minimum!" My team leader huffs out, looking thoroughly pleased. The collective cheering indicates she's not the only one thankful of this little reprieve – however long it should last.

Yep, I'm now officially that person I hate. The one who calls you and asks if you would like a new phone. The one who tells you they can give you a better utility deal. The one you always hang up on, because if you did want any of those things, you would've called them yourself.

For the last four months, I've been working in a call centre, eight until four, Monday to Friday. I always wondered what these places are like and swore I would never work in one. But considering I now exist under a shroud of secrecy, and all my identity documents are impeccable counterfeits - thank you Jeremy James' mysterious forger - beggars cannot be choosers.

When I interviewed for the job, after conceding that I couldn't hide away indefinitely - or make my savings magically stretch out - I was surprised. Not only when they didn't question my dodgy CV and equally dodgy ID, but when they said I could start on the next induction – two days later. It isn't easy, but it's highly convenient. It's convenient, because I get left alone. No one really talks to me, which means no one bothers me. But above all that, it doesn't require any type of physical contact, and that alone is priceless.

For me, there is definitely an 'I' in team.

Ten silent minutes later, I put the phone on break. This is one of the things I absolutely loathe - everything is monitored. From how long it takes to answer and deal with a call, to how long, down to the last second, you take for lunch. Even toilet breaks are timed.

Knowing I only have minutes, I grab my bag. Pressing the button on the vending machine, my phone buzzes in my handbag. These days, I take it everywhere with me, always on vibrate. There might come a time when I need it. I shake my head at Jeremy's last words echoing inside. But regardless, he's right. It isn't a case of might, it's when. And when the day of reckoning finally comes to pass, is anyone's guess.

But it's coming. Of that fact, I shall never be ignorant.

"Want anything from the canteen?" Melissa asks, popping her head around the door.

"No, thanks. I'll bring you a fresh tea," I reply, sounding like Marie. As the door closes, I bring my hand to my chest, wondering what she might be doing right now. Will she be doing this, making coffee for her and Nicki? Or will she be stood, hand on her heart, thinking of the missing link in her life, the same way I currently am? Wiping the solitary tear, I take a breath, pick up the plastic cups and leave the room.

Slipping my headset on, I pretend to concentrate on the magazine in front of me for the next hour or so.

"*Emma?*"

The familiar name ripples around my head as I close the magazine. My phone vibrates and my eyes narrow, when a number flashes up that I don't recognise.

"*Emma?*"

The movement stops, and I hold my breath, waiting for the message alert. With my concentration fully fixed on my mobile, I shriek when a hand flies down in front of my face. Instinctively, I lurch back, avoiding any sort of contact. That is another prevalent thing that has returned with a vengeance; the absolute aversion of being touched – by anyone.

"Sorry, I didn't hear you!" I rasp out, attempting to calm myself.

"I was calling you. I'm going for lunch, want anything?" Melissa asks.

"No, thank you."

She smiles, but it's guarded, like she knows I'm not really Emma. Unfortunately, my new name is still just as foreign to me as my new appearance. Remembering back to when I was Kara Dawson, it took me months to get used to it. But I did then, and I shall again.

Fed up and bored, I grab my lunch and handbag. Outside, I sit in a quiet spot. Although I'm far enough away from the smokers, I'm still close enough that it will linger on me. Pulling out my ham and cheese, I realise some things will never change - I still have the same thing day in, day out.

Retrieving my voicemail, I wait anxiously, wondering what the hell he wants, since no one else has this number. It's safe to say I still don't entirely trust him. It doesn't matter that he saved me, because he was still there, assisting in killing off the final part of me that had finally found trust again. He asked for redemption, but can I really forgive him for leaving me with the devil himself twice? Honestly, I don't know. I know the day when I'm forced to, will be the day we will see where his real loyalties lie.

"Call me back. It's important." He sounds concerned; he doesn't need to be. These last few months I've been doing just fine on my own. His forged documents have worked well for me. So well, in fact, they have procured me a job, one that has been valuable in making sure my head remains in relatively the right place.

Nibbling the sandwich, I debate what could possibly be so important that he has to do this to me, considering I haven't heard a peep since he left. Taking a long swig of my water, I collect up my belongings and head to the nearest disabled toilet. Dropping the charade of not giving a shit, I turn the phone in my palm and hit call.

"Kara?" His deep tones flow into my eardrums.

"Hello, Jeremy. To what do I owe this dubious pleasure?" Screwing my face up, I'm being unnecessarily nasty again. I don't mean to be, but these days I just can't forget. I've tried. God knows, I've tried so fucking hard, but it's futile because I remember everything.

Everything.

"Kara, John called me-"

I stare up at the ceiling. "No, we're not having this conversation!"

"Kara-"

"No. I'm done with that life and all the pain it has brought me!"

"Listen, you stubborn fucking child!"

I seethe that he has the audacity to speak to me in such a way after the integral part he played in destroying my life.

Twice.

"Jeremy, what have you done? Does he know I'm here?" I do my best to calm the rage that is desperately trying to fight its way free. The silence is thick over the line, and I shout when he remains silent. "Just answer the question!"

"Yeah, he knows!"

"Goodbye, Jeremy. Don't call me ever again-"

"Ka-"

"-because I have nothing left to say to you!" I hang up and throw the handset, causing the back and battery to scatter in opposite directions. Sinking to the floor, I kick my foot against the door as I rock back and forth, losing all control.

Glancing at my watch, I quickly splash my face and pat it dry with a wad of paper towels. Fanning my hands in front of my eyes, I pray no one questions my newly distraught appearance.

Back at my desk, I shove everything into my drawer and slide on my headset.

"You better silence that before someone hears," Melissa nods at my drawer. Retrieving my ringing phone, I'm thoroughly unimpressed, and annoyed, that he's called back - numerous times for emphasis.

If there is one thing that he and Sloan have in common, it's their insistence.

Turning it off, I deliberately change the subject. "Nice lunch?"

She is about to answer, when she huffs and flips down the microphone. Gritting out the company greeting, she rolls her eyes and taps away on the keyboard.

I breathe out, bizarrely thankful we are back in business when a beep rings in my ears. It's a blessing really, considering I had finally managed to reach sinking point on the toilet floor.

"Good afternoon, Emma speaking."

The afternoon passes by quickly, and when I glance at the clock again, it's almost four. Shutting down the computer, Melissa follows me out. Pushing through the revolving doors, I inhale deeply. Even though I've been called every name under the sun this afternoon, at least it has taken my mind off what is waiting for me. Namely, Jeremy, and how many messages he has left in his wake and revival.

"I'll see you tomorrow," I say, as she waves goodbye and jogs over to her waiting fiancé. Kissing him at length, my heart physically hurts watching their display of affection.

She waves again as they drive past, and I clench my hands into fists in my pockets. It's fucking pathetic that I'm insanely jealous of a woman who has everything I so ardently want, but fear I may never have again.

Picking up my pace, I enter the car park ten minutes later. A burning sensation plays on the back of my neck, and I turn in a perfect circle. The car park, although full, is virtually empty of life.

"You okay, love?" An attendant ticketing a windscreen asks.

"I'm fine, thanks. Just thought I saw something," I mumble. He does a quick check, before continuing to issue fines.

Climbing into my car, I lock the doors and rest back. My lungs seize up when I see a dark grey Range Rover parked not too far away. I slam my hand on the wheel, because I need to stop this. I need to find a way to bury this forever. Except, I can't put my trust in what might be false security. Truthfully, I can't say I feel safe. These days, I don't really feel anything anymore.

Slotting the key into the ignition and driving off, I'm relieved when nothing seems to follow. Although the itchy burn on my neck is still comparable to a silent warning.

I stop at the supermarket and pick up a microwave meal and a bottle of wine, totally prepared to drown my sorrows again. I'm not normally a big drinker, but these days I'm finding the only way to escape this perpetual hell I'm forcing myself to live in, is to seek solace in a bottle seven nights a week. It has to stop, but I just don't know how to at the moment.

Pulling up into a space, a black Lexus is parked in the next one over. The past comes back to haunt me, remembering the day this all started again, when Sam unknowingly invited *him* into our home and back into my life.

I make my way up the stairs, but I'm stopped short by Jeremy, who is sat on the floor with his back against my door. I grip the bottle in my hand, absolutely furious he's doing this to me. I'm trying to move on, to get by, to claw back some sort of life for myself, where no one knows who I am or what atrocities have befallen me.

"Goodbye, Jeremy!" I hiss, nudging his leg with my foot.

"Kara, we need to talk," he says, getting to his feet.

"No, you need to leave, and I need to pour this down my neck and forget all the fucked-up reasons why I'm doing it!"

I unlock the door and open it a little, just enough to slide inside and pray he isn't quick enough to make it through. My plan is thwarted when he lodges the door open with his boot, refusing to leave.

"Fine! Come in, make yourself at home. Shall we talk about the good old days? The ones that include cable ties and metal chains and my begging for clemency?" I spit out, slamming the door shut.

He looks desolate, but I refuse to feel sympathy. I leave him weighing up his thoughts and enter the kitchen. Removing the meal from the cardboard sleeve, I stab at it repeatedly, unnecessarily, while my eyes threaten to reveal my current mental state. His hand comes around and lightly grabs my wrist.

"Don't fucking touch me!" I scream in his face, then collapse on the floor.

Picking me up, my fists beat against his chest as I finally allow the pain to eviscerate me. He gently strokes his hand over my head, and I grip his back, desperate to feel affection, irrespective of whether it comes from someone who has assisted in my personal obliteration.

My cries eventually subside into silence. When he is sure I have calmed down, he leans back, assessing me. I stare into his eyes, seeing someone equally as broken as I am, also being forced to tread the same path of perdition, hoping one day he will be exonerated, and his sins will be forgiven.

"Why did you do it?" I ask quietly, finally gaining the courage to unearth the reasons why he wronged me in such ways when I had never done anything to him.

He lets go completely and sighs, moving towards the living room. I follow behind, watching while he tries to figure out how to impart the truth at long last. Picking up the battered hoodie, he runs his hand over the uni logo.

"I was high at the time; an addict..." He stops. The shame in his voice is abundant and, as expected, he doesn't continue. But yet again, his partial confession has proved something that has always been a constant in my life. Drugs have destroyed me at every turn, in every shape of man. My parents, my friend, and finally, someone who could still be my enemy.

Turning back into the kitchen, I pick up the ready meal and throw it into the microwave. "Before I kick you out, tell me why you bothered coming over here. Obviously, it isn't to relive our debauched glory days and take a trip down bad memory lane with me."

"I think it's time you went home, Kara."

I let out a preposterous laugh. "I think you're still high! I'm never going back. To live with one foot in and one foot out, praying to whatever merciful God above that the bastard doesn't come after me again? Hope the next time we meet he just ends me quickly, before he marks me up like a goddamn piece of meat and leaves me for dead! I don't think so, Jeremy. I'm not stupid enough to allow history to go full circle for a third fucking time!"

"You need to see Sam, Kara. You might not get another chance. She's still showing no signs of recovery. I'm sorry, but John and Doc thought you should know."

Turning around, I squeeze my eyes, coming to terms that she is finally withering away. I did this to her. It's obvious looking back that Deacon only wanted her to get to me. It isn't fantasy; it's fact. One that I didn't see until it was too late. She may have abetted in his assault on me, but I have assisted in her inevitable demise.

The microwave pings and I pull out the ready meal, blowing my scorched fingers. "Still not good enough," I mutter. "It's not like she would even know if I was there or not." My mind rambles, remembering our childhood. The promises we made to always be there for each other. Yet another promise I'm now breaking. My only consolation is that she broke it long before I did.

"Well, what about Marie, she's heartbroken. John can't get through to her. She's here, but not really."

I spin around, attempting to show conviction in my decision to move hundreds of miles away and hurt those I love.

"And yet again, Jeremy, it's still not good enough!" I slam my fist on the worktop. "Why are you really here?" Except, I already know the answer.

Sloan.

"Why do you think?" He rests against the wall. "He's not doing well. Doc has got him on anti-depressants, apparently."

My heart instantly breaks. "Why are you doing this to me?" I ask tearfully.

"Because there's a chance the day you finally do go back, he might not be the man you left behind. I know; I spent years hooked on anything I could get my hands on after…" he quietens, and I realise he's talking about his part in the removal of my innocence. "Look, I hear what you're saying, but you made me a promise, remember?"

I swipe my hand over my eyes, trying to hide the fact his words have breached the last remaining intact piece of my heart that has Sloan's name scrawled all over it.

"I can't go back there!"

"Tell me why? And you better fucking make it good enough!" he hisses, throwing my words back in my face, making me feel guilty, when the only thing I have to feel remorseful for is trying to preserve what little life I still have left.

"He's not safe if I'm there." I look down, because he will see right through me.

"Is that the best you've got? All I'm hearing are pitiful excuses of a frightened little girl. And you have every right to be, but that isn't good enough, and you know it."

I rip open the top of my blouse, clenching the material in my fists. "Because why would he still fucking want this? I'm damaged, Jeremy. That son of a bitch has scarred me in ways I'll never get rid of. Do you know what it's like to be repulsed by your own reflection? Do you?"

His jaw tenses. Yes, he knows exactly what it's like, and therein lies his answer.

"If I can barely look at me, how the hell is he going to?"

He sighs loudly and turns. Walking towards the door, he halts. "He'll see past the scars; the same way he did the first time. He loves you with such passion, that you being away from him will eventually kill him. Just consider what I've said. I know you'll make the right decision."

And with those words hanging thickly in the air, the door closes behind him. I rush to it, lock the bolts, and rest my head against the wood.

Padding back into the kitchen, I throw the meal back into the microwave and take a long swallow of wine. Running my fingers over my chest, I sob.

Jeremy's double confession has halted my train of thought and the direction in which I was headed. I know I shall go back to London, it's a given. There has never been any doubt in my mind it would be an eventuality.

Heading into the bedroom, I drag the Manchester University sweater with me and cocoon myself in it, knowing my journey south will be upon me sooner rather than later.

Jeremy's words, and Sloan's supposed mental state, have just validated it.

Chapter 3

"I LOVE YOU."

The room falls into blackness around me, and I smile as he reaches around and hooks my leg over his hip. A simple gesture, one he likes to act upon constantly. It's a need to feel closer, to connect, to become one. Running my hands over the contours of his back, he drags those incredible lips down the curve of my neck, delicately nipping at my collarbone, before soothing it with a gentle kiss.

"Beautiful," he murmurs, his eyes dark and meaningful, transposing his verbal declaration when there really is no need.

Rolling us into the middle of the bed, I sit astride him, admiring my idea of perfection. With a slight, but sudden movement, he groans. The sound of it fills the room, and I bring my head towards him, leaning down painfully slow. Closing my eyes, I press my mouth to his, enjoying the brush of softness and moisture as he sucks in my bottom lip.

"We're gonna play a little game, and I'm gonna win!"

I baulk as the memory tumbles around my head, and the sneer of the last word resounds continuously. Opening my eyes, the world is black.

Deacon Black.

"You ready?"

I cry out, struggling in his death grip. He laughs manically as I thrust out my arms, until he clasps my slender wrists together and fixes them with cable ties, then finally, chains.

"Please!" I beg, but it's no use. I've been here before; many times, in many ways. On a bed, up against a wall, fighting for my life and my dignity, realising they are tainted and already gone.

My body lurches sideways, and I kick out my legs, determined to fight him, irrespective of how futile and ridiculous it is inside my own head. He smothers my small body under his and drags my arms up to the headboard. The sound of metal scraping against the wood is the final assault on my hearing, before he pulls out a knife...

I vault upright the same moment the cheap, plastic alarm clock begins to ring shrilly. Snatching it up, I smash it back down until the infernal racket ceases. My shallow, terrified breathing, is heightened by the deathly silence.

Lately, it seems the nightmares of my childhood have been replaced by those of last year. The good and the amazing, and the bad and the downright torturous. Evidently, Jeremy's revelation is playing havoc with my sub-conscience. Although, if I'm honest, deep in my heart, I regret the choices I have made. At the time, when I was neither seeing nor thinking straight - not of anything other than what I had just lived through - those choices were the right ones. Except, all I've done is transition myself from one perpetual hell directly into another.

And it's time I shall never get back.

Time; it's such a beautiful thing to have. Unfortunately, mine is borrowed. Every soul-destroying nightmare confirms it, because I'm reliving it daily, unable to sleep because two men from both ends of the spectrum invade nightly, in ways I cannot control.

Unable to suppress my fear, I press my head further into the pillow. I stare up at the ceiling with a mind full to capacity, and a heart hollow from the barely existent life I'm now living once again.

It has been just over six months since I involuntarily walked into the seventh level of hell. Six months, since the last remaining shreds of my already scarred soul were left obliterated and strewn on the wind. And six long, painful, fucking months, since I last saw the man I love.

Wiping a tear from my eye, I harden my emotions and rein it in. I have to, because if I don't, I will shatter – more so than I have already.

In the last twenty-six weeks or so, I haven't seen or heard from anyone. I'm currently residing - or to put it bluntly and truthfully - hiding, hundreds of miles away, still in Yorkshire.

After walking out of the door that night, Jeremy respectfully gave me what I asked for - he left, and I haven't seen him since. *Until now.* I have no idea where he has been, or who he has been with. More curiously, I have no idea how I've not managed to fall apart completely in my new, secondary, self-imposed isolation. But yet again, I'm still completely alone.

I am also now back in that place of despondency. The place where I use my own head for company, notwithstanding how depressing and volatile it actually is when I'm forced to admit the truth. I am also regressing back into that girl who crossed the street to avoid the crowds. She who stuck to the shadows to avoid being seen. I'm no longer Sloan's strong and beautiful Kara. I'm no longer Sloan's anything. And it is heartbreaking and soul-destroying because I was once his everything.

I sob with abandon into my hands. Unable to stop the flood, I curl up and allow myself to break. It isn't often I do this. I can usually remain strong, but lately, it's becoming hard. Hard, because he completes me in ways that no one else ever will. And not seeing him for this length of time is killing me. And there is only one way to escape it, but it's a decision I fear to make.

Slamming my fist down, I grind my jaw. I had it all, and I fucked it up royally when I let my own unreasonable logic convince me it was right to run. Looking back, I admit I was wrong. That one small misgiving has proven to be catastrophic, and I will live every goddamn day in purgatory for it.

Hindsight is amazing.

And truly the biggest bastard of them all.

Dragging my hand down my face, unable to drift back asleep, I throw the duvet off and march into the kitchen. The smell of stale wine and lasagne hits me as soon as I enter. I never did make it back in after Jeremy departed. Instead, I cried myself to sleep.

I fill a glass with water, lean against the worktop and stare down at the floor. Once upon a time, I asked myself where I go from here. My destination has been one to nowhere. I'm neither living, nor existing. I'm pretending, and doing a piss poor job at that. Wiping the tear from my eye, I slosh the remaining liquid into the sink and move with no real purpose through the small flat.

Closing the bathroom door, I strip off my clothes and study my front. Flattening my palm over the healing scars, I sigh. They are another reminder of the path I've been forced to walk. A path that was mapped out at the hands of a mother and father who couldn't save me. Or wouldn't. I guess the technicalities don't really matter now.

Lifting my breast, I wince at the scars. Why I'm still shocked, I can't say. I know what they look like, and I can tell you the position of each and every one. Honestly, it's a miracle I made it out at all.

Without Jeremy's intervention, I probably never would have.

Opening the taps fully, the pipes rattle. As I perch on the edge, waiting for the bath to fill, I pray it will cleanse my mind as thoroughly as it will my skin. The water burns upon contact as I climb in, and I brace myself for tolerance. This is my penance, a self-infliction for hurting those who love me unconditionally.

Lathering up the soap in my hands, these days I make an effort not to linger. It's dangerous to my mentality, and a torture I just don't need. If I allow myself to reminisce over the times I stared at Sloan with nothing but water between us, it will break me. It will devour me completely, once and for all, removing the last part of my being that is still surviving for him.

Quickly washing my hair, I drop my head back, close my eyes and mentally walk myself back through the misery. Falling into eternal darkness, my body sinks lower as the depths of despair beckon.

My eyes enlarge the moment water seeps down my throat, and the oxygen liquefies. I convulse, slamming my hands on the edge of the bath. Choking and exhausting my breathing, I'm powerless to keep the foreign body from entering my lungs. I hold onto the side, catching my breath, and bring my hand over my face to wipe away the excess moisture. Scrambling out and panting hard, my throat raw and tender, I pull the plug and listen to the water drain away.

Getting to my feet, using the sink as ballast, I remove the condensation from the mirror. Roughly drying my shorter strands, I still don't recognise the woman staring back at me. Gone is my long brown hair, in its place is a dyed blonde bob. My irises, although still a sludgy green at the moment, will turn blue from the contacts I've been using to aid my disguise.

With my fingertip guiding the lens, I insert it, blinking a few times for it to adjust. Inserting the other, I lean back and gauge my reflection, judging the minimal transformation – the same way I do every morning.

Touching my fingers to the glass, I can see *her*. The girl I'm shielding away forever because she isn't safe in this world, not while evil still treads a free path. If I was on the outside looking in, would I recognise me? The real me? She who lives so deep inside these days, I fear she will never come back out. She who will eventually be lost in the depths of my damaged soul, fighting her way out of hell in order to finally exist again. But that will never be because Kara Petersen is dead. She died in a dirty, barren room, after being chained up under the tip of a knife's edge.

The woman staring back at me is Emma Shaw.

And just like Kara Petersen, she is also invisible.

Staring at my reflection, I sigh. One day I know I shall go the distance, as I seem to do with every other aspect of my life. One day I will stand in front of a mirror, and Emma Shaw will be dead, and Kara Petersen will be very much alive again. How long I have to wait for that day, is anyone's guess. And if the man I love so much is still waiting for his strong and beautiful Kara to return, well, that's anyone's guess, too.

Dried, dressed, and completely disinterested, I kneel down in front of the wardrobe and dig through the holdall. Sliding out the envelope that holds my life savings, I drag myself back into the kitchen. Quickly making a mug of tea and some toast, a determined beep drowns out the silence, and I look over my shoulder with caution. Devouring breakfast quickly, and damn near burning my mouth in the process, I move back into the bedroom, my mind curious.

Removing twenty pounds from the envelope and placing it back in, my finger inadvertently touches my old mobile - the one I haven't dared to use since I walked out of the suite for the last time.

Since I vanished, Sloan has called me hundreds of times. In the beginning, I would sit and stare at his name, heartbroken. Whilst I've never answered, it's equally soothing and selfish that I still have him, in some shape or form.

It's a sad fact, but casting aside everything that has come to pass, he is the first and last thing I think of every single day. I have spent more time than I care to admit just wondering what he's doing. Wondering if he has managed to forget me and move on. Wondering if he has removed every shred of me from his life. Wondering if Christy – or some other woman - has already taken my place, just like she said she would.

Ultimately, I wonder if he hates me for what I've done, and for what I allowed to be done, by fleeing in the dead of night.

The void in my heart deepens, threatening to crack and swallow me whole. How I have managed without him, I have no idea. Yet my love for him means I have sacrificed every last part of myself so that he has a future without me. One that doesn't involve incarceration for assisting in the murder of a rapist.

Brushing the abysmal, although not entirely ridiculous thought aside, my other mobile chimes again. I grab it from my handbag on the bed and stare at Jeremy's name on the screen.

"Oh, for fuck sake!" I hiss. Shoving it back inside, I quickly check all the windows are secure, shoulder my bag and lock the door behind me.

Just like my old life, I'm living in a basic, privately owned flat. It is the same place Jeremy left me in, and the one I forced him away from. It's not good, but it's cheap, and it's all my minimum wage affords me. Fortunately, while the rent is paid, my bills are not.

These days I force myself to live minimally, only buying the necessities and what I absolutely need to. The money which he left for me, is still sat untouched in a nondescript bag in the bottom of one of the kitchen cupboards – just in case there is ever a time that I need it.

Getting into the car, I lock myself in and turn the engine. Sat in the queue of traffic, rocking the biting point, I become lost in my own world. I've spent a lot of time recently debating where it all went wrong. I had it all for a time; a man who loved me, a family, and a few guardian angels in the shape of six damn good men. Now, I have nothing, except a heart full of pain and a body once again marked by violence.

And then there's Jeremy.

My unofficial protector who is on his own path to redemption, while I'm still trying to find mine.

I breathe out slowly, attempting to calm my inner thoughts. Hiding my true emotions, my feelings, is something that's easier said than done. Truthfully, I don't really feel anything tangible in my life anymore. It is back to being solitary and regimented. I can honestly say I fucking hate it, and have no idea how I made myself live in that place for so long.

But the truth of the matter is, it *was* safer. Just like I knew before Sloan bustled into my life, I was better off not knowing how amazing and wonderful it could be, because nothing good ever lasts for me.

I knew it then, and I definitely know it now.

Slipping onto the floor in the nick of time, I flop into my seat and wait for the computer to load up. I give Melissa a slight tilt of my lips, but nothing can induce me to smile today. Jeremy's admission is still running frivolously around my head, while his calls are causing me serious anxiety.

When I last looked at my phone, there were numerous missed calls from him. I know if I don't ring him back, he will most likely show up outside my door again, but I just can't. Regardless that he saved me, his care has been in vain. Because while he delivered me from evil, a few simple words have transported me right back there. He has unknowingly breached the invisible barrier I have managed to rebuild and strengthen yet again.

Saying goodbye to my first unhappy customer of the day, my phone vibrates inside my bag on the floor. Picking it up, I shake my head as he continues to call every ten minutes. I sigh inconspicuously and casually glance around. Predictably, no one has noticed my distracted demeanour. A single beep indicates the next caller, and I lift my head to the screen, smile falsely, and chime out the company greeting.

My ears burn, and I tap the pen faster and faster; my temper on the rise. Unfortunately, I know I can't lash out. I have to sit here and take it. *Repeatedly.*

"Yes, sir, I do understand." I manage to get a word in at last under his incessant ranting. "Is there anything else I can help you with today?"

"Yeah, you can fuck off!" He hangs up abruptly, and I drop my headset for a minute. This is a regular occurrence – the needing a minute after being verbally abused. Some days are worse than others.

"Are you okay?" Melissa asks, putting on her jacket and giving me a worried look. I nod, because it doesn't matter if I am or not. "Matt's meeting me for lunch."

"That's nice."

She musters a smile, but sadness overcomes her. I stare, misunderstanding, until I realise I'm wearing a look that is probably bordering on hurt.

"Have you got a boyfriend, Emma?" she asks softly, for the first time ever.

I sigh and shake my head. "I had once. I left him behind. The effects will be long-lasting." I drop my head and my eyes well up, unintentionally rehashing *his* words. A gentle hand tilts my chin, and I stiffen.

"I always believe true love prevails. Maybe one day you'll find him again." With that, she turns and leaves.

I lean back and stare at the computer screen, my finger hovering over the buttons, ready to wire myself back up to be taunted and abused. Thinking better of it, I grab my mobile and head into the breakout room.

The vendor dispenses in a trickle, while the wretched device continues to dance a determined jig on the table. I swear violently to myself that he's still clutching at straws. What more can I say to him that I haven't already? What more can I give? Does he not think I've already sacrificed enough? My heart bled out in that bastard room, believing the world could be safe, and I could have some kind of existence within it. I was wrong; we both were. The scars we harbour between us tell a story. One neither of us wants to bear witness to or speak out loud.

Staring, morbidly intrigued, yet infuriated I'm having to deal with his shit for a second day running, I answer.

"Given any more thought to what I've said?"

"No!" I lie. "I haven't thought about it full stop, now leave me alone. I mean it, if you call me or show up on my doorstep again, I'll leave. I will change my number and sell the car, and you'll never find me again!"

"Stop being ridiculous. You're not going anywhere."

"Jeremy…"

"Don't *Jeremy* me. Get your arse outside, I'm waiting." Then he hangs up. Realising I have no choice, I absentmindedly leave the room, stop at my desk and collect up my things.

Stepping outside, a relaxed Jeremy is leaning against the wall, attracting a bit of attention with his perfect, if not slightly scary, handsome looks. The sunlight captures his scar, highlighting every jagged pockmark. Like mine, it's fading, but still a reminder.

One he shall never forget. Nor I.

Rolling my shoulders, I follow him to his car, and he holds open the passenger door.

"Just one thing, are you here of your own accord or are you ordered to be here?" He makes a pissed off sound, and I carefully climb in, my suspicions confirmed.

"Ordered," he says, slamming his hand on the wheel.

"Sloan or John?"

"John. He hasn't told him. It's better this way, for now. *For you.*" He activates the child locks, and I eye him questionably. Slipping on his sunglasses, he grins. "I know how much you like to run, but your running days have just come to an end."

I throw my head to the side and snort. *Who the fuck does he think he is?*

"Do you really want an answer to that?"

Not waiting for my reply, he slowly moves off the side of the road. Driving through the city loop, he eventually pulls up. I climb out, experiencing a moment of fear when he attempts to take my hand. Shaking him off, I walk ahead into the traditional style pub. Picking out a table at the back, I settle in. Returning with two cokes, he shrugs out of his jacket.

"I ordered burgers and chips."

"Thanks. You not drinking?" I jerk my head to the glasses.

"No. Sloan would have my hide if he found out the love of his life was in my car while I was intoxicated."

I snort. "One rule for one..."

"Hmm, you know what he's like. And speaking of which, your decision?"

Glugging down a mouthful of pop, I wipe my lip. "I told you; I've not thought about it." Honestly, I haven't stopped thinking about it. I would sell my soul to the devil to feel him next to me again. And that is the underlying, devastating truth, because the devil already has my soul. And you cannot barter with something that's no longer yours.

"Bullshit! You don't lie very well. Kara, Jo-" He stops abruptly when the waitress comes over with our food. "John's threatening to come up here if you don't get your arse back down south. As far as he's concerned, you've had long enough. His boy – *your boy* - is hurting, and he can't live with that. Can you?"

"What, and I'm not? I'm not exactly living it up! I left for a reason, remember?"

He sighs out. "They know what happened." His eyes shift in guilt. "John just wants to make sure you're okay. Marie, too."

I wipe my impending tears, my heart breaking at what she must be going through, remembering the last time I saw her.

"Kara, that woman is your mother, whether she birthed you or not."

"Did John say how she was?"

"Yeah, she's falling apart – they all are. Just think about it. You don't have to say yes right away."

"Jeremy?" I lean closer, stretching my fingers to his. A tingle plays on the tips. Whether it is the thought or the actual act, I don't know. One thing I do know, is that if I do allow him to invite them up here, they can't see me like this - this broken girl I have relapsed back into.

"Kara?"

"I can't face Marie yet, but just give me some advance warning when John's on his way up." He squeezes my hand hard and releases it, but his unmistakable look of guilt is ubiquitous.

Stabbing his food, he studies me observing the other diners. Happy families; couples. "Don't think you don't deserve to have what your heart desires."

"I already had it, and I threw it away over a few omissible words. I didn't even let him explain."

"We've all done things we shouldn't have. Things we feel guilty

27

for," he confesses sadly, looking at my wrists.

I gape blankly into space, my heart inexplicably heavy. His expression turns pensive when his phone starts to ring. Looking between it and me, I know something is stirring that I'm not going to like whenever it materialises.

"I think it's time for the truth. The ID, the car, the bag of swag... The mysterious job you actually do up here, if it's up here..."

"You already know the answers. In theory, Sloan could come walking through your door anytime he wanted to."

"So why hasn't he?" I mumble, praying he would do exactly that, and carry me away from this place I seem destined to never escape from, yet can't stop imprisoning myself in. Slowly tearing a beer mat in two, I sigh. It's symbolic because this is exactly what Sloan and I are at this moment - two halves now torn apart.

"Because it's not what you want. He's many things, but he will always respect what you want. I will tell you this though, the moment you're finally back in his life, he'll never let you go again. Make no mistake of that."

Ripping the two halves to shreds, Jeremy's face drops, unimpressed. Thankfully, the waitress arrives in a timely fashion to query if our meal is satisfactory before he can lambast me for it. With my elbows on the table, I bury my head in my hands.

"Kara, for a moment, look past what's been and gone. You and Sloan are two sides of the same coin, and if you're hurting half as much as he is, then you know exactly how he's feeling."

Unresponsive, I drop my eyes back to my plate. Jeremy diverts his attention between me and whoever is trying to contact him incessantly. Slowly tucking into lunch, his words have given me far too much food for thought.

An hour later, standing on the kerb, I watch him pull away. Shifting to the rear entrance, a prickle plays upon my nape again. It's been occurring far too often lately after months of nothing. Turning on the spot, there is nothing there, but clearly, there is, if this sensation is anything to give weight to.

Sliding on my headset, the incoming beep carries an ominous tone, and instinctively, I know whoever it is isn't going to be friendly.

"Good afternoon, Emma speaking."

My stomach turns and I slouch further, bracing my hands on the chair arms. Listening to the irate woman drawl on and on in my ear, my eyes roam. I stare around at my colleagues; people I've never really bothered getting to know. Each wired to a job that neither invigorates nor inspires. Everyone wears the same expression – it's one of being stuck between a rock and a hard place. I know, it's where I seem to have spent my entire life.

Finally, the rude shrieking in my ear fades. Honestly, the need to hang up and run is so strong, I feel my body preparing to move. But I can't, because while resolution has almost been confirmed inside my heart, it could be a while before I bring it to fruition.

The dull ache in my chest feels stronger than ever. Finally facing up to my inner fears has inadvertently turned fate in the favour of my beloved kid. I don't belong here, or anywhere else. I belong inside the arms of a man who has loved me for nearly a decade. A man who might not be empathetic with my choice and reasoning when I finally have to face him again.

The only unspoken question is, will he still be waiting for me when I finally return?

Chapter 4

BALANCING THE SPLIT carrier precariously, along with my handbag and keys, I slam the car door shut. I make my way over the grassy verge, and eye the charcoal Range Rover parked on the opposite side of the road. Instinctively, I rub my hand over my neck, experiencing the chill of a cold sweat. Tapping in the security code, I stop and do a double take when I notice Jeremy's Lexus occupying a resident's space again.

Marching up the stairs, ready to let rip, I halt when two large, familiar backs face me. I instantly turn, my feet picking up the pace. The bag slips from my hand in panic, and the sound of tin cans dropping echoes until they finally stop.

The sound of heavy boots plays on the cheap, plastic tiled floor as I flee. Flinging open the door, someone grabs me, and I trip on the step. A body quickly moves in front of me, protecting my fall, and the shorn head of John Walker fills my vision, dashing my hopes of anonymity and escape. Grabbing him tightly, I turn to the side, staring wildly at the vein protruding in his forearm.

My tears fight for freedom, and the first makes a steady track down my face. Equal amounts of shame and hurt descend as his thumb drifts across my cheek. I shudder as the fine imprint of his flesh makes contact with mine.

"Blonde?" he asks incredulously, sliding his fingers through my hair.

"John, I'm sorry," I say tearful, unable to stop the pain from escaping. "I don't know what else to-"

"Don't cry, honey. You have nothing to be sorry for," he whispers, pulling me close, cradling me. I remain stiff, statue-like, as he tightens his arms, forcing me to remember. Cautiously, I reach around him; my fingertips digging into his back.

He eventually guides us back inside and his breathing eases. Turning the corner, Jeremy is collecting up my runaway items. I start to bring my hand to my face; shame carrying over every cell. His earlier worried expression gives way to sympathy, and as always, I fucking hate it.

"Let's go inside," I murmur, passing Jeremy the keys. Walker relaxes his hold and firmly grasps my hand; clearly fearful I may run.

31

Again.

Dropping everything on the kitchen worktop, Jeremy puts the kettle on and gives me a look that makes my neck prickle.

"I'm not sorry, Kara. If you're expecting me to grovel, you'll be waiting a long time. I've done the right thing this time. And regardless of how much you want to hate me, you know it's true."

Words fail me, because it is true.

Peering into the living room, Walker blatantly investigates my meagre space. He isn't impressed and looks partially revolted as he makes his way around the tiny room. It doesn't take him long. I clear my throat when he picks up Sloan's sweater.

"The last time I saw this properly, was the night I ducked into a derelict house you were squatting in. Marie saved your life that night, and now, I'm going to do it again." He slowly approaches, and I hold my hand up.

"The only way you can save me is by walking out of that door and never coming back. Forget about me entirely and never speak a word of me to anyone. Never tell him."

He lets out a mirthless laugh. "No can do, honey. I kept you apart for eight years, and I'm not proud of it. It destroyed him; he destroyed himself. He grew cold and heartless. Then last year, he finally had a reason to breathe again; he had the one person who made his life worth living."

"John, please…"

"No, I'm going give it to you straight, because I don't know any other way. So, listen up and listen good. This last year has been hard on all of us. I don't pretend to know what you're going through, but I do know this, I know if you're suffering the same way he is, then a part of you is dead already. He's closed everybody off; no one dares to mention your name in case it puts him over the edge."

"Oh, spare me the fucking lecture! I don't have to listen to this shit!" I shout, tearful.

Running into the bedroom, I slam the door hard. Sliding down the wall next to the chest of drawers, the last intact piece of my heart - the part I have kept secure for him - shatters.

A single bang kills the silence, and Walker careens into the room, uncaring in his stance. I shake involuntarily when he drops to his knees and pulls me towards him.

"I'm not saying this to make you feel guilty; I'm saying it because you need to hear it. I swear I will keep you safe. That son of a bitch won't get another chance, I promise you."

"You can't guarantee that!" I cry out. "I've heard this all before, and it's a promise that's easily broken!" I ease down when he doesn't refute my statement, still unable to see a possible way out of this situation.

Lifting me up and putting me in bed, I stare through tear burnt eyes as he sits himself down, looking thoroughly uncomfortable on the small chair.

"Marie cries every day for you. She's lost without you. What she did all these years... She took chances, grave risks that could've had dire repercussions. But she didn't care, because you were worth it in her eyes. Still are...always will be."

"Don't," I whimper.

"Don't, what? Tell you the truth? I thought that's what you always wanted from us. The truth - the sordid, ugly fucking truth that binds us all together. How quickly you realise the grass isn't greener when confronted with the reality that you're refusing to face!" His tone becomes menacing, and I curl into myself, fearful of his rage barely contained under his deteriorating façade.

"Get out." I stare at him, feeling my own rage digging its heels in. "I said, get out!" I scream, throwing off the duvet.

"Why? So you can wallow in this shitty fucking flat and drink yourself to death? Don't think I don't know about that, girl! You're wasting your life here!"

"This isn't a fucking life. It isn't even a goddamn existence! I have spent the last six months alone with my guilt. I made Jeremy leave. And if you want to know why, just look at his face! I guess you could call it karma for these!"

Throwing my wrists out in front of him, he remains emotionless as I vocalise my hatred for what I've inadvertently done.

"I'm really fucking sorry for their suffering, but I'm not exactly living it up here! Now get out!"

Ripping open the door, I stomp into the living room, and Jeremy spins round from the window. "And you can get the fuck out, too!"

I pick up the steaming mug of tea and launch it at him. He moves quickly as the porcelain shatters upon contact with the wall and liquid splatters over his sleeve. He runs at me and grabs my arms. I fight against him, kicking his shins as he tries to restrain me. I manage to loosen my hand and smack it over his scarred cheek.

"Kara! Kara, stop it!"

Fuck him! He has no right to tell me what to do. He assisted in creating this pain inside me!

I continue to beat my hand against him, until it's clear he's had enough. Letting go, he steps back, takes a deep breath, then pushes me hard.

Falling backwards, my skull hits the sideboard and shocks me back into sanity. I stare up in horror, and scramble into the corner, experiencing the burn and aftershock of his action. The rumbling of feet commences, and Walker bounds in. I stare at him from my position on the floor. Touching the back of my skull, his eyes narrow.

"Remy!" he hisses out.

"John, she's out of fucking control!"

He doesn't reply. He doesn't need to; his expression says it all. "Go home, now!"

Jeremy huffs, grabs his jacket and leaves, slamming the door on his way out.

I feel weary, out of body even, watching Walker disappear into the kitchen. I glance forlornly at the sweater and crawl to the sofa. Picking it up, I hug it to my chest.

"Come here, darling." He presses a tea towel to my crown. The ice inside stings, then gradually becomes tolerable.

"Don't hate him. I was – *am* - out of control. Truthfully, I'm barely holding it together. It wasn't through hate, it's because he cares."

"No man has a right to hurt a woman, honey - ever. Caring or not, he should be ashamed. He knows better than that." His hand runs through my hair, and I allow myself to begin to feel again, if only for a little while.

"He saved me, John. If it wasn't for him..." I squeeze my eyes, picturing a past that will always control my future.

"Look, get some sleep. We'll talk tomorrow." He stands and slides his finger over my cheek. Picking up his jacket, I follow him to the door.

"Do you not think you're wasting your time trying to convince me?"

He looks back. "No, because you don't need convincing, you need reassuring – there's a difference. Besides, your true heart resides lonely in London."

Leaning against the architrave, I hesitate. "Is the man who owns it the same one I left behind?"

He shakes his head. "No, but he'll find himself again when the woman he loves comes back to where she belongs." He leans in and kisses my forehead, inducing a ripple of awareness. "You once asked me what you give the man who has everything. My answer still stands, and inside his heart, you're the only thing that matters. I'll see you in the morning." His hand brushes down my face, then he's gone.

I close my door and rest myself against it. Hearing the heavy entrance door close downstairs, I pad back into the living room and wait at the window. Walker strides across the grass verge towards his car. Inside, the lights turn on, and he steers away, until the taillights disappear completely.

Locking the multitude of bolts on the door, a yawn escapes me. Flicking off the lights, I double, and triple check the windows, until my sanity is convinced there will be no more visitors tonight.

Switching on the bedroom lamp, I tug the hoodie over my head and strip out of my clothes. Tucking myself under the duvet, my heart is fraught with indecision. As I will my mind and body to relax, I toss and turn, until a voice sounds hauntingly in the darkness.

"I've got you, baby. Always. I'll never let you fall."

Staring up at the ceiling, my mind wanders. It carries me through the various stages of the past, and the instant my last decision become final and binding.

Unsurprisingly, I've been unable to sleep. I have laid here for hours, my mind regressing back and forth, powerless to do anything other than endure the consequences of my actions.

"You made your bed," I mutter rhetorically, battening down the pain and closing the gateway on my defunct heart. Closing my lids, I'm instantly assaulted. The image is beautiful and vivid, damaged and condemning; standing at the end of the bed, absorbing him, before I turn and run.

I'm brought back to reality when my phone rings on the bedside table. Rubbing my eyes, they feel sore through lack of sleep. Picking it up, it's six o'clock in the effing morning!

"Hello, John."

"Just making sure you haven't fled in the middle of the night!"

"I wish. The door code is one zero zero four."

I pad out of the bedroom and onto the landing. I open my front door and lean against it, as voices rib each other on the way up.

"Good morning, sunshine!" Walker says brightly, stepping inside. Closing the door, it stops midway, and Jake fills the entrance.

"Hey, stranger." I gasp as he pulls me into a hug and breathes against the side of my head. The tingling dissipates, and I hold him. "You look good, blondie." With a wink, he eases away and follows Walker down the landing, bag in hand.

Hiding in the doorway, I breathe in steadily as Walker rolls up his sleeves and moves effortlessly around my small kitchen. I smile to myself, recollecting.

"Penny for your thoughts?" I snap my head up at a smirking Jake.

"Just reminiscing."

Walker grins and drops the utensil. "The kid wears that look a lot, too. He can be sat at dinner and he'll just…smile. Although, just as quickly, it's gone."

"Seriously, how is he? Jeremy said Stuart had prescribed him anti-depressants."

Walker turns down the heat until only a faint crackle is audible. "He's…coping. He *was* on extremely low doses of meds for a month or so, but Doc refused to give him any more in case he became addicted. Naturally, he was resolute in obtaining what he thought he needed-"

"And naturally, it caused *them* to have a falling out." Jake finishes Walker's sentence with a smile while setting the table.

"Did you hit him hard?" I query softly.

"No, just enough to knock him out for the night. Well, a good fourteen hours or so. Trust me, he needed it." He grins and turns back to the hob. "Go get dressed, I'll have it waiting for you."

"Thanks, I won't be long."

Fifteen minutes later, brushing down my damp hair, I slide into my jeans and pull on a jumper. The smell of bacon and sausage invades my nostrils, and my stomach growls in anticipation. The closer I get, the more determined it becomes.

Sitting down, Jake puts a plate in front of me, while Walker brings the rest over and takes the seat opposite.

"What are you doing here?" I ask him.

"Well, when John said he was coming up to make you see sense, I thought, why not. I've never been up here, so I figured I would see what God's own country offers."

I roll my eyes. "I'm not exactly camping in the Dales, you know. It's no different than London."

"No, but this concrete jungle is a little prettier – in parts. And new. To me, anyway." He picks up his bacon butty, and I do the same.

"How's Charlie?" I query, between mouthfuls.

He smiles beautifully, completely in love. "She's great, aside from the obvious. I guess you could say that when you left, you took a part of her with you. She's just as closed off as he is."

I sniffle; my nose and eyes water simultaneously. "I'm so-" My words are dashed when he puts his hand over mine and shakes his head.

Walker rubs my shoulder, knowing it pains me to hear the truth. "Now, how's life been treating you?" he asks, taking a large bite.

Sipping my coffee, I shrug my shoulders. "Not much to tell."

"Well, lie - and make it interesting!" He smiles, and I reciprocate. It's hard to stay mad at him.

"Okay. Well, I've been working at a call centre, where the major highlight of my day is how many times I will be shouted at. Normally, I'm greeted with a 'fuck you'."

"God, that's rough!" Jake laughs, picking up his mug. "But at least I know my fakes are convincing." I roll my eyes – I knew it.

"I think I'm also insanely jealous of a woman I work with. Is that interesting enough for you?"

Walker's brows shoot up, and he stops mid-bite at my very unfortunate, but very truthful, retelling of my life alone thus far.

"Jealous? How so?"

"It's not the woman, per se, it's her life, and the fact that someone up there feels she deserves to be loved unconditionally."

He snorts. "But you *are* loved unconditionally! Nothing will ever change that. It doesn't matter what you say or do, or even that you abscond two hundred miles away. He will always love you. He's loved you from the moment he first saw you. I recognised it the instant he plucked you out of that cubbyhole."

"If I was him, I'd hate me for what I've done. Every action has a consequence. If there's one thing I have learnt well, it's that."

"True, but the question you have to ask yourself is, can you forgive *him* for not telling *you* sooner? I won't lie, yes, he's hurting, but he hates himself far more than he will ever hate you. He hates the fact he couldn't save you. Look, how much notice do you have to give at work?"

"I don't know, a week, I think. Although I can't imagine anyone would miss me if I didn't bother turning up on Monday." I shift my eyes; he doesn't need to be privy that I've already made my choice. "Why are you even asking? I haven't said I would do anything, yet."

"No, but we both know that you will. Whether you leave with me, the National Express, or drive yourself, either way, you're coming home."

Jake chuckles, while Walker shuts his mouth to eat and I openly scowl.

"I can see where he gets that from now." Peering through my lashes, he grins. Fixing his focus on his breakfast, he inhales before imparting his pearls of wisdom.

"When he was growing up, I always told him if he wanted something, he had to fight for it. He's been fighting for you for years; against the Blacks, against his mother, me, and even against himself. He wants you home - sooner rather than later. And if I don't see your backside in southern climes within a week, I'll finally send him up here to get you. I'm not playing, Kara. I don't give a toss what you say, you've had long enough."

"What do you mean 'finally'?"

They both look at each other, and my eyes slit when long minutes pass without explanation. Knowing I'm not going to get an answer, I ask the next logical question.

"What if I'm not ready?"

"Well, you better get ready! Do you want to spend another eight years without him? Still hiding away in your thirties, wondering, living in regret?" He raises his brow, and I drop my eyes back to my plate. "No, I didn't think so."

Silently picking at my food, there's nothing I can say to him, because we both know he's right. Maybe this is the boot up the arse I need to make me see the bigger picture - the one that doesn't just involve me, but all of us. That's what I have been failing to recognise, the truth that has been there all along, one which I never allowed in – until now. Whilst my heart still yearns for Sloan and Marie, I've failed to remember everyone else who gave me a life worth living. Everyone else who also loves me unconditionally.

"Ah, before I forget," Jake says, reaching down to the floor and putting a box on the table.

"It's contracted to the company, and only I have the number. Don't switch it off," Walker states, very matter of fact.

"I do still have my old phone." The new handset buzzes and starts to load.

"I know you do. But since the kid calls it and it goes straight to voicemail, I can't really put much faith in that, can I?" He runs his hand over his cropped hair and stares intensely.

"I don't know how to make it right. I can't just rock up to the front door and announce my overdue arrival!"

Jake snorts. "As far as he's concerned, you can do whatever the fuck you like. He doesn't care what it takes, he just wants you back."

"It's all so easy in theory, isn't it? Go home, knock on the door with open arms, and pray he falls into them willingly and never leaves." He drops down the bacon sandwich, but I shake my head. "I don't deserve his love. My heart is broken. He consumes so much of it. Every day I feel him. I know you think I've shown no contrition, but that's not true."

"Honey, it doesn't matter what I think. I don't have all the answers," Walker replies.

Silence overcomes the conversation yet again, until the clock chimes. Walker gets up and drops his plate and mug into the sink.

After washing up, he motions me towards him. Tenderly stroking my face, his eyes drift down my front. In a gentle action, he lowers my jumper. His expression remains passive, but his hold hardens, identifying his repulsion of a past that will never allow me peace. I close my eyes as he pulls it a little further.

"Open your eyes." His thumbs drift over my lids. "You're a strong woman, Kara. One of life's true survivors. You've been to hell and back, and you deserve your happily ever after." He smiles. "You deserve to be his wife, and all the good things it brings."

"I know," I whisper. As psychologically painful as it is, my heart urges me to make the right decision once and for all. One that involves finding my true light in the darkness again.

"I need to get back to London before the kid realises where I am. I'll call you," he says, placing a kiss on my cheek. He stops at the door and slides into his jacket.

Jake stands in front of me, arms wide open. I slink into them, but the slight burn is far too apparent. "Think about what you really want in life. Do you want to be here, alone, or inside the arms of a man who loves you? I know where I'd rather be. Remember, you've got a week to make it right, or *he* will make it for you."

I lock the door behind them and swallow hard. Picking up my mug off the table, I cradle it at the window. Sipping it slowly, watching the Range Rover leave, I know I won't be too far behind them.

Chapter 5

IT HAS BEEN eight days since Walker and Jake turned up on my doorstep, threw me a curveball, and force-fed me a few home truths. To say they have been hard, mentally and emotionally, is an understatement.

Grabbing my bag from the car, I walk wearily towards the communal entrance. My eyes cast over the car park, studying each vehicle, and although nothing seems untoward, the fine hairs on my neck are having a psychological breakdown.

Tapping in the code and pushing open the door, I take the flights up to my flat. My head has been all over the place since I left work this afternoon. Today was my last day at the lovely call centre. Melissa wasn't in today since her little boy was sick, so she won't know I'm gone until she returns tomorrow. Hopefully, she won't be too upset when she sees the flowers and chocolates I've left for her with the team leader.

This is my first right step in the last six months. It's the start of my own redemption.

Reaching my door, my hand fumbles with the key and the lock, before I slip inside and slide the bolts across. As I drop my bag down, the phone Walker left with me awakens and I fish it out.

"Kara, you there?"

"Where else would I be?" I reply sarcastically.

"Have you ever heard the term, 'time is precious'?"

"Yes. Hello to you, too."

"No time for pleasantries, my girl. Have you decided what you're going to do yet?"

"No," I lie, realising the word has rolled off my tongue far too often recently, and still it continues.

Turning my head towards the living room, I stare in bewilderment at my bags that I had dragged out last night, that all are currently sat waiting in a uniformed row.

He sighs, drawn out. "One day, when you and the kid have children of your own, you will understand the pain I'm going through as I stand by and watch my son gradually die, and there's not a fucking thing I can do to help him! I suggest you search deep inside yourself and find whatever little of that cold bastard heart of yours is still remaining."

"Fuck you!" I hang up and throw the phone down.

While my so-called cold bastard heart starts to break all over again, a knock comes to the door. I squeeze my lids shut. Has he not said enough to demoralise me, that he has to do it in person all over again just for visual effect?

Looking through the peephole, one of my neighbours is waiting patiently outside, holding something.

"Hi," I greet him through the half-open door. He smiles and holds up a few letters.

"These were delivered for you this morning." He hands over the envelopes with the dead girl's name on the front. I take them with an awfully fake smile.

"Thank you," I say, as he turns on his heel and trots back down the flight of stairs.

Clutching the envelopes to my chest, I drop them on the table and pour a glass of wine. I need some serious Dutch courage to open up whatever is inside. I slowly do a full turn around the kitchen and then the living room, all the while the ominous packages silently call to me, desperate for me to delve inside and unearth their truths.

Temptation gains the upper hand, and I down the remaining liquid and head into the kitchen. Ripping open the first, I let its secrets spill out onto the table.

Looking back at me is a dead girl; the one I mentally buried somewhere on the M1 between London and here. Staring at the picture, I shed a solitary tear for her, standing alone in the rain, soaked through to the bone. I run my hand over her heart, the one rapidly beating inside my chest, giving credence to a future I had failed to convince myself would ever be mine again.

Picking up the envelope, there's nothing further inside. I narrow my eyes, wondering what Walker thought he could achieve by sending me this. But I do know, because she is Sloan's Kara. And she's the girl buried deep inside, fighting to be free and strong once again.

Pissed off and ready to cry a river, I take a shaky breath and lift up the other envelope. Ripping open the top, I turn it upside down, and the contents drop to the table. As I pick up the pictures, the air dispels my lungs in a millisecond.

My eyes drift over the monochrome colours depicting my personal demise. From the crude chains elevating and holding me, to the blood, sweat, and tear-stained clothes adorning me. My head is hanging forward - a clear sign of my unconscious state.

Grasping the second torn envelope, my fear rises when I notice it has been posted within the city. My lungs seize painfully, and I slam my hand over my chest, because the bastard shouldn't know where I am. Yet there's only one person who could have sold me out…

Jeremy.

But would he, considering the last words he shared with his best friend of the past? Could he, when he promised he would protect me until the end?

Unable to maintain my composure, I slump into the chair. Chewing my nails, the torturous photo continues to taunt me, showing me that my life is still marked. Scraping the chair back on the floor, I snatch it up and ignite the hob. Reaching over, I run the cold water as my other hand slowly brings the picture to the flame. The corner blackens and crinkles, and I quickly drop it into the sink, watching it scorch and burn before it finally goes up in flames.

I open the window as I kick off my shoes and head into the living room. Picking up the bits of crap I have collected over the last six months, I start to put them into a bag. Dragging it behind me into the bedroom, I pull out my clothes and dump them on the bed. I rip off the hangers and stuff them inside.

Carefully clearing one room at a time, I keep a close eye on my watch. An hour later, with the pungent burnt smell still lingering, still enveloping everything it touches, I stop and look around. A patter of anxiety plays upon my heart, realising this time tomorrow, this place will be just another memory.

Pulling on the Manchester University hoodie, I curl up in bed, needing to get some much-needed sleep before the inevitable. Clutching the material to my chest, I give faith to my absolution, because the decision has definitely been set in stone.

Downing the last of the strong black coffee and twitching the drawn curtains, morning is starting to break outside.

After doing a final check of the rooms, I close the door and lock it. Sliding the keys back through the letterbox, I heft the last of my things down the stairs and into the car. Closing the book on this chapter of my life, I prepare myself to go back to desolation, to relive the past that refuses to permit me a future.

I brace my hands on the wheel and take a deep breath. I stare at what was my home when I needed a safe haven. A sanctuary that provided security in my darkest hour. But considering a few good ghosts of my past have risen from the dead in the space of nine days, I know it is only a matter of time until the other three reaffirm their place inside the troubled, volatile world they moulded perfectly around an innocent.

Stopping at the nearest petrol station, I lean against the car and fill the tank to capacity. My mind races with what kind of reception I shall receive upon my arrival back in the big city. I don't expect anyone to welcome me with open arms; initially, I might not be welcome back at all.

Whether I am or not, I belong there. I had a life there, no matter how lonely and barren it might have been once upon a time. London is my home, and setting aside the choices and foolhardiness I have endured, yesterday's unwanted reminder has verified that running just isn't a logical selection anymore.

Giving it some, the engine rumbles against my tatty trainer. Riding the biting point, I glance at the dash, it's five o'clock in the morning. With any luck - at this ungodly hour - I should hit London by eight at the latest. Fixing my eyes firmly on the road ahead, I drive through the streets; a mixture of leafy greens and concrete guide my way.

Twenty minutes later, I pull off the slip road and join the M1 South, London indicating my final destination. With my foot hard on the accelerator, I plough down the motorway with only one thing in mind.

I'm coming home.

I'm coming to reclaim my shattered heart.

Chapter 6

I PULL UP outside the hotel, and my leg shakes uncontrollably on the clutch as I watch the guests depart for the day ahead. Smart dresses and suits, wrapped up in overcoats, ready for the impending business day. Others are casual; tourists, excited for a day of sightseeing and discovery within the city.

Staring with sad eyes, I speculate if Sloan might be one of the above shortly. I inhale deeply, desperate to re-enter the world of so many firsts and dreams.

The sun glimmers over the ornate features, a brighter day forcing its way through the clouds. Leaning back, I recall the moment I sat on this very spot, seeing it all for the first time in the harsh light of day, while my stomach churned over the mysterious man in the penthouse, who found me in the cold dark of night.

Bestowing the beautiful façade with one last lingering look, I slide the gear into first. Driving through the morning rush hour, I stop in the queue. Being one of many in the tailback gives me time to procrastinate further, more so than I have already. Picking up speed, I turn off the main high street and head towards my first real home.

Bringing the car to a stop, my determination dies painfully, remembering the desperation I felt upon seeing everyone so broken only yards away. I drop my head to the wheel; I knew the moment I saw this place again I would regress. But I have to finally face my demons, because by running, I'm not just escaping pain, I'm denying myself the beauty of an eventual pain-free existence.

The lights flicker on and an undeniable sickness rises up my gullet. Shadows move behind the living room curtains, and my resolve disintegrates. I can't handle this right now. Seriously, I'm amazed I'm even back here to begin with. The day I closed my door on Walker and Jake, I didn't think by the end of the following week I'd be sat here, debating whether or not to walk up the garden path.

Turning the key in the ignition, I slowly move off. Driving with no absolution, I have three choices; the hotel, the mansion – God forbid – or the one place I've only been to a few times in the past. The final option - and what I deem to be my *only* option - wins the battle of mental wills.

Parking in the empty driveway, the house appears completely devoid of life. I reach into my bag, and fumble around inside and pull out my phone. For a moment, I consider what I'm going to say to him. Regardless of what it is, I know he'll be proud that I have returned, ready to face whatever life decides to throw at me again.

Touching my head to the rest, I close my eyes, devising my speech until a yawn escapes me. Somewhere in my impending sleepy state, the mobile slips from my hand and lands on my lap. Currently far too fatigued to retrieve it, I know I need to sleep. Honestly, it's a miracle in itself that I managed to get back here with without accident - especially since I didn't sleep at all last night through worry.

Giving myself over to it eagerly, the cold glass is heavenly on my cheek. While my shoulders sag and my body melds further into the seat, I lose the fight to stay awake.

Just ten minutes is all I need.

Just ten…

"*Kara?*"

A thud beats on the window. My head drops forward, while my drowsy brain remembers I'm in my car, outside Walker's house, catnapping. Or maybe it's full-blown unconsciousness. I really don't know.

Lifting my mobile, it's almost eleven, and there are a dozen or so missed calls awaiting my attention. Clearly, I needed more than ten minutes. Try a few hours.

The banging sounds again, and I snap my head right. The man himself glares admonishingly, and shakes his head, although he's not thoroughly displeased. With a Cheshire cat grin forming, he comes around to the passenger side, and I deactivate the locks to let him in.

"Well, when old Mr Jenkins next door called to say my house was being screwed, the last person I expected to see was you. Jake and I were actually looking forward to getting in the car and dragging your arse back down here. I'm actually quite sad, the delights of the M1 are my favourite pastime," he says sarcastically.

"I'm sorry; I didn't know where else to go. I actually went to Marie's, but a part of me just isn't ready, you know?"

"I understand, but you can't hide away forever. You've had six months; six months too long in my book."

My mind regresses to the day that was the beginning of the end. "The last time I saw her, it broke my heart."

"What do you mean?"

When I don't answer, he eventually nods, understanding something that, ideally, he should know nothing about. Although, I suspect Jeremy has probably given him a few pieces of the puzzle. He starts to look around and then latches onto the bags in the back.

"You staying then?"

I nod; I am staying – where, is another matter.

"Honey, where are you staying?"

I chortle. "I was just thinking the same thing. I don't know. I'm guessing I won't be winning the popularity contest if I waltz up to the front door and tell her I'm home." He laughs. "Honestly, what's she going to do when she sees me? Is there a possibility she'll ask me to leave?"

"Honey, anything is possible, I told you this. Regardless of what she does, she'll come around. She has to; she doesn't have a choice."

"I had a choice." I stare down, unable to say what I need to, and look upon a face that will not mollify me for my own personal assurances.

"You did what you thought was right." He looks down, slightly ashamed. "I'm sorry for the things I said to you; the manner in which I said them. I know you love the kid more than anything else." He cups my cheeks firmly.

"It's okay, I needed to hear it. And you're right, I do love him, and he's why I came back, first and foremost," I confirm resolutely. "Always. Whether he wants me now or not."

Silence engulfs us until he starts to shuffle in agitation. I turn and gauge his pained expression.

"Let's go inside and get you settled. Then I need to reassure old man J that my house is safe. The last thing I need are the police sniffing around."

"Why? I'm sure they'll be delighted to know you can supply them with arms and ammunition the next time someone decides to shoot up the middle classes," I mumble, amusing myself slightly.

Clearly, he's less than impressed when he raises a dark, assessing brow at me. Seriously, he forgets the number of times I've seen that not very well concealed weapon under his clothing. His studious look eventually relaxes into a grin and a smile curves his lips. Reciprocating, I *have* made the right choice this time.

"John, can I ask you a favour?" His brow quirks up. "If it's not too much trouble, can I stay with you? I mean, I can find somewhere else…but I don't have much money and…" I let the sentence evaporate into the ether, hopeful he will show me leniency. He holds out his hand, and I take it without hesitation, even though it does feel like a naked flame smouldering.

"I pretty much live with Marie these days, so it's no trouble at all. You can stay as long as you like… Or as long as the kid will let you." He rolls his eyes. "I wouldn't bother unpacking."

He's right; we both know it won't be long.

Climbing out of the car, he jogs over the lawn to the house next door, ready to placate his noisy old neighbour.

Moving around the dining room, I ruminate on the place where one of my many truths finally surfaced. I can still feel the tightness of Charlie's hand in mine, the sad eyes and devouring silence.

Turning to the office door, partially obscured by a wall, a chill runs through me. *Marie.* I broke her heart that night. I did it again not long after, and truthfully, sitting in this house that provokes two inciting memories, I've never been as terrified in my life as I am right now. The thought of seeing her is causing ripples of anxiety to gallop around my heart like wild horses.

"Here you go." Walker places a large mug in front of me. "What's got you all pensive and worried now?"

With a loud yawn, I slouch down. "Do you really have to ask?" I query sarcastically. He grins and laughs.

"Look, I'll talk to her, let her know you're here. There's a damn good possibility she is either going to come over and greet you with open arms, or smack your skinny arse stupid. Either way, it'll be memorable!"

My eyes shift as his words hammer home the truth. Picking up my drink, I down half of it and nurse it between my palms.

"And speaking of skinny, the kid's going to have heart failure when he sees you." He scrunches up his nose, blatantly repulsed, then politely adds, "and get rid of that shitty, nasty blonde, too, he won't like it."

I run my hand through my hair, annoyed that I've only been back a few hours, and I'm already being given life's lessons again.

"Maybe I like it. Or maybe I'll dye it red." I stare at him pointedly. He slams down his fist, his expression totally fucked off.

"We're not doing this again, Kara! Don't try my patience, girl, because you won't like who you see. Are we good?"

"Sorry," I grumble, sensing my own patience slipping under his glare.

"Kara, she's been gone for a long time. Not to mention, I don't think she would dare go another round with you." He tilts his brows, and I smile shyly and drop my head. "I'm all eyes and ears, honey."

"Hmm," I smile, remembering the lift groping and subsequent ear bashing I received in the wake of it. The only highlight was finally facing up to Christy.

The clock in the hallway starts to chime, and he gets up and puts his dirty things in the dishwasher. Returning, he picks up my bags and carries them upstairs.

After dropping the last one down, he pulls me close. "Just for today, I suggest while you still can, just go and do whatever you want to. No one knows you're here, but the second the kid finds out, your freedom will be relinquished. It's gone. Understand?"

He presses a hard kiss to my forehead and releases me. Patting my pocket, he pulls out the phone. Satisfied, he drops a key into my palm.

"Make sure that thing stays on at all times. I need to get to the office. Otherwise, the boys will wonder where I am, which means they call and harass Marie, and then she calls and harasses me! Ring if you need anything."

Turning the key in my hand, his heavy boots fade down the stairs, until the front door opens and closes, and the rotating lock indicates I'm safe.

And alone.

I lift up the first of my bags and empty it onto the bed I had last shared with Sloan. Dragging my hand across the duvet, I remember him promising me my days were going to get a hell of a lot better. I breathe out hard. My days were bloody brilliant until *I* made them a hell of a lot worse.

Hefting the last bag onto the bed, I pull out my wash bag. Housing my toiletries in the little en-suite, I notice the last strip of my pills is almost finished. I turn them in my hand, knowing eventually, life is going to revert back to normal. It's obvious I won't be bedding down here indefinitely, which means I need to get something else sorted out today.

Tiptoeing into the living room, my attention is captured by the montage of pictures on the wall. My fingers trace over the matching frames of different shapes and sizes, until I stop upon the face of my dreams. Imagining he's standing in front of me, I glide my finger over the glass. The green sash around my waist shines as he holds me tight. Stepping back, its neighbour is from the first function we attended together. I smile at the way the midnight blue gown clings to me, while I cling to him. I was so consumed by him; I was completely unaware any of these had ever been taken.

Continuing my perusal, I assess the girl in the pictures long and hard, willing her to come back to life. To fight her way out of the box I have buried her in, to find strength in the darkness to reclaim her place in his heart.

When I catch a glimpse of my reflection, I finally see exactly what Walker was referring to. The emaciated features and crappy dyed blonde hair. The real Kara is trapped in obscurity until I set her free. Until I rid myself once and for all of Emma Shaw, Kara will remain lost and alone in a place she doesn't deserve to be.

Straightening up, vowing I shall bring her back, I march out onto the hallway. Picking up my car keys, I head out.

Chapter 7

"OH, CRAP," I mutter, fumbling around for the right amount of change for the parking meter. As my terrible luck would have it, the law of sod is working beautifully – because I'm short. Sliding out my credit card - *Sloan's credit card* - I stare at it. This is the first time in six months I've contemplated using it. If I do, there's a possibility he has asked the bank to notify him. Shaking my head at my own idiocy, I slide it into the machine. There's no point in being worried anymore. He's going to find out I'm back sooner rather later.

Standing in the aisle, perusing the boxes of hair dye, I really have no idea what the differences are. The last time I did this, I just grabbed the first one that assured me it would transform me without any problems.

It worked.

Poorly.

"Hi, can I help you?" A perfectly groomed shop assistant is suddenly next to me. I hesitate, thinking she will laugh, then yield.

"I need to get rid of this," I mutter, embarrassed, pointing at my hair.

She rotates on her heel, then heads straight towards another brand of colours. "That's home bleach, right?" I nod. "Well, there's a chance it could either turn green or, provided it does take, it may not last very long." She leans back and pulls a few faces at my head. "I would suggest either buying two boxes or go to a salon. They'll be able to advise you better."

"Okay, thank you." Choosing two the nearest to my natural colour, she smiles unconvinced and leaves, obviously thinking her advice is better. But a salon isn't an option for me, because I don't have the money, and I don't care to be touched.

I browse the remaining aisles and grab some shampoo and conditioner that are on offer. Scanning the shelves, I pick up my usual box of tampons, then remember the other reason that brought me out today. I quickly collect up the rest of the things I need and join the long cashier's queue.

I dump everything on the passenger seat as my fingers tap the phone screen, searching the internet for the hospital number. Dialling the switchboard, I wait for someone to answer.

"Good morning, St Mary's NHS Teaching Hospital."

"Hi, Doctor Stuart Andrews, please."

"May I ask who's calling?" the man inquires.

"Sophie Morgan," I reply, wanting to keep the element of surprise for as long as possible. Watching life carry on around me, Mozart plays in my ear. It continually loops, and I wonder whether he is actually on duty, in the middle of surgery, or on his rounds, until it stops, and he answers.

"Hey, babe," his deep tones ring in my ears, and for a moment I feel sick. Breathing deeply, I finally speak.

"Hello, Stuart."

Silence.

"Oh shit! Kara, where are you?" His voice is an urgent whisper.

"I'm back, Stuart. Walker knows, so don't panic. I'm in town; buying, window shopping, procrastinating. I'm actually calling because I need you to do something for me." He inhales sharply, clearly worried about whatever is going to leave my lips in request of him.

"Come over, I clock off shortly." I close my eyes and drop my head back to the rest. I know I have to, but I don't want to. I don't respond and leave him hanging on, until he sighs in realisation.

"Kara, you'll have to come back here eventually. I'll even hold your hand while you bury a little piece of the past."

I scrunch my face up but can't stop the tears escaping, or the sound they are causing me to make. Sniffing back, pain reaches deep into my chest, refusing to let go.

"Don't let him win again. I'll be right here with you. I promise I'll not let you out of my sight. Come on, we can have lunch and talk." He waits to see if his coaxing method is successful.

"Okay. And thank you, by the way," I say, wanting to get it out now, rather than face to face.

"For what?"

"For saving me all those years ago."

He chuckles. "Thank me when you get here. You can buy me lunch as repayment. You'll not get a better offer than that today. I'll see you soon."

While I manoeuvre through the familiar streets, memories come flooding back, both good and bad. I gaze up at the building, my heart laden with guilt. Inside these walls lies the real reason I didn't want to come here.

Two, actually.

Gripping my bag, I slowly make my way through the warren of corridors to Stuart's office. With my hand raised, his door opens before I even knock.

"Welcome home, stranger." He gives me a big, genuine smile.

"Hi, Doc," I reply, pulling back when he attempts to grip my hand. Gauging my appearance, I suddenly feel on display. He raises his brow unimpressed at my hair, then the rest of me.

"Hmm."

I stare down my front inconspicuously. I appreciate I need to put some weight back on, but there's nothing more infuriating than it being put on display. Without any explanation, he points me towards the scales.

"I didn't come here for a medical."

"Tough, get on." I slip off my shoes and step up to the machine in annoyance.

After weighing me, taking my blood pressure, and waving that light pen around my eyes, he sits.

"Well, you seem to be okay. A little underweight, but nothing to cause me too much concern." He steeples his hands in front of him. "Although it's safe to assume Sloan might have an aneurysm when he sees you. I guess his highness doesn't know you're back yet?"

"No, I'm staying at John's. We both think it's best to leave telling him for as long as possible. At least that way I can live another day in peace."

"You keep telling yourself that," he says with a laugh. Rising up, his eyes cross, and he stares vehemently. I consciously pull at my shirt, realising he has just seen my scars. Grabbing my hand and holding it away, he unfastens a couple of buttons.

"Have you spoken to anyone about what happened?"

"No." I shake my head, pointless words failing to be heard. He lets go and jots down a number on a post-it note.

"She's a really good counsellor here."

I take it reluctantly and stuff it into my bag. One more potential shrink to add to my list.

"I'll consider it."

"Make sure you do."

Putting his hand on mine, he tugs me closer when I visibly shiver and guides us to the canteen. Standing in line with the rest of the medical professionals, he starts to lob large spoons of everything onto his plate.

"The hot pot and mash are really good, everything else you can take a view on."

Serving myself, I take a quarter of what he has. With a look of disgust, he grabs my plate, stacks it, and eventually gives it back.

I baulk. "Stuart, I'm never going to finish all this!"

He grins. "That's okay, I'm already clocked off. We can sit here all day, if need be." He picks up a couple of bottles of water, some cutlery and goes to pay. Locating a few empty tables at the back, he follows close behind, true to his word of not letting me out of his sight. I sit down and pull out my purse, but he waves his hand.

Blowing the fork full of mash, my little moan of delight rings out on the first bite.

"Told you they were good. And filling, which is what you need right now."

I scowl at him. "God, you sound like John. He gave me his thoughts on my appearance this morning, too."

"Not surprised." He grins, aware he's testing me unnecessarily.

"So, how have you been?" I ask, taking a sip of water.

"Good. I've just applied for promotion. Hopefully, if lady luck is shining on me, there might be something good to celebrate – besides your homecoming."

"That's great, I hope you get it." I drop my eyes down, wondering if I should ask about the other lady in his life.

"She's really good. She's in a better place than she was before you left. No more afternoon piss-ups. She actually works for Sloan now, since Gloria went part-time. Anyway, we're living together, and eventually, we're going to look at buying a house together. It's all very grown-up and civilised in the Andrews-Morgan house!"

I laugh. "I've missed so much. How was she after I left?" I ask, taking another bite.

"Heartbroken." He drops down his fork and takes my hand. "Look, when you finally have to face her…all of them…don't let them make you feel guilty, because they will. You can't change it. You did what you had to do to save yourself, and that's the only thing any of us can do."

I suck in my bottom lip. "She'll hate me. *He* hates me."

"Oh shit, Kara. Soph doesn't hate you, neither does Sloan. Look at me," he says when I turn away. "Don't let your insecurities manifest.

Sure, she's upset, but it won't last. As far as Sloan's concerned, all he wants is to love you. It's all he's ever wanted. Trust me, it will all work out fine."

Picking up my fork, we both recommence eating in a weird comfortable silence, until we're the only two people remaining.

"What did you want me for anyway? We seem to have gotten carried away," he asks, as I take a seat in his office, feeling five stone heavier.

"Are you able to prescribe my pill?"

He nods and pulls over his keyboard. "Sure. Have you run out or did you just stop taking it?"

"Neither, the clinic only gave me a six-month supply, and I only have a week left on my last strip. I figure it's important to get it sorted, considering..."

"Indeed, but there are other options. I can get one of the nurses to go through them with you and get it done today?"

"No, the tablets are fine."

"Right then, I'll prescribe you a years' worth, but make sure if anything *happens* in the meantime-"

"I get the idea!" I stop him, sensing myself turning crimson.

"Good." He smirks, and I divert my eyes to the window. The last thing I expected to do today was discuss my sex life with one of Sloan's best friends - doctor or not.

Handing me the prescription, he looks thoughtful. I wait for him to say it, considering there is also something else to keep me here today.

"How's Sam?" I ask sadly.

"You can see her for yourself, if you like?" he offers.

I shake my head. "No, I can't. Seriously, how is she?"

"Honestly? She seems to be on the decline lately. Some days are better than others. The nurses tend to go in and read to her since she has no visitors," he says sheepishly, not realising the impact of his statement.

"*What?* No one's come to see her, not even Marie?" I lean back in horror as he confirms she has spent all this time alone - like I have.

"I'm sorry, Kara, but at some point in the future, you'll be called upon to make a decision regarding her care and condition."

"I know." I stare down momentarily. "Look, I've got to go. I promise I'll come back and see her. Will you come in with me when I do?" He agrees and holds his door open. I reach up and hesitate to touch his arm, but drop it down when the thought overwhelms me.

As I walk through the corridors, I pause. Absentmindedly, I have entered the ICU. I lift my hand up to the door that conceals Samantha. I loiter outside, observing as an orderly sits beside her with a children's book.

Raising my finger to the glass, I trace the outline of her body, while my own starts to lose its ability to hold me upright. Unable to bear the sight of what I've involuntarily assisted with, I throw my hand to my chest and run from the building heartbroken.

Chapter 8

THE FRONT DOOR slams, and I scrunch my eyes before throwing my head back down again.

My phone has been ringing off the hook all afternoon. I haven't answered it, which means the charging up the stairs is most definitely Walker - probably making sure I'm still where he left me, and not speeding back up the M1 like I should be.

"Kara?"

"Leave me alone!" I shout, bringing the pillow over my head.

"Kara!"

The door flies open, hitting the drawers behind it. The bed dips, and he tugs off the pillow I'm practically suffocating myself with.

"Why haven't you answered? I've been calling all afternoon!" He spits out, angry as fuck.

I sit up, wondering if I'm about to say the wrong thing. Covering my face with my hands, I expound the truth.

"You all go on about how I'm this strong and determined girl, but I'm not! I went to the hospital today to see Stuart, and I passed by Sam's room when I left. I didn't even have the fucking courage to walk in there and tell her that I'm sorry!"

"Kara-"

"No! I'm not strong. I'm weak, pathetic, and above all else, I'm a bitch! I broke his fucking heart, and I'm not even woman enough to face him. Instead, I run, because that's all I can do right. This is my fault – all of it! Just leave and never look back, run far away from me-"

"Kara!"

"Because all I am is poison-"

"Kara, stop it!"

"I'm fucking poison!"

He grabs my shoulders and shakes me hard. "Right, that's it! We put an end to this shit right now. Get your fucking coat on!"

"Why?" I scream, beating my fist against the bed, finally becoming unhinged.

"Because if I can't talk some sense into you, then maybe someone else can! Now move your fucking arse!"

I remain defiant as he forcibly stands me up. Behaving like an unruly, insolent child, he throws a cardigan at my chest and shoves me out of the door. I shuffle grudgingly, making it harder for him.

"Kara, I swear to God, I'll put you over my fucking shoulder if you don't move those bastard feet!"

I stomp out of the front door towards my Golf. Getting piss wet through, I cross my arms and tap my foot. Walker's face turns grave as he waits by his Range Rover, and we commence the face-off. Completely aware I can't win; I hold my head high and slowly pad over to him.

"You are seriously trying my last fucking nerve! And this little display of insolence is not helping you in the slightest. You're a grown fucking woman – act like it!" he bellows in my face.

I climb into the car with a huff. Activating the child locks, he stares at me with that unwavering glare he conveys so easily. Ignoring him, I brace myself for the tongue-lashing Marie will be giving me in roughly twenty minutes.

Feeling positively sick, I bring the window down a little. The rain seeps in while the day slowly falls into night. The clouds sweep by overhead, and a crack of thunder and lightning illuminates in the distance. I close my eyes and count. A serene beauty, a feeling of mellow suddenly feels natural, and I ease myself into it, knowing this is definitely the calm before any storm I've ever faced before.

The car halts, jerking me awake. Groggily, I open my eyes.

"Nice timing. I hope you found your renewed strength somewhere during that little snooze." Walker raises his brows.

Rubbing my eyes, observing my surroundings, my heart immediately fails to do the most basic function it's designed for.

Emerson and Foster stands intimidatingly in front of us. Grabbing the door handle, I tug it hard, praying for divine intervention to open it for me. The moment Walker opens his door, mine releases under my hand. As I try to escape, his large arm comes around my middle, and he drags me over the handbrake. Gripping my wrist, I feel like he's going to break it, as he forces me forward under duress.

The foyer is awash with people as the evening exodus begins, but the two guards – the two I had last seen months ago – look surprised. Without being asked, one of them points towards the sky at our approach.

He's upstairs.

"How long?" Walker hollers out.

"All day!" the guard replies with zeal.

I walk blindly towards the lifts, my heart pounding, ready to break free of my rib cage and diminish beautifully for all to see. Right now, I'd rather be facing Marie's one-woman firing squad, losing all my bodily functions.

I squeeze myself into the far corner of the lift when it arrives. The cabin starts its ascension, along with my sharp breathing. This isn't a shock; confined spaces will always be the hardest thing to break free from. Harder still, when life keeps putting me back on the bastard wheel I desperately want to get off of.

The instant the doors part, I haul myself out. Slamming my back against the wall, I grab my knees, while my stomach threatens to perform a spectacular reverse action in the pristine surroundings.

"Please, don't do this," I whimper.

"Begging doesn't work on me, actions do. Now move your backside." Placing his hand on the small of my back, he forces me down the corridor.

Feminine voices cease the moment a very fucked off Walker asks where *he* is. I lift my head in shame to see Gloria and Sophie sharing looks of absolute shock.

"He's just finishing up. I think they have somewhere booked for drinks after...or maybe not," Gloria mumbles, giving me a sympathetic, but reassuring smile.

Sophie appears both angry and relieved. She starts to approach, but stops when Walker raises his hand.

"Go home, Soph. Plenty of time to see her another day." He looks at me while making his demands of her. "She's not going anywhere ever again."

Sophie looks almost ready to cry, but quickly grabs her things and hurries away with a final look over her shoulder. The hurt is clearly drawn upon her face, and I feel the first shock to my system in the wake of what is about to happen.

Commencing his pace, he strides down the corridor, literally dragging me. "That power and strength you think you don't possess... Well, you better locate it in the next five seconds, because you're gonna need it. Now walk."

I cautiously step, one foot in front of the other, until I'm in front of the glass panes. Swallowing hard, I look over each person present, until I reach the head of the room. The terrifying sensation of trepidation is doubly potent, as my heart rate surges, and I see him properly for the first time in an eternity.

I cower back when he turns, and I'm instantly overwhelmed with grief when I see the devastation of my actions. Under the boardroom lights, he looks tired, beaten. Even from my obscured view, dark circles languish under his eyes, and his skin is pale, devoid of colour. Even his smile is lacking.

He points towards a large screen filled with graphs and charts. Motioning his hands, he laughs, and the room erupts with him. I smile pitifully, happy that, for at least a short time in his day, he might have something other than emptiness to dwell over.

Holding my hand up, I watch everyone raise a glass in a toast. I close my eyes, hearing the congratulations flow until the room falls into an unnerving silence. Somewhere deep inside, something is telling me to look up, to see him. Glancing back at Walker, still leaning against the wall with his hand over his mouth, he looks remorseful, conflicted.

When I turn back, I understand why.

Sloan is now directly in front of me; only an inch of glass separates us. Mustering strength from within, I slowly rake my gaze up. Coming face to face with him, his look of absolute shock is evident. A mien of pleading slowly cascades over my features, and I press my palm to the glass. His eyes soften, but he remains dignified and exacting, considering his colleagues are looking curiously at each other behind him.

Dropping my head, my heart breaks. I move swiftly before he can see me plummet completely and ruin his life even further. Marching straight past Walker, the door slams open and Sloan's mixed baritone bellows.

"KARA!"

I continually jab the lift buttons until one arrives, all the while my name echoes around me. A caution. A threat.

"Kara!"

Turning around, Walker is holding him back, whispering to him. The doors begin to shut, and Sloan throws him off, and runs towards me. Staring into his eyes, just before they close, they reveal his pain, his guilt, and quite possibly, his absolute aversion to me now.

Finally, I let it in that I may have lost him completely.

Sprinting outside into an unknown world of my own making, the unforgiving chill of the evening stabs like knives. Wrapping the thin cardigan around my chest, I barrel into the sea of people. My body shakes as I fight my way through, each one brushing by creates a tingling effect on my flesh, adding to my burgeoning insanity.

The phone in my backside pocket vibrates like it's on fire, each pulse is an admonition. A wave of foul surface water sobers me as a car speeds by, soaking me to the bone, forcing me to snap out of it.

Breathing hard, with my hair plastered to my face, I continue to dart through the sodden streets with no hope or direction. Everyone in the vicinity runs for cover, but I halt and watch, allowing myself to finally die inside. Any hope I have carried with me diminishes painfully.

Finding shelter in a shop doorway, I cry for a man I have evidently destroyed. Slouching down the wall, pathetically trying to conceal my pitiful existence, I finally give up on the possibility of reclaiming my place in this world – in *his* world. Inside his life. Inside his heart.

I hold my knees tight, while my body shivers undeniably against the brutality of nature at its most wicked. My teeth chatter as my cardigan fails to keep out the elements, then suddenly, I'm shielded. Lifting my head, Sloan is in front of me. His look of abhorrence has been replaced by an unfathomable glare that leaves me colder than I ever thought possible.

He bends down and holds out his hand. Unable to comprehend why he isn't screaming at me – because that's what I would be doing if the roles were reversed – I scramble away. Crawling piteously from the doorway, his large strides resound in my ears while I continue to run.

"Kara? STOP!"

I spin around in the middle of the road, seeing the van hurtle towards me. I'm trapped - a deer caught in the headlights - and I wait for it to finally be over. The squealing of tyres brings me back, and the horn is all I can concentrate on.

"Get off the road, you stupid fucking bitch! You're gonna get killed!" The driver smashes his hand on the horn repeatedly, deafening me. Wiping the water from my face and grabbing my chest, my feet find life again.

Weak and still in shock, a mixture of rain and tears fog my eyes as I head towards a small, fenced park. I run through, unsure of where this choice will take me, but I need to get away from him. I want him, and regardless of what I've been advised, I may have lost him. I know

I can't stay and watch him eventually love someone else from afar. I'd rather be dead, or on my own, dreaming of what might have been.

I freeze, my body expended by heartbreak when I see Walker and his Range Rover blocking my escape. I finally surrender, knowing from now on, if I run, he will follow. He will no longer allow me the privilege of being left to my own devices. Whilst I know how to survive, I don't know how to live. I seek solace in bad things; things that I will allow to destroy me. Things that will eventually prove I am my parent's daughter.

Grabbing my knees, I breathe hard, my lungs exhausting the crippling pain that is causing them to seize up. The sound of movement behind me stops. Glancing back, I look into the dead eyes of the other half of myself who is barely a shell. Turning around, Walker nods over my shoulder and takes off his jacket. Holding it open to me, he pulls it over my body and zips it up, muttering something akin to a straitjacket, before putting me inside the car.

Walker sighs out, and I turn to the window. I can't take hearing whatever he's dying to say. I've fucked up everything. I sure as hell don't need him to spell it out to me.

Movement outside snags my attention, then Sloan's hand presses hard against the glass. Vacillating, I place mine on it. A strange look of relief spreads over him, but it quickly vanishes. He turns abruptly, his overcoat swinging out behind him, and he walks back through the park in the pouring rain. I sob uncontrollably, watching him become one of many, lost in the sea of bodies.

"Come on, you're gonna get hypothermia. Let's get you home."

I don't have a home; I have nothing. Sloan clearly despises me now – he could barely look at me.

"For fuck sake!" Walker shouts, responding to my unintentional loud lamenting. "The kid doesn't hate you! He loves you more than anything else in this world. He couldn't save you, and that cut him deep."

"John, the way he-"

"Kara, if he hadn't just secured one of the biggest deals of his life, he would be the one driving you home – *to your home.* And another thing, he's seldom been back to the hotel since you've been gone. As much as he despises the suffering they endured in that house, it's nowhere near as heartbreaking as him remembering the tone of your voice that night."

"Why didn't he come and get me, John? He knew where I was all along. Why didn't he come for me?" I cry. "Why?"

"Because I told him not to!" he shouts, then sighs. "When you finally decided to come home, it had to be because it was your choice, not because he showed up on your doorstep and begged you. Because he would have."

"But that's what you did," I mutter. "I don't understand."

"He thinks *you* hate *him*!" He screams at me, shocking me with the truth. "He thinks you blame him for what Deacon did."

"But why would he think that?" I whisper, still misunderstanding. It couldn't be further from the truth.

"You never answered his calls. You turned Rem out. What else was he meant to believe?" With a resigned sigh, he starts the car.

I cry pitifully into my hand. My lips part, ready to speak words I haven't formulated correctly yet, but he puts his finger over my mouth.

"I suggest you finally get your head out of your arse and start making this right again."

I stare into the distance as the rain beats hard on the car roof. Walker hasn't said anything further and honestly, after this evening's turn of events, it's comforting. Stopping at the kerb, I stare up at the house.

"I'll wait until you get inside."

"Are you not coming in?"

"No, you and the kid need to duke this out privately. He won't appreciate my presence. That said, call if you need me."

"Why, so you can knock him out?" I reply flippantly.

He sighs. "Look, I'll speak to him. Tell him to come around in the morning after you've both slept on it."

"I'm terrified," I confess in a whisper.

He strokes his hand over my face, and I shiver. "Don't be. This time tomorrow, it will all be back to normal again."

"That's what I'm terrified of." I stare down, contemplating.

"You know, at some point, we're going to have to talk about where we go from here." He kisses my forehead and motions for me to get out.

"Did you tell Marie I'm back?"

"No. If Soph hasn't already done it, I thought you could do that - preferably tomorrow after you've made things right." My stomach sinks, and I sense a look of fear replacing whatever expression I am wearing. "Honey, don't. The kid will be with you. Go on, get inside."

I get out wearily and hurry up the path. While I lock and bolt the door, a text comes through with the security codes on it. Arming the house, I trudge upstairs and change into a nightshirt, before getting myself comfy in bed.

Flicking through the channels, unable to find anything that holds my attention, I settle on an old repeat.

A loud yawn escapes me as I glance at the clock one last time. My eyes close of their own accord, and I allow it to take me down. While my body sinks further into the darkness, I pray in the morning I can finally stand back in the light.

Chapter 9

JOLTING AWAKE, MY fingers reach for the ringing mobile on the bedside table. Bringing it up to my face, I squint and rub my eyes.

John.

I cancel it; the last thing I want is to go over what was said earlier. Scrolling through the call log, there are more than a dozen missed calls from him. Putting it down, it chimes again.

"For crying out loud!" I grit out and grab the clock. "It's gone bloody midnight!"

I throw off the duvet, pick up the infernal thing and stand. Cancelling it again, a loud banging erupts throughout the house. Exhausted and pissed off, I yank open the bedroom door. Stomping down the stairs, the banging continues, as does my swearing.

Disarming the house, the mobile starts all over again. "John, I'm fine. Really! Come back tomorrow when I'll really flipping need you!" I shout, unlocking and flinging open the door, without looking through the peephole.

With a shaky breath, I freeze.

Sloan.

He has one hand braced on the outer frame; the other holding up John's phone. I grip my own phone tight in my hands, killing the sound again, as he slowly lifts his head.

The silence devours, until he steps inside. My body itches to move, and I stare at him, wondering if he's feeling the same. My unspoken query is confirmed, when he throws the phone down and grapples with me. Instinctively, my body wraps tight around his, as he slams the front door shut and shoves me up against it. The invisible fire I thought had diminished ignites instantly. It feels like I've been shocked back to life, but feeling such an emotive sensation is the best type of torture.

The first brush of his lips to mine is my undoing. My tongue fights against his, and I roughly drag my fingers through his hair, wanting him closer, desperate to be consumed in his passion, desperate to be forgiven. Pulling back slightly, I express the first thing to enter my head.

"You're not supposed to be here," I whisper against his cheek. His lips trail down my throat, sucking reverently. Lowering my head to the crook of his neck, I begin to drown in his intoxicating, unique scent.

"No, I should have been outside your door six fucking months ago; holding you, protecting you. I should have followed you. I should have done so many fucking things differently." His hand opens, and I lean into it, desperate to feel. "Forgive me for not coming to get you." Palming my cheek, my heart breaks.

"Why didn't you...come for me?" I dare to ask the question, but don't know if I'm strong enough to hear the answer. Truthfully, for six months I've been lost, set out to drift on an ocean of desolation, waiting for him to find me.

An ominous air permeates the space. Palpable fear scratches my insides in anticipation of the moments that will follow. Moments where my heart will either be healed, or the void will crack completely.

Looking into my eyes, his hand slides around the back of my neck. Running his nose up the length of my mine, he speaks his truth.

"Because I didn't want to hear you say that you hated me. It's always going to be my fault." Squeezing his eyes shut, a lone tear drops to earth. "Tell me you don't hate me."

"No," I whisper. "Never." Pulling him closer, his lips warm mine again in the tiniest of brushes.

"Tell me to stop. Tell me to walk away and let you live a good life you deserve. Far away from the pain I've caused."

"No." I grip him tighter, fearful he may put his own words into action.

Breathing out, his hands run down my back and stop at my bum. "That word has never sounded so goddamn good!"

Pressing me up against the wall, my legs tighten, refusing to let go. An urgent need spills over his façade, and he slams his mouth over mine. Working his way down slowly, he burrows his head into my neck, sucking on the shivering flesh. Every cell sparks to life, desperate for his everlasting touch, while every muscle clenches, horror winning the war waging inside me.

"Forgive me," I beg in a whimper.

His face twists angrily in my peripheral vision, and suddenly, every terrifying, unspoken thought comes out to play. Reluctantly lowering myself from him, and what may be concealed false hope, I sprint up the stairs.

Dashing into the bedroom, my eyes flood with tears, and my body quakes in fear. Everything is silent until a floorboard creaks outside and the door slams open. My attempt to remain strong is in vain as he thunders into the room. Looking over my things, he shakes his head, but his annoyed expression and continuing silence slay me.

"Please forgive me. I'm begging you!" I cry out.

"I told you, you will *never* beg me for anything!" He shouts, enraged, finally at the end of his tether.

Scrambling onto the bed, hugging my knees to my chest, I'm gone. I clutch the duvet as my non-existent control shatters. He moves another step, and I stare down at his feet, powerless to look upon the face that has haunted every second of my life for the last six months.

"He broke me," I confess, losing all control, until I can no longer disguise the shaking of my limbs or my tears. "The bastard fucking broke me!" I scream. Lifting my head, he recoils at my honest admission. "Please don't hate me."

He scrubs both hands over his face and roars out, before grabbing me up. "Shit, baby, no. I will never, *ever*, hate you." He continues to speak, but I can't hear anything due to the blood pulsing through my veins, putting me on the verge of what may be a premature heart attack. I crumble further, crying furiously, still pleading for his undivided compassion.

"Shush, baby, shush," he soothes.

The arms I have longed to be inside of snake around me. Falling into him, my fight to maintain a solitary existence shatters. He rocks me gently, then cups my chin and lifts my head up. Staring into his eyes, I see a part of myself. The part that has obliterated the best of him, the same way it has done me.

He slides the duvet aside, lifts me onto his lap and holds my thighs. I lean closer, desperate to feel him, not giving a damn of how irresponsible and fatal it may prove to be. His tongue slides across my lip, pressing against the closed seam, and I open autonomously. My mouth duals with his, and I suffocate on the taste of him, needing to fulfil the unbridled desire of wanting him.

He fumbles with his clothing, and I grip tighter around his waist as he strips himself of his jacket. Without warning, he stops and attempts to lift my nightshirt. I hold it forcibly and stare at the ceiling, covering my chest with my hands. Tapping my cheek tenderly, I bring my eyes to him, witnessing his combined expression of hunger and hurt. I mentally push it aside, knowing we will definitely be having words about this in the foreseeable future.

Holding my chin in his hand, he forces me to look at him. A sharp tug digs into my hip, and the tearing of fabric indicates the destruction of my underwear yet again. He drags me to the edge of the bed and drops his trousers. Spreading my legs apart, he presses into me, rubbing me against his covered erection. My head drops back, remembering the way his body feels when it connects with mine.

"More," I request breathless, needing him to erase the pain.

With his hand on my nape, he pulls back. His expression is heartbreaking, and he lifts his hand in silent request. His fingers drift down my front, over the nightshirt, and over my pubic bone. A moment that feels like forever passes, until he closes his eyes and circles my flesh, pressing a finger inside.

I jolt as he claims me; stretching me uncomfortably. Crying out, the dull pain finally awakens parts of myself that had been laid to rest the day I left. His breathing quickens under his floundering control, and I cling to his shoulders, desperate to become one with him in a way I have never before. The sexually charged fog clouding my mind clears the moment he inserts another and thrusts them steadily.

I grip his shoulders hard. "Don't stop."

"Never!" he roars out. "Mine. All fucking mine!" His eyes darken, and he palms the back of my neck, still pressing deep inside. I scoot forward, feeling him deeper. Yet mentally, it isn't deep enough. "Let go," he whispers.

"Sloan!" I gasp breathlessly.

Sliding his hand under me, I twist my legs around his, and he shuffles us back up the bed. He carefully rakes his hands up my sides and over my nightshirt, positioning them under my shoulders. My lungs stall as he sits back and studies me, taking in my blonde bob and noticeably malnourished body. Time fails to tick by, as he moves a lock of my hair and gives it a look of pure disgust. Closing my eyes tight, fear churns inside.

"Open your eyes, my love," he whispers gently, and I obey without hesitation.

Spreading my legs out, my pelvis tilts. He thrusts his fingers back in, circling my clit with his thumb. I stare up at nothing of significance, while my nails graze his back under his skill in performing an action that causes me to fall. I moan under him; all my control is gone in our combined passion for each other.

"That's it, baby. Remember how good it was and how it will be again," he grits out, adding further pressure.

"Oh, God!"

He roars out, pumping relentlessly. I clench my legs tight, attempting to draw him closer as he slows to a stroke. With a resigned expression, his outstretched hand presses against my chest in a bid to stop.

"No, I just want to hold you." I cock my brow, and he nods repeatedly. "Yes, I would like to do other things that include some forms of bodily interaction, but we have all the time in the world." My brows raise higher. "Clearly, you still think so little of me, my beautiful smart-arse Petersen." I laugh, sensing the vestige of desire radiating inside again. "Kiss me."

He doesn't need to ask me twice as I plunder his mouth, my hands devouring his skin and hair, holding him to me.

"Touch me," he breathes against my ear.

"I am touching you," I whisper, my hands gliding down his neck to his chest. I finger the buttons, contemplating whether or not to open them. Casting aside my better judgement, I rip them apart and slide my hands over his hard chest. His breathing is laboured, and his fingertips dig into my thighs. His mouth is dominant against mine, and I find myself no longer feeling him, but reciprocating his previous action and pushing him away. It kills me, but with so much left unsaid, it has to be done. Because we can't happen again, not like this.

"Sloan!"

"Baby, don't, just let me feel you, touch you. I love you so fucking much. I've been dead without you." He stops kissing me and wraps himself around me. "I love you, Kara Petersen. No matter how far you run, how well you try to hide, you'll always be mine."

"Say you forgive me."

"I do, always. I just can't forgive me."

His sad eyes endorse his honesty, and my heart falters under his expressive pain. His fingers capture my tumbling tears and my resolve snaps. I push into him, dragging my lips over his, savouring him, wanting to drown in his taste and touch, wanting to give him back his happiness and his reason for living.

"I love you, too. More than living, more than breathing. Always."

The mattress shifts as he moves beside me. Sleepily, I press back into him, insofar as possible. His arm lulls over my stomach, slowly drawing invisible circles, soothing the anxiousness stemming up from the deep fissure in my heart that has begun to fuse itself back together.

"I can't believe you're finally home," he murmurs, stroking my face.

"I can't believe you're so calm about it."

Clamping my fingers in his, I shuffle over. Coming face to face with him, the moonlight bleeds into the room, highlighting his five o'clock shadow and stunning features perfectly.

Stroking his finger down my profile, he looks a bit annoyed. "John said he came to see you. He also confessed he was quite nasty to you, too."

"He was, but it wasn't anything that I didn't deserve and something I needed to hear."

"Still, he has no place threatening you, especially when it was a joint effort to conceal the truth."

"None of that matters now."

"Yes, it does, and that's why I shall never hate you for leaving. I can't exactly play the martyr when I brought it upon myself, John neither." His expression is one of hurt and happiness all rolled into one. It's a strange sight to see him so contrite.

"I bet you told him that, too." I smile.

"I did." He rubs his jaw gingerly with a crooked grin. "I figure I have a few of his good hits still left in me before he causes serious damage." I can sense my expression change instantly.

"Don't worry, my love. I have broad enough shoulders." He bestows me with a thoughtful gaze. "And in John's eyes, he's looking out for your best interests, not mine." I start to open my mouth that it isn't right. "No, it is. Has been for a long time."

I nod as he verbally placates his own insecurity. He is burying his own pain in a bid to alleviate and eradicate mine. The little stab of doubt plagues my thoughts, and the unanswered question now really is where do we go from here?

"Talk to me, my love," he whispers, his hand pausing momentarily.

"Is this real?" I ask. He nods; his smirk begging to break free. "Please tell me I'm not imagining you. That this isn't just another fucked up dream that pulls me down and tortures me, like so many before it."

Pulling me close, he entwines our legs. "Baby, I'm very real, and very much yours. Always." He kisses me, but I'm in the zone, needing to say how I feel.

"But it isn't possible," I mutter.

"What isn't?"

"We can't just wake up in the morning and pretend none of this ever happened. We can't forget how much we've both suffered."

He sighs and brings his hand up to stroke my hair back. "Baby, of course we'll never forget, but when the sun rises tomorrow, I want to look into your eyes and start to plan the future that has been denied us both for nearly a decade."

"But I hurt you...so much. How can-"

"And I didn't do the same? I should have told you about my mother. I should have trusted you. You deserved better."

"You *did* try to tell me, but I understand why." My eyes flick down my front because I'm well aware of what *that man* is capable of.

Sloan doesn't respond, just stares curiously. Pulling at my nightshirt, I stop him. He hasn't broached the subject until now, and honestly, I don't know if I want to be the first to speak of it. It will happen, there are no two ways around it. But considering he's very subdued and reasonable at the minute; I'd rather wait to address the condition of my body until after Marie has either welcomed me or disowned me.

"Don't," I warn before he can say anything.

"We need to talk about this."

"And we will, but I'm not the same girl anymore." His eyes narrow suspiciously. "I'm dead, Sloan. Deacon broke me. What he did to me... He didn't do that to hurt me, he did it to hurt you. He even said so, so now I'm through being kept in the dark."

"Baby, I-"

"No. I've made mistakes, huge fucking mistakes, but at the same time, I've made some damn good choices, too. I made the choice not to throw your card away. I made the choice to have dinner with you, knowing exactly what would happen. We've both omitted the truth from day one, and that day began over nine years ago."

"I know, but how could I ever tell you?"

"You couldn't, because I didn't remember. You want me to hand over my trust again, but that cuts both ways." I stare with determination, needing him to see that the woman he loves will one day come back, stronger than she was before.

"Okay," he mumbles, then shivers. Instead of pulling over the duvet, I quickly shuffle off the bed and grab the sweater – his sweater – and hold it out to him. "I didn't think I'd ever be wearing this again," he says, taking it from me.

"No, but I guess you could say it has gone full circle, like we have. It's time its rightful owner reclaimed it. I don't need it anymore to feel at peace. I have…" I look down, the words wedged in my throat.

His finger lifts under my chin. "You have what? What were you going to say, my love?"

I sigh. "I have…you. Or had. I don't know…"

An uncomfortable silence sweeps in, and he sits up. Cradling my face, he stares ardently. "You do have me; you've always had me."

I smile and rub my cheek to his palm. "Sorry, I caused you problems tonight."

"John didn't tell me you were back. Heading up that boardroom, giving the speech of my life, I thought someone was playing a cruel joke when I saw… a ghost outside."

"I didn't want you to find out like that."

He smiles beautifully. "I know. Finally seeing you again, it was like a lead weight had just been lifted from my chest, then you ran."

I start to open my mouth, but he shakes his head.

"When I found you shivering in that doorway, then I chased you down the street, and you were nearly hit by that van… Jesus Christ! I wanted to scream at you, shake you, tell you how fucking stupid you'd just been. But I couldn't. All I wanted to do was pick you up and never let go, but I'd just deserted my clients." He strokes my cheek, capturing my falling tears. "I love you. I've always loved you. I am angry, but it will never be at you."

"But I want you to be."

"Well, you'll be waiting a very long time. I'm many things, but I'm not a heartless prick."

His hands rub up and down my sides, and an uncomfortable chill befits me when I look into his eyes. I know this look all too well. And it's one that is making my heart miss a beat – for all the wrong reasons.

Manipulating me towards him, I reciprocate cautiously and bring a hand to my chest. The light kiss deepens, challenging me to a battle of lips and tongues. The colossal need to be ignited in passion is too much and, as much as it pains me, I push him away. Clutching my front, trying - and failing - to ignore the anguish he's directing at me, I roll to the other side.

"I love you," I murmur. Positioning myself to sleep beside him for the first night in a proverbial eternity, I feel at peace. My eyes fail to stay open, and his body presses hard into mine; his desire still evident and alert.

In the misty haze wrapping itself around me, inducing my body to relax and my sanity to ease, I can sense movement. Floating away into the abyss, the inexplicable weightlessness is overwhelming, and I feel like I'm being elevated. Turning around, the sound of his content heartbeat resounds in my ear.

"Sleep, my love, I've got you. I'll never let you fall."

Chapter 10

THE SOUND OF nothingness rouses me. Instinctively, I run my hand over the other side of the bed, but as already anticipated, I'm alone. Fear grips me, realising last night probably was just false hope. Sitting upright, keeping the tears at bay, I rub my face in confusion as the mansion bedroom gains clarity.

"Right," I mutter, realising the floating sensations I experienced were not a bloody dream, and that he hasn't banished me to the dark side as I feared.

Sloan's clothes from yesterday hang over the chair; his shoes placed neatly underneath it. I quickly bring my hand to my front; thankful he hasn't undressed me. Although who's to say he hasn't already looked when I was comatose to the world. Let's face it, he managed to transport me here from Walker's spare bedroom without my knowledge.

I pull on the yoga pants - which he has left on the end of the bed - and whistle as the chill of the vast room makes my skin goosebump. The Manchester University sweater is folded atop the chest of drawers, and I pick it up on my way out.

Peering out of the landing window, morning is still breaking outside, bringing with it the start of a new day. One in which I will receive the biggest bollocking known to man, and one which Sloan and I still need to thrash out the true devastation of my leaving.

Today, I will suffer. We all will.

Descending the stairs, I smile, somewhat relieved. The place appears to be exactly the same. Why I thought it would be any different, I can't say.

I hesitate and stall when I see the kitchen door open. Sloan is leant over the worktop, flipping through a broadsheet, drinking coffee. My eyes widen for two reasons; firstly, the fact his behaviour seems so normal, considering my return has once again changed everything; and secondly, the way he devours such a vast amount of space in a fairly large area.

I linger quietly, drinking him in. His bare feet and muscular thighs. His toned backside, all the way up to his strong chest and shoulders. Intuitively, he turns in my direction. His look sears me, but I'm too enthralled by the raw, evident hunger he is invoking in me.

Pushing off the island, he swaggers towards me, a different type of spring in his step. The invisible flames stoke between us and my body tingles with a mixture of passion and calm. I tighten my hand atop the bannister, steadying myself.

"Why did you bring me here last night?"

"Because deep down, the true reason why you returned, is because you wanted to come home." Clutching my hand, his touch ignites my senses and heats my blood – not that it hasn't already.

"Actually, I came back to claim what I'd left behind. I came back for you." Smiling timidly, he squeezes my hand, and I move closer to the man I owe all my firsts and lasts, and who will be my one and only.

Lifting my head, I feel the tears beckon. They don't seem to be doing anything else these days. I still have a lot to cry over and come to terms with. Namely, the part of myself that is still doubtful, uncertain of what may - *will* - still befall me in times to come.

He clears his throat and tucks me into him. Gradually moving down the hallway, without direction or intention, I'm battered by past images flooding my senses. We stop outside the pool room door, and I raise my hand. My fingers drift over the wood along with my memories. Looking up, Sloan is pensive and intrigued.

"Just remembering," I mumble, as I move again, my eyes re-familiarising themselves with the beautiful pictures I had loved so much upon first sight.

Re-entering the kitchen, I tiptoe to the doors and look out. Once again, the treeline sways; its random shapes casting shadows. I turn and am instantly drawn to the lamp table – *my lamp table* – from my old flat.

"That doesn't really go in here – or anywhere in this house, actually."

He shrugs his shoulders. "It belongs here, just as much as you do. This is your home."

I can't control my grin. "Yes, it *is* my home. In my heart, it always has been, because the man I love to the bottom of my soul is here."

He clearly loves my answer, when he smirks, raises his brows and motions for me to come hither. I slide closer, oddly light on my feet. Grabbing my nightshirt, the top button comes undone, and I quickly refasten it before he sees. I know I said we would talk, but he never stipulated when, and it's time I fear I may need to unburden myself of the trauma I currently hold inside.

He picks me up and carries me into the living room. Like so many times previously, he lowers me onto the sofa. Expecting him to sit and coax me to straddle him, he surprises me when he drops on his haunches. Fisting his hand in front of his mouth, I wait while he tries to organise his thoughts. Gently rubbing my knees, he sighs.

"I can't change the past. I can't erase what's been said and done, and I can't right wrongs." I stare at him, unwavering. "I once offered you forever. Notwithstanding what has come to pass, I still want forever, and I know you're lying if you say you don't want the same."

I breathe out and run my hands over my thighs. "I just... I don't know how to act with you anymore. I keep thinking any minute the illusion will shatter. That this isn't actually real, and it's just a dream I will wake up from alone."

Mouthing *no*, he presses his lips to mine. He retracts, glides his fingers through my hair and sighs. "I feel like I'm cheating with this blonde, my love."

I laugh. "I'll dye it back."

"You don't have to. I confess I prefer you on the dark side, but I'll have you any way I can get you."

I crawl closer, and he cautiously unbuttons my blouse again. Unable to watch, I tilt my head to the side, horror consuming me. Noting my reaction, his hand claws at the fabric, and I scramble off the sofa in panic.

"Baby?" His look of confusion is irrefutable, and he edges towards me.

Shaking my head, he halts, concern and annoyance flash over him. These have always been his two most identifiable visual emotions. Terrified, I turn back into the hallway, charge up the stairs in tears and into the bedroom.

On the bed, I pull my legs up to my chest, knowing the moment of truth is finally here, and it's make or break for us.

For me.

The door creaks as I continue to wallow in self-pity. Strong, familiar arms encircle my waist, caging me in their loving embrace.

"Baby, don't cry," he says, forcing me to look at him. My fingers toy with the buttons, and I slowly start to unfasten them. My tears fall harder and echo hauntingly. "Shush, calm down. Calm down," he coaxes, rubbing my back.

"'*Calm down?*'" I pull the shirt apart at my front. "This is what he did to me!" I look down at my damaged, defiled flesh. "This is what

I'll always have to live with!" Falling apart, my small, balled, fists beat constantly against his chest, until the fight in me gradually dies. "I'm just a fucking victim. I'm nothing. *I. Am. Nothing!*" I scream hysterically until I'm hoarse and can no longer verbalise.

Ignoring my protests, he holds me until he's satisfied I'm not going to strike out further. Turning me in his arms, he holds my chin and kisses my nose.

"You can lash out as much as you like, but I'm not going anywhere." He leans back and frowns. "This is all my fault. If I'd given Franklin what he wanted years ago, maybe... I don't know, maybe you and Charlie wouldn't be suffering in silence now. I'm the one to blame for all of this." He sweeps his hand over my forehead delicately. "You may think I deserve someone better than you, but truthfully, *you* deserve someone better than *me*. I promised I would keep you safe, and I've failed twice. Trust me, you *do* deserve more than I can give you."

I rapidly shake my head. Yes, I'm angry and I want to blame everyone, but I know the responsibility lies at my door. I did this to myself. I could have fought against my selfishness and listened to him, but I didn't.

"How can you still love this? How can you look at me and not see...this?" I ask disgusted, in a distraught, messy state. Tightening his arm, he wipes his thumbs under my eyes, before capturing my bottom lip and soothing it.

He brings his hand to my chest, and I nod my acceptance of his action and stare over his shoulder while he slowly strips me bare. He gasps, seeing the true devastation for the first time.

"Is this okay?" he queries softly, conflict raging inside his eyes. I neither confirm nor deny, because I don't have a choice. It has to be.

His hands finally glide over my shoulders, taking the fabric with them. He pauses, and I draw my arms over my front, praying he will see past the carved up, emancipated body before him. His desolate, unforgiving expression, while I let out my anguish and the absolute diabolical loathing of my appearance now, is evident.

"Please let me look."

I drop my hands, as he stands me up and circles around. Stopping at my back, his fingers stroke the second round of marks Deacon left behind. He then fumbles with my yoga pants, until they fall to the floor. Kicking them away, a shiver swathes my skin, and I wait for him to come back to face me. My tears are now fully-fledged, and the urgent need to coil myself around him and forget is so strong, so palpable. So very conflicted. He makes the choice for me when he picks me up.

"Say the words, my love."

I run my hand over his face, easing his poorly concealed anxiety. "Prove you still want me. Make love to me."

"Always. I'll never deny you, but we both know the moment we connect; all bets are off."

"It's a gamble I'm willing to take." My lips softly press his.

"Baby, you find a way to tell me if you're uncomfortable or hurting," he urges.

"Stop talking," I murmur, tugging his bottom lip. Without further persuasion, he slams his mouth over mine. A faint, metallic taste envelops and we lose ourselves in a moment we have waited far too long for.

Grabbing my backside, I wrap my legs around him, and he lowers us to the bed. Tensing my thighs, holding him as close as possible, he comes to life again. My hand grips the sheet as he begins his slow descent. My eyes close involuntarily the moment I feel him reach the start of the abrasions, and I whimper when he kisses each in turn. His free hand entwines with mine, clenching it tightly.

Delicately tracing over the lines, I wince a little each time he touches a new one, until he gradually stops. I lift up on my elbows, wondering what's troubling him. My eyes meet his, then drift down to my breast – the one bearing the worst scar of them all. Another disfiguration; a painful souvenir that will need to be reconstructed.

"Baby, I.. I-" I place my hand over his mouth. There's nothing he can say to make this right. We have to go through this hell to come out of the other side. This isn't his doing. In my eyes, there is nothing he needs to redeem himself for. His expression turns dark, contemplating something, before he speaks again.

"May I touch you?" His eyes are simultaneously wanting and empty. I nod eagerly, as he slowly invades the space separating us and claims my lips.

As he deepens the kiss, the feel of his perfect weight on top of me is all-consuming. My lips part further, and my tongue breaches the threshold, until I'm massaging mine against his. His hand slides up my stomach, finally reaching my chest, and he tenderly squeezes one breast. Rolling my nipple, I sound out timidly.

"Sorry," he says into my mouth.

"It doesn't hurt, not anymore." His irises enlarge, clearly stumped. There's no point in lying, we've both done too much of that already. And it has got us absolutely nowhere. "Please," I plead. He gives me a small smile and drops his head. I remain slightly upright, needing to see whether he's truly disgusted. He continues pressing further soft kisses to my belly button, before looking up again.

"You're worrying too much, my love. Lay back and close your eyes." I breathe out, obeying. No sooner am I comfortable, his skilled mouth sucks my abdomen. I lower my hand, guiding him further down my body.

"We have all the time in the world," he chuckles. "First and last, my love."

"I know, but… It's been a long time."

"That it has," he confirms, rubbing circles on my inner thighs. He slowly crawls up my body, and I lose myself and my indecision in the moment, ready to give him back all of me again.

And this time, I shall not take it away.

He turns us over and sits on his shins. With his hand around my backside, he eases me against his groin. His other hand progresses down my neck, lower and lower, until he reaches the conclave of my belly button and rims it with his finger.

I close my eyes, enjoying his exploration, teasing my flesh to perfection. My head falls back; six months of pure need explodes on the surface. My shivers of happiness mix with sobs, as he works his fingers further until they are hovering at my opening, inching in a fraction, waiting for my consent.

Opening my eyes, he stares at me. Refusing to break the precious visual contact, I copy his actions precisely and bring my hand down his front, stopping at his belly button. My fingers toy tentatively, drifting lower until I feel him throb under my touch. He grins and hooks his free hand around the base of my head.

"Make us remember, my love."

Taking his length in my palm, I hold soft and secure; he's both steel and silk. Hesitantly, I shift, performing his wish. He hisses, as I harden my grip and run it up his shaft. I touch my forehead to his and close my eyes. I don't want to watch; I want to feel. I want to reconnect emotionally and spiritually with the side of myself I had shown the door to months ago.

My breathing becomes laboured, and the giveaway signs beat down on me as he massages my folds, before sliding his fingers completely inside. His motions are quick, forceful, designed to bring us to fruition.

"Oh, God!" Euphoria cloaks me and tips me over the edge. Crying out intermittently, he pulsates in my hand but doesn't release. "Let go," I whisper.

"Only inside you," he replies. Dropping my head back, he lavishes my aching nipples, in turn, causing the ecstasy to peak once again.

"Make love to me," I sigh out.

Lifting up on his knees, he guides me back down and pulls my legs around his back. "Condom," he mutters, looking around.

"I'm still on the pill." An instant expression of shock falls into place. "I never stopped taking it. I was always coming back to you. Only you." I smile, but the look is still there. I shuffle, because maybe this look isn't aimed at me at all. Maybe... Oh God, do I really want to know? No, but I'm a glutton for punishment, and the burn for knowledge is flaying me.

"I don't even want to ask," I whisper. He smiles; the first real smile I have seen thus far.

"There's been no one, but you." He teasingly nips my skin. "And this funny blonde looking at me right now. Take me, Ms Petersen. Reclaim what's always been yours."

Without further verbal interference, he gently guides himself inside. The tenderness of feeling this full causes me to squirm, but my body definitely remembers. I attempt to manipulate him lower, but he remains resolute in his control. Swiping his tongue against mine, he glides in a little deeper, but not deep enough. Eventually sheathed inside me, I try hard not to whimper at the slight stinging he's creating deep in my heat.

With both hands cupping my face, he rotates his hips, touching parts of me that have been dormant, patiently waiting for him. I arch my back higher under his fluid rhythm. Moving under him, I fight back the burn, finding my own tempo again.

Entwining his fingers in mine and bringing our hands to the headboard, I hold tight. My legs fall to the sides, allowing him more room to bring me to my peak. With his mouth on mine, he muffles the sound of potent desire ripping through me, firing every cell. Swelling inside me, he rolls us over.

"Fuck me, baby."

I move uncomfortably atop of him. This has never been something that goes hand in hand for me. It's something I'm still unsure of, regardless that we've done it plenty of times prior to today. Lowering myself up and down nervously, his fingers dig into my flesh and separate my cheeks, opening me up further. Grabbing my hips, he lifts me hard and fast, never wavering or losing speed. I quiver the moment my body spasms, and I scream out his name until my throat burns.

"Oh, fuck!" he roars beneath me, and I flop onto him, replete and satisfied. My eyes drift shut; my body no longer used to this type of activity.

"I'm not done with you yet," he says slyly.

He pushes me back, and I bounce against the mattress. Stretching and tangling my hands in the sheet, his hot breath fans down my body, causing the pleasure to soar, while he reaffirms his mouth with my nipples again.

Parting my knees, he lowers his head and breathes against my centre. I tighten as he slowly kisses my inner thigh, inching further towards where I really want to feel him. Moving his lips with delicate precision, each time it is met with my vocal acceptance. His tongue touches my core, and I cry out, unable to control myself. This will never be enough – for him, or for me.

I throw my arm over my face and exhale hard, fearing my lungs will give out any minute through overexertion. He flicks his tongue repeatedly, and I know I can't hold on much longer. Taking a single bite to my flesh, I fill the hollow space with rapturous sound again.

Smoothing aside the damp strands from my cheek, he smiles beautifully. "I want back all the time that we've missed together. Including yesterday, we still have five months, three weeks, and five days to make up for. And I intend on getting every last minute's worth."

Pulling the duvet over us, I grab his hands and wrap them around my front. Relaxing behind me, our bodies align perfectly. His gentle kisses to my neck encourage me to forget the turmoil and devastation, because he has given me back what I thought I had lost.

He has given me back his heart.

Chapter 11

SLOAN LOOKS AROUND fastidiously, his brain working overtime, as we drive towards Marie's. I watch inconspicuously at his true persona filtering back through. I knew it wouldn't take long.

He turns with a contradictory grin, and I furrow my brow in reciprocation. Rubbing my palm over my thigh, the apprehension beckons further. As I rest my hand on my knee, his fingers squeeze mine soothingly, inadvertently touching the flimsy, cheap trousers. Looking down, his expression darkens, and he diverts his eyes between my leg and the road.

"You should have bought some better clothes," he mumbles under his breath.

I press my lips together in infuriation; he knows he's just upset me when he pulls over.

"How dare you? I've been back a little more than twenty-four hours, and you're already laying down the law. For your information, designer clothes don't pay the bills. These cheap clothes are all my pitiful, minimum wage afforded me!"

He starts to shake his head. "Kara, I didn't mean-"

"No. I'm sorry if these are less than favourable to you, but I had more important things to be concerned about than clothing!" I spit out. He reaches over my shoulder and starts to massage the back of my neck.

"Baby, I'm not saying it to embarrass you, but we gave Remy that money so you wouldn't have to struggle. I knew you wouldn't touch it."

"Of course, I wouldn't touch it!" I scrub my hands over my face. "Can you just drop it? I've got bigger problems right now."

The house looks ominous as we progress further down the street, until we gradually stop. Hesitating, the urge to tell him to floor it is immense. I shift and watch him; the way his eyes drift over the house, checking for anything untoward or not quite right. He's not exactly filling me with hope here.

"I saw you," I whisper. "When Deacon... He was parked over there." I point. "I watched as life finally broke you – as *I* finally broke you. I was so stupid."

He gets out of the car as I sob into my hand, accepting that the life I wanted so much with him has been torn away by my own actions. The door opens and he bends down and brushes my cheek.

"Again, something else we will talk about today. I'm as guilty as you are - more so, even. If I hadn't kept you in the dark, then maybe none of this would have happened. Just don't hold back when you tell me. No matter how painful, I want every detail." I nod; I will be honest, because I owe it to him. And myself.

Getting out of the car, my heart is thumping in my chest. "God, I really don't want to do this," I admit, edging up the path. "I'll call you when I'm ready to leave." It's going to take longer than an hour to climb this mountain.

He looks confused and shakes his head. "I'm not going anywhere."

Approaching, a determined shiver runs rampant, and the door opens before we are even within knocking distance. Walker appears on the other side looking pleased, although his face depicts a foreign anxiousness.

"Welcome home, honey."

"I'm scared," I confess, praying she will be lenient on me. He ushers us inside, smiles and strokes my cheek.

"Remember, make it right. You look better, kid." He slaps Sloan's back and moves down the hallway. I study him swaggering away, entirely at ease in this house - pretty much like he is everywhere else. He stops, winks, and knocks on the living room door.

"Hey, angel, I've got a belated Christmas present for you."

Sloan's arms come around my middle, and I drop my hands onto them, ready for the verbal battering I'm about to be on the receiving end of.

Marie's sigh resounds, the door opens, and she steps out. Looking at her profile, she is more lined, prematurely aged due to unnecessary stress. She turns with a huff and then breathes in sharply, her eyes widening.

"Hi," I whisper, since one of us needs to break the ice.

Her expression morphs from heartbreak, then shock, and then delight. "Oh my God!" she gasps, running towards me.

Taking me into her arms, she holds me with the fierce protectiveness of a mother being given back her child. I squeeze tight, refusing to let go, while her tears puncture the silence of the hallway.

Smiling, I notice Walker gripping Sloan's neck and tugging him away.

"Come on, no one's taking her away again." Walker shuffles him into the kitchen. His query of where his phone is, is the last thing I hear before the door closes.

The hallway clock ticks loudly, masking the sound of our combined sobs. Eventually, she pulls back, palming my face and staring intently, trying to decide if I'm actually here, or just a cruel figment of the imagination.

I inhale deeply, coaxing out a tiny fragment of the strong girl that everyone identifies, but I never do. "I love you, and I'm sorry."

She shakes her head, her expression profound. "You will never, ever, have to explain yourself to me, but I just need to understand. You could have called, written, emailed – anything! I would never have made you come back, you know that."

I do know that, but I also know if I had done any of those things, the men in the adjacent room would have coerced her into working things their way. Her knowing look towards the door confirms we both already know that to be the unspoken truth.

She stares expectantly, waiting for me to absolve myself of the reasons why they have all walked invisibly alongside me through hell these last few months.

I touch my collarbone reflectively; can I show her and not mentally fall apart when she does? Can I remain strong under her inevitable breakdown?

Moving into the living room, her confusion is apparent when I close the door and stand behind it. Untucking the fabric from my trousers, the waistband drops. She looks horrified at what I've allowed myself to become.

"Honey, what are you doing?" she asks, concerned. Unfastening the buttons, the blouse slides down my arms.

The room turns silent, but her gasp indicates she's still breathing. Our eyes meet, and she reaches out her hand; a gentle finger grazes my skin delicately. She concentrates hard, feeling along the raised lines, but her frontage is crumbling, until her composure finally withers, and she openly sobs.

I close my eyes, yielding under her touch. As disconcerting as this is, it's nowhere near as uncomfortable as hearing her cry for me.

When the perusing stops, my eyes flutter open. She's red-eyed and wet-cheeked, staring at my bra, which is exposing the scar that streaks over my areola. I put my hand over it and reach for my blouse. Sliding it on, she begins to button me up. She stops before my brutalised breast and gently lowers the fabric.

"Now I understand. Has Sloan seen them?" she queries, securing the last button.

I nod. "Nothing escapes his attention."

She laughs, but it's quickly lost. "God, I feel so overwhelmed and heartbroken, but at the same time, I'm grateful. I'm grateful that I'm not getting a call to say you've been found dead in a gutter." Her expression brightens somewhat, and she rolls her shoulders, although her eyes cross when her hand drifts over my shoddily dyed hair.

Awkward and not knowing what to say, I pad across to the sideboard and pick up my old school picture – one taken not long after she had taken me in. I sigh because I'm her again. Still that damaged child inside a woman's body. Carefully putting it back down, I look at the pictures of our family. Our *acquired* family. The one that embraced us both without explanation for reasons unknown. Although the reasons unknown, are now open and clear.

Approaching hesitantly, I hate that I flinch the moment the fine hair on her arm touches mine. For so long I had fought to empower myself, and with the love of a good man, I achieved it for a time. Now it has deserted me again, like so many things in life that have preceded it.

"Talk to me, honey," she whispers, ignoring my displeasure as she pulls me to sit down.

"He broke me, Marie. I spent eight years trying to forge a life for myself. I walked the streets; I stole to eat. I did everything I could to survive before you. And he's taken it all away from me again. I feel like that girl who sat in that lorry, wondering what London would bring. I was dreaming when I thought I could escape a past that will never let me go."

"Baby, he made a mistake, one that he will live with for the rest of his life."

I turn, shaking my head for emphasis. "Not Sloan, Deacon! I should've asked questions. I should've demanded Sloan to tell me the truth right off the bat, but I didn't." She holds me tighter. "I spent weeks, months, too terrified to tell him anything, because I feared he would be disgusted, yet he already knew."

She stays silent as she judges me until she breaks it. "Sloan and John have kept tabs on you for nearly a decade. Do you honestly think they would've done it that way if they knew how the end was to come about that night?" I shake my head. "He's a good man, honey, and you deserve him. He hasn't done things the right way, just like I didn't, but by God, I would never change it." She smiles and kisses my cheek, then purses her lips.

"What?" I narrow my eyes, as she shifts a strand of hair from my face.

"How about we talk about some good stuff – for now?"

"I'd like that," I say, happy to have a little piece of normality back.

"Well, a lot has happened since you've been gone. Stuart and Sophie are living together. Can you believe it? He's removed all things pink, and boy, did she tell me about it. Livid she was!" She laughs, recollecting. "Dev and Nicki are still together - we think. They don't talk about it, and we don't ask!"

"And Charlie?"

"She's in New York with her mum, although I imagine she'll be coming back soon considering. I doubt Jake has kept her in the dark again."

I suck in my bottom lip; being in the dark is where these men like to keep us fragile, damaged women.

"Good. I haven't dared to ask in case it puts him over the edge."

"Honey, you're the only one who could do that. There were some days, in the beginning, when we couldn't even think about you without him noticing."

I cross my legs, my expression turning serious. "I want him to hate me, but he won't. He's hurting, and I'm the cause of it – I'm always the cause of it. When I left the suite, if I'd have known what I was unknowingly..." I breathe out, still pondering the big *what if*.

"Hindsight is a beautiful thing."

"She's also a beautiful bitch!"

She laughs, opening the door. "She's that, too, but we learn from our mistakes."

"Do we?"

She sighs loudly but doesn't answer. "Let's go and have some tea. God, I still can't believe you're here!"

"Thank John for that. He said you were all heartbroken, and it was my fault."

"No, that's not fair. He had no right to make you feel bad." She marches towards the kitchen, and the sound of Sloan and Walker ribbing each other is infectious.

"Hey," Walker greets as we enter, fiddling with his broken mobile.

Sloan quickly pulls out two stools. Marie takes the one next to Walker and gives him a look that means business. I know, because I've been the recipient of it many, many times in the past.

"You owe my daughter an apology!"

"For what?" he asks, choking on his coffee and her audacity.

"For telling her lies! Just to jog your memory, sunshine, she didn't create this mess on her own." My face enflames under her chiding. I stare down at the table, drawing patterns with my fingertips until he takes a breath.

"Kara, I'm sorry. But seriously, does it really matter? You're home now." I raise my head and see Marie looking a little guilty. "Let's put it this way," he says and stares straight at me. "I was merely putting into action what they didn't have the balls to do. And it worked, didn't it?"

"It did."

"See, I told you everything would be right." He winks and throws me a custard cream. Pulling it apart, Marie begins to question Sloan about last night's almost ruined deal. I have no desire to talk shop with them and delicately touch Walker's hand.

"Thank you for making me come back. For your reassurance."

"The day you finally believe it, say it to me again."

After spending most of the morning talking about random stuff, Marie ups the ante with the most preposterous question of them all.

"Honey, where are you going to live? You can come back here, you know," she says with a huge smile, pouring another mug of tea, while Sloan almost spits his out. I raise my hand to my mouth, realising she has just touched upon a subject of contention of which the silent decision has already been determined.

"I *was* staying at John's. That is until I fell asleep in the spare room last night and woke up in the mansion this morning." I quickly glance around, just in time to see Sloan looking confident and Walker nodding, surprisingly impressed with his kid's achievement.

"Well, I couldn't have you getting too used to that idea, my love," Sloan declares.

Walker clears his throat, his expression solemn. "Kara, we still need to talk about what we do now. History has proven your ways of protecting yourself don't work particularly well. Now, we do it our way again."

"John, he's going to come back – they always come back. It's my constant."

Sloan slams his mug down. "I've already spoken to the guys. You'll be manned indefinitely. Fighting and arguing it is not an option."

"What about work? Marie doesn't want them in the office all day, do you?"

She gives me a tight, worried smile. "It's fine because you won't be in the office," she says, her eyes fixed on the tea she is stirring the life out of.

My forehead creases. "What are you saying?"

"I'm saying…you don't work for me anymore. Honey, it's been six months, and we've talked about this." She gets up and starts to wash the plates.

Glancing between the woman who can't even look at me, and the two egotistical, self-righteous arseholes, I huff out. Of all the things I jotted on my mental to-do list, the Jobcentre wasn't one of them. And, apparently, that was a grave oversight on my part. But really, what did I expect?

The table remains quiet, and Sloan and Walker do that thing where they conduct a silent conversation with flicks of their eyes and random expressions. My absconding has evidently done nothing to stop the trail of deceit from ending.

When the silence continues to devour, I stand, grab my bag and tug Sloan's hand. "I think it's time we left."

A plate smashes on the floor, and Marie rotates around, ready to open her mouth.

"Don't look at me like that! I just wanted something from my old life back. I've spent the last six months alone – and I mean *alone*. I got up, went to work, and then went home. There was no aberration. I lived off cereal and ready meals, and I downed half a bottle of cheap wine every night. Don't think for one minute I was swanning around living the good life!"

"Kara, I-"

I hold my hand up. "No. It's pretty fucking low that I have to finally admit how far down I really did sink!" I stomp out of the house and slam the door behind me.

Leaning against the car, the front door opens, and Sloan kisses Marie goodbye. Striding towards me, he deactivates the locks, and I slide inside the same moment he does.

"Well, that went well," he mutters.

I turn and lift my brows, daring him. "I'm sorry. I didn't mean to speak to her like that. I need to apologise."

"She understands."

"I know; she *understands* me far too much," I admit. Lifting his hand and kissing it, I smile sadly. "Take us home."

Holding my hand to his chest, he replies, "Always."

Chapter 12

SLOWLY OPENING MY eyes in the darkness of the living room, a faint glimmer of light bleeds from the hallway. I stretch out; my body feels tight, possibly drugged by the abnormal amount of sleep I've had over the last couple of days.

Tip-toeing up each stair rung, I step into the bedroom. It's empty, but skimming over the floor, our clothing from this morning is gone. I smile to myself that his undiagnosed OCD is still prevalent, then turn and follow the trail of light to the man who will be waiting at the other end of it.

Latching onto the door handle, acid rises in my chest, and I swallow it back down. Once I have finally exorcised my demons of the last few months, the harder I will become. Unfortunately, it means I have to endure these undeniable, stomach-churning moments to get there.

I curve my head around the spine, and Sloan appears positively stressed out, grabbing numerous bags and emptying them onto the island. His beautiful and expensive array of watches and cufflinks are strewn to one side, along with my jewellery.

"Hi," I murmur, putting one foot in front of the other.

His head whips up, and he drags his fingers through his hair. "Hey, my love." He holds out his hand, and I take it firmly. With his beautiful, signature grin, he pulls me closer and slides his back down the island. Positioning me on his lap, he meticulously fixes my legs to the sides of his hips.

"What are you doing?" I ask, feeling bizarrely content.

"I'm looking for something."

I glance around the bags; yet again those personal shoppers of his have been busy – and frivolous.

"Sloan…"

"Fine! I was looking for your gifts." He strokes his finger down my face, gentle and emotive.

"What gifts?"

"Christmas, Valentine's Day and your birthday," he says, a slight choking in his voice, while his words smart my eyes.

Overcome with guilt, I kiss his temple and ease back again. "You didn't have to do that," I whisper.

"Yes, I did. You're the woman I love, and I take care of what's mine." Curling myself into him, he tilts his head and coils his arms tight. "There were days I just sat here alone. I could always see you so clearly. It was more than a memory, and more than I knew it could ever be. Your scent drifted for weeks afterwards, and I consoled myself within it." He turns away with glassy eyes.

I tap his cheek, and he looks back at me. "John told me you've rarely been back to the hotel since that night."

"No. Truthfully, I just couldn't bear it. You were everywhere and nowhere. Lost and found, both dead and alive."

I lean forward and kiss his lips, alleviating the downturn of them. "Outside Marie's, when Deacon had me bound and gagged in his car, I prayed for you to look. You never did."

Slamming his head against the island, his jaw grinds. "Baby, I'll never forgive myself."

"No, I did this. I did. I took the easy option, but all I've done is unintentionally damage us. John was right, my ways of protecting myself just don't work."

"I beg to differ, because in some regard, your ways are right. Just not when it involves the psychopathic Blacks." He looks tired, but strangely relieved.

"Franklin didn't want to hurt me. He said he only wanted what was rightfully his, and when he had it, he would let me go. He knows about your mum. Is she safe?"

"She's fine. She's still in New York."

He draws me closer, pressing my body hard. I attempt to shuffle away, but he is having none of it and tightens his hands on my bum.

"He called John to say he had you. John called his bluff, even though we knew he wasn't lying. He said he would email through some evidence, but it never came." I shudder, because it did. And it went up in smoke in my kitchen.

Stroking my face delicately, I squeeze my eyes tight and surrender. "No," I whisper, concealing. "Deacon came in and he…" Tears careen down my cheeks as hesitant fingers pull the fabric away.

The cold air envelops my front, and a whisper of pain emits his mouth. Opening my eyes, he's looking over my torso. The fading marks are as clear as day, randomly crossing over my flesh, yet another constant reminder. Eventually, they're going to turn into silver, raised patterns, and join the rest of the scars he left me with nearly a decade ago.

His hand caresses my jaw, and I finally admit the truth.

"These are a representation of the life I have lived; the path I have walked. It also depicts the evil that has graced it far too many times." I look away, but he tugs my chin, disabling me. "When I left, I wanted you to disown me. And as painful as it was, I wanted you to move on. At least then I wouldn't have had a problem in masking myself under the charade of being a bitter, twisted girl that the world had wronged in so many ways. But my dreams prevailed. If I was to die right now, it would be worth it, because you still love me."

He carefully wipes away my fallen tears, evidently lost for words, but each one is true. Wanting him and needing him runs so deep in my veins, that it wouldn't have taken long for the mental and physical loss to amalgamate and drag me under. I would've forfeited myself completely.

With a delicate touch, he adjusts my top and glides his thumb over the nipple that stands out like a fractured piece of glass.

"Every time I see these, I'm reminded of his depravity. I've never asked you for anything, but I need to ask you for something now; something I'll never be able to afford." His eyes lift, encouraging me to continue. "Eventually, I want them all gone. The one on my thigh, my wrists, these." I point to my breasts. "I want them gone."

He nods; leans back down and begins to kiss each scar individually. Time passes slowly, until he reaches the last one just under my collarbone. He shifts us around and carefully lays me down. Crawling up my body until we are face to face, I run my hand through his messy, ebony hair.

"Can I ask you something?"

"Of course," he says nonchalantly, pressing his core to mine, ensuring I feel it. "What's wrong?"

"Nothing, I just wanted to know…" I stop. Can I really ruin this moment by bringing up the woman he loves to hate with a passion? Unapologetically, I must. I need to know the truth - not that I would ever accuse Doc of lying to me.

"I didn't want to ask at Marie's, but yesterday, Stuart said that no one has been to see Sam. You and Sophie, I understand, but Marie? Why has no one been to see her?"

He sighs and plays with my hair, still repulsed by the brassy hack job. "Baby, I saw her once, with Marie. She made a comment that it could be you in that bed somewhere. After hearing that, I just couldn't go back. If it's any consolation, Stuart has kept me informed.

We were going to get her transferred, but red tape halted it since only you are allowed to make that choice."

"What?"

"Hmm, John made the guys clear out the house she'd been staying at. They found a power of attorney. It was official, sworn by a solicitor. At some point in the future, you know what's going to be asked of you, don't you?"

I lift my brow; I'm abundantly aware. Her life is currently hanging precariously in the balance, and one day, I will be the one to decide whether she lives or dies. Who gave me the right to play judge, jury and executioner with her life? Although some might say, I've already performed all three of those roles, in some shape or form.

"Let's do something together tomorrow," he says, noticing my pensive state, and the fact I'm dwelling on something that is still to materialise.

"Why? Are you planning on skiving?" He adjusts us and rearranges my limbs. "You like sitting like this, don't you?"

He chuckles. "Indeed, it allows me to feel you in all the good ways. And as far as work goes, I can do what I please. Unless you have something else you want to do without me." He gives me a sad look, and his blues overemphasise it.

"Actually, there is something, and it comes with one request." He furrows his brow. "I want to see Sophie. *Alone.*" He starts to shake his head. "Please. I don't want an audience while I plead for her forgiveness."

His face runs through a variety of emotions, until he swipes his hand through his hair in agitation and concedes.

"Fine, but if anything looks suspicious, you call me, John, the police, the goddamn army, if need be, but you get the fuck out of there! Understood?"

"Thank you," I reply, relieved. "She looked so hurt when I saw her the other night. Gloria, too."

"She'll be fine, as will Gloria. The poor woman was at her wits' end about what to do with us both moping. Having to deal with me was bad enough, but when Sophie started, I think she was ready to start digging up the patio."

I laugh. "I'm sorry."

"Don't be. Just make sure you drop by the office and see her. She's been really worried about you."

"I will." I kiss him and stand, wrapping my arms around him.

"God, how I've longed to hold you like this again."

Glancing around the room, I smile at all the gorgeous items I have been reunited with. But unfortunately, some may never be worn again, because they will expose what I want to keep hidden. Shuffling away, I walk out with an idea in mind.

"Let's take a bath," I suggest. He moves towards me, his suspicious smirk growing. "Well, we need to talk, and the last time we had a serious, life-changing conversation, it was in the bath."

He picks me up and strides into the en-suite. Sitting me on the toilet, he starts to run the water. Fumbling around in the drawers, he pulls out one bottle after another. None meet with his approval, until he grabs one and pours it in.

"Why were you at the hospital yesterday?"

Shuffling off the toilet, I kneel on the floor and dig through the drawer. *My drawer.* It's still stocked with so-called essentials I shall probably never use. Picking up the contraceptive boxes, I turn one in my hand.

"This is why. I wasn't sure if you might've binned them and it was easier than making an appointment," I reply, holding up a little box. "I also figured you wouldn't tolerate me sleeping anywhere else again."

"You're damn right!" he confirms.

Picking me up, he peels off my clothes. I instantly bring my arms around my front, and he cocks his head in annoyance. Except, until I can look upon myself and feel satisfied, this is the reaction he will always receive.

I quickly hurry into the almost full bath and turn off the taps. Bringing my knees up, the water moves as he slides in behind me. He leans back with his arm just under my breasts and pulls me down with him. Running my hands over my chest, I urge my emotional side to harden. I try to think of the right words to say, words that won't obliterate the last twenty-four hours.

"Talk to me." He breaks the tension, considering I've been silent for far too long when this was my grand idea.

"I didn't think I'd ever see you again," I whisper, pain consuming me that I'm going to give him the honest truth. "When Deacon had me in the car, I really did think that was the end. I gave up; I gave up on us. I didn't want to go back to being the old Kara, but I knew if he did *that* to me again, I would."

"Baby, I don't think I can listen to this."

"You have to. I once told you that the day we become one, was the day we spoke of life's horrific moments that we didn't want to. Please just listen and don't stop me, because if you do, I might not have the courage to speak of it again."

He stills behind me, and only the hollow ripple of water resounds.

"When I finally woke up, Jeremy was with me. He told me I was stupid for running; that I was the bait. Frankie then came in, and he said he'd let me go. Hope bloomed in my chest that maybe I would live through it. I vowed to myself that I would. I was determined to see you again, but after he left and Deacon..." Catching my breath, I feel myself falling into despair. "How could I ever face you again, looking like this?" I whimper.

"Hearing your voice over the phone, I was so confused. I remember thinking you were asleep next to me, until I realised I was alone. The fear in your voice was terrifying…and I *knew*."

Turning around, the water sways at my sides. I lean forward, with my hands around the back of his neck, and I stare at him.

"This is the only time I will ask you this question, and I want you to be honest." My eyelids close in resignation, waiting for the inevitable.

"Open your eyes, my love."

Obeying, they liquefy.

"Did that bastard rape you?" I turn away, ashamed. "Kara, look me. Answer me."

I shake my head. "He inferred it, there was a moment when he made me believe it, but instead, he did this." I stroke my chest lightly.

He drops his head in my neck, while his hands tightening on my waist. "Baby, did he touch you?"

"Yes," I whisper, mortified.

"*Where?*" The venom lacing his tone turns my resolve to ash, and I don't know if I should face him. I don't know if I can handle seeing how he will look upon me now.

I inhale shakily. "He grabbed my…" I bring my hands to my breasts, showing him what I cannot articulate. "And he touched…" I glance down my stomach and then meet his sad, vindictive eyes. "He didn't pene…enter…"

"Thank God." Hauling me close, the water splashes over the edge in a mini tidal wave, and he kisses my tumbling tears. "I'm sorry, my love. I keep on saying it, but I don't know what to do to make this right. Tell me how I can make this right."

"You can't. There's absolutely nothing you can do because I remember everything now. Except, when I do, I think of everything amazing and wonderful we've experienced together. Just like before, the only thing that can help me now is knowing you're still mine."

"Always." Studying my chest, he picks up a flannel from my corner of the bath, soaks it and dabs it over my skin. He glides his thumb over my lips, eventually easing his fingers at the back of my neck. The flannel slaps the water's surface, and he starts to slide down the bath. Pointing behind him, I narrow my eyes. I have no clue of what he is requesting.

"I want you to lay over me, and we're going to stay here until we are cold and wrinkly."

I laugh loudly. Sliding over him, I bring my leg across his hip, feeling him spark to life intimately. "I would love to grow wrinkly with you, Sloan Foster."

"I'm glad to hear it because you won't be growing wrinkly with anyone else!"

I rest my head against his chest, placing a slight kiss on his nipple. My ultimate wish is definitely being fulfilled.

My aim was to reclaim whatever was left of the shattered heart I had left in my wake. Listening to it beat strong and determined beneath me, I haven't just reclaimed it, I've brought it back to life.

Chapter 13

MY LEG SHAKES nervously, and I slam my hand over my knee, trying, ineffectively, to stop the reflex action. Averting my eyes to the house with acute anxiety, I consciously chew my nails. As I repeat over and over what I'm going to say, I sigh. It all sounds so brilliantly executed inside my head, but I'm not an idiot. After all these years, I know she will make me grovel – that's if my cheek doesn't fall foul of her hand first.

Getting out of the Evoque, I walk timidly up the driveway. I clutch my bag and observe diligently, obeying the explicit instruction I have been given.

Raising my arm, I dither, my fist only inches from the wood. My stomach roils, and I swallow back the waters in my mouth before knocking. Time passes by, and the sky starts to darken as grey clouds begin to build momentum above. I stare up, wondering if I should risk knocking again - although I'm probably pushing my luck by doing it in the first place.

I pull out my phone, ready to let Sloan know I'm on my way back, when the handle rattles from the inside. I inch away cautiously and drop my head in shame.

The door opens, and the first thing I see are fluffy slippers. Soph takes a shaky breath as I finally meet her line of sight. With her lips pursed together, and her hands clenched in anger, she speaks.

"Well, the prodigal best friend returns."

"I'm sorry, Soph."

She moves her head from side to side and chortles. "Is that all you've got to say? Hmm? We've been going out of our fucking minds, yet all you can say is *'I'm sorry'*? Tell it to someone who gives a shit!"

The door slams in my face, and I stare at the wood in absolute, yet expected, shock.

Running back to the car, inside I drop my forehead to the wheel and cry furiously. I never expected her to be all open arms and gushing at my reappearance. I didn't even expect her to be happy to see me, but out of everyone, I expected her to have an ounce of compassion. Yet, obviously, compassion cannot be conveyed when it's clear she is unaware of the circumstances surrounding the event.

I start the engine, ready to drop the handbrake, as my door opens. Sophie reaches in, pulls out the key and grabs my bag from the passenger seat. She remains solemn as she walks back up the driveway and stands in front of the door. Folding her arms over her chest, she waits for me to follow.

"Are you coming in or not?" she calls out, annoyed and impatient.

I shuffle back out; my eyes trained on the paving stones until I reach the house. She activates the car locks and slams the door shut again. I flinch and turn, ready for it. Instead, she pushes my bag into my chest and leaves me at the front door.

Hanging my coat on the rack, I muster a smile when I see Stuart's boots and jackets alongside hers. Removing my phone, I leave my handbag on the small table and follow dutifully.

As I make my way into the kitchen, I notice most of her stuff has been replaced by items that are definitely manlier. As per Marie's extrapolation, Stuart has already put his own stamp on the place.

My aim to be quiet and introvert, collecting my thoughts, is lost when my boot heel clicks on the tiled floor. She stands by the sink, waiting for the kettle to boil, saving me from pleading benevolence straight off the bat. While I desperately want her forgiveness, I will not grovel again for doing what I deemed to be right in a moment of stupidity that has cost me everything I hold dear.

"Why?"

The silence is shattered, yet I can't answer. All my good intentions of explaining disappeared the moment she slammed the door in my face.

"Of all the shit that has happened, why did you do it? Six fucking months and nothing!" She thumps her hand down on the worktop.

"I don't know," I whisper, my conviction gone, flailing in the wind.

"Yes, you do! Why?"

Unable to say the words, I slide onto the stool and tuck my chin in, keeping my eyes low. The first tear splashes the surface, making way for the rest that are sure to follow. An eerie silence cloaks the room, and the only sounds are my anguish and Soph's anger.

"Kara, stop falling apart. I called you every day, wondering where you were. You could have been dead somewhere!"

"I know," I utter in absolute ignominy. She rubs her thumb and forefinger over her eyelids, pinching the bridge of her nose.

"This isn't going to work, is it?" she probes softly, placing the drinks down.

She slides onto the stool next to me and turns the mug between her fingers. My heart is beating wildly, then suddenly, she whips around. Tugging me close, she starts to cry into my shivering neck.

"I missed you so much," she whispers. "I needed you, and you weren't here, but I *do* understand why. They told me what happened when you were a teenager – what Deacon did and subsequently what Marie did. They told me everything." She pulls away, roughly wiping her eyes. "At least now I understand the name change, and why when anyone called you Dawson sometimes you didn't answer!" I snort, while her thumbs capture my tears.

"I wanted to tell you for so long, but I couldn't. If anyone had found out about me…"

"I understand, babe." She picks up her mug and takes a long draw. "What?" she asks, and I wonder what expression I'm wearing. Clearly, they haven't told her everything as she seems to believe.

"What did they say, exactly?" I feel my forehead crease, knowing I'm going to have to fill in the blanks.

Lots of them.

"Erm, just what I've said. Why?"

"Okay," I say slowly, punctuating the letters. "We went to see Sam in hospital, and Deacon showed up. He kept calling Sloan *brother,* and I missed it. Actually, I missed it twice, but that's irrelevant. Deacon gloated about what he'd done when I was fifteen, and I broke down." I stare at her, seeing beyond the glassy, sorrow-filled eyes.

"Go on." Holding the mug to her chest, she nods her head to continue.

"Back in the suite that night, I overheard John asking Sloan if I knew, and I lost it. After what happened with Sam and Christy, it was a natural reaction to think the worst. Long story short, his mother isn't dead. She's very much alive, living in New York."

She slams down the mug and lets out a mirthless laugh. "They didn't tell me this!"

I put my hand over hers, experiencing a dull twinge. "No, they wouldn't, because of her ex-husband, Charlie's father. Throughout my childhood, my own dad *worked* for a man called Franklin Black. Supplying drugs and what other screwed up shit they could make a quick grand from. He's the reason why Deacon snatched me, or maybe half the reason since that bastard has his own deranged motives."

"Kara, I don't understand…"

"I was repeatedly raped throughout my teens by Deacon, because my father wasn't strong enough to protect me. It also happened because he was frightened of Franklin, so he allowed me to be abused to keep the peace as such."

"Jesus Christ!" She slowly puts her hand over her mouth, before lowering it. "But I still don't-"

"Franklin is Charlie's father." Soph's mouth starts to open again, but I put my finger over it. "He tied me up in a filthy fucking room because when Sloan's mother divorced him, he didn't get a penny. He thought he could use me to get what he thinks is his."

Sophie's mouth finally drops open, and she appears to be thinking, absorbing what I've said. Until it becomes clear, yet again, she still doesn't understand.

"And how does this Deacon fit into all of this?"

"He's Franklin's son," I acknowledge pitifully. "They never told me. I had to find it out for myself just before he injected me with shit and tied me up in that place."

"Oh fuck, babe, I didn't know!" She looks horrified, but just like me, they have kept her in consummate darkness. But unlike me, at least she knew before the bastard ever turned up at her door, looking to exact revenge on those she loves more than life.

"That's not the worst of it. The things he did to me, things he wanted to… I'm not exaggerating when I say I'm lucky I didn't leave there in a box." I remain emotionless as a veil of water runs down my cheeks.

Sophie's hands encase mine. "He didn't ra… God, I can't even say it!"

I shake my head. "No, he inferred it, but instead he cut…"

"What?"

I impulsively raise my hand to my chest, while her fingers move the fabric. She breathes out in shock, as a mark, probably smaller than a fingernail, is revealed. She hastily tries to move the rest of my top, but I stop her.

"Please, don't."

Her hand retracts instantly. "Are they worse than the ones on your back?"

I nod. I won't lie, because at some point she's going to see them, and when that happens, I know we will come back to this place. The place where I want to conceal myself and not expose the tribulations that have been and gone and still cruelly remain.

The room falls back into silence. Watching her turn the mug in her hand, I remember the other reason why I also made it my mission to come here today. I ease off the stool, and she turns abruptly.

"Where are you going?" I hold up a finger and dart down the hallway. Digging into my bag, I pull out the hair dye. Back in the kitchen, I shake the box in front of her.

"Want to do some beauty school bonding?" She lifts a section of my hair, pulling a repulsed face.

"It does look pretty bad." She laughs. "I wasn't going to say anything."

"No, of course you wouldn't." I laugh with her, as she slings her arm over my shoulder.

"I'm guessing Sloan doesn't like it?"

I roll my eyes. "No, he feels like he's cheating, apparently."

"Babe, you changed it for a reason. I can always do a better job than this, if need be."

"I know you can, but considering I'm back now makes the reason null and void." Nodding in agreement, she snatches up the box, then my hand and leads me up the stairs.

Sitting cross-legged on the floor, I face her, sitting on the toilet, studying the instructions.

"You picked a crappy one by the way. Crappiest and most expensive. This is going to take over half an hour for the colour to take. Maybe longer." She gives me an awkward look. "Promise you won't go off on one if it turns your hair green?"

I laugh. Clearly, she and the shop assistant know far more about beauty standards than I do.

"I promise I won't!"

"Good. And another thing?" I furrow my brow, challenging her to say anything further. "I love the shorter do on you. Very cute, and it'll finish up very sexy when you get back to the natural you. Right, put this over your shoulders," she says, throwing me an old towel and snapping on the plastic gloves.

Marching up and down the landing, since I'm forbidden to set foot anywhere else in case I splash, I sigh, bored. Scratching the side of my plastic-covered head, I'm positive this stuff has something thermal in it. My head is on goddamn fire.

"Is it meant to feel hot?"

Soph hurries towards me with her make-up case and lifts the cover. "I don't know. Just let me know if you feel faint. Come on, sit down." She tugs me back into the bathroom and kneels in front of me. Rummaging through the box, she pulls out some concealer.

"I need more than that for this sleep-deprived look!" I comment flippantly, and she glares, unimpressed.

"It's not for the bags," she mutters, her hand loitering near my chest. "I want to see if I can cover that."

Delicately applying the concealer, she starts to blend it meticulously. Scrunching her face a little, judging whether or not she can still see it, a few strokes later, she appears to be satisfied.

"Well, it's barely visible now, although I don't think the standard stuff will cover them completely." She hands over the tube and starts to pull out more. "Here, take them home and practice. I think we might have to see what else we can buy."

"Soph, you're looking at the girl who doesn't like having to buy a dress, can you imagine if I have to go shopping to cover the signs of torture?"

She grimaces. "You're over-exaggerating!" I roll my eyes in response. "Okay, maybe not, but it's got to be better than worrying if anyone can see them, right?"

I huff, causing my lips to reverberate. "True, but I can't afford a fancy cosmetics shop. I'm virtually penniless."

She looks at me like I've lost my mind. "Is there something my boss needs to tell me? Did he suddenly become bankrupt overnight? Look at what your man's worth! There's no way he would deny you anything. Kara, I know you don't like spending his money, but it's yours now. You know, I was furious when Stuart removed all my stuff and replaced it with better. He did it, because just like Sloan, he takes care of what's his. Buck it up, babe, because this is your life now!"

"Soph-"

"No, I refuse to listen. Now, be quiet and let's see if the old Kara is ready to present herself!"

"So, what's this Deacon like?" Soph asks quietly, running the straighteners through my hair.

"Terrifying," I admit in a whisper, capturing her eyes in the mirror.

"Stuart keeps telling me to watch for anyone suspicious, but since I have no idea who he is, how am I supposed to know?" She shrugs.

"I'll see if John can get a picture of him, but seriously, you'll know when you see him. And if you ever do, you run." She sprays me copiously, and I close my eyes as I taste chemicals.

Smiling, satisfied she has brought me back, she pulls me up. "Do you want to stay and have lunch?"

"I'd love to, but Sloan's keeping me on a tight rein at the moment."

"I'm surprised he even let you come over here." She looks sympathetic.

I nod mutely. "It didn't go without disagreement. Although it won't last long, especially when I tell him I'm job hunting."

"You've seen Marie, then? How was she?"

"Good. And she didn't slam the door in my face!"

"Sorry, babe," she replies, embarrassed.

"Don't be. So, how's working for Sloan going for you?"

"Really good. The other staff are nice, and it's abundantly clear he doesn't hire arseholes. I also like that I'll be seeing more of you in the future." She grins coyly. "Although how much *more* is debatable!"

"What do you mean?" I ask suspiciously.

"Oh, nothing, but Gloria warned me!" I shake my head, missing the point as usual. "There'll be no funny business on my watch! And you can tell that man of yours, too!" I gasp in shock. "Okay, so she didn't tell me exactly, I *overheard* a comment she made to his highness."

"And you put two and two together and actually came up with four?"

"Precisely!"

"Well, I wouldn't worry. He let down his guard today, but who knows how he'll be tomorrow," I comment, taking each rung down to the hallway.

"He's lived and breathed your memory from the moment you left, chick." She smiles, stroking my hair, letting the newly dark strands ripple through her fingers. "And they'll be no holding back now his true girl has returned."

"Thank you - for forgiving me, for colouring me, and for still being my best friend."

"Well, someone's got to do it!" She lets me go, and I step outside.

Gazing up at the sky, my world is bizarrely bright again.

Chapter 14

"KARA?"

I LOOK towards the door from my cross-legged position on the floor. I've been sat here for a while, staring at my old mobile, debating whether or not to call my mother. I want to, I really do, but I fear if I give in to temptation, fate will find a way to overrule and prove to be the consistent, dominant force. It means the wheel will never stop turning, and I shall be drawn back into the place of my nightmares, torn between the past and the present that will ultimately play a hand my future.

"Kara?" I scramble up, identifying the urgency in his tone.

"One minute!" I run out of the spare room and malinger at the top of stairs. Seconds later, he jogs up, looking relieved to see me – the real me.

"Hey, how did it go?" he queries. Gazing at me longingly, he touches my newly dyed hair. "There's my girl. Welcome home, my love." I come over shy and put my hand on his, bringing it down my shorter lengths.

"You like?"

"No," he says, nodding his head. "I love." He cups my chin, easing me into him. "I've always loved and will always love. And I'm definitely not sorry to see the blonde imposter gone!"

He really bloody hated it! Admittedly, I wasn't overly keen, but sometimes we must make sacrifices in order to survive.

He studies me, still expressing his look of adoration. Stepping a fraction closer, my stare focuses on his mouth. I've waited a long time to taste those lips again as Kara Petersen.

"May I?" he asks. Pursing my lips shyly, I nod. He's asking a silly question, and his cocky grin confirms it.

He slowly rakes his hands down my back, his touch awakening me. It feels different than it did last night, and that's because it is. Last night, I was still pretending to be someone I'm not. Now, I am truly Kara Petersen. His Kara Petersen; the girl I banished into purgatory that he forever releases from her invisible prison.

The heat of his mouth warms mine before we are even touching. Softly brushing his thumb over my bottom lip, he finally quenches his desire to feel, and I moan into him the moment his tongue requests more. Grabbing the bannister, I rub my free hand over his back, reaching up on my toes.

He groans deep in his throat and clutches me harder. Shrugging out of his suit jacket, he walks us backwards, until the wall halts his endeavour. I open my eyes, and his darken. Trailing my fingers south, his pupils dilate, and he grins with understanding.

"You want?"

I demonstrate my enthusiasm by dragging his tie and wrapping it around my hand. My shirt is torn clean from my body, and he shakes his head at it. Taking his lead, my hands fumble with his buttons, until he rips that open, too.

"Too slow, my love."

I move towards his beautiful chest and tentatively stroke my tongue over his nipple. He hisses instantly and fixes his hand on my nape, circling hypnotically. Exploring every muscle, ridge and flaw, I reach his abdomen. He glides his hand under my chin and lifts my head; concern furrows his brow.

"Easy, slowly," he says, touching my lips.

"Please don't make me stop," I whimper.

Desire radiates through me seeing him turned on and wanting. Undoing his belt, his trousers and shorts drop simultaneously, exposing his already aroused appendage. Consumed with both excitement and fear, I lower. My tongue darts forward and swipes his head. He shudders upon first contact, exhaling heavily. Assured, with my confidence growing, I take in the first inch. Running my lips up and down, I acclimatise myself with him all over again.

He constantly shifts under my administration, throbbing against my tongue, until his hand tightens in my hair.

"Shit baby, you need to let go!" he strains out, his tone laced with passion. I grab his thighs with all my might, because letting go isn't an option I possess anymore. I did it once; it destroyed me. I will not make that mistake again. Not when it concerns the way we live, and definitely not when it concerns the way we love.

Roaring out my name, his hips move fluidly while liquid heat infuses my mouth. I swallow, urging my gag reflex to behave itself. Continuing to mark what's already mine, the final heady ripples of pleasure leave him breathless, proud and tall above me, unable to communicate what his heart truly craves.

I lift up on my hands, and tenderly place one last kiss on his stomach and bring my hand over my mouth, feeling my lips tingle pleasantly. Picking myself up from the floor, he remains motionless, and I creep into the bedroom.

I stare at the door; I don't know if I've just done the right thing. When he jogged up those stairs, he wanted life to revert back to the way it once was, he wanted back his dominance over me. Instead, I shifted the equilibrium by giving myself the man I sacrificed selfishly. The quiet calm of the situation heightens my procrastination, until I can no longer think.

Padding into the bathroom, the crazy demeanour I displayed on the landing disintegrates with each lonely second that ticks by. Discarding my clothing, I step under the shower and watch the dark remnants of dye seep down the drain.

The glass door eventually opens, and Sloan's unique scent swirls around the space. I twist my head to the side, and a large hand comes around my middle and grips my waist. Resting his chin on my shoulder, he slowly kisses my neck, up to my temple. Pivoting to face him, I whimper with sensation when he slides against me.

"Mine," he growls, tugging my bottom lip between his teeth. Our eyes meet; his fierceness is captivating. He runs his tongue down my chin and neck, reaching the swell of my chest. "Mine," he says again, equally determined. "I want words, my love."

"Yours," I confirm, gripping his hand. He clenches our fists together and presses me up against the wall. Bending, he squeezes both breasts hard, then takes a nipple into his mouth. I gasp out at the sensation he's eliciting. Looking down, he gazes expectantly.

"Yours," I whimper.

He sucks reverently, soothing the sting he has just invoked. Working down my body, I lean back, allowing him to conduct both pleasure and pain to alleviate himself of whatever is possessing him.

He kneels down in front of me, then lifts my leg and puts it over his shoulder. Pressing his head into my apex, nipping my skin, I yelp when he slides his tongue through my folds. My heart spasms under his control; the power he has over me never falters.

He starts to move faster, harder, bringing us both to the edge and beyond. Holding him firmly, my muscles feel like they are ready to explode, while I try to maintain my stance and give in to the congenial force driving me.

"Oh, God!" I spit out, accidentally smacking my skull on the tiles. "More," I demand, unashamed, forgetting the discomfort. His talented tongue instantly obliges, unleashing my hidden, passionate side.

The room is filled with sound; my cries, his grunts, and the water hitting the floor. Bracing my arms out to the sides, my fingers slide along the grout. My chest heaves and my body feels weak, having gone from an abundance of physical activity to nothing for six months, and now back again in a matter of days.

He studies me, then runs his nose up and down my neck. Considering his impending action, he places his hands on my back and lowers us to the shower floor.

"I'll never have control with you. The only time I feel alive is when you're near me. When I can feel your heat and when your body is connected to mine. Today, you come back to life for me. "

"Make love to me. Remove the last shred of lingering doubt from here." I press his hand over my heart.

"Hold on," he whispers, and I accommodate willingly, slapping my hands on his shoulders. He lifts us up and positions my centre on his tip. Guiding me down, I feel every hard inch as we fuse together. "Ride me."

Slanting my mouth over his, bracing my legs for leverage, I move with urgency. I need to reach the finish, not because I want the act to be over, but because I want this internal pain we have both carried since that night banished indefinitely. It doesn't deserve to have a place in our lives, or in our future.

"That's it, baby, feel me."

Riding his length, I cry silent tears of joy while his passion penetrates deep into my soul, making me heady and sublime. "Tell me you love me."

He reaches up and turns off the water, before thrusting up with force.

"I love you," he grits out. "So fucking much, it could finish me!" Taking my scarred nipple between his lips, he lavishes it with kisses.

"Oh!" I moan out, clenching my thighs, holding him deeper.

"Come. Eyes on me." I stare at him, seeing beyond the damaged man I have assisted in creating, and into the other half of my being.

"Oh. My. God!" I feel out of control, but it doesn't matter, because the last twenty minutes have corroborated what I needed to hear.

"Squeeze, my love," he murmurs. I clamp my internal muscles around his length, and his lids start to droop as the rapture of release builds.

"Eyes on me when you come," I order playfully, in the same tone he bestows upon me. He growls out, thrusting himself deeper to the point of pain.

"Always, my love." True to his word, he stares wide-eyed as we reach the peak and float back down together. Dropping his head to my chest, his breathing stabilises, until he finally looks up and around. I shuffle off of him, and he staggers up and reaches down for me. Turning the water back on, he appears sated.

"Thank you for letting me come home."

Stepping closer, he starts to wash me, doing what has become so easy and natural.

"This has always been your home, long before you even knew it existed. But until you eventually arrived, it was just a house. A house that had been the subject of many nightmares. This might be our home, but your true home will always be here." He presses my hand to his heart.

"Notwithstanding how many times I destroy it through my own idiocy?" I step back, but he stops me.

"Yes, and let's not forget I always seem to achieve equal destruction through mine." I wrap my arms around him. "I should have told you the first night I met you, but I couldn't because I needed something from you." Gauging me with caution, he continues. "I needed you to fall in love with me. It wasn't malicious or misleading, but I had been in love with you for years. I knew if you loved me, you would always come home, regardless of the reasons for staying away."

I soap my hands, then carefully slide them down his front. He makes a few noises; still affected by my touch.

"Always mine," I whisper.

"Yep, you did a number on me the first moment I saw you. Every time I see you, even now. It's like the room fades out and you are the light. *My light*." I smile and bite my lip, happiness threatening to expose itself through my eyes.

"Don't do that. I hate to see you cry. Let's get you dried." I open the door as he playfully slaps my backside.

Wrapping myself, I dry my hair, while watching his reflection in the partially condensed mirror. He shuts off the water and steps out, and I approach holding a towel open.

"Are you reversing the roles here?"

"Hmm, I thought it might be nice to take care of you for a change."

"That's a delightful gesture, but it's never going to happen."

He quickly takes it and covers himself. As always - and not that I would expect anything less - he picks me up and carries me into the bedroom.

He drops me on the bed, then walks towards the drawers and pulls out a t-shirt. With a mischievous smirk, he fumbles around in another and balls something up in his hand. Coming back to me, he crooks his finger.

"Closer," he whispers.

My heart is on the verge of shattering as I crawl towards him, still clutching the fabric at my front.

"Drop it!"

My arms shoot up, and the towel lays redundant on the duvet. I breathe out, thoroughly at ease as he lowers the t-shirt over my head. I attempt to pull it down, but he slaps my hands away.

"Stop it. Stand."

Slowly getting to my feet, I balance myself on the bed. Seeing my awkwardness, he runs his palms up my sides and circles my nipples under the material. I mellow and sigh out. *This,* I have missed so much, and clearly, my body is ecstatic to be back in that place of sexual fulfilment again.

My eyes widen when he brushes something soft over my areola. His hand reappears from under the t-shirt, and he holds up a black lace thong.

Holding it at my feet, I step in, and he slides it up my legs. Wiggling while he positions the band, he kisses the front, then cradles me in his arms. His laugh is infectious, as he spins us around the room until I feel nauseous.

Laying us back on the bed, he curves my leg over his hip. His breath blows blissfully while peppering my skin with gentle kisses.

"Go to sleep, my love."

His hands rub small circles over my belly, assisting to eradicate my anxiety. As my eyes flutter shut, ready to see morning and the man I love in a new light of forever, the darkness slowly devours. My sub-conscience shudders, as a triad of figures emerge from the subliminal darkness. My body instantly convulses, causing his hands to wrap tighter.

"You don't have to be frightened any more, no one will hurt you again."

With his words drifting over me, the shadows blend and fade, waiting until they are ready to reveal themselves again.

I grab his hand in mine, constantly rubbing it. My heart is beating rapidly, and it isn't the man holding me who is the cause of it, it's the memory of the monsters who devoured their prey in the dark and left her in desolation.

It's the fear of a future that is yet to unfold.

Chapter 15

THE FRONT DOOR slams and I tilt my head up from the computer screen. Numerous voices puncture the quiet, and then one set of heavy feet bang on the stairs.

I sigh out, taking a sip of my tea. It's cold and bitter. Ignoring the infernal racket, I return to scrolling through the website.

"Hey, baby." Sloan's voice resonates through the room. I look up - not that I need to - and smile.

"Hi," I answer, my attention diverted, as he moves into the centre and starts to look around.

My day hasn't been completely taken up with job hunting, I've also managed to house some of my old furniture here and there.

He narrows his eyes with interest at my old landing table, that is now housing the printer, a lamp, and his old uni books. I stop and look over the top of the screen, my curiosity piqued. He runs his hand over the second-hand wood and smiles.

"I like it. What else have you done today?" he asks, striding over and twisting the monitor. "Besides pointless job hunting."

I swipe my hand over my head and glare at him. "I will not live off your purse strings, Foster!" Now that gets his attention sharpish, but I don't care, because I don't want him putting the Queen's head in my pocket.

"And if we had kids, what would you do then? Work with one on your hip?" He throws his hands up for emphasis.

Sarcastic git!

"That's different, and you know it!"

He scratches his chin, deep in thought. "Fine. If you want to work, I'll give you a job."

I gasp, needing to remain intolerant of the position he's putting me in. He doesn't need to know that I already have an interview lined up.

"It wouldn't be ethical for me to work in your office."

He grins slyly. "No, but it would be awfully convenient."

"And very weird. And technically, it would still be your money."

Standing directly in front of me, he leans down. "Actually, it's all my mother's money. Does that make you feel better?"

"Not in the slightest!" I huff out, as he lifts me up and sits himself down, positioning me as per his usual preference. He rubs his hand over my forehead studiously, before pillaging my mouth.

A deep throat clearing breaks us apart. Walker lobs himself into one of the big, comfy chairs and crosses his legs, wearing an expression that is borderline arrogant.

"Don't stop on my account, children. Kara, I should be thanking you, this last fortnight has been heavenly. I swear I've heard cherubs draw a chorus!"

My face tinges a darker shade of pink, while Sloan is clearly unenthused by his verbal intervention.

"Piss off! Come back in a few hours, better yet, a few days. We still have five months, one week, and four days to make up for! And take the heathens downstairs with you!"

"Jesus, sunshine, give the girl a break! Honey, how are you doing?"

I wriggle out of Sloan's arms, as he mutters incessantly about unwanted guests and being eaten out of house and home. Curling into the adjacent seat, I tuck my legs underneath myself.

"I'm okay, just fed up. You know, I now appreciate it when I hear that there are two point whatever million unemployed. And because of you two, I'm now one of them. Thank you so much!"

Honestly, my days of taking up residence in the hotel restaurant with the laptop might just be on the horizon again. That is still something to discuss, along with the more important matter of my independence. I haven't pushed it these last two weeks, only going over to Sophie's and Marie's, and that's it. I know my ability to roam the city unmanned is out of the question. I also know Mr Overbearing is going to have a coronary when he finds out what employment tricks I have up my sleeve.

"Baby, you're not one of them!" Sloan mutters from the desk. I roll my eyes and ignore him. Walker grips my hand, gives the kid a sly look, then stands.

"Yeah, well, there's a shed load of takeaway downstairs. I'd like to say I'm here purely for a social catch up, but that would be lying. Instead, I've invited myself for dinner. Fortunately, or unfortunately – whichever way you want to look at it – I've brought some guests." Commotion from downstairs causes him to roll his eyes. "Come on, before the fat bastards eat it all, and I have to roll them out of the door!"

He disappears out of the room as Sloan moves and throws his arm around me. He then pulls my chin so he can continue where he left off. "I've got a surprise for you in the living room." He turns on his heel and leaves me in confusion.

I follow them and stop outside the living room door, wondering what on earth is in here. Pushing it back, Charlie's strawberry blonde hair is the first thing I see. Suddenly, this room is a place I neither want to enter, nor run away from. Inside this room stands the other half of my emotional self, someone who will not condone nor condemn. She has walked the same path of pain and brutality alongside me, long before we knew the other existed.

Staring into her glassy, lifeless eyes, it feels like the oxygen has been ripped from me. She looks so young and vulnerable, yet frail and partially aged. This is a common theme in the women who love me - aged through my abandonment of them.

"Oh my God," she whispers, barely moving her lips. Time fails to move, and seconds feel like hours while her eyes drift up and down. "Oh my God!" She moves swiftly, wrapping her arms around me.

The burn garners prominence from my head to my toes. Tolerating it, I bury my head in her shoulder, dampening her blouse with my tears. Inhaling her scent, I pray my sins will be absolved when she finally lets me go and speaks of her own personal suffering.

"I never thought I'd see you again. I've missed you so much. Sloan was-"

She doesn't finish as the man himself appears in the doorway. He strides over and tilts his little sister's face up. Ever so gently with his thumbs, he wipes her tears. I stand off to the side, feeling intrusive in this very private moment between the siblings. She whispers something to him, looking hopeful. After a few tense moments, he groans and gives in.

"Fine, but only for tonight."

They walk as one, and Sloan holds out his other arm for me. Leaving the living room, Charlie begins to tell me random, meaningless stuff. It's her way of breaking the proverbial iceberg wedged between us. Letting us go, Sloan holds open the door.

"Hi," I greet, entering the dining room and pulling out a chair. Sloan takes his seat beside me, while Charlie takes the other.

I run my eyes over everyone. Tommy and Parker are both giving me heartfelt smiles, and I reciprocate nervously. A nudge on my shoulder startles me, and I turn quickly to find Devlin at my side. Rising up to him, he takes me in his arms and holds firm.

"Lay one on me, little lady." He points to his cheek. I hesitate, but he puts a sloppy kiss on my forehead and steps back, waiting for the admonishment of touching me.

"Boss, you might need to disinfect her before you go there again!" Parker calls out, causing Tommy to howl with laughter.

"Arsehole!" Dev replies, flipping him the middle finger.

"I see some people haven't changed," I murmur.

Parker stands and rolls over a can of coke. "I will have you know I *have* changed. I no longer only supply one night stands now, Kara - I send them on their way with a twenty for a taxi and breakfast, too!"

Walker veers around the table and smacks his head. "Shut up, Si! And don't you say a word!" He points at Tommy.

"I wasn't…but twenty is a bit steep. I thought the last one only got ten quid, you tight bastard!"

"Well said, son!" Jake shouts on his way in from the kitchen. He comes over and kisses my forehead. "Welcome home at last." I bring my hand to my mouth, ready to burst into tears. Until the bedlam starts again.

"Devlin, where's Nicki?" I query, needing a change of subject before I launch my drink at something. *Or someone.* These raucous men are trying my last nerve, and they've only been here five minutes!

He puts down the slice of half-devoured pizza, turns to Walker, then back again. "Your mother made her drive to Surrey with her all because of a goddamn, frigging cake!"

"Check the attitude, sunshine," Walker admonishes him.

"When did you get back?" Parker speaks up with a mouthful to Charlie.

"This morning," she replies sarcastically, expecting him to already know.

Sloan grins, a pizza box in his hand. "The flight didn't get cancelled, much to my mother's delight. Clearly, she didn't listen when I offered a timeshare on you!"

The table erupts in male laughter, but Charlie just shakes her head and piles up our plates. Bizarrely, I feel very much at ease again. More so, since she is definitely not avoiding me this time.

Sloan tilts my chin and winks. "Well, I guess I'm going to have to get my fill of you while I can, because now I won't get a look in."

An easy conversation begins to take over, and I study each man in turn, until Devlin eventually stands and holds up his beer.

"Welcome home, little lady, but do us all a favour? Hang up those bloody tatty trainers!" Everyone laughs, but it's joyless, because my reasons for sprinting like the wind were valid and just.

Walker and Sloan stare at each other, having an unmistakeable wordless conversation. It infuriates me abundantly, but I realise it will never stop - and I'll probably never question it, even if it does raise my blood pressure a notch.

"To family." Walker holds up his beer. "And to missing loved ones who eventually find their way home."

They all mutter the words and the door swings open. Stuart comes marching in, dishevelled, flustered, and still in his scrubs. "Hey, guys." He drops a case of lager on the table and hastily grabs a box.

"Hi. Where's Soph?" I ask, looking into the empty space behind him, already knowing where the other ladies in these men's lives are.

With a full mouth, Stuart swallows quickly then gasps. "Her mother's."

Fond memories of Mr and Mrs Morgan skip to the forefront of my mind. Remembering when we sprawled out on their living room floor during GCSE time.

"She's nice, and Soph is definitely her mother's daughter!"

Garrulous *is* a Morgan family trait.

The evening passes by slowly. I'm thoroughly up to date with everything that is happening in everyone's lives. Tommy and Parker, as already noted, are still moving from bed to bed, looking after their *dates* with a kiss and a twenty. Devlin, although keeping it to himself, seems to be happy to chat a little about Nicki. The tender looks as he speaks warms my heart. Regardless of his love to hate you relationship with Sloan, I adore him, and the things he did for me; for Sam.

An idea pops into my head, and I bite down on the inside of my cheek, wondering if it will be given the green light or bright red tape. Turning, I hesitantly tap Sloan's arm.

"Are you okay?"

"Fine, but I need to ask you something. I know you'll refuse, but she has no one else." Turning away, I catch Stuart's knowing brow lift, and lean across the table and gently touch Dev's hand, dragging back when I have his attention.

"Yeah, honey?"

"Would you mind taking me to see Sam again? I know she doesn't have any visitors, so I'd like to see more of her while I still can. I appreciate it might not be long."

Dev drops his beer, and his eyes flit between his uncle and Sloan rather worryingly. I dare not look at them, because they will not be sympathetic to my plight. And who can blame them? In different circumstances, I certainly wouldn't, but I will not give up on her. Not until the day comes when I have to play God with her life. I bristle, knowing one day will be an eventuality, and I won't be able to run and hide. I will have to make decisions that will haunt me forever.

One day, I will have to sacrifice her to set her free.

I stare around the table as eight pairs of eyes give out guilty glances before averting elsewhere. I can't stand to look at them and feel guilty for asking to do something for someone currently helpless. I assisted in putting her there, just as much as she did. But unlike them, I shall not brush her under the goddamn carpet until she is no more.

Glancing at Sloan, ready to speak the unthinkable, the table remains deathly quiet.

"Please. I'd rather have your blessing than be deceitful," I beg under my breath. A loud sigh rumbles from him, and his hand slides up my arm.

"We'll be a minute." He tugs me up and towards the living room. As soon as we are alone, he presses me into him. "Fine, but you *will* be manned. And if anything looks relatively untoward, going back will not be an option." He rubs his fingertips over my temples and down to my shoulders.

"I'm sorry I embarrassed you," I confess, ashamed that I used his friends against him in order to get my own way. "My safety is paramount, and it causes you to be blindsided."

"You didn't. And yes, it does, for damn good reason." He slants his mouth over mine and pulls back. "I love you, and I would never deny you anything, not even this."

As we re-enter the dining room, the sympathetic expressions are evident, but I allow them to disintegrate.

Looking pointedly between each person present, am I fooling myself again? Believing in dreams that may turn into nightmares. Planning a future that isn't on the cards for me. I had it once, and as far as the man next to me goes, he still thinks we do, but I know better. Until the Black nightmare is gone forever, I shall never feel completely at peace. The incessant burn of being touched and confined spaces is ebbing again, only to be replaced by an anxious patter inside my chest. It isn't something that burns, knowing that the man beside me still loves me, still wants a life and an uncertain future with me; it's the constant fear of looking over my shoulder. It's the fear that one, or both of them, could step out of the shadows at any given moment to re-enact the misery and pain, and show me that I'm still forever doomed inside the place I fear. Only now it is tainted and evil, and the sound of metal holding me to my fate is a moment of clarity I remember above anything else that came before it.

The sound of a glass smashing stops my mind rambling. Lifting my head up from staring, trying to placate myself, I feel the fury. It doesn't quite register what I have done. Shifting back, shocked and dazed, my first reaction is Sloan. His anguish is devastating, and my heart sinks.

"Oh God, I'm sorry!" I apologise, covering my face with my hands. "You weren't supposed to hear that."

Gliding his hand over my cheek, he quickly turns me, inspecting my face. His features turn hard, knowing he can't react in the way he desperately wants to.

"I had to hear it. We all did."

An uncomfortable silence ripples around the room, cold and uninviting. Walker, sensing they have all outstayed their welcome, rises. "I think it's time for us to leave, boys." They all murmur their gratitude for my hospitality, of which I agree for the sake of it, then file out.

Standing at the door with Jake and Charlie, and Sloan's arms firmly around my waist, I watch the numerous vehicles ascend up the driveway.

No sooner is the door closed, Charlie tugs me towards the stairs. "Let's talk."

Laying parallel, my heart aches seeing her again after so long away.

"How's Samantha? Sophie never mentioned her whenever she called," she says with disinterest, but I know this game, it's one of easing us both in before the truth is told.

"She's not good. It's just a matter of waiting for the inevitable, I guess." Her hand massages mine, and I reciprocate cautiously. "It's okay," I admit. "I've made my peace with it."

She runs her fingers through my hair and down the side of my face. Her eyes drop, and she softly touches just near my collarbone, over my abused skin.

"I can't believe you're actually here."

"Nor I," I whisper, sliding my hand into hers, bringing it away from my neck to rest in between us. "I was so scared to come back. Inside, I still am," I confess.

"I'm scared, too. How can we not be? You know who my father and brother are; what they're capable of." She puts her arm around my waist, and with a simple kiss on my forehead, she closes her eyes and just holds me.

The door moves a fraction, and I look up to see Sloan, holding the spine, watching us – or namely his sister, interacting with me again. I purse my lips together in a kiss, before he closes the door behind him.

My eyes remain open, and I tighten my arms, fighting the unease. I know she isn't asleep; I can feel her eyelashes brush against my skin.

"I'm sorry, Charlotte," I confess in a whisper. "Please forgive-" Her finger on my mouth scuppers the words I have spoken far too much of recently.

She looks up, thoughtful. "No."

I press back and furrow my brow. For two weeks, I have grovelled to everyone. I have felt my heart break on more than one occasion, and the only person who truly understands is now telling me no.

"After Deacon raped me, I lied to everyone, Kara. I didn't want them to know, because I didn't want to look at myself and feel guilty that it was something I had done to deserve it. I didn't. All I was guilty of was being in the wrong place at the wrong time. The same way you were."

"Do you really believe that?" I query, croakily. "That if it wasn't us, then it might have been someone else?" I stare at her questionably, until she sighs. If she says yes, she is more of a pathetic liar than I am. Yet the truth is, there was someone else, two that I have seen with my own eyes.

"No, but I have to believe something. Otherwise, I would still be looking at that girl in the hospital mirror, telling her I'm sorry. Back then, I never apologised for lying to them, or doing what was right for me at the time. Please don't insult me by doing the same." I start to smile, but her expression turns serious.

"But don't think it gets you off the hook for not contacting any of us! I was furious when Sloan ordered me to go to Mum's. It was weeks until Jake finally told me you had run. Sloan just disappeared off the face of the earth, holed himself up here and didn't speak to anyone. So not only did I lose you, I lost him for a time, too."

"For that I am sorry. I thought I was doing right. Even Jeremy told me I was wrong."

She looks sympathetic. "I know you don't have a lot of faith in him, but he's a good man, Kara. He's made mistakes, but he's not like that now. Trust him, like I do." I nod, hoping she doesn't see that my heart isn't fully in it.

"Deacon cut him straight down his face; the scar must be at least four inches long. It makes him look mean. Attractive, but mean."

Seeing her eyes widen, evidently unable to express anything to that statement, I change the subject to something she may find a little more palatable.

"I love you," I acknowledge sincerely, holding her tight, fighting back the tingle.

"I love you, too. I love that one day you will be my brother's wife. And better than that, you'll be my sister." She giggles, noting I am speechless.

The tiredness overwhelms, and I feel myself drifting while she talks the hind legs off a horse about everything New York has to offer.

I wake with a yawn as Jake picks up a sleeping Charlie from beside me. Turning my wrist, it's past midnight. Sloan's shadow casts over the floor, and he exits the en-suite and holds the bedroom door open as Jake carries his sister out.

Shutting it firmly, I watch drowsily as he goes back into the bathroom and requests my presence. Wearily, I enter, and he hands me my toothbrush. Diverting his attention from me to the mirror, we carry out an act of normality. One I want more than anything else.

Carrying me over to the bed, my head feels heavy, and my eyes close again. Feeling his body warm mine, the heat both intoxicates and calms my inner disquiet.

"Kiss."

I relinquish the fight with my fatigue, while the mounting excitement makes me shiver.

"I'll have you warm in no time!" He grins beautifully. Positioned above me, he pulls off my bottoms and pushes my knees apart. My feet rub up his legs and over his hips, guiding him closer.

"Tell me what you want, baby." His eyes darken, and I sigh out and arch my spine.

"I want you to make love to me until sunrise. I want everything," I murmur seductively. Adjusting, he engorges between us, and I press my hand to his chest as rationality kicks in. "Your sister and her boyfriend are down the landing." He ignores my protests and quickly strips off my top and bra, lavishing my breast with a tantalising tug.

"Oh, God!" I gasp, feeling the change commence. Rolling my nipple between his fingers, he pinches until I sound out again. "Oh! No, they'll hear!"

He lovingly growls at me for saying his favourite miscreant of a word. "Well, I guess that means Jake will learn something new tonight then!"

Sliding his hands around my hips, he rubs them over my arse, opening me further.

"No, this is so wrong!" I force him over and straddle him, unable to commit to my own reasoning.

"No, this is so right." Sliding me down his hard length, I keen out, rotating my hips forward, then back. He laces his hands under his head lazily, basking in his victory.

"Ride me, baby. I've got you."

Chapter 16

THE SOUND OF chains clinking together pierces my hearing. They no longer exist or elevate me, but they resound as though they are still secured around my wrists; holding me captive, keeping me prisoner – taking away any hope I have of a future.

I writhe against them, pathetically hoping to change the course of the dream. The nightmare. But it's in vain. I know how this ends... And I know what comes before and after.

This nightmare will never change.

"Eyes down and fucking watch!"

The knife trails down my front, and the first sharp pain digs into my flesh...

Bolting upright, a strong, undeniable feeling of trepidation psychologically slays me, and my body wilts from the memory. Rubbing my hands over my face, I know what I finally have to do to make it stop. To have some kind of hope that makes it worthwhile. I've known it for a long time.

I glide my hand over the pillow; Sloan's side is cold. Pulling the duvet aside, the door opens simultaneously to reveal the man himself, almost dressed, fumbling with his tie. I smile a little, but it's still filled with sorrow.

"Morning. Did I wake you?" he asks cautiously. I shake my head and stretch out my arms. Mentally, I still might be lost in this thing I call my life, but physically, I'm right where I belong.

"No," I whisper.

He cups my face and his eyes narrow. "Are you still having nightmares?"

My eyes smart as I shake my head in confirmation.

"Childhood?"

"No. I no longer dream about that," I whisper. He drops his forehead to mine.

"Baby, I think you need to go see-" I put my finger over his mouth. I know exactly who I need to see, but I don't know if I can.

Yet.

"Are you going to work?" I hastily divert the conversation. Looking at his immaculate suit, I know he can't stay at home with me

125

forever. But in times gone by, whenever turmoil has reared its ugly head, he's made the exception.

"Unfortunately, then the bank. Maybe that isn't so unfortunate," he says coyly. Sitting on the bed, he shuffles closer. He strokes my hair, then regards me with adoration.

"Is everything okay?" I ask, a hint of worry in my tone. He smiles, gently cradling my head, placing a much-wanted kiss to my parched lips.

"Everything is…as it should be. How it was always meant to be." He slides his hands under my arms and stands us up. "Wrap." I narrow my eyes. Realising we're not on the same page, he playfully slaps my thigh. "Legs around me, baby."

My legs obey and snake around his hips. My head lulls against his shoulder, and he carries me into the dressing room.

He sits me on the island, and déjà vu cuts a path through my thoughts as he lays out my phones – all three of them – beside me. Slapping his hands on either side, he cages me in.

"We've walked a rough road, haven't we?" Words fail to materialise, and instead, I nod, feeling my eyes turn to liquid. "Baby, don't cry. I've seen your tears enough these last nine months, and I'm usually the reason behind them."

"That's not true-" He puts his finger over my mouth and pulls down my bottom lip.

"No, it is. I've wondered so many times if things would've been different if I'd been honest from the off. I know it doesn't matter now, but I altered your future, and I did it the moment I walked into that pink, sparse bedroom." He bites his bottom lip and breathes out. It's not an annoyed sound, it's one of contentment.

"I love you. I loved you the moment you kicked me out. The moment you refused to leave the hospital, and the moment I walked out of the hotel suite. I never stopped loving you."

Gently kissing my temple, his eyes drop back down. I glance over the handsets, feeling like the most popular, yet unpopular girl on the planet. I run my hand over the one he gave me last year and grip it tight. He motions his approval and picks up my original phone, the one that wreaks havoc every time I switch the damn thing on.

"They're your parents… I swear I won't dictate or demand-"

"But?" I ask, knowing he just can't help himself. We'll see just how long his promise of not dictating or demanding actually lasts, shall we?

"But there is a tried and tested method, and bizarrely, it actually works, until I fuck it up."

I huff out - that's a little harsh. "Sorry, it's equal opportunities in this relationship. I'm sure if we tally it up, I've done my fair share of the same." I drop my head down, but he lifts it back up.

"You're expressing the *look* again." He raises his brows, and I push myself off the island, my body sliding down his, feeling every inch of him from soft to hard caress my front.

I shuffle towards my side, and finger the clothing, keeping up the pretence. "Devlin?"

"Hmm," Sloan replies, deep in thought, and continues to dress. Edging closer, I'm well acquainted with the taciturn side of him. He straightens his waistcoat and winks. "I'll see you downstairs." He flounces out of the room.

Quickly walking after him, I divert into the bedroom for my robe and hurry down the stairs. The kitchen is empty when I enter. Looking around, voices emanate from the office, and I follow them to find Devlin sitting at the desk, looking over some paperwork.

"Are you positive you want to do this? If he doesn't eventually get what he wants, and he finds out, it will give him leverage-" Dev quietens when he sees me loitering in the doorway. "Morning."

I smile and step inside. Sloan turns around with a file in his hand. He moves towards the desk and snatches up the papers, then stuffs them under his arm along with the wallet.

"Are you going to be out all day?" I query.

"The majority. I need to tie up a deal, and then there's something else I need to do. Why?"

I drop into the tub chair and curl up. "Oh, I was going to go see Marie." I divert my eyes to Dev, and his narrow in question. He's actually spoilt my morning without knowing it. Now I'm getting him into it. *Again.*

Unbeknown to my beloved kid, today – with Marie's assistance - I have sorted myself out an interview. Unfortunately, I've had to bargain for her complicity, and shortly, I will have to do the same with Dev.

Sloan packs the documents into his bag and shoulders it. He approaches and looks towards Devlin, who sees the clear indication in his boss's face to leave. He leisurely saunters towards the door and slams it on the way out.

"I never thought I'd say this, but I think I might prefer you with Tom or Park. At least they know when to stop trying my patience."

I giggle. "You love him, really. Jeremy said you were all like brothers. And he's right."

"I guess you could say that. He's doing okay, you know. He called earlier in the week, wanted to know how you were."

I nod and bite my lip. "He protected me, and Deacon cut him for his betrayal." I touch from my temple down to my lip. "From here to here. Scarred him for life."

He pulls me close, gripping me with determination. "I know, my love. He told me what the bastard did. I promise I will never, ever, hold it against you."

"How many times do I have to say you're a good man, Sloan Foster?"

He rubs his hands up and down my back, eventually breaking free of my hold.

"I'm going to be late, but you do provide the best distraction." He smiles and leads us out.

As he strides down the hallway, he stops at the pool room door and winks. "How about six?"

I nod innocently and up the stakes. "Make it five-thirty, and I'll consider it."

"You're on, my beautiful smart-arse, Petersen."

Entering the kitchen again, Devlin is tapping away on an iPad, cursing up a storm. I climb onto a stool, as Sloan quickly pulls out my usual cereal, milk, and a bowl.

"Tight git!" Dev exclaims, and I do a double take. He looks sheepish. "Sorry. Cheap client!"

I grin; I remember those very well.

Sloan moves around to him and removes the tablet. "Remember the rules, sunshine? Make sure you adhere to them." Devlin flicks him the middle finger, and Sloan grins. "Good idea. Forget them, and that's the first thing you lose!"

Sloan hands him back the tablet and slides into his jacket. Crooking his finger at me, I follow him to the door.

"The rules?"

"No going off on my own, and Dev's word is final?"

"Good enough." He kisses me one last time before yanking open the door. "Five thirty, I'm coming to collect. Literally."

I lean against the frame as he reverses the Aston and cuts a path up the driveway until he is out of sight. Shutting the door behind me, I lock all the bolts on the other side and venture back into the kitchen

Dev's head tilts to one side. "Do I even want to know?"

I shake my head and run upstairs to get ready, while his *'oh shit'* resounds behind me.

"Well, it's been lovely to meet you, Miss Petersen. Provided your reference is satisfactory, I will be in touch," the Human Resources Manager says to me, as I offer my hand, ready to feel spontaneous public combustion.

"Thank you, Mr Owens," I respond. Grimacing a smile and shaking his hand firmly, I count the seconds until he releases it.

Inside, I already know Sloan isn't going to take the news very well. I haven't mentioned job hunting to him since the night of my impromptu welcome home dinner, but at the same time, I haven't bothered to delete my web history either. Having a hand in his pocket is a serious problem for me. I've worked hard for everything I've ever had, and that will never change. Something else he already knows. Every time I've raised the issue of my financial independence, he has ignored my protesting. After hearing 'you don't need to work' for the hundredth time, I internally snapped. Hence why I'm here now, feeling the fire of a thousand fiery suns heating my bloodstream and smiling like an idiot to conceal it. After a few more pleasantries, I leave with a spring in my step.

I climb into the car as Dev grimaces. "He's been calling."

I nod; I'd be surprised if he hadn't. Rummaging through my bag, ready to call my surrogate mum, I note my missed calls. No doubt his tracking devices are working overtime again. Yes, I'm definitely in for a bollocking when he sees me later.

Clearing the screen, I look up to the sky. The clouds float by, revealing the early afternoon sun. Dialling, I wait for Marie to answer.

"Hey, honey. How did it go?" she asks, full of fake excitement. I know it's fake because she wasn't too impressed to lie for me. Actually, I'll say it how it is, she was downright, effing livid. Although she seems to have developed acute memory loss, considering she gave me the number of another catering company looking for an office assistant. After much bargaining and coercing, she succumbed, realising today was incumbent on her duplicity. And my overall sanity.

"Really good, I think. Thank you for setting it up."

"Well, I can't say I'm pleased you might be working for my competition, but I understand your reasoning. Just remember, if they ask-"

"You didn't know," I finish, not wanting to drop her in the shit.

As she continues to speak, a sharp twinge plays on my neck, creating an awareness that comes in the sign of a warning. I hiss as it burns deeper.

"You okay?" Dev whispers.

I lie and mouth *yes*, as a black Lexus glides through the car park, finally stopping in the opposite space. Balancing the phone between my head and shoulder, I watch the vehicle with suspicion.

"Sloan called this morning, wanting to speak to you," Marie continues. "I lied and said you were indisposed. Honey, he told me in no uncertain terms was I to give you a reference. I thought you should know."

"Huh," I reply, still transfixed. "Do you know if Jeremy's back?" I ask her but turn to Dev, who sighs loudly, knowing I'm not easily fooled.

"Erm, I don't think so, but John doesn't really tell me anything." I nod, completely unappeased in the harsh reality coming back to haunt. "Oh shit! John just pulled up; he doesn't look happy. I'll speak to you later." She hangs up in a hurry.

"Bye," I whisper, although she's already gone. "Devlin?" He huffs and slams his hand down.

"No, he isn't back, Kara."

My phone beeps as he starts the ignition. I roll my eyes when a text from Charlie says she and Sophie are in the pub.

"Fancy a beer?" I ask him.

"Absolutely. Might be the last time I can drink without assistance!"

Sticking the gear into reverse and rolling back, the Lexus opposite rocks against the biting point. Driving slower than usual, Devlin gives way and waits for a gap in the oncoming traffic. I glance into the wing mirror and the damn car is directly behind us.

Still waiting for a break in the steady stream, my mobile buzzes, and Sloan's name glows like a warning light.

Shit!

I keep a close watch on the ominous car as it maintains a constant presence behind us, allowing other cars to overtake it. Three separate us, but it isn't enough – it never will be.

"Why the fuck can't you leave me alone?" I swear under my breath. And therein lies the real crux of this lifetime of pain, because until one of us no longer breathes, he never will.

And I have no idea why.

The old swaying sign for The Swan comes into view, and we drive in. Approaching the entrance, Jake is sat outside, sunglasses on, reading a paper with a pint of coke in front of him.

"Hey, man," Dev greets him, but he doesn't look happy.

"Hi," I say, squinting from the sun. He's about to answer when he lifts his ringing phone up.

"He's been calling everyone all morning." He brushes his cheek. "Please speak to him, before I go over there and ram this fucking thing down his throat to shut him up!" Losing his exasperation, he looks me up and down and smirks. "And now I understand why! You do realise you're gonna gain a third hole, right?" he says to Dev.

"He's been threatening that for the last ten years!" Dev replies flippantly.

"I wouldn't worry, it's dependant on Marie's reference," I say, seeing a reflection in the window behind him.

"Yeah, good luck with that!" Jake laughs, then stares curiously over my shoulder. Looking at what has him spooked, I refuse to turn. He rakes his hand through his fair hair and shares a look with Dev, who pulls out his phone.

"Get in!" Jake's tone leaves no room for argument, and I do as I am told, because these days, I know better. A lot better.

The undeniable smell of ale and gastropub food is like an artery-clogging smack in the face, as I step inside. Spotting Sophie's perfectly styled locks at the bar, I tiptoe behind her.

"Triple vodka, please," I request half-heartedly, causing her to jump and drop the money.

"You scared the shit out of me!" she admonishes, picking up the twenty. She slides a large glass of lemonade over and smiles. "Pretend it's laced! How did it go?"

"Fine, but I won't get it."

"Of course you will. You're brilliant!" she replies with zeal and a worried expression.

"Sloan's been calling everyone all morning. Did you tell your boss I had an interview?"

She instantly looks down and starts to mumble.

She did!

It's times like these I could gag her.

"Sophie?" I utter softly.

Animatedly, with her hands, she replies, "It just popped out there!"

"Soph, nothing just pops out there!"

She scurries over to the table where Charlie is sat, looking partially pleased at the tablet screen. Except I have no interest in knowing what material object is brightening her day, when I'm more concerned over how my own is panning out thus far.

"Kara, I didn't tell him per se, he overheard me talking to Marie this morning." She downs a mouthful of wine, followed by a sigh of relief that she has cleansed her guilty conscience.

"It's okay," I comfort, wondering how Marie is fairing up with her unreasonable other half right now. "So, you're on his shit list then?" She nods with a smile. "Well, I think I might have just taken the next spot, with Dev right behind me." I sigh aloud as my phone rings, knowing it's Sloan.

Taking a sip of my pop, I figure I might as well get it over with. I bite my bottom lip, scraping it with my teeth.

"Hi." I make my way to an empty table. Looking out of the window, Jake's eyes are trained on the car, still waiting.

"I'm just wondering how my wife's secret interview went?" he asks sarcastically.

I chortle, making sure he hears it. "Very well, thank you for asking. Oh, and I'm not your wife."

Now it's his turn to be amazed, as he chuckles heartily. "Correct, you're far more than that. That title is nowhere near accurate in describing what you are to me." Before I can say anything further, he inhales. "Are you in The Swan?"

Still watching Jake, he starts to stride over the tarmac towards the car, which is now pulling away. I stare at it as it manoeuvres into the line of traffic and eventually disappears. Jake, unaware of my prying eyes, has his phone to his ear in seconds. Except this way - *their way* - isn't how to stop him. It never has been, and today, I'm going to correct that.

"Baby?"

"Yes," I reply, preoccupied with events outside.

"Please tell me you haven't abandoned Devlin."

"No, he's here with Jake."

A throat clears, and an old man sits on the worn leather bench with his pint. I grin, instantly knowing this is his regular table, and move over while he nods his gratitude.

"Are you coming over?"

"Ten minutes," he replies and hangs up.

Dropping myself back into my seat, a small hand touches mine. I rip it back and feel guilty when Charlie holds up hers. Unable to feel complacent, I stare at the door as the minutes pass by, until Jake and Dev enter, Sloan at their rear. Striding inside, he demonstrates his best runway model impression in his perfectly fitted trousers and waistcoat. His jacket is flung over his shoulder; his tie slack, and his collar partially undone. Quickly getting up, I move over to him and grab his arms.

"Right then, tell me about this job."

"It doesn't matter. There's something I need to do. Right now. And I want you there holding my hand." I reach down for my bag.

"Okay," he replies, a little suspicious. "While I'm not complaining, why am I going to be holding your hand?"

Taking a deep breath, I train my stare on Charlie and Jake, aware that by the end of today, she may be that broken girl again. I might be, too.

"It's time," I say firmly. Sloan looks between his sister and me since I haven't removed my stare. "Deacon followed us here. There's only one way to make it stop. I need to report what he did."

Charlie gasps and darts out of the building. Jake runs after her, while Sloan motions for Sophie to get up.

Outside, Charlie is by her car, wiping her eyes. "Why?" she spits out. "I've done this before, and it achieved nothing! I can't go through that again. We don't even know if it's him!" she shouts, showing me a side of her I've never seen before.

"Don't we? You want to live like this forever, Charlie? He raped and beat us because he hates Sloan, which means he hates everyone by association. Including his sister."

"No..."

"Yes, he told me! And just for completeness, how long do you think it will be before he gets bored of toying me with and moves back to you?"

"Kara, we should discuss this!"

"What's to discuss? What it felt like when the bastard touched me? Or the pain I experienced when he dragged a knife over my chest? Or when he beat you into submission for hours? What exactly do you want to discuss, Charlotte?" I shout out in the empty car park, finally finding my voice. Charlie covers her face, and Sophie tucks her into her chest, as her soft whimpers resound in time with the birdsong.

I start to approach, but Sloan holds out his hand, and Jake grabs my elbow. Sophie, sensing she's in the way, walks back towards us. Sloan tilts his sister's chin, revealing her red-eyed, snotty appearance. They speak in low tones, barely audible to my ears.

Jake's phone starts to ring, and he answers. The words 'police', 'report', and 'rape', are the only things I hear, until Charlie is suddenly in front of me with a renewed strength about her.

"I know this is hard, but I need you. My assault was never reported because I was a runaway. I would've been taken into care and left to rot. Please, you have more credibility than I do. I need you."

She nods compliantly and walks in silence towards her car. Sitting in the passenger seat, Jake starts to move, but Sloan drags him back.

"Whatever is said, don't let it change how you feel about her. I mean it," he says, pointing vehemently.

Jake looks at the car, then back to him. "It never will."

He climbs into the driver's seat, and Charlie nestles into him, ready to bare her soul for the second time in her life.

Sophie, not really knowing what to do with herself, loiters on the spot.

"Take the rest of the day off. Dev will follow you home. Call me when you get in and lock the door," Sloan says, passing her my car keys. She nods and hugs me, apologising when I stiffen.

Watching the back end of the vehicles leave, Sloan kisses my forehead. "How much are you going to tell them?"

"Everything," I reply, holding his gaze.

"Your parents?"

I nod. My father is the easy one – he likes to live on the edge of the law, and now he will feel the brunt of it. My mother, however, is the hard choice.

"Jeremy?" he queries.

Another hard choice.

I bring my hand to my mouth, the unknown part he played is very likely monstrous, but without knowing the real facts, I have no basis for having him incarcerated. The scars on my wrists are all him, but hearing it leave Deacon's mouth is not enough for me to turn him over.

"I asked him…"

"But he didn't tell you," he replies in an answer, not a question.

"No. I can't make accusations based on theory, so no, I will not be reporting him. Yet." Sloan's hand comes around my neck, and he kneads unrelenting. It isn't comforting; it's an awakening of what I'm finally going to do.

I clutch my bag to my chest, while I stare at the aged buildings lining the route. Following behind Charlie's car, my absolution is strengthened and robust.

This is what I should have done years ago. The day I turned eighteen, this should have been my first stop. I should have done this when Deacon battered me last year, instead of lying my way through the police's questions. And it's another thing I should have done, the day Jeremy saved me with a new realisation of how truly evil some really are.

And Jeremy, for all his flaws, was right. They can't take me into care anymore, and this might be the only way I can eventually find peace. When the time comes, and his truth is finally aired, I don't know what I will do, but he saved me, and that has to count for something in this sad life.

"We're here," Sloan says, devoid of all emotion. Climbing out, I instantly move to Charlie and grip her hand, forgetting the sensation peaking.

"Together," she whispers, as I stare up the seventies façade. Entering, an officer smiles, ready to listen.

"Can I help you?" he asks, slightly amused, wondering which one of the overindulged, wealthy-looking women carrying designer handbags has lost her purse.

"Yes. I'd like to report a rape," I say firmly, watching his expression harden.

"Whose?"

"Ours," Charlie replies with conviction.

Splashing cold water on my face, I stare at myself, seeing the teenager still trapped inside the woman's body. Hours later, my eyes are still red, inflamed through tears as I finally dispelled the truth.

Since we arrived back, Sloan has shut himself away in his office. Hearing his raised tones with Walker's on speakerphone, makes me wonder if he's angry at me, or whether I have pushed it too far, taking away whatever vigilante justice they were seeking to exact.

I malinger in the bedroom doorway, where he is treading a path in the carpet. Shutting the door, he spins around and rushes towards me. Wordlessly, he picks me up and holds me tight. He lays me down, and divests himself of his clothing and climbs in. Eventually, the silent treatment proves to be too much, and I sob.

"I made the right choice," I murmur, because for once, I really have. I've thrown my own father to the wolves in order to eventually have a life that I can walk through without fear. Whilst I spared my mother, I can't control what might be said whenever the police question them.

The room illuminates, and he turns me over. Arranging me atop of him, he continually strokes my head.

"Please don't be angry with me."

"No, don't ever think that. Honestly? I didn't want to listen. To hear those things leave your mouth..."

"You've avoided me since we walked back through the door," I confess my fear. "I needed you."

"Today affirmed what I already knew. I'm not enough to save you. I never have been."

"But you did save me, because you love me. Unconditionally."

Rolling me over, his soft lips graze my neck. "I will always love you, but my life without you in it...I won't go through it a third time. I will do whatever it takes to ensure that one day we can tell our children how love can span a lifetime."

Closing my eyes and counting the beat of his heart, I sigh, hopeful.

"I'm going to hold you to that."

Chapter 17

RUNNING INTO THE dressing room, I flip through the rails and pull out a matching suit. I fasten the skirt, and the waistband drops down an inch as I stand in front of the mirror. Gazing at myself, I'm nowhere near as starved looking as I was. While still indubitably skinny, my shape has started to fill out again.

I slide on a crisp, white blouse and tuck it in, taking note of how much it covers. Wrapping a thin belt around my middle, I judge critically.

Today, I have another interview. One which Sloan has organised, considering his fury at hearing I had intervened in my own future and set the wheels in motion previously. Needless to say, the *disagreement* we had over it – days after the actual event, for obvious reasons - was lost when he put Marie in a tight spot when the nice Mr Owens finally requested a reference for my abilities.

She said yes.

He said no – not very politely – hence why I have finally given in.

While Sloan has remained tight-lipped and provided no valuable insight, I figure it has to be better than leaning on him financially. It also means I will have something other than my own misery to think about day in, day out.

Whilst I have spoken to the police a couple of times since giving them my statement, no real progress has been made. I haven't heard from either of my parents, and I wonder just how seriously the police are taking it, considering how long ago it happened, and the fact I never reported the two assaults from last year. I also can't help but feel I have strained my relationship with Charlotte and caused unnecessary strife for everyone else around me.

Still, I have made the right choice. It's my new mantra, words I repeat when I feel otherwise.

I have made the right choice.

"Are you ready?" Sloan calls from the bedroom.

"Nearly!"

The door opens, and he watches with a smile, while I continue to critique my appearance. Grabbing the jacket, I breathe out. I look presentable enough. Hopefully, my new, would-be employer will think so, too.

"Do I look nervous? Seriously, what do you think? Would you hire me?"

Moving behind me in his own suit, complete with the obligatory waistcoat, he cradles his chin, with a thoughtful, flirty look.

"I would hire you for lots of things, but never to type letters and answer the phone." He does a turn around me. "I would hire you to sit in my chair and look pretty all day."

I smile as he runs his hand down my front, prising open a few buttons.

"I would hire you to keep me entertained and satisfied. To grace my office whenever the need arose, and to warm the edge of my desk while our bodies connected perfectly." He grins knowingly, and my breathing rises a notch.

"Well, therein lies a future problem." He lifts his brows. "Your new PA has already told me the rules of the game now she is in command of your affairs."

Pressing against him, his hardness penetrates through the fabric, and I feel myself reacting desirously to it, my body urging me to strip off these stuffy suits and feel his flesh on mine again.

"Really? And what has the verbose Ms Morgan said on the subject of keeping me entertained and satisfied?" Walking my fingers up his tie, I place a kiss on his chin.

"None of the above. Not on her watch." Giving him my best innocent look, he mulls something over in his head.

"I see. I guess a lunchtime rendezvous is out of the question then?" I nod. "What a shame. I was looking forward to seeing you laid bare over my desk on a dismal, unsatisfactory day."

"Against it, not over it," I correct him.

"That, too. I think I'm going to have to find ways to keep her busy outside the office from now on."

I shake my head. "You won't hear the end of it if you do."

"Oh, but that's where you're wrong. She forgets who puts that nice, triple the average salary into her account each month. One of her job descriptions is discretion. Don't worry, I'll make sure the good doc educates her, sooner rather than later."

I close my eyes, my body feeling the effects of him in all the good places...and all the bad. Lifting me up, he moves towards the island and drops me down. Pushing my skirt up a little, he stands between my legs, stroking high on my thighs.

"I'm going to be late," I remark, my body heat rising in time with my heart rate.

With that gorgeous grin firmly in place, he steps back and moves towards the drawers. Retrieving a jewellery box, he returns, an easy, playful swagger in his stride. Back between my thighs, he opens it and delicately removes the bracelet he had presented me with a lifetime ago. I hold my hand out, and he massages my wrist. Fingering the scars, both old and new, he dresses it with his timeless gift of adoration.

"Now you're ready for work," he says, full of pride. He slides his arm under my legs and drops me down. Standing in front of the mirror, my attention is divided between the gems capturing the light, accentuating my simple, yet smart look, and him. Always him.

"You know, normal people don't go to work wearing hundreds of pounds' worth of diamonds."

I grab my belly, feeling slightly sick. His hand comes around my other wrist, and he slips a watch over it. I refuse to look. I don't want to see what it is or be left guessing its monetary worth. I'm abundantly aware I'm already wearing enough material cash that will guarantee I don't step outside for fear of being robbed. *Or worse.* Or maybe that's the undisclosed intention here – bling her up and lock her down.

"My wife does. She deserves the best of everything, and she will have it, whether she disagrees or not," he says, very matter of fact, in the tone he likes to spit out whenever he feels he will be shot down in flames.

"I'm not your wife." I turn and hold his lapels, sliding my fingers down the fabric.

"Not yet," he mutters under his breath. He stares at me confidently, and a glimmer of something highlights his eyes. His look of knowing is concise. I could try to dig to the bottom, but I know he'll never divulge, not until he is ready anyway.

Minutes later, he guides us out of the bedroom and down the stairs. At the bottom, I spy my Prada bag and purse on one of the tables. I carefully open it and look inside. As expected, my usual two phones are in there.

"John said that you called and left me messages."

"I did. Numerous times, declaring numerous things." I nod, feeling my eyes spike with impending tears. Grabbing the phone, his hand comes over mine. "I don't want you to listen to them. Instead, I'll say them to your face when you're ready," he whispers.

"I was always coming back to you. It isn't the way I anticipated, but between John and Jeremy…" I can't continue, because my heart is breaking in the best way possible. Truthfully, I was always going to find my way home.

His thumbs swipe my cheeks, and I bring my hands up, using my flat palms, very unladylike to assist. "Do I look like I've been crying?" He tells me no but shakes his head yes. His smile is glorious, and for the first time since I've been back, I have absolution in my choice to return and face the future that has yet to unravel.

"Good, I need to make the right impression."

"Stop worrying, it's in the bag," he says, walking off down the hallway.

"Sloan, I appreciate you don't have to worry about trivial matters like money, but I do. How am I supposed to earn a living if I'm unemployed?" He spins around just before the kitchen door and marches towards me, his frustration firmly back in place.

"*'Earn a living?'* What are you, lodging here?"

I run my hand over my brow, exasperated as he currently sounds. "You know what I mean!"

"No, I don't!" He quickly holds up his finger, when he sees my mouth adjust. "But I'll let it go for now." He throws his arm around me and glides the other down my front.

"These are still a little big," he sighs out, tugging my waistband. I know it hurts him to witness my decline, so I remain mute.

Sitting at the table, my eyes slit when I see only one plate – a serving plate, holding enough food for four. I glance around the worktops, thoroughly impressed at their spotlessness.

"Is this takeaway with a difference again?"

"No, smart-arse, everything is in the dishwasher. I'm not completely inept, you know," he replies, holding one set of cutlery. He sits close and picks at the various cheeses, cold meats, and bread.

We stare at each other, judging each other, while he randomly feeds me, then himself. He still looks partially annoyed, but is, thankfully, letting it go.

If only I could.

"I didn't mean to offend. I just want to be able to buy something and say, 'that's mine', not 'that's Sloan's', that's all."

"I know, baby. I know you'll dig your heels in every time until the end of our days, and truthfully, I actually like it." He puts down the fork and runs his thumb over my lip. "I like my fired up, passionate, spirited Kara. And today is the first time she has come back out to play properly. Let her stay - I don't want her being too scared to say how she feels or what she wants. I want my strong-headed, stand her ground, and never let it go, girl." He grips my shoulders. "I want *her* standing in front of me in eight weeks' time, not that girl who ran from my boardroom, terrified of living again. *I. Want. You.*"

"What's happening in eight weeks?"

He shakes his head, keeping his secrets, and I watch in suspicion as he bins the leftover food.

"Trust me?" He turns and cocks his brow.

Climbing down off the stool and smoothing down my clothes, he passes me my jacket, and I saunter out. "Absolutely not."

I wait anxiously beside the Aston as he locks up the house.

"Catch!" He throws something at me, and I clench my palm around it. Opening my hand, my BMW key is sat there.

I hastily move towards the car and climb inside. "I guess you drove this for a while again?" I query, starting the process of adjusting everything.

"You know me, I like to keep you close, whether near or far."

I tap the accelerator, and the engine growls at me. Before setting off, I turn to him. "What happened to my Golf?"

He grins. "It's Sophie's now. Although if *someone* comes between me and what I want, that will be something else I'll be using as leverage."

Slowly inching up the driveway, I can't help but retort. "She's a force to be reckoned with. You can throw whatever you want at her, and she will laugh it - and you - off. It doesn't matter that you're now her boss, she sees you as being her best friend's boyfriend, first and foremost. Not to mention you mistakenly told her she talked sense the first time you met."

He inhales slowly. "Hmm, that was a schoolboy error. But it's fine because I also have a few tricks up my sleeve. Let's just say, I'm expecting some arguments. As a matter of fact, I'm looking forward to them."

I exhale loudly and smile to myself. "It's good to be back."

His hand comes over mine on the gearstick and squeezes hard.

"You're right about that."

Killing the engine, I stare out at the eight-foot-high metal fencing and security cameras. Leaning forward in my seat, I study the ominous building façade. I glance at Sloan, who is completely relaxed, considering the area of the city we are currently parked in.

"Are you sure this is the right place? It looks derelict," I utter questionably.

"This is it."

Sliding out of the car, he takes a cursory look around. Holding my seat belt firmly, I'm not impressed. Not because it doesn't look good enough, but because I don't fancy being stuck on an industrial estate when the nights eventually start to draw in.

"Come on, my love." Leaning in, he slaps my hands away from the belt and lifts me out. My whole body clenches, and I grip my handbag tight.

"Cold?"

"Nervous." And absolutely terrified of where this job is located. Maybe pulling on his purse strings is a more attractive prospect after all.

I follow him, still gauging the area, still unimpressed. Doing a full turn, numerous vehicles, including a few Range Rovers, are dotted around inside the fencing. I shudder, because they're not helping my psyche one bit. I watch as he taps in a code for the door, then steps inside. A long corridor lays ahead, and I tentatively walk through.

"Stop it," he says, rubbing my shoulder, guiding us towards a decrepit looking lift.

"I can't get in there, it doesn't look safe," I protest, shaking my head. There is no way in hell I'm getting in that thing. It's bad enough with the hotel and his office.

"It's completely safe." He smirks. "Trust me."

That's his answer for everything. *Bloody trust him!*

I groan out, grip my bag straps and enter. Looking up at the light, it flickers, and the doors strain shut before it rattles to life. And I mean, *rattles*.

"Worst case scenario, it stops." He drags me towards him and lets his hands roam. "I can't think of anything better than being stuck in a confined space with you."

He can speak for himself. Confined spaces are not attractive to me, especially this one.

"Stop it, you're rumpling me again!" I reply, concerned. Patting down my clothes, beads of sweat form across my neck. I need to make a good impression today.

"A little *rumpling* will do you a world of good. Me, too." My mouth forms an O, and I shake my head. "I can't help it! We still have-"

"Three months, three weeks, and two days to make up for. I'm keeping tabs, too!" I sigh. "Now please quit with the innuendos, I need to look professional!"

"Baby, the job's already yours. Don't make me say it again."

"Good, I won't! Why are you not concerned about where this *job in the bag* is located? Did you see outside? The old Sloan would have me shut up in the car and speeding off in plumes of smoke."

Chuckling to himself, he digs into his pocket. "Here," he says, putting a key in my palm. "That's yours. The door code downstairs is my date of birth. The code upstairs is Charlie's. See the picture forming here?" I stare at his back, attempting to slot the pieces together. Yet I'm failing in this task, because I feel like the air is being stripped from my lungs the longer I remain inside a moving box that is smaller than my old Fiesta.

The doors creak open, sounding as though they are finally going to give up the ghost, and I hurry out. Mr Unconcerned strolls out leisurely and grabs my hand. Tapping in the second code on the panel, he leads me down another long corridor.

"A bit security conscious this guy, isn't he?" I query rhetorically, realising this is also someone else who probably flies close to the wind at times.

I push back an eighties style full glass door, enter cautiously, and look around the office. Taking in the room, it's reminiscent of Marie's – crap all over and stacks of paperwork mounting up. Studying everything closely, noise from outside resounds, and Sloan kisses my head before leaving. Putting down my bag, I look up at the army medals displayed on a shelf. They are the only things sparklingly clean amid the chaos.

Male voices echo outside, and Sloan pops his head around the door. With a wink, he motions me towards him.

"He's ready for you, right over there," he says, pointing to the opposite door. I swallow, terrified that maybe this isn't as *in the bag* as he assumes. Straightening my jacket, I grab my bag and remove my

CV and reference. As I edge out, I yelp the moment he pulls me back. He can't do this to me now, not when so much depends on it.

"Just be yourself. He'll love you," he says with an air of surety.

"Easy for you to say," I mutter, receiving his kiss and grabbing the handle. "Are you not going to wish me good luck?"

He steps back, wearing a perfected look of absolute confidence. "No."

Inhaling deeply, I blow it out and open the door.

And my mouth drops open instantly.

Tommy, Parker, and Walker are all leant over a desk with plans and drawings in front of them.

"I should have known." I drop my bag on the floor and gracefully pull out a chair. I sit, decreasing my skirt and my homicidal thoughts.

"Well, you see, honey," Walker starts, rubbing his chin. "My boys had, what they thought, was a brilliant idea – one I had already set into play. The truth is, you need a job, and we need a secretary slash accountant slash personal assistant."

"Kara, you're our new girl Friday!" Parker says sarcastically. He smiles, his teeth beautiful and white against his rich, dark skin. And right now, I just want to scream at him; all three – four – of them, since Jake has just entered with a grin and a tray of steaming mugs. I turn to the door in disbelief and fold my arms.

"Well, at least you don't need a tea lady."

Jake glares and picks up his drink. "Kara, did you honestly think we would have you working for just anyone?" I don't reply and calmly observe the room. My eyes narrow when I see more piles of papers, half my height, stacked on the floor.

The door opens, and Sloan enters, passing me one of the two mugs he's carrying. Taking it, the desire to douse it over him is immense.

And it wouldn't be the first time I've done it… I think grimly.

"Did she pass?" he asks sarcastically, sitting next to Tommy.

"Very funny! Do I have a choice?" I ask, but already know the answer.

"No. I want you somewhere I know you will be safe. These guys need someone who can organise an office-"

"And someone who will make them fall in line," Walker says after him, pulling up a seat next to me.

I acquiesce, annoyed that they have planned my life again, but relieved that I have people who care unequivocally. I feel conflicted and confused. Truthfully, I don't know how I should be feeling, but you have to take the rough with the smooth, and unfortunately, I'm in no position to throw down ultimatums. Or tantrums.

"You will have your own office, your own space. You can kick these guys around as much as you like, I won't say a word. All I ask is that you take someone with you whenever you want to go out. That's it."

I look around, my stomach sinking. "Will this be my space?"

"No," he laughs. "This is where we dump all the shit we say we'll get around to later. Your office is next door to mine. Come on, I'll show you." He takes my hand, and I stiffen. Furrowing his brow, he tugs me out of the door and into another room.

It's clean, bright, and freshly painted. The large window overlooks the street, and I gaze out at the galvanised fencing and electric gates, feeling safer than I should in this creaky, old, past-its-condemn-date, building.

"What are you thinking, Kara?" I look over my shoulder at Dev, smiling in the doorway.

"I don't know."

He strides towards me and takes my hand. "What do you say, little lady?" he cajoles, using his favourite moniker. "Want to work with the army throwbacks? It's more interesting than ordering stale sandwiches and sour cream cakes!"

I laugh. "I'd love to work with you guys, but I do have some conditions," I say, needing to lay down my own set of rules from the off. Sloan stands away from the others, smiling, proud that I still have the strength to be heard when everything is against me.

"When that door is closed, you don't just walk in. You say this is my office, and you will treat me with respect when in it."

They all nod.

"I expect to have a full lunch hour, regardless if something is urgent or not. Clearly, you have survived without an *assistant* for this long, and so another hour will not kill you."

Again, more nodding.

"You might see me as your *girl Friday*, but I'm not your personal skivvy."

"Oh, you'll fit in nicely here," Walker chuckles. "I'll give Marie my love for raising you to stand your ground."

"I think you'll find yourself sleeping in your own bed when you do!"

"Yep, sounds about right. Right then, back to it. You can all ogle the new girl tomorrow." He winks, and they all file out.

"Good speech." Sloan sits on the desk, grabs my hand, and reels me in. I stand between his knees, enjoying the silence.

"Ask me how good it is when they fail to remember."

"No, they respect you, my love. Not because you are mine, but because you are strong, and you've proved it to them year after year. They were the ones following you, watching you. They admire your strength and determination."

I have no idea how to respond to that, and instead, take another glance around my new, partially bare office, then back to the corridor.

"The dumping ground over there? Are there any more rooms like that?"

He laughs and rubs his chin. "Fuck knows! It's safer not to ask!"

"Are you going to work now?"

He nods. "Unfortunately. I'll get one of these to take me in."

My eyes flit again, because I know he isn't going to be happy when I make my request.

"You want to see Sam," he says knowingly. "Absolutely fine." Stroking his hands over my back, he kisses my forehead. "Dev?"

The door opens to reveal Tommy. "He's gone to quote a job. I'll see you outside." The door swings shut.

"Still angry?"

"Not so much, but you can make it up to me later."

"You can count on it."

Chapter 18

WE STOP OUTSIDE Sloan's office, and he subtly glances over to the adjacent building. I sigh aloud; he knows he's expecting too much considering I've refused once already, and I shall again until *I'm* ready.

"Small steps," I murmur.

"Okay. I'll see you around five." He kisses my forehead and gets out, and I follow and climb into the front with Tommy. We both sit and watch as he disappears into his office.

"That man's been lost without you."

"I know. Jeremy said the same." I stare at the people coming and going, lost in memories. Tommy's eyes drift to my chest, and he raises his hand to my blouse. Moving it aside a little, the tendons in his neck protrude, and his teeth grind.

"I'm sorry we failed you again, Kara."

I muster a sad grin, because they didn't; I did. And there's no use crying over it now.

He leans forward, turns the ignition, and drives into traffic towards the hospital.

"Wait here," he orders, getting out. He blatantly scans the car park, his hand in his pocket, holding his concealed weapon. Happy, he eventually comes around to my side. Holding out his hand, I take it and shiver, making him squeeze harder.

"Should you be bringing that thing in here?"

He raises his brows at me. "Would you feel safer if I didn't?" Mutely, I stare up at the façade, remembering. "Thought so."

Heading towards Stuart's office, his door opens when we are near, and he steps out with another doctor.

"Hey, I didn't expect to see you today. You look good; very much his wife in this getup."

"Thanks. I actually had an interview, so I dressed the part." Stuart nods, until his eyes narrow.

"Expensive jewellery for playing in the sandpit with these reprobates." Clearly, he also knew of my fate today.

I touch my hand to my wrist, a little embarrassed. "It wasn't my idea."

"After all these years, I know exactly what he's like. Remember, it's easier to agree."

"Hey, Doc." Tommy thumps fists with Stuart.

"Devlin been demoted?"

"Nah, I offered. Gets me out of the office and keeps me in the boss's good books."

I take a seat as Stuart moves to the filing cabinet and runs his fingers over the tops of the documents.

"Right," he says, with a folder in his hand.

"Stuart, remember I don't understand medical terms or Latin."

"Well, in simple terms, she's technically still the same. I won't lie - it doesn't look good. She isn't showing any signs of recovery, and her neurological function is weakening."

"What does that mean?"

"It means if she does recover, she may need assistance. There's a possibility of permanent brain damage, which means there could also be deficiencies physically, mentally, and verbally. Again, there's no way of knowing of any lasting effects until she regains consciousness."

I bring my hand to my mouth. There isn't a single fucking thing I can say in response.

Stuart leans back. "I'm sorry, Kara. I wish I could tell you something different." He looks forlorn and pulls out a sheet of paper. "A letter was found in her house."

I quickly turn to Tommy, who looks blasé, since he and Parker had found the stuff.

"Stuart, I know about what was found, but Sloan has chosen not to tell me, and so I don't think it's a good idea to show me that."

"Well, I do. As a medical professional, one who may be calling you to ask for your authority to end her life, I think you do need to know, considering her condition."

"Tommy?" I ask worriedly.

"It's fine. I also think you need to see it, but mine, Park and Dev's opinions were overruled on the subject. I'm gonna get a coffee, you guys want one?"

Stuart and I both say please at the same time, and he leaves.

"Do you think he's calling them?"

"No, he's good like that. You know, you'll see him in the office more than anyone else."

My eyes squint. "Why?"

"After we removed you from your parents' house all those years ago, he became somewhat passive. After seeing you, he made the conscious decision to remain in the office, insofar as he could. He doesn't talk about his past, but I know he lost someone close to him, in more or less the same circumstances. I don't really know that much. John does, of course, but he would never betray his boy's confidence. He's acts like a dickhead, both him and Parker, but they're not. Beneath it, they're all suffering something. It's what binds them all together."

"Misery loves company, doesn't it?"

His eyes narrow, and he gazes at the triangle of flesh that my blouse is exposing. "Have you call that number yet?"

"No," I answer sharply, tentatively touching the documents.

With a resigned sigh, he pulls out some medical reports and lays them out. He starts to explain each one, but I have no idea what he's talking about. Fortunately, Tommy returns carrying drinks and crisps and drops them on the desk.

"Let's go see her, shall we?"

Walking slowly towards the ICU, my stomach curdles loudly, and I slam my hand over it. "I think I'm going to be sick."

"She looks exactly the same, there's nothing to be frightened of," Stuart says.

Peering into her room, a nurse is taking her vitals. My heart is failing already, and I've not even set foot inside.

"Tommy?"

He runs his hand through his hair, then jerks his head. "I'll be in the waiting room."

The nurse comes out, greets us, and moves on to the next. Forcing myself to walk the line and face up to what is now a cold, harsh reality, I step inside. Suddenly, it feels freezing, and I can't quite fathom if it's the room or me. Stuart, realising I'm regressing, gently presses my lower back. I turn to him, ready to burst into tears.

The slow, pulsating beep resounds spasmodically through the thick, tense atmosphere. The sound is both soothing and damning to my mentality.

"We've got a visitor for you, Sam," he says. "Stay strong, Kara. Forget everything that has happened and just talk to her. You may not get a second chance." I shudder as I lean over and stare at her face.

Second chances. I know all about those. I've had more than I feel I deserve. I had a second chance at a childhood in Marie's care. And I had a second chance at finding my true self the moment Sloan stepped into my life. This is Sam's second chance – whether she knows it or not.

"Hi," I whisper, pulling the chair to the edge of the bed. I reach for her hand and stop. Quickly turning to Stuart, he nods.

"You can touch her." He picks up her records and inconspicuously moves to the other side of the room, studying them ostensibly.

"I don't know what to say to you. I can't find the right ways to apologise. All I seem to be doing lately is saying sorry; sorry for leaving, sorry for returning. I don't think there's anything left to be sorry for."

My eyes track the tubes and wires, and I wonder if I had called her when I arrived down here, would her life have been better. Would Marie have taken us both in? Lost inside pointless thoughts, the door opens, and a young nurse steps inside.

"Sorry, Dr Andrews, I'll come back later."

Stuart nods and approaches. "There'll never be an easy way to bring this up, but we have to be realistic." He sits on the bed and hands me some paperwork. I take it grudgingly, because it feels wrong to be holding something akin to her death warrant when I have inadvertently caused it.

"I want you to take them and read them thoroughly. If there's anything you don't understand, have Sloan get one of his solicitors to talk you through them. One day, you might have to sign them."

Shivering, I release a shaky breath. "Do you think she knew?"

"About?"

"The past. When I last saw her, she told me to never forget. At the time, I didn't understand, but now I have to ask. Do you?"

"I don't know, Kara. That's the truth. The rat bastard might have inferred something. She might have pieced it together. The best person to ask would be Remy when he comes back."

The machines beep in the background, and I run my hand over hers, holding it, circling it, beating down the fear and loathing.

"What were you all like back then, before all this became your lives?" I ask, still staring at the woman in front of me, remembering the past that brought us both together so many years ago.

"I was in my last year of med school when I first met Sloan. He was sharp and astute. We lived together for a time until he came back down here after…" He gives me a pointed look, indicating the past that joins us cruelly.

"We were what you would expect - two guys living together, away from the prying eyes of parents. We weren't saints, Kara."

"I didn't imagine you would be," I reply, dividing my attention between the sound of his voice and the machine maintaining life. "I often wonder what life would've been like if none of this had happened."

A knock comes to the door and Stuart turns and sighs. "We'll never know. Come on, they want to bathe her, and we're interrupting their schedule." Kissing her cheek, I smooth my thumb over her hairline.

"Are visiting hours still the same?"

"Yeah," he replies. He holds the door open and greets the nurses as they enter. Outside, I take one last look, until the blind is snapped shut.

Walking towards the waiting room, Tommy looks to be almost asleep in the chair. Stuart nudges me.

"You better get him back to the office. I doubt he will still be in the bosses' good books if he falls asleep on the job. I'll see you later."

I watch him leave, then slowly walk over to Tommy and flop down beside him. He straightens up, looking remarkably alert. Passing him the documents, I lean back.

"You know if you love someone you set them free."

I raise my brows at him. "What if I can't? What if the day comes, and I know I have to, but I can't?"

"You will, and if not, the good doc will make the decision for you." He slowly wraps his arm around me. "They always do." I turn, but his focus remains straight ahead.

Dropping my cheek to his shoulder, we both sit staring at the wall, dwelling upon decisions that have yet to be made. Or quite possibly, somewhere in Tommy's past, have already been made, deciphering the extent of his insinuation.

Chapter 19

"YOU SURE YOU want to do this?"

I stare nervously around the foyer. Squeezing Tommy's hand, the burn seeps up, culminating at my elbow. When I first suggested we come here, he was hesitant.

And he's still hesitant.

"Why not? I've exorcised every other demon, I might as well get this one over and done with, too." Shaking him off, I move towards the front desk. Laura's look of shock is unavoidable.

"Oh my God, Kara. It's so good to see you!" she exclaims genuinely. She comes around and shrewdly glances at Tommy. Her eyes twinkle, then narrow. "Is Mr Foster with you?"

I shake my head. "No, just me. Please can I have the master key for the suite?"

She slowly walks back around the front desk and fishes the key out from somewhere. Visibly cautious of handing it over, she gives Tommy a terrified expression.

"What?" I query.

"He told me not to give it out without his consent. Not even to you," she mumbles.

Tommy motions me towards the small seating area, and Laura follows, fisting the key firmly. Sitting down, the two of them shoot looks all over the place, evidently not wanting anyone to hear.

"The suite's a little different from what you remember," Tommy states. "The last night you were here, he, hmm…"

"Redesigned his living space," Laura continues for him.

"But John said he hasn't been back," I reply, confused.

"No, he hasn't. Aside from moving the…damaged…he refused to have anyone touch it, or even clean it. You might be a little shocked when you enter." Looking between us, she relents and opens her palm. "Here, I keep it under the desk for emergencies. If he asks-"

"I took the opportunity upon myself. Thanks, L." Tommy winks at her, but still looks uneasy. She wearily moves back to the guests awaiting her assistance, while we approach the lift bank. I tap my foot, equally anxious to be getting inside, and nauseous at what the penthouse will greet me with.

The doors slide shut, and the oxygen is ripped from the inside. My lungs feel like they are about to seize up and fail. The combination of this and the impending visual of the suite is sickening. I stare at the floor, wondering if it will still be unspoilt before I get out. Counting my customary one to ten, I reach six as the bell dings.

Stepping out into the intimate foyer, I glance over at the other door and then back to the suite. My hands begin to sweat profusely, terrified of what I may find when I step into the home of so many of my firsts.

"Do you remember the code?" Tommy asks, inserting the key.

My fingers move over the numbers nervously. Pressing the last one, the door latch releases, and he pushes it back.

A ghostly silence greets us. Crossing the threshold, an atmospheric tension grows inside, because it feels wrong to be standing here, knowing I didn't gain his consent to obtain entry. But the reasons why are not lost on me; I ripped his fucking heart out in this place.

As I drop my bag on the table, it disturbs the amalgamation of thick dust. Moving further inside, the open plan living room comes into view. I gasp when I witness the true devastation of what his *redesigning* must have entailed.

Aside from the leather sofas and a stand-up lamp, the room is empty. My eyes trail across the floor, imagining the destruction I left in my wake. Gliding my fingers over the top of the sofa and down the arm, I remove the dust with them. I slip off my heels and rub my foot on the rug in front of the fire, my mind relapsing. It's almost a year since we started my firsts, and over seven months since I remained consistent and ran.

Pressing my lips together, I bypass a subdued Tommy. With my foot on the first step, I slowly walk up the stairs, punishing myself to return to the scene of the crime.

Outside the bedroom door, I take a breath before entering. My eyes expand, and my heart breaks when I see the room I have so many amazing and beautiful memories of. Notwithstanding the thick layers of grime, the place looks like it has never been lived in. The bed is naked; the mattress new, still in its cellophane. It all looks so barren and cold.

I furrow my brow as Tommy's footsteps stop outside. I'm grateful for his discretion, because I need to absorb this on my own.

A glimmer of light from the walk-in captures my attention, and I hesitantly enter. The first thing I see is a pair of shiny scissors sitting innocuously on the island, standing out horrendously alongside his expensive, shiny watches. I pinch my nose, confused as to why they are there at all. Walking the interior, my eyes drift. Just like the bed linen, all of Sloan's suits are gone.

Glancing back to the island, I understand why.

With my hand over my mouth, trying to fight the shriek desperate to break free, I turn to my side. It's empty, but there, hanging bizarrely in front of the naked rails, is the midnight blue gown.

"Are you okay?" Tommy asks the most fucked-up question.

"No!" Ready to break down, I shove the scissors into his hand. Marching past him, fighting to stay strong, I quickly shrug out of my jacket.

"Can you ask Laura to get someone to bring up some fresh bed linen and cleaning stuff?"

"Kara, you don't have to do this. I'll get a team sent up."

"No! I did this, and I have to make it right!"

Defeated, he agrees, unimpressed, and quickly leaves the way he came.

My tears come calling when I rip the plastic off the mattress. The sound of multiple footsteps resound, and Tommy returns with Laura behind him.

"I'll help you," she says, putting down the requested items and offering a weak smile. She places her hand on mine, aware I'm falling apart at what, possibly, unknown to her, I reduced him to. It's abundantly clear now why Stuart medicated him – and why Walker knocked him out.

Tommy's phone starts to ring, and an ashen look befalls him. "It's John," he confirms, then leaves. His voice echoes from the landing, but I concentrate on putting a little piece of my life back together again.

Glancing at my watch, it's almost six. I have spent the biggest part of the afternoon cleaning and straightening up the suite. Standing in the living room, I look around at the almost presentable space. Granted, it will never be what it was, but at least the signs of past destruction have been vanquished.

After nearly an hour of ignoring Tommy's request to leave it, and my constant refusal to do so until I was satisfied, he left. I'm grateful, but every good memory I have is now marred and tainted.

And I have no one to thank but myself.

Pulling out my phone, I scroll through the missed calls from Walker and Sloan. Holding it to my chest on speakerphone, I wait until someone picks up.

"Walker Security?"

"Hi, John, it's me."

"Hey, honey. How you feeling?"

"Better, kind of. I don't know, it was hard to see this. I wish you had warned me."

A deafening silence cuts the conversation, until he breathes in. "It wouldn't have changed anything. Can you honestly tell me you wouldn't have reacted the same?" I don't respond because we both know I would. "Honey, the reason I wouldn't let him come and get you is because he wasn't in a fit state to. It would have killed him to hear you say no."

"I know," I whisper, finally understanding why he never came for me, like I always thought he would. It's a lonely truth, but broken can't mend broken.

"Look, I don't know if you've spoken to him, but he's on his way over." A knock comes to the door, and I tilt my head with a smile.

"I think he's already here."

"Have a good night. I'll see you tomorrow."

I peep into the spy hole to see Sloan waiting outside with a bottle of champagne, a bunch of flowers, and a smile that goes on for miles. Slowly opening the door, I lean against it.

"You're late!"

Bypassing me entirely, he drops everything down on the newly clean table and spins back around. Raising his hand, he pushes the door shut behind my head, and I coil myself around him as he shoves me up against it.

"No, baby, I'm right on fucking time! Now, let's create some new memories," he murmurs into my neck. I tighten myself around him as he takes my lips in his. Holding firmly, I giggle at the scratching on my jaw, courtesy of his five o'clock shadow. "Bedroom or living room?"

"Living room," I whisper, feeling him harden between us.

"Grab the champagne, baby."

Sliding me around his hip, I reach out my hand as we move into the living room. I hug the chilled bottle to my chest, wanting to set the scene of times gone by and equally cool down my body temperature.

I ground myself as he leaves momentarily and returns carrying tea lights. Lighting and positioning them sporadically, he flicks off the light, and the room glows softly from the minuscule flames.

He removes the bottle from my hand, and his lips brush against mine in the most exquisite of touches. Cradling his head, I stretch my neck back, silently requesting his kiss. Obeying, he sucks gingerly while I reminisce.

Falling back onto the floor, he rises up above me, touching my face. His eyes move from side to side reflectively, while his mouth starts to curve. I put my hand over his, feeling very self-conscious.

"What?"

"Marry me. Now. Let's just get in the car, drive somewhere no one can find us, and be married by sunrise."

I pull him close, my heart beating rapidly. "I would love to be your Mrs Foster, but not like that."

"Then how? How would our perfect day play out in these beautiful eyes?"

"Well, let's see." I stare into his midnight blues, smiling innocently. His hand strokes down, pausing at my collarbone. "Firstly, it would be a small affair." He cocks his head. "An intimate gathering," I elaborate, gliding my hand through his hair.

"Hmm, I can definitely do intimate, my love."

He unbuttons my shirt, taking his time, treasuring the moment, as he proves he can do intimacy - with me - very well. Deftly removing my bra, he licks a solitary line from the base of my neck to my breast. His pain is evident as he repeatedly traces a prominent scar.

"Don't," I whisper. "Don't bring him back into this perfect place with us." Resigned, he kisses the offending mark.

"What else?" he asks, his tone emotional.

"The build-up would be slow, thorough, and a moment to savour." I rub my hands down his chest, before untucking his shirt, starting the process of discovery again.

"Hallelujah," he whispers against my skin, shrugging his arms from the material.

We simultaneously undress each other, and he drags my skirt off whilst I push down his trousers. He effortlessly kicks them away, along with his shorts, and throws them into the surrounding darkness.

Manoeuvring us easily, our bodies press together, and my nipples slide over his chest. He opens the bottle, and I watch in delight as the cork pops and disappears into the void.

I smile shyly and purse my lips. "There would be celebratory champagne," I murmur, licking my bottom lip. He tilts my head and pours the cool, crisp liquid down my inflamed throat, then his own. "Lots of it," I purr, pressing closer. Pressurising my mouth in an open kiss, he transfers the fizz, reliving our first.

Lowering me back down, he pours the alcohol slowly over the length of my body, lapping and stopping at my belly button. My back arches under his methodical, tender nipping of my flesh.

"There would be good f-food-d," I stutter when he shifts my knickers aside, and his tongue carefully slides over my skin, teasing me beautifully.

"And the best, most exquisite dessert I've ever tasted."

"Cheesecake," I mumble to myself, quivering, growing mindless.

"No, my wife." My legs stiffen at his statement, as he rips the material and slides the destroyed fabric down my leg.

"Stop talking," I rasp out. With a grunt, he pinches my clit playfully, his normal action when he doesn't like my response. I'd like to say it hurts and makes me annoyed, but I think he fails to realise it just makes me more lightheaded and aberrantly brazen.

"Nope, keep talking."

"Why?" I ask, elevating my hips, desperate to squeeze his head between my thighs and keep him there for a while. Indefinitely, actually. "Why are you even asking?"

"Just getting an idea."

"Your ideas are dangerous. Besides, you've not asked properly, and when you do, I might say...*no*."

"What was that?" He jerks up, hand to his ear, laughing, pretending to be annoyed.

Yep, if there's one way to ensure a game of cat and mouse, it's to say one, simple, little word. Usually, I would laugh, too, but not when I'm on the verge of release, and he rudely cuts it short.

"Hmm, a challenge. One I quite like the sound of." He climbs up my body, meeting me face to face. "Do you want more?"

"Yes," I admit lasciviously.

"What are you willing to barter, my love? We've been at this impasse before, and I think I won."

Holding each other close, he waits patiently for my response. I run my fingers over his strong, muscular chest, delighting in the smooth texture of his skin. As expected, I don't have anything ingenious to impart, because I have already bartered everything precious to be back in this position. I have nothing left to give that he doesn't already own. My eyelashes flutter, while my body falls back into the sea of euphoria.

"Eyes open, baby. I'm not letting you off that easy."

Still blind, I feel for his shoulders. Connecting limb to limb, my fingers find his arms. Caressing every contour and ridge, I breathe steadily, while my centre ignites, teasing every cell in the vicinity.

"What would *you* choose for this imaginary wedding?" I ask, opening my eyes, wanting to distract him so I can revel in the hidden ecstasy penetrating me beautifully.

"Who said it's imaginary?" He smirks, running his finger down my front. I gasp when he drifts lower, over my abdomen, and finally, through my folds. I wiggle, determined to feel him in all the areas silently screaming for him.

Circling his finger deep, he breathes in. "I would choose the perfect venue; hidden away, timeless and memorable."

"Hmm," I murmur, delicately riding him. Pulling his nape close, I kiss him deep and roll his tongue with mine, sucking his bottom lip, then letting go. "Hidden is good. All the best, most delightful things are hidden," I confer, referring to something else entirely. The dull light of the room does nothing to hide his smug grin.

"Maybe not that well," he comments knowingly, before sliding another finger inside, making me vocalise rhythmically.

Manipulating us to the floor, I run my palms over his cheeks and toy with his hair. He kisses my breast, the one marred and prominently damaged, then grabs the back of my knee, adjusting my leg over his hip.

"You would wear a stunning white dress-"

"Simple and elegantly cut," I smile, thinking of what I would look like if I was to ever grace this body in a dress of such significance.

"You don't want layers?" he queries suspiciously.

I shake my head. The idea is sour. "I have layers; far too many for my own good."

"Noted."

He rolls us over and positions me precisely, then glides my body down his length. I tighten my hands over his as he fills me with perfection. Seeking a comfortable rhythm, he swells deep within, tilting his pelvis in silent demand. Putting his hands under his head, he looks completely relaxed, in a sexually induced kind of way. I still, staring at him, until his knee pushes my arse from behind, jerking me forward, and I groan.

"Let's talk about lingerie. I want descriptive detail here," he says cockily. I roll my hips, the pressure building. Grabbing what were previously my knickers, I hold them up with one finger.

"They'll be white and lace...and shredded on the floor!" I smile broadly, proud that I've just got the upper hand.

"Damn right!" He quickly sits up, rocking me back and forth.

"Oh, God!" Breathless, I rotate, riding him, giving him what he wants. With one hand under my arse and the other on the back of my neck, his perspired skin slides over mine.

Biting my lip, he pulls back and lets it go with a pop. "Will you honour me?" I stare at him, breathing hard, comprehending the double edge sword of his question.

"Yes!" I gasp out, feeling my core tighten, desiring immediate release.

"For richer, for poorer?"

"Yes!"

He speeds up our movement, slamming me down on him repeatedly, holding my ribcage as I begin the journey of shattering beautifully.

"In sickness and in health?" He starts to roar out his release.

"Always!" Sensation floods my abdomen.

"Til' death us do part?"

I cry out, my body eviscerating in timely passion. "Sloan..."

"I will, baby. I always will!"

He holds me as the simultaneous shuddering reaches its peak. His arms stay strong and substantial, but I grow lax and compliant. Stroking my damp hair from my cheek, his finger glides over my lip. My tongue instinctively darts out to lick it, and his eyes smoulder, full of expression and desire.

"I will, too, and it's terrifying."

"Is the prospect of growing old with me not fulfilling?" He gives me his best harmless, midnight stare.

"It's more than fulfilling, but it's so...eternal." I admit, because he's seriously making me think of the underlying truth that he is still offering me.

"Love will set you free."

He holds me close, and his hipbone rubs over my centre, infusing further friction. Kissing the curve of his neck, he slowly walks us up the stairs, never removing his stare. Just outside the bedroom door, he smiles sadly.

"Say something, my love." Tenderly moving my finger down his nose, I pause while he kisses the pad.

"It's already set me free."

Cradling my head into his neck, he sighs out content and kicks open the bedroom door. I watch with sleepy eyes as he tugs back the duvet and settles me down. Climbing in beside me, he cocoons us together.

"Marry me. Let's create our ultimate memory," he whispers.

I leave his request to evaporate into the ether. Placing his hand on my breast, I close my eyes.

"Thank you, for giving me back another amazing memory."

"You know me, I'm all about the memories...and the firsts...and ultimately, the end game," he affirms.

I smile to myself in the darkness as he kisses the back of my neck, getting himself comfortable.

"I love you, my future Mrs Foster."

"I haven't said yes."

"But you'll never say no."

Turning away, I'm consumed by thoughts of the past. The times we've shared together; in this room, in this bed, creating, what are to me, also ultimate memories. The good ones, the amazing ones. Ones that define exactly who we are, and the love we share in this volatile, messy, unpredictable world.

With a smile on my face, I close my eyes and see myself in white, inside eyes the colour of a beautiful, dark night's sky.

Correct in his assumption, inside my heart, I've already said yes.

Chapter 20

SHIFTING OVER, THE delicate touch continues across my forehead. My sleep has been tormented with dream Sloan again, followed by the imaginary wedding we verbally fashioned yesterday.

I grumble, slap away the hand and turn over. Something around me moves, and I burrow my head into the pillow. I'm exhausted beyond belief. The last few weeks have been arduous, to say the least. Not to mention my body is falling back into that place of continual sexual fulfilment with him. Apart from the slight soreness, it feels like I've never been away.

He shifts me, until I'm laid on top of him. "You feel nice. Perfect, even," he whispers.

Leaning down, our noses touch, and he kisses me fervently, sliding his tongue against mine. Entwining our legs, I drop my head to his neck, experiencing a lull inside that is causing me to drift off again.

"You've got a big day ahead."

"Hmm," I murmur.

"I'm going to get in the shower, care to join me?" His coyness tells me we could be in there a while if I do.

"No," I whisper.

He clucks his tongue in fake admonishment. "I still don't like that word. However, don't fall back asleep."

He slides me off of him; his hard length pressing into my hip. Tugging his pillow to my chest, I absorb his scent. His unique aroma consumes my senses, and I pretend he is still under me, as dream Sloan takes the place of the real man shutting the en-suite door.

The shower starts to run while I fall back into my dreams.

"I thought I told you not to fall asleep?" I rub my eyes, taking in a distorted looking Sloan minus a towel.

The fire in my blood heats a notch, causing me to become more alert. My eyes widen at his beautiful, water glistening flesh. Sitting up, I roll my bottom lip into my mouth, my head filling with ideas.

"Hungry?" he asks innocently, and his unambiguous question fires inside me.

"I'm hungry for lots of things." I reach out for him, but he shifts. "That's not fair."

"Neither are you when you're wanting, hoping for more that I am definitely willing to give you." He breathes out, content, the moment my hand connects with his, and I entwine his little finger with mine and tug him towards me. "Let's change the subject before it gets too hot in here, and I have to call down for a do not disturb sign."

"What you don't already have one?" I mock shock.

His chuckle fills the room. "No, but do you think the arseholes would pay attention if I did?"

"Absolutely not. You're all John's boys through and through! No awareness of boundaries or personal space between you all." I roll my eyes.

He holds me close; curling a strand of my hair around his finger. "Speaking of John's boys, are you looking forward to your first day?"

I groan out. "Honestly? Yes and no. I appreciate it won't be half as stressful as a *normal* job, but I'm just... I'm worried..." I glance away.

"What's wrong, baby?" He gives me that concerned look he seems to wear regularly when I procrastinate wildly. He worries about me more than I do, which is saying something.

"I don't know, everything really. I'm sure once I'm settled in, probably ready to kill one of them by the end of the day, I'll be fine. Are you going to work today?" He nods, and I stare down his body and giggle. "You might give all the ladies a really good free show," I murmur, drifting my hand down his stomach, until it encases his growing hardness gently, causing him to hiss.

"Hmm, that's nice, my love, but the only lady I'll be giving a free show to is you."

"I like that reply," I confirm, letting him go. "But seriously, you'll be underdressed. You...you destroyed everything in there." I look towards the walk-in, and a subtle chill overcomes me.

"I was going to tell you. I just couldn't... I lost it." He shakes his head, clearly ashamed that he had something similar to a breakdown. "How could I be strong for you when I was barely on the edge of sanity myself?"

Whether he realises it or not, I appreciate exactly how hard that is. To be strong. I've tried and failed so many times to be that for him, both before and after tribulation.

"I understand. But you're still going to be stark bollock naked!" I slyly tilt my head, finding amusement in pain. "Unless you want to wear a lovely blue dress?" He throws his head back and laughs loudly.

"Still amusing, my beautiful smart-arse Petersen. Actually, yesterday's suit is being dried as we speak." He looks unimpressed. "And Dev's on his way over. He's bringing you some jeans and trainers since I moved most of your things out. I think you might be safer in them until you get that fucked-up house of theirs in order!"

My face drops, wondering just how disorganised their house actually is, until he lifts my chin back up.

"Let's go have breakfast downstairs. I'm sure James will be happy to see you; Laura, too. She told me about yesterday. Thank you."

Staring at him, I promised to always give him the truth. Working my eyes from the walls to the furniture - or the lack of it - I breathe in.

"Actually, it was for my benefit more than yours." He raises his brows, misunderstanding. "Well, this and the mansion are the true homes of all my firsts. Leaving it in chaos just didn't sit right with me."

He looks thoughtful and starts to pace up and down in front of the bed. I sigh out; he still has the ability to see through me like no one else.

"That wasn't just it, though, was it?" He smiles joylessly. "Doc called me."

I drop my head in my hands, the moment he simultaneously kneels in front of me. "She doesn't look good. I mean she looks better, healthier than she has for years, but the prognosis is indisputably bleak."

"We just have to hope she gets better."

"Don't be a hypocrite." His jaw works tirelessly, and I ease his annoyance a fraction. "Seriously, if she was well, I probably would've washed my hands of her, too. But she needs me because she doesn't have anyone else – she hasn't for years. That's what made me stay and suffer all this time. I lucked out with Marie, but we both know that could've been a very different story entirely."

"Okay baby, I'll stop lying and say that I fucking hate her, but I will tolerate this for you. It's the only reason I didn't throw her drugged-up arse out that night."

I arch up on the balls of my feet and kiss him. "I know. Let's have breakfast."

Walking me back towards the walk-in, he diverts me to the drawers and lifts me atop of them. Kneeling down, he kisses a tender

165

line from my ankle to my knee, looking up slyly. Almost reaching my apex, he grunts.

"My breakfast is served. What are you having?" He grins, and I playfully nudge his head away.

"Stop it! I think you've stretched me out enough already!"

"I don't think so, my love. By my calculation, we still have four months-" I place my finger over his lips.

"Yes, but not all now!"

"Are you kidding? This is the best make up sex ever!"

"Baby, please."

He grudgingly stands, relaxing his hands on the back of my head. Leaning forward, his rubs between my legs, reaffirming my choice is the wrong one.

"Find us a couple of robes to wear."

"Sloan, there's no way we can go downstairs and eat with the patrons, who are paying an arm and a leg to stay at this fine establishment. I'm pretty sure they don't want to look at my pasty legs over breakfast!" I laugh.

"I own this fine establishment, and my wife and I can do whatever the fuck we like. But if it makes you feel better, call down and have them bring something up." He turns back to the bathroom, then pauses. "Oh, and I adore your pasty legs... especially wrapped around me!"

He quickly ducks into the bathroom as my pillow flies by his head.

Sitting at the island, I feel content as Sloan holds me close, feeding me little bites. Aside from the curious expressions he is giving out intermittently, he's thoroughly relaxed. Evidently, he banished his demons from here last night, too.

Picking up the last piece of toast, the landline starts to ring. He groans out, exiting the room as I move to retrieve it.

"His timing is fucking flawless!" he calls out as he goes.

"Hello?"

"Morning, I'm on my way up."

"Okay." I head into the office, where Sloan is currently collecting up whatever he needs. "I'm just going to get a quick shower."

Holding up his finger, he grins lazily and motions me forward. "Kiss." I shuffle over until he reaches out and pulls me onto his lap.

Long minutes tick by until the doorbell chimes. Pulling away, I lean over him, my hands on either arm. "I." Kiss. "Love." Kiss. "You."

I lightly scratch my finger over his jaw, before turning with a flirty sway and sashay out of the room.

I stop at the suite door, and Devlin is on the other side, looking wide awake as usual. He stomps in in his worn leather jacket, jeans, and heavy boots over the hems.

"You're a little underdressed this morning," he says, engaging the security system. "Here." He passes me the bag. Looking inside there are jeans, a jumper, and my trainers. My cheeks redden when I see the clean underwear.

"I didn't rifle through your drawers. Unlike *someone else*, I have more respect than that."

"Thanks," I answer dryly.

"Where is he?"

"In the office, also underdressed. I won't be long."

He waves me off, calling out for his favourite half-brit. I love that he pushes Sloan's buttons – the same way that Sloan pushes mine. He really is unimpressed when the shoe is on the other foot.

As I sit on the bed, drying my hair, I listen to the muted voices downstairs. For once they sound jovial, and I hope that if anything good has come out of all this, it is that they are getting along better. There is no doubt in mind that deep down they actually do love each other, but in the past, it was hard to be the pawn between them, especially when Devlin did something he thought was right and Sloan failed to agree. I wander over and shut the door, my days of eavesdropping are over; it gets me into shit every time.

Slipping on my trainers and jacket, I grab my bag from the floor. "Great," I mutter when I can't find my phone. Eyes studying the room, it's lying innocuously on the bedside table. Picking it up, I realise at some point I'm going to have to listen to the voicemails on my old mobile and delete them. And, quite possibly, make it redundant once and for all.

If there is one thing this last year has taught me, it's that the past should stay precisely where it is; in the past. It has no right to plague a future I didn't think I'd ever be in receipt of.

"Baby?" Sloan shouts up at me.

"Coming!" I shout back, trotting down the stairs. He meets me at the bottom with his hand out.

"Not in company you're not!" He smirks, and I scowl, realising what I have just verbally walked in to.

"You have such a one-track mind!"

"*Me?* You're the one making insinuations, my love. But if that's what you think, when we get home tonight, I'll show you exactly how one-track my mind really is. Are you game?" I tut out and ignore his hand, while his chuckle resonates behind me.

"Let's go, little lady, it's almost eight. John will skin my arse if I'm late." Devlin breezes by us and marches out of the door.

Waiting patiently in the Range Rover, Sloan opens my door and twists me in the seat.

"I'll see you later." Leaning in to kiss me, I allow him to claim what's his. Eventually, he gets into his beloved Aston, guns the engine, and reverses out and away.

Devlin climbs in, and the door locks activate. I stare ominously at the handle. Being inside this vehicle - which seems to be the car of choice for these men, and *others* - strikes the fear of God into my soul. Just like my childhood cubbyhole is the place where pain started and ended, these 4x4's are the fear equivalent.

"Don't worry, nothing bad is going to happen."

I nod, unable to find faith in his statement. Especially when we all know it's only a matter of time until the dark clouds come rolling through and blacken out the light again.

Chapter 21

SCRUNCHING UP MY nose, I gasp and spit out the dust that I have, unfortunately, just swallowed. I throw down the pile of papers and brush down my front. Why the hell I agreed to this gig, I have no idea. Actually, I do - I wasn't exactly given a bloody choice in the matter!

It's my third day on the job, and I'm almost two rooms down, with about four to go! After day one of just being sat at my desk, watching the barren landscape, having already established they didn't need anyone to run their office, I gave in and decided to tackle the rooms. Two hours in, Sloan was right; it was better not to ask. Even though they have all told me to leave them more than once, I can't.

Already fed up, I stick my head out of the door. Rock music floats down the corridor from Walker's office. The sound of him and Tommy discussing last night's *date* in great detail is all I've heard intermittently since Sloan dropped me off.

I block out some of the unnecessary things that have shocked my eardrums this morning and reach up to the last shelf. Prising off the final box, a lifetime of dust and papers fall in succession. As I rub the grit from my eyes, the landline starts to ring, but I ignore it and wrestle the box onto the desk.

Scrambling around on the floor, I collect up the last of the strays. The phone continues to go unanswered, and I puff out, annoyed, as the music blares beneath the bantering.

Unsure of how these men work their office, considering they just threw me in at the deep end and offered no real training, and the fact it could be whatever legal, or maybe illegal business they conduct, I pick it up.

"Good afternoon, Walker Security." I cradle the handset on my shoulder and pick up the files, sliding my finger under the flap with curiosity. I wait for the caller to speak, but it never comes. "Hello?" Silence, but whoever it is is still there. Listening. Learning. I hang up quickly as a deadly chill erupts, because the call has just validated what is already fact; it isn't over – maybe it never will be.

Dialling one four seven one, predictably the number is withheld. I sigh out, sat on the edge of the desk, in between the year's old paperwork and crap. I cast my eyes over the room, but my heart is conflicted between the ominous call and the files laying innocuously at my side. Something urges me to look at them. Picking them up, my intention is cut short once more by the intrusive phone.

When the caller fails to identify themselves, I disconnect it quickly. I tap the digits in a second time, hoping it might be a wrong number or a call centre, but again, it's still withheld. Slamming it down, I massage my temple, fighting back the fear.

The bastard knows I'm here.

Again, I have to ask the question of how he knows. And yet again, only one person could have sold me out.

I pace the room in my unspoken misery, when it rings again, and I snatch it up, finally at the end of my tether. "*Yes?*"

"Erm, hi. Is John there?" a man asks, surprised.

"No, he's unavailable." What else can I say? He's down the corridor discussing promiscuous women and listening to fucking music while I'm being silently hunted? "Can I take a message and ask him to call you back?" I offer instead.

"Sure, it's Dominic Archer. He has my number," he says with an air of authority.

"Okay, that's great. I'll get him to call you," I reply courteously.

"Thanks, have a nice day, Miss Petersen."

"Hey, how do you-" He hangs up before I can finish. "Okay," I say to myself, collecting up the files.

"Kara?"

"Come in."

Walker throws the door back and smiles. "Hey, how's it going?"

"Fine," I answer; the files in hand.

His narrow eyes fix on them. "Where did you find those?"

"They fell from the shelf." I point. "Why?"

"No reason," he says awkwardly, taking them from me. "Everything okay?"

I sigh; I can't conceal shit from these men. "Fine," I execute as positively as I can, hoping to God he won't see through it. "Someone called twice, but the number was withheld. One four seven one doesn't work."

"Okay," he says suspiciously. "Probably nothing, but I'll get Parker to have a dig around on the system." Satisfied, he glances around the room, giving it an impressed look. "If anyone else calls, just take a message."

"Oh, a Dominic Archer called." I gauge his expression.

"Great. Thanks, honey," he says and starts to turn away.

"John?" He halts, and a resigned sigh escapes him; as if he already knew I was going to pry. "He used my full name, but I never gave it. Do I know him?"

He looks down at the files in his hands and moves closer. "No, he's an old friend." Grinding his jaw, he's lying through his teeth.

I look from the man to the files and back again, as the secrecy starts to punch through once more. As we stand glaring at each other, waiting for the other to ask the next question, his eyes harden. Like so many times over the last eleven months, it's the look that tells me to forget it. Unfortunately, that isn't an option anymore, but quite clearly, I will be wasting my breath even trying.

Truly fucking fed up, I leave the room. Marching back into my office, I slam the door in frustration. Rocking in my seat, heavy feet stop outside.

"Kara?" I drop my head in defeat, but don't utter a word. "Can I come in?" I get up and open it - an invitation for him to enter.

I exhale a shaky breath. "I have no right to ask, but-"

"That's right. As a paid employee, you have no right whatsoever. While I'm putting a salary in your pocket, you will not delve into business that isn't yours. Understood?" His tone carries a menacing lilt, but he doesn't wait for my reply as he thunders down the corridor.

I smash my fist down on the cupboard and take a breath. How many times have I heard their lies and concealment before? What will it take to stop the wicked web of deceit from spinning? What more do I have to go through to get a little fucking honesty and rectitude?

"Kara, we need to go out for a while. Won't be long," Tommy calls out.

I stick my head around the architrave as he approaches Parker, who is already twirling the car keys around his finger at the security door. I slam my own door shut once more and the sound echoes in the stillness.

Loitering at the window, still relatively unimpressed with the concrete landscape, the sunlight blinds me as the trio stride across the car park and climb into Tommy's 4x4. Counting silently in my head, I watch as the gates close and lock, and they disappear into the maze of streets.

A glimmer of light intrigues me, and I gaze down, seeing an old banger of a Micra slowing to a stop outside. My breathing hitches as I watch it until it moves again towards the scrappers. Dropping the blind halfway down, I pick up my mug.

The phone starts to ring while I pour the last bit of coffee. Holding the handle tightly, I enter Tommy's office and grab up the handset the same moment the sound ceases.

Glancing around, my eyes are automatically drawn to the confiscated files, poorly concealed under the chaos of plans and handwritten quotes. My heart quickens as pick up the first file and slide out a document naming and shaming my father. I drop it in shock and quickly leave, because whatever is in them will not be good for my current mentality.

My fingertips feel numb as I finish typing up the last quote. Taking a sip of coffee, I instantly hiss at the vile strength of it. Having been so incensed by what those files might represent, I have completely forgotten about it.

A faint rumbling resounds from my desk, and I grab my mobile to find Sloan has texted. My dark, gloomy mood brightens instantly when a picture of his desk and a bottle of champagne appear. Replying with a capitalised *no*, I put it back down. Shuffling in my seat, I'm half tempted to tell him to come over here since I'm still alone. It's been a few hours since everyone left. Aside from a few insignificant calls; one from Jake, and one from Charlie begging me to meet her for lunch – regardless of the embargo we both have on us - I haven't heard a peep.

Rubbing my forehead, the ringtone of my old mobile begins to chime. A portentous air of dread causes bile to seep up my oesophagus. Slowly opening my top drawer, the screen is glowing. Still not finding the courage to listen to it, today is the first day I have actually turned it back on in months. Invisible red warning signs flash behind my eyes. I know I should ignore him, but it's futile. The only way to finally make this stop is to sever all ties completely.

Throwing it on my desk, it rings again. Pressing the call button, I hold it away from my ear as my father drawls out my name.

"Sweets?"

I shiver under the sound. It's the same tone he would use just before he handed me over to the devil. Pressing it to my ear, I yield.

"Yes?"

"You got me fucking arrested! I'm fucking dead because of you!" he shouts.

I walk an invisible line, considering how to reply. "I don't care!" is the first thing in my head and out of my mouth. Although a part of me is relieved, because whilst the police acted like they didn't give a toss, thankfully, they did.

"I'm outside, sweets."

"What do you mean? How do you know where I am?" He doesn't reply, and I rush to the window, pressing my cheek to the glass. Looking up and down the street, I cannot see him, until the battered Micra pulls up outside the gates and he steps out.

"I'm not leaving until you call them and tell them you were lying!"

I exhale incredulously. "No! When will you accept that you are nothing to me?"

"Kara?" his tone lowers.

"I'm not your fucking Kara! I stopped being anything to you the moment you handed me over to that bastard! You never cared about my mother or me!"

"She's the reason why I'm here!" he hollers. I close my eyes, because he has just levied the one thing that will make me submit.

Unbeknown to Sloan, I didn't sell my mother down the river. I lied and told them she was unaware of the systematic abuse I was suffering. It was wrong not to make her pay, but she was just as much of a victim as I was, and I can't have that on my conscience. She'd never survive in prison.

Grabbing my jacket, I march out of the room. The corridors feel hollow as I make my way through them. I grip my phone as I open the door, and slowly approach the gates. The sound of electricity floats over the air, and I look up to see a security camera tracking my movement. Unfortunately, there's no time to ponder the ramifications, as my father holds the bars on the other side.

I take in his appearance; gaunt, sick looking in a way that will never be cured. His clothes are worn at the vital areas; hems, knees and cuffs. His skin is darker, not by the sun, but tainted by life's hardship. A smattering of grey highlights his temples. Combined with the grey streaking his unkempt facial hair, it makes him look older than his time. Worn and lived. Yet staring into his eyes, I have no sympathy. He destroyed the side of me that was able to forgive years before I finally learned the truth.

"How did you find me here?"

"I followed that blonde bit you used to work for." I inhale inconspicuously, although wonder if that's true.

"Look, John will be back any minute. You need to leave now," I say harshly. "If you don't, I'll call the police and have you arrested again."

"Sweets, please…" he begins to plead.

"And I'll do it again, and again, until they lock you up indefinitely."

The silence times out between us. His eyes work the area behind me, looking up at the metal separating us, to the all-seeing eye of the camera; still moving, still spying.

"You need to tell them you were lying. You need to-" I throw my hands up as the atmosphere tenses around us. He looks down to the pavement, ashen and bewildered.

"How dare you? You have no right!" I hiss from the safety of the fencing and two feet of air. This is as close as it's going to get, because who knows what he's planning inside that screwed up head of his. He's only ever cared about saving his own skin – my body is confirmation of it.

He reaches out, and I step back. "This is the last time I want to see you. When I turn away, I want you to crawl back into the hole you surfaced from and never come back."

"Frankie's going to kill me," he whispers. "I said no. I told him I couldn't. I ran, sweets. Your mother…" he rambles, saying things that make no sense.

Curiosity tries to get the better of me, but I hold my hand up and slowly turn.

"Please Kara, she's sick!"

I laugh out. How many fucking stories can he spout out to influence his power? Well, no more. I'm done.

"No! I'm not a little child who will believe anything anymore. Stop doing this to me!" Tears wet my eyes, and I fight so hard to keep them contained. "You lost me long ago, but she always put you first."

"No…" he shakes his head.

"Yes! You know I begged her to come here with me nine years ago, but she wouldn't leave you!"

"But she is leaving! She's dying!"

I lift my head, horror infusing my body and holding it captive. "You're lying!" I scream at him. "Stop fucking lying to me!"

Reaching into his pocket, he pulls out a well-read, crumpled letter and stuffs it through the railings into my shoulder. My eyes skim over it; glazed by my own devastation.

"Sweets, please."

"You're dead to me." I don't recognise my own voice as the words tumble out without a hint of emotion.

From the corner of my eye, he walks back to his car and finally leaves.

Listing to the drone of the engine fade, my tears fall. For the first time in his life, he has given me the truth. And in doing so, he has finally broken my heart and the pieces of my soul that I could never hate. As much as I wanted to, I never could, because I will always love my mother, and the half of me that is the half of her.

After everything that has paved the way for the life she couldn't escape from - the one she couldn't protect me from - I realise she wasn't lying when we last spoke. She wasn't doing his bidding. She wasn't even pretending to keep the peace. She was being honest because she might not get another chance. Because the paper in my hand verifies it.

She *was* saying goodbye.

I scurry back into the building, crying irrepressibly and slipping on the stairs. Ripping off my jacket, I run into one of the barren rooms, lock the door and throw myself onto a makeshift camp bed.

Lost, and further losing myself in a world of grief, I cry into the paper. The ink bleeds under my tears, while my heart bleeds under the pain. Truthfully, I had lost her years ago, but a part of me would never let go. Never allow the possibility to grow life.

Heavy feet echo inside the building, and I lift my head. The door slams open and I turn in time to see Tommy's boot lower, as Walker quickly grabs my shoulders and shakes me.

"What the hell were you doing, Kara? I want an explanation, and it better be fucking good!"

I turn my back on him; I'm tired of explaining and listening. His mobile rings loudly, cutting through the tension thickening between us.

"I'll call you back."

"Kara?!" Walker shouts again, as Jake appears behind him and grabs him.

"John..."

He shrugs him off. "I saw him on the live feed."

Just as I thought.

I scramble back on the bed, pick up the letter and shove it into his chest. I whimper as my bodily functions break down once more. His eyes drift over the paper, until he pulls me close and rocks me. I cry against him; my heart and mind broken. My fingertips dig into his back, trying to feel something other than imminent loss.

Laying me back down, he strokes my face tenderly. His sympathetic expression is too much.

"Honey, I'm sorry, but I promised to keep you safe. And that includes from your own father. Get some rest, I'll call the kid."

The bed rises, the light fades away, and the door closes. I shut my eyes, just wanting to wake up feeling refreshed, less tired, less troubled – less anything.

Grabbing fistfuls of fabric, I disintegrate into the perpetual, agonising darkness. As it beckons me closer, I dream of my mother.

Standing in front of me, she is the way I remember when I was young, no more than five or six. She is youthful and pretty, and I see so much of myself in her. I reach out, and my chubby fingers touch hers as she whispers goodbye. Giggling, wanting to play the game, I run after her. She doesn't turn, and she doesn't hear my calls. Suddenly, she is gone, and everything around me is black. As I panic and spin on the spot, shadows move towards me, and I scream.

"I love you." Sloan's mixed tone sounds pained as his cheek rubs against mine. "Come back to me."

Rubbing my eyes, he shifts me closer, his hand curling my thigh around his hip. Becoming one with him, I kiss the column of his neck.

"Want to talk about it?" I ease away from him, but he refuses to let me have space I so desperately want. "I'm not angry," he whispers, and I feel strangely relieved, happy that my actions today are not going to cause an all-out war with my inability to follow simple orders.

"You'd have been proud of me. I didn't back down."

"I know you didn't, and I'll always be proud of you."

"But you shouldn't be, because I've killed them both. Sam, my mum…" I whisper, holding him tighter, too ashamed to speak it aloud for fear it might infect like the plague, and I may lose more than currently at stake.

"No, baby, no."

My body shakes involuntarily, and he lifts my chin. Caressing my face softly, I can't stand to feel such tenderness when I have inadvertently caused such anarchy. Meeting his eyes, the tiny glow of light from the glass reveals his anguish.

"I remember how much it hurts...to lose those you love," he whispers. Kissing him, he rolls me over. "Just let me hold you."

"Make me forget. Just for a while, take it all away."

Lowering his lips to mine, he presses his hand to my chest and bequeaths my wish.

Chapter 22

WELL, IT'S BEEN three long weeks since my father announced the most painful of admissions and left. And three since Walker gave me my dressing down in the wake of it.

The following day, I hesitated whether or not I still wanted to work for the man. And also, because those who shouldn't know where I am, do. But given that it was either come into the office and find something productive to do with myself, or stay at home bored out of my mind, taking Sloan's money but not actually earning it, the office won.

"That's the last one," Jake says, slapping an invoice on the desk. My eyes feel sore just looking at it.

"Wow, I don't think I've ever seen so many numbers." I continue to stare, wondering what their percentage is. "How the other half live," I mumble.

Jake snorts. "Kara, you *are* the other half!"

Rolling my eyes, he clears his throat, knowing he has said the wrong thing, and then edges towards the door.

"Coffee?"

"Please," I murmur, tapping away on the keyboard again.

My mobile buzzes across the desk and I grin broadly. "Hello, stranger!"

Apart from a visit or two, Marie has pretty much left me to get back into a routine again. Business has also picked up for her recently, so it hasn't left us much time to see each other.

"Are you busy, honey?" she queries.

I look around at the non-existent work. "Not really. I have a few things I could do, but I'm saving them for when I'm really depressed," I reply sarcastically. "Why?"

"I'm coming over for a girls' afternoon. I'll see you soon." She hangs up, and I lean back in my seat, wondering what, exactly, this afternoon is going to entail.

Whilst the men in my life have become a little more loquacious than usual, the women have done a role reversal. Even Sophie is showing prudence and reining it in these days, but it's clear they are planning something. Their looks and gestures all point towards scheming.

Waiting for her to arrive, I yank open my desk drawer and fish out my old mobile. I rest my head in my hands as it shows yet another missed call from my beloved father.

Sloan, newly intolerant of my being left in the dark, which is a triumph in itself, hasn't addressed the issue of him, or my apparently dying mother again. Although just to be sure, he had Stuart snoop through the NHS database to confirm what I had been given was official. And, sadly, after the good doc's protesting about ethics, conduct and blatant abuse of his position, he finally relented and confirmed it was, but refused to elaborate any further on her condition.

Needless to say, I'm actually heartbroken, and I have spent more time alone, crying to myself for a mother that was never given a chance to nurture in the misery that surrounded her. Nonetheless, I still can't find it in my heart to speak to her. If I do, it means I have to face reality, and a side of me has to forgive completely.

Shoving it into my bag, Marie's heels click down the corridor. Watching her throw the door back, illuminating the room in a way only she can, she floats in. Immaculate, in a perfectly fitted trouser suit and not a hair out of place, she drops into the seat opposite and looks around.

"You've really made this your office." She continues to stare, picking up the picture of Sloan and me. She smiles and repositions it meticulously. "Come here, honey. It's been too long since I've seen you properly."

Rounding the desk, I calmly move into her open arms, breathing in the scent of her perfume and the faint aroma of shampoo.

"I've missed you," I whisper.

Letting go, she carefully touches the sides of my head. Like everyone else, she has also skirted the issue of my real mother, although unknown to everyone else, she has insisted numerous times that I should call her. Like Stuart, she said I may not get another chance. Gauging me, still stroking my face, I know it hurts her to hear of the past and my parents, especially when she risked imprisonment to be that for me.

"I love you."

"I love you, too. I know we don't say it enough, but I love you as my own."

An expression of heartbreak consumes her perfect features, and it is more than a tell of the honest truth. I'm about to ask, when the door opens, and Walker fills the space. She turns and smiles, and I witness his change immediately. He's always been different in her presence. The hardened, rugged exterior evaporates with a single flick of her lashes. He's a goner when she's around.

"Why, hello!" she says, meeting him somewhere in the middle. He pulls her close - completely forgetting that I'm present - lifts her off the ground and kisses her until she stops him.

Yes, this is my office you are almost fornicating in.

"I'd like to believe you're here to see me, but that would be wishful thinking, my angel." He drops her on her feet, and she quickly straightens herself up.

"You see me enough! I thought I'd take my girl out for the afternoon. Do you mind?" She presses her hands to his chest, while he moves his head from side to side. "Good. Let's go, honey."

"Not so fast, angel. Sloan doesn't want-"

Marie's hands find her hips. "I don't care! We spent years doing just fine on our own before you boys invaded our lives."

I smile, but he looks annoyed that he's being put in a precarious position between two people he loves.

"Baby, please. We don't have much time," she whispers, thinking I can't hear.

Walker lets out a long, infuriated sigh. "Fine, but only because..." he stops, looking at me closely. "Just make sure you check in every hour, on the hour. Otherwise, I'm sending out the cavalry. Clear?"

"Crystal!" she replies sarcastically, leaning up to kiss him. "Thank you. I love you."

I turn involuntarily at her declaration. Whenever I raised the subject of boyfriends in the past, she would skirt the question. The same when I last broached the subject of children, it's a topic that is off-limits. Seeing this new side of her is enlightening.

She turns with a devilish wink. "Don't say a word!"

Walker grins and takes her in his arms again, just to prove the point. "I love you, too, angel." He releases her and holds up *those* files. "After you ladies have done...whatever, Kara, can you take these to the kid?" Passing them over, he eyeballs me. Whatever else is in these, I figure it's best not knowing.

Yet.

"Sure," I confirm, putting them in my bag for safekeeping. He moves out of the office, slapping Marie's backside as he goes.

"I'll see you later."

"No, you won't," he laughs. "The kid will make sure of it!"

"Ready?"

"How do you do it?"

"Do what?" Marie asks, swinging her bag over her shoulder, hurrying down the corridor before our emancipation is revoked.

"Why is it you can get him to relent on the whole bodyguard issue and I can't?"

"Ways and means, honey. Ways and means."

Stepping outside, my eyes flick over the steel fencing, capturing a familiar Range Rover parked a few hundred yards down the street.

"You okay?" she asks, noticing my apprehension and divergence of attention.

"Fine." I climb into the car, and stall with my hand on the handle as my eyes skim over the sleek bodywork of the Mercedes 4x4. "Is this yours?"

"Hmm, don't ask. I was *won over* on the subject of it."

"Really?" I query, surprised. Clicking on the seat belt, my eyes are drawn back down the street.

"Well, when his highness buys you anything, I now appreciate how much of a fight it is for you. When John pulled up in this beautiful tank, for days I refused to drive it. One morning, the sly git took away my old car keys, shoved me inside and sent me on my jolly way."

"It's nice. Safe, too, which is probably the real reason behind it," I rattle on, still concentrating.

"Kara, what are you looking at?" she asks, exasperated, and I turn in trepidation, pointing at the car.

"So? The scrappers and a showroom are just around the corner."

"I know, but-"

"Honey, in this city Range Rovers are like tourists – they're everywhere! Little man syndrome. You should know, you work with five of them!"

I halt my train of thought, then burst out laughing. "True. What are we doing today, anyway?"

"You'll see," she replies with a grin.

"Marie…"

"Ask no questions, I'll tell you no lies!" The car roars to life, and she rolls up to the opening gates and edges out.

Driving past the car, I stare straight into it, although futile due to the illegal tinting. I grind my teeth inconspicuously. *What is it with these bleeding dark windows!*

As I stare in my wing mirror, it follows us down the street until we hit the main road. Keeping a close eye on it, it tails us for a couple of miles, before turning off.

My hands tighten as I clutch my bag in my lap. I pray for something completely different to what I'm currently romanticising inside my head. Even so, nothing is to be trusted. Between the three bastards who have demoralised and obliterated me each in their own way, I know time isn't an ally on my side.

"So, who's the cake for?" I ask, flicking through the wedding catering magazine that we have picked up along the way since Marie wanted a third opinion.

"Just a client. They want my advice," she replies far too quickly.

Looking down, a five-tier cake that the confetti threw up, on fills the two-page spread. Dropping my head to the side, I flick over a few more pages, horrified that some of these nasty monstrosities are the price equivalent of a small second-hand car.

She walks up behind me and peruses the pages over my shoulder. "Which one would you pick?"

"I don't know. That one's quite nice," I say, pointing at a simple, elegant, multi-layered white thing.

"Hmm," she replies and strolls away. I follow behind her, dog-ear the page, then pass it back to her.

"What do you think?" she queries, as she holds up a suit. I do a double take and finger the soft, cream material.

"It's nice, but it's not exactly a colour for your line of work, is it?" I turn away and start to look around, doing the one thing I do absolutely detest.

"I think I'll buy it," she says proudly, grabbing up the two-piece and laying it over her arm. "Aren't you tempted by anything?"

I scrunch my nose up, the answer is no. Truthfully, I'm just glad to have a day free of male order. These last three weeks, I haven't set foot outside the office alone. I'm surprised I can even visit the little girl's room without having an armed guard. And that right there is another problem - the fact that these boys always carry a weapon. Apparently, it has escaped their attention that not even the police carry unless absolutely necessary.

"Let's go and have a look at lingerie." She waltzes off before I have a second to process what she's just said.

Walking around the department, I stop when I see a beautiful set on display. I delicately skim my fingers over the satin and lace, admiring its stunning simplicity and how it feels. Marie's warm breath flutters against my neck.

"They're nice. I'm sure Sloan will like them." My cheeks flush crimson. "Stop it, Kara. You're a grown woman in love. Wanting to look nice for your man is normal." I grin, wondering what reaction she would get if she was to flounce around in front of a certain ex-military man in such a barely-there set. "And stop that way of thought, too!"

"If John ever asked you to marry him, would you?" I query, turning back to the rail, trying to locate my sizes.

"Why do you ask?" she answers, in that panicked, brainwashed tone from last year.

"Sloan asked me again. I want to say yes, but it just doesn't feel right. Not with everything that is still to materialise."

With a tender huff, she shakes her head. "Honey, you don't know what the future holds, none of us do. Go on, buy them." She nudges my arm.

"Marie, it's bridal lingerie," I reply, getting a better look at the labels.

"And? Soon you'll be getting married, and it's one less thing for me to organise," she says, trying to conceal her grin like she has just let the cat out of the bag.

It's no big secret that, eventually, I will be Mrs Foster, but the way she's talking, I'll be barefoot, pregnant, and tied to the kitchen sink before the year is out.

"Something you need to tell me?" I put a hand on my hip, the other still suspended above the beautiful bras.

"Nope," she mutters, waving her hand.

Watching her scurry off, my suspicion piqued, I grab the bra, a matching thong, and a very cheeky pair of lacy shorts. Holding them up, I wonder how long it will be – whenever I might be wearing them – that Sloan will ensure they are on a first-name basis with the bin the following day. With that thought in mind, I move back and grab another pair.

Hindsight; it's wonderful when you have it.

I look around, trying to locate Marie, when I see Charlie, phone pinned to her ear, running through the knicker department. A grin forms on my cheeks, until *something* captures the corner of my eye.

There, three displays over, is the lovely Christy, with her equally lovely friend. Even worse, I have to pass them to get to Marie.

Perfect.

Fantastic.

This day can't get any better, can it?

Of all the shops she had to be in right now, it's this one. Although it's definitely a sign of the financial times. I can't imagine a year ago she would have been in a high street department store with the rest of the great unwashed.

My spine straightens, like there is an invisible piece of string being pulled from the heavens, and I move.

"Hello, Kara." Her vicious tongue swings into action the moment I'm in range.

I give her a forced smile. "Christy."

She gazes down at my occupied hand, and I keep my expression neutral as Charlie rushes towards us; her grin of excitement is unmistakable.

"I've been looking all over for you!" She winks and throws her arm over me. My shoulders do a jig as I slowly let go of the apprehension. "Christy, how are you?" Her arm tightens. "Still trying to find wealthy men to sail you through life? Prostitution might be a more secure source of employment, you know."

I close my eyes in provocation. As detrimental as it was to my heart when she flung her verbal shit at me – *twice* – it's nothing in comparison to the discomfort of hearing Charlie stoop to her level. But she does love to wind her up, and unfortunately, I'm now slap bang in the middle of the latest episode.

Christy, still staring maniacally at my hand, completely ignores Charlie and gets up in my face.

"Still hanging in there I see," she says maliciously, touching the garments. "Considering I haven't seen you for months, and he was on my arm for the last few events, I thought he'd finally been shocked back to sense." I step back, absolutely hating the lies she is spewing out again. "I'll give it six months. Don't worry, when he doesn't come home one night, and he's in my bed again, I'll be sure to call you at the pivotal moment!" She sticks her head in the air, almost knocking me over as she shoulders by, her sniggering friend two steps behind.

The rage that I am barely keeping tethered under my skin inflames me, but this is not the time nor the place. I quickly turn back to the rail and exchange the garments.

"Why are you changing them?" Charlie asks in confusion.

"She touched them!" I close my eyes and inhale.

Charlie grabs my shoulder. "Kara, he never-"

I rapidly shake my head. "I know he didn't! He's many things, but I *know* he isn't a cheat. I'm going to have to deal with her for the rest of my life, aren't I? It doesn't matter if I have his ring on my finger, or his child in my belly, she will always find a way to twist the knife!"

She sighs, silently concurring my assumption, before pulling out her phone as Marie comes over. My eyes are fixed on Charlie, who is tapping away furiously, obviously checking in the latest upheaval with big brother dearest. The thought of having to go to the office and drop off *those* files is looking less appealing by the minute.

"You okay?" Marie asks, although she knows I'm not.

"Debateable!" I answer sarcastically, virtually running towards the cashier.

Four scraps of material and an obscene amount of cash later, I finally put my purse away.

"How's being back at the office?" Marie asks Charlie, as we step onto the escalator.

"Fine, but it's work. At least Sophie is there now to listen to me. All we need is for Kara to join and it will be a family affair!"

Ah! No way in effing hell is my backside warming his desk on a daily basis, because I sure as hell won't be typing his letters or answering his bloody phone!

As we walk around the shopping centre, I listen to them chat randomly and feel myself drifting further away. Except, rather than catch them up, I halt when the fine hair on the back of my neck stands to attention. Rotating, much to the delight of a grumpy old bloke behind me, I study the faces of everyone passing by. Nothing is standing out, but my neck is still doing a jig.

"Kara?"

I take one last look around, then quickly make my way over to Charlie, who is holding open the coffee shop door, playing footman to everyone coming and going.

I shuffle my bum across the leather bench and wait for Marie to bring my usual over. Charlie is still fiddling with her phone, and I try to play dumb. My own phone vibrates in my pocket to show another missed call from my father. Stuffing it into my bag, I know it only brings pain - pain I can't sustain any longer. It's stopping me from living. It has for a long time, but now it's time to let it go.

"...there's another fundraiser coming up soon. Did John tell you about it?" Charlie's eager tones ripple through my eardrums.

"Maybe you'll be able to wear that cream suit then," I mutter casually, whilst my phone continues to buzz.

"Cream suit?" Charlie asks, and Marie shows her a little of the dress. "Is that for..." She stops, and I raise my brows, silently challenging her to elaborate further.

I'm not stupid. Between the mother of the bride suit, the wedding cake query, and the lingerie she insisted I buy, I know they are planning my wedding, and honestly, they can get on with it, because I have more pressing issues right now. Namely, the pressing issue of my phone that seems to have developed a connection to the national switchboard again.

"Are you going to answer that?" Marie asks, finally getting annoyed at the constant vibrations coming from my side.

"No," I retort, disregarding their questionable expressions. I pick at the sugar waffle on the saucer and slouch down in the seat, the weight of the world bearing down on my already broken shoulders.

The silence falls into place easily. Between Marie, who is now, apparently, Walker's girlfriend through and through, judging by her secrecy; to Charlie, who, like me, is still so frightened of what may come to pass, reports in dutifully to big brother every five minutes.

My phone comes to life once more, and for some asinine reason, I actually do want to see my father again. Hoping that the next time he will do as requested. Call it closure, or maybe just call it what it really is: self-infliction. Either way, I know it will see the light of day. It has to, because if it doesn't, I will always come back to this place. The place where I ask why and wonder until one of us is no more. Lost in my thoughts, Marie swears.

"Shit, I forgot to check in!" She brings the phone up, and I listen to her bargaining.

Yes, John; no, John; three bags full, John.

"We need to go." Collecting up our empties, Marie grabs me. "Sloan isn't happy you came out unmanned. John asked me not to say anything."

I chortle; that man is never happy when it comes to my welfare, or the lack of self-preservation he seems to think I have in regard to it.

We walk over to the car, and I climb inside. Marie, as paranoid as she can sometimes be, always parks in the quietest spot. It means walking for an age, but at least you don't have to be stick thin trying to slide in if other drivers can't put their vehicle in between two white lines properly.

Her words, not mine.

Belting up, I gaze out of the window. My hands tighten on the ominous files, while the familiar, scenic route to Sloan's office finally appears around us.

Chapter 23

MY FEET CLICK over on the marble foyer floor as I step into the lift. The sinking sensation culminates the instant movement begins. Charlie squeezes my hand, and I blow out my breath, making a sound similar to a whistle, while my stomach threatens to expose its contents. No matter how much I've tried to shove aside my anxiety of cramped spaces, it's no use. I shall always carry a fear of them, purely because they draw out memories I shall now never forget.

Ever.

We stop on the top floor and pad down the corridor. Chitter-chatter is ascertainable, and I smile when Gloria comes into view. She clicks off speakerphone immediately when she sees us.

"Hello, darling!" she greets. Swinging out her arms, she grabs on and holds tight. "I've been wondering how long it would be before I saw you again. I'm so glad you're finally back." She pulls away and clenches her arm around my waist, guiding us towards the desk.

The sound of the boardroom door closing, and Sophie's grumbling voice, muttering about the unreasonable arsehole, is unmistakable. She then squeals, runs on her four-inch heels, and I drop the files when she subsequently squeezes the life out me.

"Ken's looking for you!" Gloria quips at Charlie, who groans at the statement.

"I'll see you later, Kara," she says, undoubtedly glum, but still smiling, walking back to the lifts.

"I didn't know you were coming over. His majesty is in the boardroom. He won't be long," Soph says, finally releasing me. "But don't be getting any ideas now!" I purse my lips, ready to pick up the fallen files and wallop her over the head. Gloria, appreciating my discomfort, collects up her effects.

"Kara, it's been lovely seeing you, but I hope you will come back another day when it isn't my early finish." She squeezes my hand. "Take care of him." She walks to the lifts calling out goodbye. As soon as the doors close, I spin around and glare at Sophie.

"What?" she asks innocently. I bite my lip, watching her move around the space. She really does look like the CEO's personal assistant.

I flop down onto the leather sofa, grab a magazine and check my watch. Three o'clock. Thumbing through the pages, I wait.

"Well, here's to a great deal all around, gentlemen," an older voice speaks jovially, the same moment the heavy doors open. "Are you up for a celebratory drink, young Foster?"

I tilt my head back when Sloan steps out of the boardroom in the three-piece pinstripe I picked out this morning. With his mouth slightly open, he turns instinctively. Even from this distance, I can see his eyes darken, holding a cacophony of mystery, laced with desire.

"I'm afraid I'll have to decline, my four o'clock is here," he says candidly, with a hint of anticipation. And exactly what he's anticipating, I don't have to guess.

I stand and subtly brush down my front. I'm glad he insisted I wear a suit this morning. I would be feeling very much out of place in my jeans and trainers right now.

"While you're all here," he says to the five men following their leader. "I'd like to introduce my fiancée, Kara Petersen." He grins devilishly, and I hear Sophie mutter *bullshit* from her corner. Refusing to turn, such that I will burst out laughing, I straighten my shoulders and curve my hand in his.

"Hello," I greet shyly. His hand drifts from mine, further and further, until it's groping my backside inappropriately.

A little flustered, with my body reacting, they all greet me. After a few minutes of job descriptions, congratulations, and dinner invites, they all board the lift. Sloan salutes as the doors close and drags my body to his.

"Now my day really begins." He growls low in the back of his throat, gathers up my hair and claims my lips. Plundering my mouth, completely forgetting the huffing and puffing behind us, he leans back. "What now?" he asks annoyed.

Sophie bestows a stern look upon both of us. When she just stands there, the slight movement of her hip indicating she's tapping her foot behind the desk, I'm impressed. Either, Sloan has done what he so eloquently said he would, and forced her to get educated in his – *our* – affairs, or she is learning that he is her boss, first and foremost.

"Go home," he orders her, but peering back down at me, thoughtful and calculated.

"But I have all these documents to copy and certify!" she says hotly, pointing at the stack she exited the boardroom with earlier.

"Then pretend there's a 'do not disturb' sign, right over there!" He motions towards the boardroom door handle. With a little gasp, she starts to open her mouth, her voluble tongue desperate to be heard.

Sloan, evidently fed up of wasting time, marches towards her. "Sophie, if you want to see no evil and hear no evil, go shopping." He digs into his wallet and throws a credit card at her. "Better yet, call Doc. Do something, *anything*, just be anywhere but here, for the rest of the day." He turns and cages my head in his hands, his thoughtful, loving expression trained hard on me. "We still have four months to catch up on. Not to mention my boardroom is dying to experience a new first for both of us!" he says gleefully, picking me up and carrying me down the corridor.

"Oh my God!" Sophie exclaims, but it is ignored with the slamming and locking of the door. Sloan sits me on the table and spreads my knees. Angling his head, he listens as the lift bell finally dings.

I lean back and marvel at the view of the London skyline in the full glass panes, then deride at the used china still sat on the table.

"Baby?" I point towards the teapot.

"Good point. I want to fuck you, not cut you!" He quickly gathers up the empties and stacks them on a tray and deposits it under the table.

"That's so crude!"

Hands on my knees, he drags me forward, until my backside is on the edge and he pulls up a seat in front of me.

"True, but it doesn't change the fact it's what we both want." Pressing a simple kiss to each knee, he scrunches his nose. "I curse the woman who invented *these*," he says, snapping my tights and reaching up to my waist.

"It was probably a man, *young Foster*," I retort.

With an amused grin, he slides them down. I grasp the edge of the table and lift as he peels them down my backside. Wiggling, like a snake shedding its skin, he fakes disgust and throws them aside.

"I think we need to have a policy on what is acceptable to wear in my office, *smart-arse Petersen*."

I snigger. "Well, I guess I should be thankful I don't work in your office then."

He brings my ankles over his shoulders, then loosens his tie and unbuttons the top of his shirt. "Ah, but technically you *do* work in my office," he says, so very conceited, shrugging out of his jacket. I squirm, so very turned on. The sight of him patently aroused does it every time. I'm like a moth to the flame; desperate to feel the fire, uncaring if I am eventually burnt.

My fingers pressurise onto the wood while my core starts to feel a little weak. Weakened by him and what I know he's planning to do in the next thirty minutes or so.

Arching my back, the blissful, reverent sensation begins to gain momentum inside me. It's laughable, he doesn't even have to touch me; just a few words of insinuation will also do it every time. Sensing my body becoming boneless, I start to lean back.

"Stay where you are. I want you to watch." My eyes immediately locate the ceiling, as he takes the first tender nip on my inner thigh. "Eyes on me, my love."

I brace myself for the onslaught of visual and physical sensation. I peer down, until my eyes catch something that is giving me absolute cause for concern, because regardless, I'm still no exhibitionist.

"The glass." He looks up with a blank expression. "Someone might come up. I'm sure you don't want this broadcasted all over the office." I point out logically, already adjusting my skirt back down my exposed thighs. Tapping my legs to stay put, he looks frustrated as he moves away and picks something up from the windowsill. He grins as he walks back over.

"Watch," he says, and the clear panes frost over. "Better?" I nod, as he sits again and leans back, looking every inch the powerful and commanding CEO.

"What?" I ask, feeling a little nervous that he's just sitting there, gauging me, like he has done so many times in the past. Cradling his chin between his finger and thumb, he's thoughtful.

"I like this; you, waiting patiently." His hands rub over my knees, each movement slowly pulling them further apart.

Staring into his eyes, my grin widens. "I like me like this, too, but who said I'm patient?"

"Definitely not the person who said it was a virtue!" He chuckles and starts the slow, painful game of reaching the pinnacle. With a soft, suckling kiss to my thigh, we begin.

A comforting ripple spans the length of my body. Reaching the back of my skirt, I shuffle on either cheek, and he rids me of it in seconds. Prising my thighs further apart, he licks his way to my apex, each stroke more forceful than the last. My hands automatically find his hair, and I bring him closer to where I want him.

My fingers clench tighter when the first touch of his tongue surprises me. Feeling him circle my opening, he spears me with delicate precision, inducing my body to sag compliantly.

"Tell me what you want," he whispers against my folds, leaving a delicious vibration in his wake.

"I-I want," I gasp out, stuttering, transforming into his Kara again. Failing to comprehend what it is I'm actually requesting; he takes it upon himself to deliver my silent wish.

When he pulls away, I look down, worried. He grins beautifully, easing my indecision. "Trust me?" He tilts his brow, and rather than fight him, I agree. "Good. Lay back."

Easing down on my elbows, my back slides over the table. In a split second, his mouth is covering my centre. His urgency is reflected in the way he sucks and then penetrates me amazingly. I slam my hands down on the wood, unable to gain purchase. My muscles tighten, and I cry out. Arching my back, I press myself deeper to where we are perfectly connected.

The tug of my thong is predictable, and he drags it down my legs. "Impressed?" he asks, holding it up intact. I grin, grateful that at least one pair of knickers have survived longer than the rest have so far. Still, I won't get my hopes up just yet.

Thrusting his tongue, I move against him. Finding our own rhythm has always been easy, effortless. Instinctive.

My body spasms and the first jolt of bliss envelops me. With one last, deep penetration, I unravel spectacularly under his skilful, wicked mouth. He grunts, pleased, while pleasure soars through me, and I cry out his name reverently.

Completely out of body, the chair scraps, piercing my hearing, and I glance down as he stands and drops his trousers and shorts with synchronicity. Hard and proud in front of me, he motions me up with one finger, while the other toys with his waistcoat buttons. Shrugging the garment down his arms, followed in quick succession by his shirt, my fingers dip into the ridges of his chest.

Allowing me to play with him, he deftly strips me of my remaining, intrusive clothing, until I'm wearing nothing but my bra. I stare up at him as he massages my back, until my breasts are falling free from their confines. Carefully removing my bra, he places it on the chair and then picks up his jacket. My nipples press against his as he holds my back, and he throws his jacket over the table behind me.

"Always considerate," I laugh, aware that regardless of how expensive his jacket is, my spine maybe a little bruised in the morning.

"I'm always the consummate gentleman," he says proudly, stroking my jaw.

He picks up the remote again and points it skyward. The room dims, until only a glimmer of light remains, creating a different sort of ambience.

I shuffle back, and my knees drop to the sides as he climbs in between them, allowing me to cradle him.

Guiding my head towards his mouth, he slowly inches inside me. I slide my legs tighter around him, caging him to me. His expression is heart-stopping; enduringly beautiful under the mood lightening. Never turning away, he presses deeper. With a low, possessive growl, he takes a nipple into his mouth and sucks it hard and long.

"More." The word leaves my mouth breathlessly. He reciprocates by taking the other with a hardened resolve, biting and soothing. "More," I demand again, digging my heels into him, showing him exactly what my definition of *more* is since he has been nothing but still.

"Say the words, my love."

Grabbing his face, the shadow of a smile is there, knowing he's requesting me to say things that still feel foreign.

"Fuck me," I whisper.

My tongue slides into his mouth and dances alongside his. Without further indecision, he slowly moves. Holding behind his neck, I stare at him, ready to be immersed in passion.

His hands rake down and stop at my hips. On his knees, he adjusts me so that my shoulders and neck are the only parts touching the table. I hold my breath as he thrusts inside. Repeating the action, he gains momentum, guiding me back and forth on his length, firmly gripping my lower back to ensure minimal bruising. True to his word, he's taking care of what's his.

"Squeeze, my love," he growls out.

I clamp around him, draining him with everything I have. Using my outstretched arms as leverage, I arch my body up further and curl my leg around him. His throbbing penetrates deeper, and he digs his fingertips into my skin almost painfully.

"Let go, baby," he says, his hips working tirelessly.

"Sloan!" I cry out. "Don't stop, don't stop!" I lift up and press into him, needing to feel his slick skin against mine. He shudders, and a drop of perspiration runs down his temple to his jaw.

"Fuck!" he roars out.

I hold him close and suck the curve of his neck as he rocks us, drawing it out until the bitter end. Kissing my forehead, his fingers twist mine of significance.

"Please say yes," he requests, and I grin against his chest.

He throws his jacket on the floor, then lowers us down. A tangled mess of limbs curled around each other, restricting movement, the sound of our breathing echoes in the vast space. Sadness strikes and digs its unwanted claws in, and I can sense Sloan already wondering what's wrong. His body gives him away without his knowing it.

"Baby?"

My heart feels physically wounded at the tone of his voice. Refusing to allow my damning thoughts to grow life, I close my eyes.

As I fall deeper into my own world of self-denial and never-ending misery, I see myself on the outside, looking in. Watching with subconscious eyes, seeing myself through various different stages of my life, I vow again that I will make it through. I will be his Mrs Foster, because it's all I'll ever want and deserve.

Even if it kills me.

"Open your eyes, my gorgeous girl."

Waking, I am instantly chilled when the heat of his body leaves mine. I pull the blanket over my front and realise it's actually his jacket that he has covered me with.

"Come on, you'll get cold." Picking me up, he quickly dresses me, minus my underwear and tights. Sticking his head out of the door, he wraps an arm around my shoulders and hurries us into his office. Tiredness gets the better of me, and I flop onto the sofa. Joining me, he curls me against his side.

"Do you want to tell me what happened today?"

I furrow my brow. "Christy happened. She did the usual; berated me, told me I was still holding on," I confess with a huff.

"What else?" he asks, tightening his jaw, wanting me to speak the words his sister has definitely already informed him of.

"She...she said you and her... Please don't make me repeat her lies."

Dragging me onto his knee, he snatches up his mobile. "Sophie, I want everything on the Spencer's sat on my desk by lunch tomorrow. And invite them to the event. Special guests. Thank you." He hangs up and throws down his phone.

"What are you doing?"

"If the bitch wants to play hardball with me, I'll fucking give it to her. I'm through with her petty shit!"

My days of sympathy for this woman are over. I might have broken a little piece of my heart when I realised Sloan owned her father's arse financially, but I refuse to feel anything anymore.

"If it's not my father, it's the Blacks; if it's not them, it's her. It always feels like something is trying to stop us."

"I know, but in a few months, it won't matter, because nothing that anyone can say or do will affect us."

"What's happening in a few months?" I ask suspiciously. He taps his nose, thinking he's being clever. He isn't. I have an idea of sorts. Whether or not it becomes a reality, I'll have to wait and see.

"Let's go home."

Carrying me out of the office and into the lift, he presses me against the wall. He rubs his hand over mine, paying particular attention to my fingers. "Not much longer."

I rest my head on his shoulder, battening down my fear of small spaces. "No, we'll be home soon."

The doors open, and the car park lights flicker on. Depositing me into the passenger seat, he bends and strokes my face.

"That not what I meant," he says slyly, shutting the door. Watching him get in, his look is all-knowing under the fading interior light.

While he reverses out of his space, I slowly turn, and there, loitering in the shadows, is a figure waiting with intent. I quickly glance at Sloan, who halts the car, either because he has seen, or because he's noticed my abrupt change.

"What is it?"

Looking back, the space is empty.

"Nothing," I whisper, hoping it's only my head manifesting my worst fears from the depths of a broken world - one that still lurks ominously in my despondent, ravaged mind.

Chapter 24

"I'LL BE IN the waiting room."

I look over my shoulder, and smile timidly at Dev. "You don't have to wait. I'll call you when I'm ready." His head and brows raise simultaneously; we both know he would never leave me.

I shut the door softly, remove my coat and hang it over the chair. Placing my coffee down on the bedside table, followed by my gifts, I tilt the blinds to allow the sun to penetrate the room.

Staring down at Samantha, she looks serene. A tear is trying to fight its way free, appreciating that, inevitably, one day it will be permanent.

Like my mother, one day she will finally be at peace.

And just like my mother, judgement will come sooner than expected.

Pulling out the chair, I grab my bag from across her body. Clenching my fingers around the disposable coffee cup, I position the book on my lap and start to read.

Lost in the pages, a knock comes to the door, and Stuart enters. "Hi," he says, looking at the cover. "The Snow Queen, huh?"

"Yeah," I reply, looking at the book, a little embarrassed. "It was one of my favourites growing up. We used to read it together when we were little." He sits and touches the gift bag that I've actually forgotten about. He tilts his head in request. "Go ahead."

Opening up the bag, he removes the box. Picking out the silver bracelet, he slides it over Sam's wrist. "It's beautiful. I'm sure she'll love it."

I lean back and look around the room. "Has anything changed recently?"

He's about to answer when the door opens, and Devlin smiles. "Your man's here. I'll see you later," he says, sidestepping Sloan, who's in very casual dress of jeans, biker boots, and a jacket.

"Everything okay?" I ask since I was meant to be meeting him at the office. He veers around and picks me up. Sitting on his lap, Doc watches us intently. I shuffle off his knee and retrieve my bag from the end of the bed.

"Stuart, I've read through the forms." I risk a look at Sloan, observing his expression turn grave. "And I've signed them. I know there is no real hope for her, and the longer we all keep speaking like there is, it's only giving me false security that I know isn't there. When the time comes, I want to be here. Promise me you won't do anything until I'm here." Stuart stands, holds out his arms, and I willing walk into them, ignoring the fading burn.

"I promise, honey," he whispers over my head.

As he releases me, Sloan replaces him in my embrace. Walking through the corridors, my eyes flicker, recalling every terrible thing that has played out in this place. *Sloan carrying us almost naked into my room. My father, pressing my buttons. And Deacon.* I ran for my life in these sterile corridors, and I still couldn't save it.

Sloan's mobile rings as soon as we leave the building, and he sighs, exasperated. "What, right now?" He rakes his hand through his hair, then turns, studying the car park. "Yeah, let me make a few calls," he groans. Something is obviously happening that is going to require his undivided attention today.

"Everything okay?"

"Fine!" he answers harshly, striding off in front.

As always, evasive, one-word answers are more telling than he divulges. They are indicative I'm about to be thrown into something that I'm trying to run away from.

With the phone to his ear again, he rattles on about what he does and doesn't want. I lean against the side of the car, letting the sun warm me, studying him flex and tense with each movement. He hangs up and grabs under my arms. Carefully gauging me, he cradles my head firmly.

"Whatever is said today, you stay strong."

"Sloan?" I ask, unaware of what he's implicating. He shakes his head and moves around the bonnet. "Sloan?"

Ignoring my querying, he disappears into the car. The power of the engine disrupts the quiet, and I pull open my door. Hanging back, a vibration comes from my bag, and I narrow my eyes at it, instinctively knowing who it is. My hand takes on a life of its own, cautiously removing the offending instrument.

I chortle to myself, disbelieving that Ian would sink to such levels that he has to use my mother's phone to call and torture me from afar. Although not completely surprising, considering I've avoided all communication since he blighted my world. Wondering if I should answer, thinking it might actually be her, something inside my heart tells me I should. Something deep inside is telling me this might be the last time. With a hardened resolve, I hit answer, but she's already gone.

"Is he still calling?" Sloan asks. I bring the phone to my chest and nod. There's no need to conceal it anymore.

"That was my mum." I stare at him, contemplating, giving in. "I never told you, but she rang me just before your birthday last year. She called to say she was leaving him." I stare out of the windscreen. "It sounded like she was saying goodbye. I need to speak to her, but I don't know what to say."

He gently moves his hand through my hair. "You say whatever is in your heart. I know you want rid of it, but for now, I think you should keep the phone. It's the only connection you have with her."

"All this does is create pain and animosity. For all of us." I shove it into my bag, as he slides his finger down my cheek, stopping at my flawed chest. His eyes fill with sorrow, and he slips on his aviators and turns to the windscreen.

Watching the city pass by around us, a muted vibration fills the car. Sloan's attention is captured, but I shift my eyes away from my bag and subtly ignore it – insofar as I can - because I know I can't forever.

Slowing down outside a modern tower block, the car park gates creak open. Parking the Aston in a free space, a black Lexus is sat alongside. Getting out, Sloan comes around and grips my hand. The way he's holding and massaging it gives me cause for concern.

Boarding the lift, we make our way up to the eighth floor. My stomach is queasy, and I grab the bar at the rear, curling my fingers around it tight.

"What's going on?" I query, knowing he had a casual meeting today that was fundamental to a deal that is near its completion. His eyes flick to the display, and he opens his mouth the second the box dings.

How very convenient.

Striding out, he stops outside one of the doors, and looks down with distress etched over his face. He still remains mute as male tones leak from inside.

"Who lives here?"

Raising his hand to the wood, he knocks twice. The tension mounts until the lock turns and Walker opens it.

I step inside. My eyes, my expression, my entire demeanour trained on him. I can feel the rage already starting to build. Moving down the hallway, I stop, because there, in the middle of the living room, along with everyone else, is Jeremy James.

"Hi, Kara," he says with a small, tight smile.

Devoured by my own escalating emotions, I waltz down the hallway and into the kitchen, slamming the door behind me.

Loitering at the sink, I can feel myself breaking down slowly. I didn't expect to see him today, although I probably should have expected it since Sloan is not where he should be right now.

I fight back my anguish, because of all the things that Jeremy has done, both good and bad, I'm more ashamed of myself and how I can so easily forget all he did for me. He risked his life to ensure I could still live mine. And what did I do? I called him every name under the sun, ignored him and then burnt him. Just seeing him standing there, carrying the war wound he will never be able to cover, I feel my own shame more than ever.

Truthfully, how can I give him his precious redemption, when inside, I fear I shall never be liberated enough to grant it?

The door opens and closes; the soft clicking of the lock is deafening. Quickly wiping my eyes, strong arms come around my middle, and his chin rests on my shoulder.

"He doesn't expect you to be all open arms, my love."

"I know!" I turn and rest myself against the worktop. "He wants deliverance...salvation. He wants to walk through this life knowing I don't hate him, but I can't. I can't because I have no idea why he did that to me. He saved me, but it doesn't erase the fact that he'd already assisted in destroying me."

He rocks us, coiling himself around me. "You'll finally get your answers today. He always said when he told his story, he would only do it the once. Only Tommy and John know the truth so, unfortunately, you will have to hear it with everyone else. Promise me something?" I lift my head up, feeling the strain in my neck. "When we leave here today, I leave with *you*, not that girl you used to be." I shrug my shoulders and nod, unable to confirm which girl he will get after today is through.

Kissing my hand, my heart beats a tattoo in my chest as I edge back into the living room. I sit in the corner - it's a calculated decision. It means I can escape pain quickly when the truth is laid at my door and proves to be more than I can handle. My knee shakes uncontrollably as I try to regain power over my muscle function. But it's no use; I'm already past saving.

Jeremy stands and turns to the window. I wait because if there is one thing I have learned this past year, is that when a normally taciturn, stoic man is ready to talk, ready to speak of the horrific pain and torture he carries inside, you let him.

My eyes close the moment the ominous silence breaks under his intake of breath, and he finally verbalises the promise he made to the men in this room.

"I was a foolish teenager, easily swayed. All I ever wanted was to fit in. I came from a broken home, and my mother was raising me on her own. I wasn't the easiest of sons. I wanted to blame her for everything; for doing shit in school, for my father leaving. Everything." Sitting on the sofa arm, he tents his hands in front of him. "I grew up with Sloan and Deacon; went to school with them. More often than not, I used to end up living with them. Sloan always told me to be wary, but I just thought he was jealous since Deacon was the centre of everything, and Sloan was, well, outwardly social, but extremely guarded."

I feel as detached as he sounds; the way he talks about Sloan like he isn't here, and I'm the only one present. But I know this is the only way he can finally unburden himself of the diabolical shame he has carried as long as I have. To pretend that the man who adores me, and ideally, should detest him, isn't here.

"Deacon revelled in the fact he had the best of everything since Julia's money was in abundance, and he and his father liked to spend it frivolously." He stares at me, realising I'm not entirely informed.

"Julia is my mother," Sloan says, approaching, before he stops. He turns to Jeremy to continue.

"As you know, she was eventually diagnosed with cancer and decided to divorce Frankie. Times were hard back then, the amount of shit that Black did was unimaginable. After a while, he finally left empty-handed and took Deacon with him. We didn't see them again."

He paces in front of the window. The action alone tells me he can't look me in the eye as he airs the next truth.

"About nine years ago, I got a call from Deacon saying he was living in Manchester. I didn't have anything to keep me here, and Sloan had just started uni up there. Thinking it would be just like old times, I hopped on the first train up. A few months later, with no real job prospects, I started dealing Frankie's shit to anyone who wanted it. For a while, it was okay, until one night John called and asked where I was. It transpired that Deacon had raped Charlie in Sloan's digs. I didn't want to believe it. I couldn't. When he finally came home that night, he was gloating about what a great time he'd had. I asked where he'd been, and he said he was in a bar watching football. Foolishly, I believed him. I didn't have a reason not to, so I brushed John's words aside."

His phone starts to ring inside his pocket, and he pulls it out. Rejecting the call, he throws it down on the sofa.

"Kara, I'm sorry," he says, clearly upset.

"Be sorry when you've finished," I answer dejectedly, capturing Walker's weary attention.

As per my request, Jeremy inhales and continues.

"Months later, Deacon told me we were going to a party. I was already high, addicted to the shit I was meant to be selling. It probably seemed like the best suggestion in the world at the time. When we got to the house, he started acting weird. On edge, constantly looking around, until he eventually approached a man. He was prematurely aged, like life had weathered him, beaten him. There was an altercation, and I clearly remember the man saying no. Deacon pushed him into a corner, and although I don't know what was being said, it was enough that the man looked like his world had just fallen apart. Deacon returned and grinned, saying the party was upstairs. I was still coming down and wasn't sober enough to know any different."

My tears start to fall away. Sloan quickly moves and crouches in front of me, holding my hands as I shake from the burning sensation coursing through my body at unfathomable speed.

"Kara..."

"Finish it!" I spit out. I push Sloan's hands away and get up, needing to separate myself from him and the awful truth that I'm finally going to be given.

"Deacon went into the room, and I lingered on the landing. I didn't want to hear him screwing some drunken tart. A tortured cry rang out, and I went inside. He was on top of some girl, but I couldn't see her face. He slapped her around a bit, until he punched her hard, causing her to stop moving. I can't remember what I was thinking, but he threw some cable ties at me and said she likes it rough."

He starts to shake and breathes in deeply, turning his pained gaze towards me.

"Don't look at me like that! I knew what kind of girls Deacon brought back to our place, and I was too far fucking gone to think any different." He looks towards my wrists conflicted and hurt. "The same moment I fastened the last one, he pulled out a needle, and my brain found clarity. As I looked around the room, finally understanding what was about to happen, I realised you were only a teenager. I didn't know what to do, so I just ran and stood outside. Listening helpless, unable to lift a fucking finger, I finally saw the truth in what John had said."

A chilling silence emanates around the room, but I refuse to look at these men and have them feel sympathy for me. Or Charlie. We're survivors. We have lived through hell and made it out of the other side. Albeit, not entirely unscathed.

Jeremy slowly reaches his hand out towards me. "God, you'll carry those scars forever because of me." I turn away and bring my hand to my mouth, needing to hear the second truth.

"And the night he..." I find my voice, then subsequently lose it when he remains silent. "Why?"

He slowly glances over each man - each brother - sat in the room. "Deacon called me, and I debated whether or not to go, but I knew I had to. Frankie had already told him not to touch you. Believe it or not, that heartless cunt actually likes you. Shocking, because he couldn't give a shit about his own daughter. All Frankie wants is money. It's all he's ever wanted. He thought by getting his son to get you he would finally have his millions. He was wrong. I was just too late to get you out of there before he gave you those." I instinctively raise my hand to my chest, gripping the fabric.

"Thank you," I say, my eyes fixed on a nail in the wall. I don't know what I'm thanking him for, exactly, but I have to say something. Just the same way I don't know why that rusty nail has piqued my attention, but again, I have to look at something. Something that is inanimate and won't reek of sympathy.

Jake stands, grabbing his head in his hands and paces around the room. His expression and concurrent sighs are identical to those of Devlin and Parker.

"How far do you want this to go?" Dev rises, wearing a glare that is by no means meant for me.

"I don't understand what you're asking of me," I reply pathetically. There's no equivocation in my mind what these men are enquiring, and I wonder how long I can play dumb for.

"Where does it end?" Walker speaks up.

I bring my hand to my mouth, shaking. "John, this isn't the right way. I can't justify ending a man's life, regardless of who or what that man is."

"And what about your life? He's already taken the best part of your teens, your early twenties. The next time he might not leave you with anything at all."

"I can't have any of you suffering a future of incarceration due to my father's failures."

"We're not going to kill him. The Blacks have enough enemies to take that level of criminality away from us. What exactly do you think we do, Kara?"

"You carry a gun. You all do. Someone only carries a weapon if they intend to use it."

"We carry – legally - for our own protection. Even Sloan has a gun in his safe, and it isn't to protect himself; it's to protect you. That said, if I was forced to choose between my life and those I love or the rat bastard, there would be no indecision."

I stare at the barren, bleak wall in front of me. "I hate him. Despise him. I hate that he took away my freedom and that he's still controlling it. I absolutely despise that he was actually my first, and that I still carry the scars and witness the nightmares even in broad daylight. Is it wrong to say I want him to suffer, painfully, for what he has done to me, Charlie, Sam, Emily, and every other poor woman who has ever had the misfortune of meeting him?"

I lift my head up and look around them, lastly staring at a vengeful Sloan. He moves closer and I start to shake my head. My tears blind me that I can speak such horrible things and feel nothing, not even shame that I'm thinking them.

I snatch up a set of keys and run out. Charging down the stairs, I look around the grey concrete car park. Clicking the remote, the locks release on Walker's car, and I quickly lock myself inside and drop my head to the wheel. A thump on my window shocks me, and Sloan is standing with both hands on the glass.

"Please let me go," I whimper.

Resigned, he steps back, walks to the gate control pad and taps in the code. Adjusting the seat and putting my foot down, I reverse back and lurch forward.

Driven by my tears and heartbreak, I smash my hand against the wheel. Staring at a red light, I was right – the truth is more than I can handle. Navigating a sharp left turn, I take every shortcut fathomable until I reach my destination.

The front door is thrown open, and Marie charges down the driveway. I rush out and fall into her arms, needing the support that, sometimes, only she can provide.

Sitting in the kitchen, I listen as she conducts her conversation openly. "She's fine. Upset, but fine," she says, raising her brows, lying for me. "I love you, too. Tell him not to worry. We'll see you soon."

I pick up a scone she has made and pull it apart, imagining it's my life. How amazing it would be to pick out the bad shit and leave only the good. To remove everything that is imperfect and damaged...

"...Honey?" I whip my head up, unable to even fake a smile. Not that she would believe it anyway. She, too, will always see through the façade. "Do I want to know?"

"No," I whisper. I don't want to taint her image of what was finally confessed today – my own confession included. I know she will find out. Walker will ensure she is aware. But until he sees fit to impart the ugliness of it, I shall not be the one to speak it aloud.

"I thought I'd be able to handle it...the truth, but when it finally comes down to it, I run."

"You haven't run, baby. He knows that. What happened?"

I slump back on the stool, fold my arms on the table and drop my head onto them. "Jeremy's back. He confessed. *Everything*." She looks horrified. "And it made me remember. Every night I close my eyes and try not to. I haven't told Sloan because he wouldn't understand."

She slides her hand over to me. I grip it tightly; thankful I can finally do this with her again without the fear of being burnt.

"No, I think he would. Some of the things that John told me about when he first met them... I think he will understand completely. You do him a disservice thinking that he won't. Maybe you just need to convince yourself. Look, why don't you get a few hours' rest. They'll be back later."

"Okay," I whisper, feeling defeated.

I dally at the top of the stairs, before I enter my old bedroom. I smile, recollecting some of the best memories of my teens, and the day Sloan became the one and only boy to grace this personal space.

Pulling back the duvet, I strip off my clothes and slide inside. As I fall into a deep sleep, my mind runs through the tragedy of the life that I was born into.

One I fear I shall never have any control over.

My eyes flutter open, and I slowly stare from the ceiling to the window, seeing the sunset on the horizon. Sitting up and rubbing my eyes, the house is extraordinarily quiet.

I slip back into my jeans and top, pop my head around the door and trudge out onto the landing. Tiptoeing down the stairs, Walker comes out of the dining room.

"Hey, honey." He sounds tired, and I smile, insofar as I'm able, considering the confessions of the day. "You okay?"

I shrug and turn, as Sloan and Marie appear from the kitchen. "What time is it?" I ask as he scoops me up in his arms. Guiding my lips to his, he coaxes me with kisses. "It's quarter to seven."

"Is Jeremy still here?"

"Yeah, he's staying," he confirms.

Well, at least I know where I can find him when I finally figure out how to say I'm sorry for his care and sacrifice.

I enter the dining room, pull out my usual chair and grab the bowl of pasta. Looking over Sloan's shoulder, my attention is snagged by the picture of Charlie on the sideboard. She was blindsided, wrong in her observation that if it wasn't us, then it might have been someone else suffering. There was someone else, who knows how many of them there have been over the years.

Filling my own head with fantasies, I barely listen to the words being spoken around me. Sloan clears his throat, and I shift timidly, wondering if he realises I'm procrastinating, mentally drowning under the damning revelations.

As I silently continue to pick at my food, today's revelations aren't the only issues causing me pain.

I was correct in my assumption; Jeremy's part was monstrous. And tomorrow, I will face the heartache of having to decide whether or not I want to throw him under the bus of culpability for his actions.

Inside, a part of me prays that tomorrow never comes.

Chapter 25

"HEY."

MISBEHAVING PALMS snake over my tum and I slap them away. With a curious smirk, Sloan surveys my organised chaos.

"Need a hand?"

I squint suspiciously, as the sun penetrates through the trees.

"Hmm. Several, actually. Why don't you stuff that bird," I answer thoughtlessly. He grins and spins me around. Thoroughly distracted, and with my nipples on the rise, I giggle when he gropes my bum.

"That's the best offer I've ever had. But how about we up the stakes, because the only bird I plan on stuffing is you!" I pierce him with a glare. "Stop with the *look*, my love. You'll like this game. Let's just say I'm going to *ring* in the changes, starting in the next few minutes. Come." He holds out his hand.

"Please be serious for once! I want this to be perfect." I swipe my hand over my forehead, my worry already coming out to play.

Today is my belated Christmas Day. Sloan has indulged me by allowing me to invite everyone around. When he casually enquired what I actually did on the day in question, I remained mute. He doesn't need to know that I sat and cried for him, while staring out of the window at the families visiting my neighbours.

"Okay," he says, running his cold hands up the hem of my top and sliding them over my skin.

"No!" I admonish playfully.

"What was that?" he feigns ignorance, but his baritone laugh echoes beautifully. It fades when he leaves to makes a nuisance of himself elsewhere.

I blow the hair from my face as music drifts in, and I wash my hands, my attention snared. Entering the living room, I stop when I see the man I adore with every inch of my being, stood in a form-fitting tux, holding a box in his palm.

"I was going to give you this last year, but in my haste to hide it, I misplaced it."

I smile, remembering how hopelessly frustrated he was the day I was finally allowed to go back to work, and he fumbled around the drawers to no avail.

I edge forward, and he grins. "Closer," he commands, and I comply far too easily; an unknown force reeling me in. Swiping one arm around me, he hooks the other under my thigh and levitates me around his waist. "There's nothing at risk of burning is there?"

"No," I whisper, running my nose up his cheek.

"Good." He smiles, enjoying the game he's setting in motion - one which I don't know the rules of play.

He carries me to the French doors and outside. Looking down my legs, his expression deems he isn't particularly happy with my bare feet, but they will have to do. Wiggling in his arms, I'm definitely vying for it. But I have bigger things to worry about right now; such as why is he leading me down the bloody garden path again.

"Put me down! I can assure you there's nothing wrong with my legs. Anyone would think I'm an invalid with the way you act sometimes. You're worse now than you ever were before!"

He grips my chin and shuts me up with a kiss. I float off into it, while he leads us further into the woodland trail, until he drops me down at the foot of the small clearing.

"Close your eyes, baby," he whispers in my ear, kissing beneath it. I inhale deeply and acquiesce, feeling him move before he commits to the action. Shivering, I wrap my arms around myself, inwardly cursing that I didn't bring a sweater out with me. Then again, I wasn't expecting to be dragged out here either.

"Sloan?" Nothing. "Sloan?"

"Will you marry me, Kara Petersen?" His voice echoes around the space, intermingling with the sounds of nature. My eyes shoot open, and he is on one knee in front of me, both palms holding the box out.

My breath lodges in my throat. It's one thing to ask this when we are lost in passion between the sheets, but this is something else entirely. I stare into his eyes; the expectant and loving expression they are casting back at me is mesmerising.

Slowly standing, appreciating I'm definitely speechless, he casually opens the box – like he makes a show of offering rings of eternal commitment daily.

The sun captures the stone, and small prisms of light reflect beautifully. I smile, seeing what he has chosen. A simple white gold - or maybe platinum, ring - showcasing a fairly simple diamond. I don't know the cut or clarity, and I don't care. I don't need his ring on my finger, or a piece of paper to denote the intense, all-consuming emotions I shall carry for him until the day I die.

"This is very beautiful, and incredibly understated for you," I murmur, my finger skimming the stone gently.

"Last night, you asked me what my belated Christmas wish was. Well, this is it, this moment and hopefully, the one that comes after it. *You* are my ultimate wish. Please say yes." He cradles my cheeks; his eyes are intense, filled with unspoken promise. I slide my hand around the back of his neck and press my lips to his, hard and unforgiving.

"Is that a yes?"

Shaking my head no, I squeal in delight. "Yes!"

He sighs out in relief, scoops me up and spins me around. Wrapping myself around him, the sound of our kisses heightens. He is still wearing that intense look, and the way he's holding me is more than indicative of his desire right now.

I squeeze harder as he jogs us back to the house. His lips fight against mine, and I massage my tongue over his, wanting more than I'm able to impart. I want forever. And the ring that now resides on my finger is symbolic that forever is finally here.

Marching down the hallway, my legs dangle by his sides. He laughs in that rich tone that always signifies he is truly happy.

"I think you better send out a text to tell them all that dinner will be delayed." I chortle and shake my head. "No? How about cancelled? Cancelled sounds so much better."

Slapping his back, my hand loses its direction and hits those amazing shoulder muscles. "We're not cancelling this dinner!"

"What if I promised a day of staying warm, practising pre-marital sex?"

"Not a chance!" He eases me down, urging me upstairs. Halfway up, he pulls out his phone and starts texting with one hand.

I turn inside the bedroom and watch him enter. He motions down my body with one finger and jerks his thumb.

Slowly, seductively, I slide down my bottoms. Pooling at my feet, I kick them off and crook my finger. The electricity sizzles between us, as he closes the distance and shrugs off his jacket. Holding his arms open, I reach up on my tiptoes and suck on his bottom lip. He growls and drags my pelvis into his. This alone quickens my pulse, and I hastily unfasten his buttons and pull his shirt apart. His chest heaves, and he rakes his hands down my sides, then drags my top over my head. He smiles boyishly and thumbs my nipples.

"This is very pretty lingerie, my love. Do you like them?"

I throw my head back and laugh. "Depends. Will they live to tell the tale?"

With a shrewd tilt of his brows, he bends and gently tugs my nipple. Pure pleasure and pain courses through me, while he effortlessly locates the fastener and slides my bra down my arms.

"Lay back," he says hoarsely.

As I steady myself, feeling like I'm about to explode, I watch, bewitched, while he slowly strips off. Standing at the foot of the bed, he brings his hand to his mouth with a determined stare.

He rocks a knee onto the mattress, then delicately grips my calf. Kissing the ball of my ankle, he slowly tracks up my inner thigh. Pausing just above my knee, he murmurs while I run my hand through his unruly hair, longing to feel it brush against my flesh. My body temperature is simmering near boiling point, and my back arches involuntarily in contemplation.

"All in good time. Show me those beautiful greens." Lowering my eyes, I meet his with a fierce hunger and a desperate need to be completed.

His head drops, and he drags his tongue from my knee, all the way up to my apex. His hot breath fans me intimately, until it stops.

"Now, let's see how many times I can make my fiancée scream."

A sweep of excitement primes me beautifully. I observe his mass of dark hair, wondering what's holding him back, when his tongue swipes over my core and I hiss at the impact of it.

My back lifts off the bed, and I clench my fingers around the sheets, fisting them as he breaches my core. With passion devouring me, he grips my hips. Each thrust claims me, owns me; taking away all rational thought.

"God!" I cry out and convulse under him. Pressing his hand to my stomach, he lowers me back down. I throw my arm over my eyes when he pinches my folds.

"Eyes, baby. Sit up." I shuffle up as he moves closer; pilfering my kisses, enjoying the chase each time I refuse to give them up. "Too tempting." His hand strokes lower and lower, until he runs his fingertip between my cheeks. I stare into his eyes, before brushing my lips over his.

"Please," I whimper, needing him inside me - however that may be.

Positioning my legs, he leans over my back. His hair tickles my neck as he draws out the tension. I groan uncontrollably when he circles his finger. Moving it from front to back, using my own arousal, he gently presses in.

Closing my eyes, I fantasise. My body, electrified by his actions, rocks back and forth, building towards the peak. This is the most taboo, but most intimate act there is. And although I have no other experience aside from him, this feels so right. Still slightly uncomfortable, but incredibly right.

"Come for me, baby," he murmurs behind me, sounding equally affected.

"More," I breathe out. "I need more." Understanding what I'm asking, his finger leaves me cold, to be replaced moments later by him. He stretches me out fraction by fraction, entering slowly. His strong legs press against me, and I lift up and glance back. More of his weight bears down, and he holds the side of my face and brings his mouth to mine. His speed increases at a comfortable pace, thrusting his tongue inside and out, emulating the speed of our bodies connecting perfectly.

I gasp as ecstasy shakes up my entire being. My thighs contract and release under the sensation rising up from cells unknown.

"Fuck!" he moans out; his actions firmer, harder. A little raw even. Coming back to meet him, rear to hips, he grips my sides and holds me, roaring out in sync with my own release.

He separates our bodies and rolls over on the bed. I curve myself into him and kiss his damp, spent chest.

"Cancelling would have been so worth it! How do you feel, my love?"

"Well and truly stuffed!"

The faint sound of electricity echoes from outside. Leaning on my elbow, I push down the sheet and admire him. Slowly moving my forefinger around his nipple and down his stomach, he doesn't flinch or make any kind of movement. I'm unsure as to whether or not he's actually asleep, or just pretending to be. Testing his limits, I curl my hand around his semi-hard length. With his eyes still closed, he removes my hand and places it on his equally hard stomach.

Glancing at my watch, it's nearly midday. Soon the beautiful, resident tranquillity of last night - and this morning - will be shattered.

Lost in my thoughts, he shifts and slowly starts to grin. "You're wearing the *look*," he stipulates, very matter of bloody fact, considering he still has his eyes closed.

"How do you know? You can't see me."

"I always see you." He turns and pulls me into him, his body tight against mine, feeling every inch of him spark to life.

"No, everyone will be here soon," I say, a little depressed. There is nothing I would like more than to stay in bed and practice the art of marital intimacy. *Repeatedly.* I'll never tell him this, but I would've loved to have cancelled and spent all day up here, constantly rediscovering my favourite parts.

He holds up my hand up and rotates my wrist, caressing the scars. Capturing the sun illuminating the room, I admire his physical sign of undying love for me.

"I'm impressed with your choice. I expected something huge and garish."

"Well, initially, that's what you would've had. I really should have bought the rock. This looks so small and insignificant."

"Oh, I don't know. It's dainty and beautiful, and something I would have chosen for myself. It's perfect," I reply, sliding up his body.

"Baby, I had the best one picked out. The jeweller looked ready to get on his knees and kiss my feet, until Sophie pointed out you wouldn't be impressed and showed me the error of my ways. I have to admit, the error of my ways cost me a ridiculously expensive lunch and an afternoon, in which I marched around every jeweller in the city, listening to her quite entertaining views on our relationship. All the while I was still paying her!"

"No wonder she loves working for you. I wish my boss would let me flirt around on company time."

"Your boss will probably say no, but his boss will always say yes, especially if he's the one to be flirted with."

Laying over his front, I roll my pelvis to get comfortable, and he rubs his palms up and down my back. I breath out satisfied, then gently rock; nothing more, nothing less. Staring, we maintain the intense visual as the impending combined throb quickens. His hands run up my front, before he stops at the sides of my breasts, and tenderly rubs both nipples in synchronicity.

"This is another first," he murmurs, between groans and shudders.

"How so?" I respond, breathless, wondering why we are having a conversation now.

"I've never made love to my fiancée before."

The room falls into the growing darkness around us, and the only thing I see is him. Digging my hands into his chest, my hips move faster, harder, needing to consume and complete every inch of my being that is on fire underneath my skin. The same fire he reignited after the flame had died out.

Pressing his hips up underneath me, determined to feel more, he jolts upright. My body slides against his, while my belly aches deliciously.

"Oh God, that's too good," I breath out.

Forcing me to look at him, he smiles, like he's seeing me for the first time. "It'll never be anything less for you," he replies. "Now, are you ready to keep those eyes open for me?"

I grin enthusiastically and rest my forearms on either side of his neck, clasping my hands at the back.

"Eyes on me, my love," I whisper, mimicking him, while he slams my pelvis forward. My elated body ignites, leaving me high and flying and never wanting to come down. "Oh, God!" I hiss, while he plunges in and out.

"I own this. Every fucking inch is mine!" he roars with fierce determination. Lifting up and down, we push and pull against each other, caught up in the last vestiges of fire, until depletion beckons.

"Sloan!" I cry out.

"Let go, baby. I've got you."

My legs tighten around him as my core throbs and releases. Sliding my hands down his back, a cold draught caresses my backside. Tilting back, my eyes enlarge in horror the moment I see a shocked Marie fill the doorway.

"Oh shit!" Walker whispers from behind her, quickly turning away in embarrassment.

Sloan looks at me confused, as I drag the sheet up and over me. "Baby, what are you doing?" He yanks it back down. "We're not done yet!"

I quickly grip his jaw and guide his head towards the door.

"*What the fuck?*" He hastily pulls the sheet all the way over my head. "Get the fuck out now!" he bellows.

The door quickly slams shut, and the sound of Marie and Walker coming to blows outside is enlightening.

"She's a grown woman. You're overreacting!" John's says, muted.

"'*Overreacting?*' That's my daughter! I don't give a shit if she's an adult; I still wouldn't give a shit if she was seventy!" Marie, as stubborn as I am, stands her ground as Walker huffs out.

"Angel, calm down!"

"I am calm!" she shouts angrily.

"That's the problem, I know you are. I've seen you angry enough!" The hint of sarcasm is indicative in his tone.

We continue to sit tight and listen to them outside, until their steps retreat. Sloan finally laughs out hysterically, and I, being so amenable to him, enable him through reciprocation. Falling against his damp chest, I touch my lips to the valley in between his pectorals.

"That was an entertaining first," I laugh with mortification, then admit my truth. "We really should have cancelled."

Still laughing, he grabs my ankles and brings them around his back. "Hold tight," he says, moving us off the bed and into the en-suite.

He slides me down, then stands in front of me and waits for the water to heat up. Quickly washing me, then himself, he spends more time afterwards just staring at me.

While I dry my hair, feeling conscious of what, exactly, he's looking at, I turn to the mirror. Staring at myself, I gaze down my chest. While the marks that ravage my heart are invisible, I can't say which is worse. One leaves you with mental scars, whereas the other leaves you with physical ones. Refusing to allow those dark thoughts to consume me again, I concentrate on Sloan, who steps behind me.

"They look so much better. I think we need to see someone if you still want them gone." I nod, feeling my heart swell that he's going to do this for me.

He clasps his hand in mine, and we hurry into the dressing room. Picking out our respective clothing choices, the sound of Marie and Walker still going at it downstairs is loud.

"Don't be too long, fiancée." He kisses me and leaves.

I grip the bannister, as the sound of Marie and Sloan now going at it greets me on my way towards the kitchen.

"Oh, come on, Marie!" Sloan cajoles her. I hope he realises he's prodding the bear.

"If you want to stay on my good side, Foster, shut your mouth while you're ahead! The last thing I expected to see when I walked up those stairs was my daughter like…that!"

"She might be your daughter, but she's now my fiancée," he mutters, showing her his back and peering into the fridge. "I also don't need to remind you that this is our house."

I cover my face with my hand, and he turns and grins at me. Removing a plate of Marie's finest cheesecake – my favourite - he wiggles his brows and mouths *later*. I turn away embarrassed, while Marie continues huffing and puffing.

"She won't be your anything if you can't keep your dick to yourself!"

"MARIE!" Walker and I shout simultaneously.

Horrified, I slam my fist down. She suddenly grows sombre, and I take the opportunity to air my views.

"You know, you once told me I would find someone who made me feel comfortable, and I have. I'm sorry you had to see us like that, but to reiterate, this is our house, and as always, everyone just walks in whenever they please. So, in essence, it was your fault, not ours."

I pour a couple of glasses of champagne and hand one to her. Her eyes widen, and she takes the glass and then my proffered, ringed hand.

"Oh my God!" She puts her hand on her face and laughs.

Sloan enfolds me in his arms and rests his chin on my shoulder. Touching my glass to his, we both grin at each other.

"Cheers."

Chapter 26

STRETCHING MY ARMS out, I malinger around the house. It's nearly three o'clock, and I have spent the majority of the day bored and alone, with my hands covered in Marigolds.

Leaning over the island in the dressing room, I pull a face, deeming what will be appropriate to wear tonight. My hand hovers over the vast array of jewels, pausing at the diamonds. Their significance is unrivalled. Fingering one stud, I sigh, happy that life has reverted back to some degree of normality.

It is almost four months since I returned. My initial apprehension was unfounded, because his arms were always going to be open. Always ready for me to fall back into them.

Another thing that has fallen back into place, is the altruistic, humanitarian side of Mr Foster.

Tonight is the hotel's annual fundraiser for abuse. It's the same event that I first met him at last year, although it has been significantly delayed, for obvious reasons. He confessed he didn't want reminders of a future I couldn't partake in. Whilst a little overkill, even for him, I understand completely. His memories would have been parallel to that night and each thereafter.

I can't say I'm overly ecstatic to be attending - not with my history - but as it is pointed out to me on a regular basis, this is my man's life. A cacophony of future balls, dinners, and the finest things money can buy. It's overwhelming in a way I cannot explain, because, this too, is now my life. And it has been since the day he propositioned me on the back steps and wore me down.

When he made the impossible, possible.

When he made me fall in love with him.

I wander onto the landing, reminiscing on the days when love was a new entity for me. Pushing back the door of the spare bedroom that currently resembles a charity shop, I glance over my possessions from a life that feels a million years away from my own. Touching over the top of my old chest of drawers, I snort. The memory of him twirling my underwear around his finger that very first night is forever burned in my mind.

"And so it began," I mumble rhetorically.

The landline rings, echoing throughout the house. I pick it up from its base just outside the door, as Sophie's name flashes. She and Marie have taken it upon themselves to come over and help me get ready for tonight. Honestly, they can do whatever they want; I never get a say in these things anyway. And these black-tie dinners have never really been my thing. Too many people invading my space, too many people trying to climb the social ladder. Just too much everything really.

"You're early!" I admonish.

The event doesn't start for another four hours, and I very much doubt it's going to take that long to make me look passable as the CEO's missus.

"Hey, babe, give us authorisation to pass the gatekeeper!"

I laugh on my way into the study to check the security cameras – a Sloan instruction that I'm actually able to abide by. Sophie is waving into the camera and pulling funny faces, while an annoyed-looking Max takes the mobile from her.

"Afternoon, Miss Petersen. Shall I let her in?" he asks seriously.

"Well, that's up to you. If you want to reply to someone that seldom requires a response, and ignores even your boss, keep her out there."

"I'll let her in," he deadpans.

Yep, he has definitely experienced Sophie Morgan prior to today.

"Thanks, Max."

On the front steps, I watch in horror as Sophie pretends she's at Silverstone and speeds down, before slamming all on, spraying my legs with soil and gravel. She climbs out nonchalantly as I brush down my jammie bottoms.

"That's dangerous!" I shout as Marie gets out of the other side, clearly nauseous. "Are you okay?" She nods, holding her stomach, and I watch with concern while she rushes into the house. The sound of a bag dropping and heels clicking up the stairs tells me she is far from it.

"Sorry, but I always wanted to do that!" Sophie exclaims.

My jaw slackens as she flounces inside, not recognising anything remotely wrong in what she has just done.

Closing the door behind her, the smell of the fresh flowers that Sloan had delivered this morning permeates the hallway.

"Don't you ever do that again!" Marie shouts, descending the stairs gracefully in her annoyance. She removes her jacket and gives me a knowing grin, as stares at the bouquet. "Is he in the bad books?"

Needless to say, I haven't been bought flowers that often, but even I'm mentally questioning the reason behind them. Indeed, there's a concealed possibility that later on, he could well be.

"Why are you both here so early?" I ask, ignoring her question and head into the kitchen to find Sophie pulling out three mugs from the cabinet. Marie sits at the island while I lean over it, my head resting in my hands.

"Well, since the men decided to have a boys' day – whatever that is – we decided to go shopping. We didn't invite you because we knew you'd say no."

"What do you mean – boys' day?" I ask as she gives me a look that tells me to use my head. Instead, I shake it. "It's starting again, isn't it? I'm being kept in the dark again! Why I ever thought he would allow me to bask in the light was goddamn idiotic!"

"Kara-" Marie starts, but I hold my hand up. "Where is he, allegedly?"

I stare down at the marble. "He said he had to meet some clients."

"On a Sunday? I didn't see anything in his diary," Sophie confirms over the boiling kettle. I lull my head to the side – yes, it's utterly ridiculous in retrospect.

"Business doesn't stop, apparently."

Marie's hand warms my back. "Honey, whatever they're doing, there's a reason they didn't tell us. John said he was going to meet a client, too. Look, just get showered and dressed, and forget about it for now." She pats my bum to send me on my way.

"I'll forget about it because, after all this time, I've learnt how to. But you two? Ask yourself what they're doing that requires Stuart to be with them. You forget how I met him the first time. That poor girl's battered body is forever ingrained in my memory." Sophie's face drops, and I scurry away.

It's cruel, but she needs to face up to the reality that sometimes he will assist in the shady shit that Walker and his boys do from time to time. The same way Sloan does. Except, unlike the rest of them, Sloan and Stuart stand to lose more if it turns out badly.

I pull out my mobile and dial. Sloan picks up almost instantly, and I speak before he can. "Are you with John and Stuart?" He sighs on the other end. "A simple yes or no will suffice. Marie and Sophie are here. I need to know what to say to them if they should ask."

"Don't worry, baby, just tying up a few loose ends." I pull the phone away from my ear, blink at it, then bring it back.

"Sloan?"

"Seriously, don't worry, my love. I'll be back soon to escort you to the ball." He hangs up, and I drop the phone on the bed. I repeat his words over and over, disbelieving he tells me not to worry when he knows I shall.

Frustrated, but with nothing further I can do to remedy the situation, I pick up a couple of towels and proceed to the bathroom to start the prep.

Looking at my condensed reflection, I slowly touch the glass. My eyes drop to my chest and gently, with my middle finger and thumb joined together, I slide them down. He's right; they do look better. A thought comes to mind, and I hurry out, wrapped in a towel.

"Soph?" I shout over the bannister, bending further until a shadow moves in my direction.

"What?" She looks up with expectation.

"I need you."

She jobs up the stairs, but halts instantly, finally witnessing the full extent and devastation of my skin. Walking towards me, her eyes remain fixed on my chest. Her hand comes out, but she stops.

"Marie, can you bring my bag up?" she shouts down the stairs.

Leading me into the bedroom, she sits me on the bed. "One lunch, I went to a dermatological shop that sells camouflage make-up. Gloria found it, and the boss happily handed over his money. Sorry, I meant to tell you, but with all the excitement of you being back, and then the engagement and...whatever."

Marie walks through the door, a tray of drinks in one hand, Sophie's handbag in the other. "Here."

"Apparently, this one is best for new sca...blemishes." She pulls out a tube, and I leave her to it and stare off into space. A few minutes later, she sounds frustrated. "Kara, this isn't going to work."

I quickly look down at the streak of thick concealer on my chest. "What isn't?"

"You, sat like this. Lay down, head towards me." As requested, I lay back. Closing my eyes, I drift away while fire alights my front with each delicate touch.

"Hey, wake up," Soph's voice filters through quietly. I smile, as he who I dream about holds me close, promising forever. He bestows me with such passion and intensity, it could burn through the dream world and into the real one... Until the hard nudge in my side pisses me off royally.

"Hey! You interrupted a really good dream." Rubbing my eyes, she's tapping her foot.

"Hmm, sounded like it. As long as it's kept in this house and your head, and not in his office again, that's fine."

Marie starts laughing, and Sophie and I give each other a look and watch her until the penny finally drops.

"I beg your pardon?"

Sophie starts to grin and edges away. I groan, because Little Miss Loquacious has no idea what Marie walked in on not so long back. She's going to open her big mouth and divulge things that will get me in trouble.

Again.

"Yep, your girl here was over his boardroom table sans her knickers!" She turns with a wicked smile.

"No, shut up! I don't want to hear about my brother like this! Oh, my God, I've got a mental image!" Charlie's shrieking tone startles me, and I wonder when she arrived. And whether I should smile or shy away.

Humiliated, I huff out loudly. "Soph, have you had this conversation with your boss yet? I'm sure he'll be able to impart a more determined perspective. One which he will eventually force you to agree with." She doesn't retort and stands next to Marie, both of them giving me looks of absolute annoyance - for two very different reasons.

Marie, still visibly horrified, wipes her brow. "Later!" she says in that perfected, motherly tone; her index finger admonishing me wickedly.

I blatantly sulk.

I'm engaged. I'm getting married. Not to reiterate, I'm twenty bloody four for crying out loud!

"I don't care!" the motherly tone replies.

Eventually, she regains her composure, and comes closer. Forgetting the verbal showdown, she concentrates on my chest, or namely the brilliance of Sophie's handiwork.

"You know, darling, I think you picked the wrong career. They look good, barely noticeable." Marie's eyes slit, obviously trying to find one that looks far worse than the rest.

"This will set it, but don't get it wet." Sophie pulls out the powder, passing it to me on my way into the dressing room.

In front of the rails, I never thought I'd say this, but I really do wish they had invited me shopping. Aside from working these events, the only times I've attended as a guest, Sloan has sorted out my attire.

"Is this what you're looking for?" Marie asks, coming through the door with Charlie two steps behind, carrying a dress.

"Another Sloan choice. And now one less dress cluttering my wardrobe." I furrow my brow, but she taps her nose. "You know, I'm not angry about what Sophie said. You're a grown woman, soon to be married, with a man who loves you more than life itself. I can't say I'm particularly pleased his office furniture has been acquainted with your bare backside, just like I can't say I'm pleased I have seen it atop of him, but I can't be mad at you for it, either. There was once a time we both thought you'd never get to this place."

"Thank you," I reply, although still embarrassed.

I hold the dress to my front, still amazed with his faultless taste. Looking between her and the fabric flooding my hands, I might be overdressed. Laying it down over the chair, I flip through the rails.

"Are you working this event tonight?" I query since she looks immaculate in a strapless, black number.

"No. Well, yes, but I've left Nicki in charge. Although I think she'll be pulling double-time with Dev being there. I don't mind - the only time she musters a smile is when he's around." She lifts her vibrating mobile from a concealed pocket and smiles on her way out. "They're almost here."

Working my eyes over the shoe racks, the door creaks and Sloan enters, adjusting his bow tie. "If you stare at them for long enough, they might sing and dance!"

I gaze at him, disbelieving he has showered and dressed and then had Walker drive them back out here. I stare down at his hands, wondering about their covert 'boys' day'. I grip his palms, then flip them over.

"Are they clean?"

"Spotless. I would never do anything to jeopardise my future with you. You promised you would trust my judgement."

"I do," I say, fingering his bow tie and smoothing my hands down his lapels. "You didn't have to come back for me."

"No, I did. I have something for you."

I shake my head. "I don't want it."

He grins, tipping my chin. "Oh, I think you will." He digs into his pocket and pulls out a silver bangle. "My father bought this for my mother when they first started seeing each other. Like everything else, it cost very little, but my mum wanted you to have it."

My heart is ready to combust as I hastily slip it on. Extending my wrist, the metal reflects a lifetime's worth of wear and memories.

Sloan snorts behind me. "I'm hurt that you like that more than what I buy you."

I turn and wrap my arms around his neck. "I didn't say that. It's just nice to know I can wear something that doesn't cost the earth. Besides," I continue, "it carries sentimental value, and you can't put a price on that."

I placate his lips with mine and he grins, boyishly, rotating his hips. I quirk a brow. He's wishing a little too hard – quite literally.

"Fine! But tonight, we're having pre-marital make up sex!"

Playfully slapping my backside, he moves away, his walk a little awkward. I watch curiously as he picks up the original dress – his choice – that I left on the chair. He shakes his head, then starts to rifle through the rails, seemingly nothing takes his fancy in this gorgeous collection that is definitely wasted on me.

"Is there any other kind we have these days? And not to state the bleeding obvious, but we have nothing to make up for."

I walk over and pull one out. It doesn't matter which. I tug it off the hanger, as he points for me to lift my arms up. Sliding the dress over me, I wiggle into the fabric. With a pensive look, he circles, outwardly displeased.

"No, but a lot can happen between now and then." He smirks, inching his hands up my spine.

"Like what?"

"Like this!" He rips it straight down the back, and my mouth falls open, having no idea how to react. He has just recklessly destroyed who knows how much, just so he can have his precious, uncalled for, make up sex.

As I step out of the tattered remains, I pick it up and throw it at him. He catches it effortlessly, while his eyes roam my scantily clad self appreciatively. From the strapless bra that makes me look two cups bigger, to the knickers that fabric forgot, and finally, the awful suspender belt, because the stupid stockings are definitely not self-supporting!

"I think I'm really going to enjoy you tonight. How about we arrive fashionably late?" he queries, teasing a finger over the front of my mesh knickers.

Pushing away his probing hand, I pull out another plain, nondescript dress. He slinks towards me and nestles me into him. My body yields and betrays me when a desirous shiver gallops through me.

"I don't like this one either!" he says, pointing at the rail. "Or any of them. I like you wet, naked, and nothing else!"

I wiggle away, hot, flustered, and undeniably aroused. He laughs, hands up in surrender and steps back. His dark eyes are brooding, and I hesitate in getting dressed. It almost feels like he's waiting for me to put on a show for him.

With his delectable arse perched on the island, he folds his arms over his chest and cocks his head. Yes, he definitely wants a show. Again, well out of my comfort zone, I clutch the dress to my front and bring my arm around my waist. Sloan, visibly upset, drops his hands and his attitude instantly.

"Come here, my love."

Shuffling towards him, I keep the dress tight to my chest. He lifts my chin, his other hand massaging one needy rear cheek.

"You never have to be embarrassed with me."

"I know."

"You look stunning and sexy and all mine." He takes the dress from me and places it next to him. I rub my thighs together as liquid heat gains momentum from his scent alone.

Dropping to his knees, he kisses my pubic bone. Ascending slowly, his tongue dips into my navel momentarily and continues to rise. Instinctively, I grab his nape, guiding him, until I stretch back giving him room to explore my neck. He holds my head with a smouldering look.

Eventually sliding into the dress, he zips me up and assesses me. He opens his mouth, but nothing comes out. And considering what got us into this predicament in the first place, I make my request known.

"You owe me a dress!"

"Baby, I'll give you sexual recompense, but I have one stipula-"

"Kid?" Walker shouts up to us.

"*Yes?*" Sloan replies tersely.

"Thought so!"

I laugh and rest my head against his chest. "Doesn't miss a trick, does he?"

Sloan chuckles. "No, he's probably got cameras in every room." My head jerks up instantly. "I'm joking!"

My eyes scan every inch of vacant wall space, looking for anything remotely tech. Still amused, he picks up my jacket and escorts me downstairs.

"What was your stipulation?"

"You'll find out later. Trust me."

There's that word again. But since I know his stipulation is going to be something that will either shock me or please me to my core, I let it go.

Climbing into the back of the car, he clamps our hands in his lap - so close, I can feel his hardness peak. A gentle stream of breath blows over my neatly tied back hair, then his palm snakes up my leg, and he leans into my ear.

"I can't wait to feel these against me when I'm inside you tonight."

Please me to my core it is, then.

Chapter 27

THE HOTEL LOOKS magnificent as we pull up outside. Spotlights streak up the exterior in a rainbow of colours, highlighting the ornate features and sconces.

My heart rate accelerates when George opens the car door. Smiling at me proudly, he gently kisses my hand. "Have a lovely evening, Kara."

I involuntarily curl my fingers around his. "Thank you, George."

Easing out, ensuring I don't flash anything inappropriately, Sloan stands behind me, straightening himself up the best he can in his current, semi-aroused state.

It has gotten worse on the journey over. His own doing, since he has given me a blunt rundown of how our night will really start once this portion of it is over. I'd like to say I want to see him suffer, but, I too, am now of the same mindset. And the way he's continuously snapped the stupid suspender belt on my thigh has not helped, either.

Curving me firmly into his side, the obligatory flashing blinds me as we pass the reporters until we are stopped at the entrance by James.

"Good evening, Mr Foster, Miss Petersen," James greets, appearing entirely uncomfortable.

"Evening, James. Is something wrong?" Sloan queries, relaxed and unaffected, unlike previous times we have been made to endure the intrusive gauntlet outside.

"No, sir, everything is fantastic! Except I have received numerous requests as to the validity of your rumoured, impending nuptials."

Sloan laughs and kisses my ring finger, his eyes sparkling. "By whom?"

"Everyone."

My heart races as he and James talk. This is precisely what I was fearing. Although our engagement isn't something we are intentionally hiding, outside of his staff, family and friends, it isn't something that has been publicly announced, either. After much deliberation, we agreed on a mutual silence, since we are both fiercely protective. Him, because of his status, and more so, the contempt that will no doubt be centred and aimed at me. And me, because I have no interest in the world knowing my every private moment, just because

I happen to be in love with a man who is obscenely wealthy and moves in affluent circles.

That discussion has now been in vain because, by the end of tonight, everyone will know. Judgement will be mine; levelled at every angle, from everyone of good standing who looks at me like the gold digger they wrongly assume I am.

A gentle tap on my cheek breaks my crazy thoughts. Sloan stares, unimpressed. "You really need to stop with the verbal opinions, my love." His tone isn't angry, just calm and understanding.

"I'm only thinking what they're going to say," I admit, a part of my heart shattering that the glitterati will think there is some ulterior motive in our impending union. "And they're right, there's an underlying reason – a love forged through a lifetime of pain, loss and wanting."

"Baby, I don't give a damn what they think, and neither should you. We know the truth; let them concoct anything they like. Besides, if they print absolute shit, I'll threaten them with slander and defamation, and have them publicly retract and apologise."

God, he makes it sound so easy, but the damage would have already been done. No amount of control would be necessary, because people always remember the bad, never the good.

Locking down the inevitable to come, he tenderly kisses me and walks off with James. I smile when Sophie appears at my side. Linking arms, we enter the foyer.

My anxiety is currently all over the place, and although everything has been relatively peaceful lately, I'm not foolish enough to think tonight will pass without event. Nothing ever does.

Marie prods my side, and I slowly bring my jacket down my shoulders and pass it to Parker. Thanking him, I make my way through the throng of people in the crowded foyer. My eyes scan the area, looking for the other half of me.

"He's right over there," a familiar voice says.

I turn to find Jeremy standing behind me. I step back, not through fear, but shock. His appearance tonight is striking, and judging the sultry smiles of a few women, they have also noticed this rather hot, if not a little scary, handsome man. Taking in his perfectly presented black suit, tie and waistcoat, he looks a complete gentleman. If you can forgive the hair that's at least six months past a cut, that is.

I step closer and reach out to him. "I'm sor-" His eyes close and he mouths *no*. I quieten, because words will never heal history for us.

"He's waiting for you. Nine years and counting, I think he's waited long enough. Go," he says softly. I start to turn, but then do something that would've been inconceivable months ago; I hold him.

"Thank you. For everything," I whisper, and he visibly relaxes. Enfolding my arm through his, he slowly walks me towards my man, waiting poised at the front of the reception desk.

Jeremy grins, inducing his scar to move and kisses my hand. "Save a dance for me, Kara."

"I will," I agree, as he walks away.

Rotating back to Mr Foster, I start at the bottom. I giggle when I see he has taken off his shoes and replaced them with a pair of battered old trainers.

"And just when I thought this was an upmarket establishment, you lower the tone again," I comment flippantly, baiting him, drawing him out.

My eyes continue, over his strong thighs, that hold me securely when they are curled around mine. To his incredible, narrow hips, that rotate in ways that leave me mindless. Staring at his chest, my heart skips a beat. His ribcage heaves, and I continue to track up to his arms and shoulders.

Taking another step, he splays his hand wide over my back. I press my hands into his chest, and he grunts and bends. My lips part and his breath seeps into my mouth. Falling deeper into the moment, the only thing I see his him. He's all that matters to me. In the beginning, I refused to admit it for a long time, but it's true.

"Open your eyes, my love."

A wash of colour highlights his features, and he looks down. His hand holds out my own equally battered Converse by their laces. Cradling me firmly, peppering me with kisses, he walks us towards a large comfy sofa, hidden away in a corner under the staircase.

"You know, if you wanted to steal my kisses, you'd never have to bribe them."

Slipping off my shoes, he puts my trainers on. "I know, but I want tonight to be perfect, and you, my future bride, are once again very naked." He drags the chair, and me, forward. "Five days. God, it's going to kill me."

"What is?"

He taps his nose, then casts his eyes over three boxes on the table. He smirks; that extraordinary, beautiful smirk I do secretly love.

"The gifts," he declares, picking up a box.

Opening it, he carefully removes a dark purple stoned earring. Delicately sucking my lobe, he positions the stud. He then removes the other and repeats the action. He leans back in reflection and brushes his thumbs over my ears. Tracing a finger behind each, he glides them down my chest. I blow out my breath under his maddening touch.

"Christmas."

Picking up the second box, he removes a pendant. A solitary stone of the same colour dangles beautifully from the end. He kisses my chest while he fastens and centres it meticulously.

"Valentine's Day."

I run my tongue over my dry lips; my heart is heavy and full. "Sloan ..."

"Shush, one more to go," he whispers. "Birthday."

He opens the final box, which reveals a bracelet of stones and intricate detail. I hold out my scarred wrist, the one he always adorns with something beautiful and reflective of his love, to cover the hurt and pain of the unforgettable past we share.

I'm on the verge of crying. I have missed so much time with him...days that should have been memorable, days that held meaning. Days he still carried hope when mine had all but left me.

"Past, present and future," he whispers. "We have a lifetime of Christmases, birthdays and Valentine's Day's to celebrate together. But tonight, I want to celebrate our impending marriage." The muted lights shadow his absolute pleasure this evening, while I do my best to disguise my anxiety.

Forgetting the impossible, I let him lead me into the ballroom. My step falters when I see hundreds of guests socialising. Clutching his hand, he twirls me around, observing the dress he bought yet doesn't like, and the ratty trainers that really don't go.

"Acceptable?"

Pinching my chin, he shakes his head and grins. "It will be when it's on the bedroom floor!"

I playfully slap his chest, and a few murmurs of surprise are identifiable around us. Sidestepping through the crowd, trying my best not to touch them, he guides us effortlessly. He entwines his hands over my stomach, and I hold them firmly to ensure he keeps us respectable.

Pointing towards a table, I slide myself into a seat and smooth my hands down my thighs. Sloan's teeth tug his lip, clearly in naughty thought, and his brows flick up to the ceiling.

"No." I shake my head at his feigned annoyance.

Thankfully, Charlie and Jake appear carrying glasses and bottles of champagne. She is dressed in a short, flirty number, and Jake is thoroughly enjoying watching her rear move in it. I suck in my lips and glance at Sloan, who just rolls his eyes and laughs.

"When they first met, I didn't want him anywhere near her. Now I couldn't imagine her with anyone else." I smile at them both, openly embracing.

A waitress approaches with the damn hors d'oeuvres I used to detest ordering. To be hospitable, I politely refuse the finger food. Sloan roars out laughing and takes two, popping one into his mouth and then mine. I suck on his finger a little too conspicuously, liking the way his eyes darken with promise.

I avert my wayward gaze when I spot Marie on the opposite side of the room, chatting up a storm with some patrons. As previous nights have already proven, pitching her business is always top priority, and she does it well. And where else to do it than with those who can clearly afford it.

"A toast!" Walker shouts, leading up the front of our loved ones. Each takes a seat and a glass, as Sophie and Charlie pour the fizz. "To Kara and Sloan...and the torture that will proceed this night!" Everyone raises their glasses, much to the intrigue of the other occupied tables.

I watch the unspoken truth between surrogate father and son, as I sip my champagne. Walker's eyes are inquisitive, and Sloan has a smile on his face that he cannot conceal.

Knocking back the champagne, Tommy motions, and I follow his line of sight across the room to Jeremy. His head darts up, and he discreetly shows us the finger as he eases his hand over the back of the woman who is holding his attention.

"Interesting," Sloan says with intrigue.

"Why, who is she?"

"She's the daughter of a client. I doubt that Daddy will approve of someone like Remy, though." He snags some glasses of water from one of the waitresses.

"Maybe she likes a bit of rough. God knows that scar is a mean mother," Tommy interrupts, his eyes following the waitress's backside disappear into the mob. He turns back when Parker comes upon us. Where there's one, the other isn't too far behind. I do worry about them sometimes.

"Hands in your pockets, boys! No free booze and food tonight!" Sloan tells them with a laugh.

"And women, don't forget the women!" Parker digs around in his pocket and pulls out a couple of tenners. Sloan gives him a disgusted expression and shoves them back at him.

"Jeremy isn't rough," I comment. Once upon a time, I might have agreed, but after what he's done, his heart is in the right place, even if his head sometimes isn't.

"No, not really, but he isn't smooth around the edges, either," Sloan retorts; all of us still observing an annoyed Jeremy, who keeps glaring from us to the stunning woman in front of him.

"And you are?" I ask incredulously, sipping my water, realising I've just involuntarily upped the stakes.

"I'm smooth where it counts, baby. And tonight, you *will* count the ways!"

I laugh out, as Walker sneaks up behind him and steals his glass. Downing it in one, he gives it back to him.

"Why, thanks, Dad!"

"You're welcome. Excess alcohol hinders performance, sunshine!" My eyes narrow; that statement in itself is enough to stop my world spinning. Walker grins, then quietens when he sees what we're all looking at. "Well, I never."

"John, who's Emma Shaw?" His smile fades instantly, and I look between him and my beloved kid, who has now dropped his self-righteous smirk, wondering where I'm going with this.

"Why do you ask?"

"Because that's the name you forged an identity for."

He stares at Jeremy, a sadness ensuing. "She was a girl he was very much in love with a long time ago."

"When, a long time ago?"

"When he was high and unhinged. She died of an overdose, Kara. Accidental, definitely not his fault."

"That's really sad," I confess. Sloan manipulates me, and I balance my toes on his as he carefully sways us. "No wonder he's so closed off." A hard squeeze to my bum sobers me.

"Do you want to talk about him, or shall we dance?" His eyes darken and smoulder, and while I'll never be a social butterfly by

Sophie's standards, I grab his hand and move us to the dance floor. "I thought you preferred invisible."

"I do," I reply and cup his jaw. "But I don't want to stay in the dark anymore. I want to bathe in your light."

"And you shall. Forever."

He pulls us into the centre, and I smile, recognising a few faces of events past. Twirling around the dance floor, I lose myself, letting go of my fear and inhibition.

Song number five, or maybe number six, finally fades out. My feet are aching - even in my well walked trainers - but it has been a long time since I've been on them this long.

Sloan guides us to a table, occupied mainly by his business associates that I had met that unforgettable day at his office.

Sitting down, I adjust my dress hem. Bringing my legs up, Sloan removes my trainers and rubs my soles, much to the amusement of his colleagues, who clearly dare not say anything. It's overwhelming just how much power he has in this domain.

He drags my chair closer, then whispers, "I think you're wanted." He points to the other side of the room, where Charlie and Sophie are now waving me over. I roll my eyes and slip my shoes back on.

"Come and find me when you're ready, baby."

"You can count on it." With a pat on my backside, I slink away.

Approaching the twosome, they meet me in the middle and huddle around me. "No, no, no! My feet already hurt!"

"Whatever!" Sophie says, grabbing my hand, which I'm desperate to shake off.

"Just one dance together!" Charlie says, waving at the band who start to play something more upbeat – well, as upbeat as they can!

One dance, my arse!

Twirling on the spot, a few glasses of champagne lining my stomach, I feel like the best dancer in the world right now. Sloan is off to the side of the floor, watching with an amused, raised brow. I giggle as he reaches out for Sophie, who is floating around the perimeter, clearly a little pissed.

I slump into a seat and rub my tired feet as Stuart approaches. He passes me a bottle of water and tips his head to the dance floor, where I left my man and his woman verbally facing off in a battle of wills. By all accounts, they're playing nice. Although it's clear there is still a power struggle going on as to who is actually leading who.

"You can guess who wears the trousers in our relationship," Stuart laughs, swigging the beer Jeremy has just handed him.

"My dance card is almost full," Jeremy says, leaning his head towards the small group of women twenty feet away. I smile slyly, until they part and expose a very annoyed looking Christy. I instantly seek out Sloan, whose attention is still being monopolised by Soph.

Jeremy stands in the middle of the dance floor, waiting for me to join him. Slowly approaching, a heavy hand slaps down on my shoulder. As I rotate, feeling the fire burn out of control, something is slammed into my stomach. Christy smiles viciously, while liquid drenches my front.

"I'm sorry, I thought you were the waitress. Guess I was wrong!" she quips innocently and holds up the now empty glass.

"Quite!" I hiss through gritted teeth.

"You know, I heard a little rumour that congratulations are in order. Not that I believe them, of course. It's not like he's announced it, ashamed more like. Is it a shotgun wedding? Did you get yourself pregnant to trick him?" She sniggers maliciously, as her bitchy friend appears by her side. I subtly shake my head. First-hand experience proves she is unable to act out this bullshit on her own; she always needs an army to back her up.

She leans down and laughs. "You think he's completely yours? Did you honestly think he would wait for you? An ugly, poor, pathetic slut like you?"

I hold my head high, maintaining my composure and fighting back my anger at her lies.

"Oh, look, he made you believe it!"

My retort is lodged in my throat. I'm ready to run away, failing to find the girl that once stood up to her. Looking across the floor again, Jeremy is speaking to Sloan, whose head jerks up instantly. The venom is potent in his glare, and Christy, the brazen bitch, blows him a kiss and licks her lips.

Times like this, seeing how vindictive she is, I actually can't believe he had a long-term whatever it was with her. But he did, and she will always ensure she rubs my nose in it. I will never escape her, like so many other things.

Sloan scans the room, until he finds the table where her parents are chatting animatedly with another couple. Removing Soph from the dance floor and into the Doc's waiting arms, he approaches the table and bends down to Mr Spencer. The old man starts to talk, but Sloan stamps down his power and stops him. He then strides over to us, leaving her father looking ashen and worried.

"Hello, lover!" Christy greets gleefully.

"Hello, Miss Spencer. I hope you are enjoying the evening," he says coldly, formally addressing her. Probably something he has never done before, judging the way her smile fades.

They are no longer lovers, just acquaintances.

She reaches out to him, but he snatches her wrist and tightens his grip. "You're hurting me!" she hisses.

"This shit ends now!" He glares as she writhes out of his hold.

Delicately taking my hand, panic laces my gut as he literally drags me to the front of the room. "I didn't-" He puts his finger over my lip, gently pulling it down.

"Not you, my love. *Her!*" Motioning his hand to the band, they slowly stop playing. With the room descending into silence, he takes the microphone.

"Ladies and gentlemen, may I have your attention please?" Everyone instantly stops, and you can hear a pin drop. "Thank you for attending tonight, and for your generous donations thus far. Please keep them coming!" The room erupts into laughter.

As he continues to speak of good causes and those less fortunate, my eyes meet Marie's. Equally confused as I am as to why I'm front and centre, she leans into Walker. Replying to whatever she has asked, he stares at Christy with a glare that could turn her to ash. Marie's responding look is one of horror. Pulling away, she moves towards us. My body begins to quiver as Sloan continues, until he says the words that cause the room to finally wake up.

"Tonight, is also cause for another type of celebration, one that is eternal and forever. Ladies and gentlemen, please raise your glasses to my future Mrs Foster!"

My smile is immediate, concentrating on the applause, praying it doesn't appear fake. My eyes instantly seek out his ex, noting the way hers are narrowing in absolute fucking anger.

His hand glides up my back, and I wrap my arms around his neck, forgetting the audience. Kissing me, he pulls back, and runs his hand through my hair. His mouth opens, but I press my lips to his.

"I love you," I whisper.

"And I you. Always."

Walking back onto the dance floor, the band starts up again, playing good old Frank. Sloan turns me out into a spin, and my line of sight lands on Christy, whose hatred is firmly in place on her scowling face. There's no hiding that she truly hates me in a way that is inconceivable. Ignoring her and continuing to dance with my beloved kid, we stop momentarily to accept the abundance of welcome wishes.

"Right, my gorgeous wife, are you ready to get hot and exhausted with me?" he asks coyly.

"Of course," I quip back with a loud yawn.

"Tired?"

"No." My body proves I'm lying when I yawn again.

Sloan guides us off the floor and seats us at a table full of jolly men. He tugs my feet onto his lap and starts to rub my ankles, inducing a lovely state of bliss.

"Don't let my missus see you doing that, she'll expect the same treatment!"

Chuckling, he continues with more zeal. "Kara, this is Andrew Blake. Andy, Kara."

"Hi, nice to meet you."

"And you," I reply, embarrassed that everyone seems to be fixed on the side of him that many will never see. The amazing, the brilliant, and completely empathic man, whose reputation precedes him, who has currently got his hands on my sore feet.

Again.

Another man gets up and taps his glass with a knife. "To Sloan and Kara!" The embarrassment dithers away as each person shakes his hand until the table finally clears, and everyone is up dancing.

Motioning over a waiter, Sloan pops a fresh bottle of champagne and fills two flutes. Passing one to me and entwining our arms, we bring the glasses to our lips.

"Past, present and future, Mrs Foster. Are you ready to start counting the ways?"

I smile and extend my hand to claim what's mine. Kissing me slowly, the cool liquid floods my mouth, dampening the heat.

"That's one!"

Pulling me off the chair, he grabs my bum and places me on his knee. I should be worried but considering I'm already on the verge of letting go, all I feel is pleasure.

"That's nice," I admit.

"You're damn right it is, and this is two," he says firmly, wrapping his hand around my hair. His grin slips away the moment his eyes lift up behind me.

"I'm sorry to disturb you, sir, but there's an issue that requires your immediate attention."

I glance back to see James. His eyes work over me, and for the first time in a year, he bestows that low, condescending stare he had first introduced me with. Sloan doesn't notice, but I do. And I realise why he's expressing it again; because he has seen something that proves I don't belong here.

"This better be good!"

"Unfortunately, it isn't."

Separating myself and hardening my heart, I march out of the room, bypassing the curious, hate-filled stare Christy is proverbially burning me with. I halt the instant my father's back greets me. Resting my hand on my forehead, I approach him. He turns, and it's startling to witness how he has declined further since the last time I saw him. As much as it hurts me, I grab his arm and force him towards the conference rooms.

"Kara?" Sloan's call is a warning behind me.

I slam my hand on the door plate as I lead him inside. Seconds later, Sloan darts in and yanks me behind him - as far away from my father as he feels necessary. Pointing Ian deeper into the room, he lets me go.

"Have you got any weapons on you?" My father shakes his head. "If you're lying to me-"

"I haven't got fuck all!" he replies.

"Good, let's go upstairs." Sloan turns, but I stop him.

"I don't want him in our home," I whisper, and he nods and rubs my nape before he turns back.

"What do you want, Mr Petersen?" Sloan asks harshly, hands on his hips. I grab the back of a chair for leverage, while my father mumbles incoherently.

"Sweets?"

"Don't fucking call me that!"

"Kara, please!"

Sloan's head shoots around. "Please? How dare you, you bastard! Did you hear your frightened daughter when she was begging please?"

I block out the sound of the truth while my feet find life, and I stand in front of the window, staring out at the dark street. Wrapping my hands around myself, a deathly cold claims me. Tears roll down my face, all the while Sloan continues his verbal attack. Hearing my father beg and plead with him is too much, and I spin around.

"Stop it!" I scream.

The door slams open and shut, and Walker and Jeremy march in, taking up a sentry position behind the man begging for my clemency.

"Franklin's going to kill me," Ian mumbles, his voice rocky, terrified. Hearing it transports me back to the childhood I never wanted to remember. "I told him no," he says repeatedly.

"What do you mean?" Walker speaks up, and my father visually cowers.

Jeremy steps forward. "Last year, he finally said no to the bastard. You were too late in growing a backbone. Where is he? Where's Franklin?"

"I don't know."

Jeremy's jaw grinds, and he slams my father against the wall. "You're lying! Where the fuck is he?" I run towards them, putting myself in the middle of the faceoff. "Kara, move!" I shake my head, because this has to stop, and it stops now.

Lowering his hand, in a motion that is clearly testing his disposition, he steps back grudgingly. "Why are you protecting him? He fucking destroyed you!"

"I know!" I scream back, throwing my hands in the air. Sloan comes over and wraps an arm around my waist. He waves his hand, indicating for Ian to move.

"What do you want from me?" I ask, not caring for the true reasons why he's here. He doesn't respond, but my heart - the one that had banished him away years ago - feels remorseful, plagued by a deepening evil that shouldn't be mine.

"I'm sorry," he finally says. "I'm sorry for everything. I'm sorry for you, your mother..." he trails off, and I squeeze my eyes shut. "I want...I need-"

"No!" I cut him off, because it's always about him, never anyone else. Just him. "*You* want? *You* need?" I repeat, my voice laced with malicious sarcasm. "And what about what *I* wanted? What *I* needed? *I* wanted parents who loved me unconditionally, and what did I get? I got a son of a bitch who cared more about drugs and money than the child who sat at home crying in the dark. I needed you, and you didn't even know I existed half the time. And do you know what it did to me? It made me hate you. I hate you so fucking much, I can't even articulate it!"

"Kara, please?" he whimpers, and I close my eyes at the pitiful sound I've never heard from him before. When I open them again, he's slumped in a chair, almost lifeless.

"Talk," Sloan commands, finally having had enough.

"I remember the first time I held you. I loved you the moment I saw you. You were so little and beautiful. I swore to give you a better life than I'd had, but I couldn't...I fucked everything up when Franklin came back up north... I've been helpless my entire life." His voice is thick, pained, and unshed tears lace each word clearly.

Sitting at the far end of the conference table, listening to my father speak the words I never thought I would hear, is heart rendering. To listen to his reasons why he *gave* me to a monster is truly the hardest thing. Finally, I see him for what he really is, a weak man, someone who will do anything for an easy ride through life. I shall never understand, but I realise when you have nothing in life, you do what you can to make it better, whether by ill-fated gain or not. Unfortunately, he has paid the ultimate price; he's not only lost his child, but he's lost his wife. And I have lost the mother I never really had.

And it was all for nothing.

Ian lifts his head up to Walker. "I'm the one who called you eight years ago, but it doesn't matter because I'm dead now." He stands, but Sloan stops him. He leaves the room, and minutes later he returns and throws a thick envelope down on the table. I shake my head in despair, because the last thing you do to an alcoholic and drug user is feed their habit. Yet I can't voice it, because in so many ways, my father is just like Franklin – he will take the money and run.

Until it runs out.

A short time later, watching my father leave by the back door, for fear the upstanding, wealthy patrons will see up close and personal the type of man their money assists, makes me feel ashamed.

I am his daughter after all.

And it feels like only yesterday that I was walking down the back alley with nowhere to turn and no one to care.

Making our way into the foyer, Sloan has remained silent since we left the conference suite. Standing at the door with his jacket draped over my shoulders, he imparts his gratitude to each guest departing.

Sophie approaches, looking worse for wear, although not stinking drunk, just tired. And chatty.

"Oh, I'm so excited!" she gushes about whatever has got her knickers in a twist now.

I give her a half-hearted smile and turn to the annoyed-looking men. Stuart pats Sloan's back and whispers something to him, until Sophie's mouth finds life again.

"Kara, wait until you see your-" Stuart grimaces and quickly puts his hand over her mouth. He nods at his friend and turns back to me.

"Thank you for an amazing night, my friend. Kara, I'll see you in five days." He assists getting Soph into her jacket, and they walk out arm in arm.

"Sloan?"

"Hmm?"

"Five days?" I ask, uncaring, still tormented that the night has turned to shit. He fidgets a little, then sighs, comprehending he isn't getting out of this one.

"No, I like my surprises. Let's go to bed."

And isn't that the best idea to enter his head tonight. Taking his arm, I just want to forget all about my father's impromptu visit and sleep the stress away.

"I love you." I yawn aloud, resting against him.

"I love you, too, my Mrs Foster."

Chapter 28

"WHAT NUMBER DID we get to downstairs?" he queries, mischievously.

"Three?" I shrug and hazard a guess, the same second the doors pull back.

Entering the private foyer, wrapped around each other, a drunken Christy is banging on the adjacent suite door. She continually slaps the wood and rattles the handle.

"What the fuck are you doing up here?" Sloan roars out, and she spins around, cowering under his tone.

"What does she do for you that I can't? Does she fuck you better than I do?"

"Christy!" he hisses in anger. Bringing his phone to his ear, his gaze flits between us. "James, get up here now!"

"It wasn't so long ago that I was in your bed!" she shouts again.

My whole world feels like it has fallen apart. Was she telling the truth? Did he lie to me? Holding my hand to my chest, I refuse to believe it, but I can barely look at him. His past has never really been an issue for me, but it's completely different having it paraded in your face.

Procrastinating, twisting the ring on my finger, I lift my eyes to Sloan's, seeing his enlarge at what I'm doing.

The lift bell rings, and James hurriedly enters the fray. He is clearly stumped as to what is going on, but before he can ask, Christy's tirade continues.

"Tell her, baby! Tell her how I was the one fucking you all these months she's been gone. The dumb, ugly slut needs to know the truth. I've shared your bed more times than she ever has!" She glides her hand down the door in front of her.

I step back in confusion, because I have no idea what lays behind that door. Or the reason why his past conquest thinks he lives there. I run my own finger down the other suite door, the home of my firsts. Meeting her eyes, the whites are almost as red as her hair. Watching her wilt down the wood, makes me feel sorry for her, more than I do myself, because clearly that suite was never meant for me – it's something he is ashamed of.

Sloan, wearing the look I had personally witnessed the day I begged him on this very spot when he kicked me out, crouches down and glowers.

"I've loved her for nine years, long before you ever knew me." Risking a look, he smiles sadly at me. "Everyone woman in this suite has been her. It's her face I've seen and sought solace in, regardless if it wasn't her body."

"No, you're lying! What we had was good. You wanted me until she turned up!" She beats her fists against his chest, until he grabs them and holds them in front of her.

"Christy, as much as it hurts, you were faceless; a body to relieve the pain of loss and nothing more."

Still incensed and not quite finished, she rises clumsily. "You don't mean that! Look at her!" Rushing towards me, I flinch when her breath washes over me. "How dare you take him from me, you fucking bitch!" Her hand strikes my face hard.

I stand in utter shock. Slowly registering what has just happened, I quickly punch in the code to the suite and slam the door shut. Sliding down the wall, holding my burning cheek, she continues to scream outside. My pain is fully-fledged, and my body sinks further, until I'm balled up, consoling myself. I always wondered what that door was, and now I know.

And it's breaking my fucking heart.

"Get your goddamn hands off me!" She continues to scream, while I lose my sanity in private.

"Call the fucking police!" Sloan shouts. "I want *it* out of here, now!"

Christy's wailing makes my own pitiful tears sound indistinguishable.

"Christy? Christy! You ever, *ever*, show up here again, or come within spitting distance of my wife, I'll pull the fucking rug once and for all. There'll be no sweet deal on the table for your father. I will ensure he suffers. He won't have a fucking thing left, and he will have you to thank for it!"

"Please, don't do this!" she begs.

His loud, drawn-out breath is indicative that the decision has been made.

"It's done."

"Sloan? Sloan!"

The bells ding and the silence overwhelms both inside and out. In the foetal position, everything clenches when the door opens and closes. Long minutes pass, then familiar arms pick me up. My body is deplete, and I have no control over my muscles as he wraps an arm around my back and one under my legs.

He carries me into the bathroom, sits me on the vanity and cups my cheeks. Catching sight of myself, I'm horrified. My face is the visual proof of the way my heart has just been ripped from my chest and stabbed to death in front of me.

Pulling out the make-up remover, he does the most normal thing he possibly can, and starts the process of removing the panda eyes and running mascara. The atmosphere is tense; thick with his shame, thick with my sadness. Lifting me down, he holds me close.

"It's finally time to show you."

As we stand in front of the door, he slips a key into the lock, and the air feels like it has been squeezed from my lungs again. It would certainly explain the difficulty I seem to be experiencing breathing.

The stale smell of months' old dust swirls through my nostrils as he pushes the door back. With a heavy heart, I walk through the open space, and take in the plastic-covered hard and soft furnishings, knowing exactly what this is. This is something else he has kept hidden from me. Hidden in full view, I might add. And like everything else I never addressed; this should have been the first.

Yet another string on my bow of errors in this relationship. I sigh, refusing to allow this to overshadow my love for him. My impending vows, the ones I intend to carry to the grave, will not be spoiled by this. I slowly take his hand, and his loving, but very solemn blues meet mine and stay.

"Remember when I told you if I wanted a woman I would take her to a room in the hotel?" I nod, remembering that conversation a little too clearly. "Well, this is it."

Edging deeper into the suite, it's identical to the one next door. Lifting the decorator's plastic, I run my hand over the furniture, disturbing the thick dust with my fingertips.

"Why didn't you tell me? I would never have judged you for it."

"I know, but John's words just kept repeating over and over-"

"What words?" I stop him.

"He once asked me how I would explain this to you, or stop Christy from telling you. Every time I tried to justify it in my head, I realised he was right. There's nothing I can say to defend how I behaved back then. I wasn't lying outside. It was always you that I saw. It isn't right, but it's the truth."

Turning a little, because I don't want him to see me cry, I inhale deeply. "What are you going to do with it?"

"Refurbish it for guests, probably. It's surplus to requirements these days. It has been for a long time."

Without answering, I look over the sofa and then the stairs, wondering how many women have graced each. Except, just like the girl I used to be, the man he once was doesn't exist anymore.

"What she said-"

"She was lying. I trust you, more than I should sometimes. You're many things; amazing, overbearing, even a little frustrating, but I know you'd never cheat on me. If I did, I wouldn't have agreed to marry you. This is certain to me."

"I never wanted you to find out like this."

"Thank you, for finally being honest."

"Baby, I'm not doing it to be honest, I'm trying to rid myself of my past indiscretions."

I stare at him, wondering if I can do the same. He already knew of my darkest days and nights, the ones I feared telling him about. The ones I was sure as soon as he knew he would run far, far away. I was foolish. The truth was right in front of me the whole time. It wouldn't have taken much to scratch the surface.

"One of the things I hid from you all those months was the truth behind my attack, but you already knew. I guess I always thought it would be my past that would be the death of us. Seeing this suite and what it symbolises… I know I'm not the only woman you've ever been with, and it's something I've always accepted, whether it showed up, treat me like shit and threw it in my face for its own self-esteem and entertainment."

Painfully slow, I shuffle closer to the man I adore. He fixes his dark gaze on me, and I shudder.

"You once told me I was the only woman to grace your bed, here and the house, is that true?"

"Yes," he says firmly. Reaching up on my toes, I can still see the conflict in his eyes.

"I meant what I said. I don't want to constantly come back to this each time I hear something new, something you've never told me. You had a past before me, and if I hadn't have come back, eventually you would've had a future without me."

He turns off the lights and guides us out. With one last look behind me, this door in his life has now closed.

But for me, it has just been opened.

The room gradually comes into focus. Sleep hasn't stayed for long enough. My sub-conscience is still lagging behind, too subdued and compliant to the tender stroking on my spine.

It's a complete contrast to the way I fell asleep last night; drowning in my own poorly concealed tears, experiencing a sensation I can only compare to the way it feels to have your heart torn to shreds.

Sloan, thoroughly concerned for my welfare that a seedy part of his past had just been aired, did his absolute best to console me. But when you are already shattered, nothing can fix you.

I shouldn't be as upset as I am, but it hurts like nothing else ever has, because she has had some of his best years. Years that should have been ours.

Raising my hand inconspicuously, I wipe the tear from my cheek.

"Baby?" His deep, husky voice calls to me. He isn't stupid, he knows it has cut me to the bone, but I don't want to look into his eyes and let him see that she has won again.

"I'm sorry, my love. I'm sorry for the past I can't change, for a woman I never should have gotten involved with. It was wrong, but I was so lonely. The one thing I wanted I could never have." The mattress shifts behind me. Enfolding my arms over the pillow, a subtle, soft line is drawn up my back with his tongue.

I let loose an involuntary groan, unable to stop it from escaping, or my body from reacting. As I arch my spine, I curl my fingers around the headboard. His strong forearm slides between me and the sheet, lifting my hips. Obeying perfectly on my knees and parting my thighs, the hair on his legs brushes against mine. I harden my stance as he spreads his hand over my lower back. Time stands still waiting for his next move. I don't have to wait long when he swipes his tongue over me, and I jolt hard.

"Easy," he whispers, returning his mouth to my core, lavishing it fervently. Tightening my hands on the iron, the cold is the complete opposite of how my body is reaching the point of combustion.

I clench my thighs hard, when he slides his fingers inside me. My body responds in the most basic way possible, and I press back to meet him, needing him to complete me. I close my eyes, willing the tingle to take fruition. Encouraged by his deep, staccato breathing, I want more.

"Harder," I breathe out, resting my forehead on the pillow. Fulfilling my wish, his tongue reaffirms itself with my flesh, and he slides it inside. "Oh!" I moan, continuing to move with him.

"Come," he says, devouring me, before I give him his request.

My legs spasm when I cry out and apply pressure to the sides of his head. As always, he flicks my sensitive flesh, and I slacken them - although not for long. Quickly flipping me over, he positions us; chest to chest, legs to hips. Grazing my lips down his neck, he stops me.

"That's three." I pull back, wondering what on earth he's talking about. "Counting the ways, my gorgeous girl. Ready for four?" I lick my lip, run my hands down his sides and grab whatever I can of his backside. "Hand."

Bringing our palms together and in between us, I wrap my hand around his length, stroking up and down, loving the way he pulsates in my caress. Entirely consumed, I jump when his finger circles my already sensitive skin and presses inside. Fixing my passion-driven stare on him, I dare not look away as he loses control under my touch.

"Fuck!" he spits out.

He kisses me fiercely, and the room is alive with the sound of carnal pleasure as we simultaneously bring each other to climax. Without warning, my body falls back. Holding aside one knee, he rocks into me in a swift motion, and I cry out, digging my fingers into his shoulder. My hands claw against the sheets, seeking leverage while he rotates his hips.

"Come on, baby, you've got another in you." I grip the back of his head and push mine back.

"Oh, God!"

He buries his head into my shoulder, thrusting hard, roaring out his release. He carefully bites my nipple, ensuring desire courses through me, leaving me exhausted.

"Did I hurt you?" he whispers, kissing a line from my ear to jaw. With my chin between his fingers, he coerces me to look at him, evidently thinking I shall lie.

"Yes," I reply unequivocally. He has hurt me, and I will only be insulting his intelligence to lie. He starts to speak, but I stop him. "But I'll always forgive you."

"There's a chance this might bruise." He tenderly strokes my cheek.

I murmur, but I don't want to talk about her. Fastening my arms around his waist, he starts to turn flaccid against my skin. Slyly, I reach down and touch him, but he groans and slaps me away.

"Baby, I don't think I can withstand five right now."

I laugh out loud, surprised he has just refused. "I'm sure there are other things I can do that don't require you to move."

With my hand on his shoulder, I roll him over. Straddling his waist, I rub myself down him thoroughly as I edge back.

"You're going to fucking kill me!" he mutters.

"No, just bring you to the edge," I reply, and he instantly comes to life again. "I think you're lying to me. I think you can definitely withstand this."

Touching his sensitive tip with my lips, his hand massages my hurt cheek. I flick my eyes up to his, and they darken and sparkle beautifully as I proceed to test out my ability to give him number five.

Chapter 29

A HAND SLAMS over my stomach, holding me down, as I shift and turn wildly, bound to the nightmares that alter the perception inside my dreams. The image is brutal, far too real inside my head. Between the memories of my childhood and those of my adulthood, it's too much to control any longer.

Deacon smiles malevolently as he reaches for me and drags me out of the cubbyhole. I kick out my legs as he throws me onto the bed, and I'm unable to move as he pins me down painfully.

"Stop fucking fighting! We're gonna play a game!" he sneers, and my eyes are drawn to the knife in his palm.

With my arms outstretched, my legs parted underneath his, I use the only weapon I have left - my voice. Taking a deep breath, I scream.

"Kara? Kara!"

I jolt upright, still hysterical, and scramble off the bed. Running into the bathroom, I lock the door behind me and brace my hands on the sink. I drop my head and my eyes capture the glint of the diamond gracing my finger. Splashing my face, the splintering of wood fills the room, and the door flies back, revealing a wild-looking Sloan.

I rest my backside against the sink, but I can barely look at him as he enters and heads straight to the shower. Turning it on, he advances on me, his face expressionless. He carefully undresses me, then he drops everything onto the floor and walks backwards, grasping my hand firmly. We step into the cubicle and the atmosphere is palpable; the unspoken truth ready to be aired aloud. Under the flow, he opens his arms, and I collapse into them.

"When were you going to tell me you were still having nightmares?" he asks softly, pushing aside my wet hair.

"I wanted to be better for you, stronger, but with Sam and..." The water washes away my tears, but he knows. Wiping my eyes, he holds me tight against him.

Squeezing the body wash into his palm, he starts the meticulous cleansing of my skin. Eventually, after spending far too long on my body parts, he turns the water off. As usual, he wraps me up first and then himself.

He drops me on my feet in the dressing room, strokes my face, and then leaves me to get dressed. Slipping the t-shirt over my head, my eyes capture his as he rests his chin in his hand on the island. After long minutes pass in companionable silence, I approach, caress his stomach with my hand and kiss him.

"I love you," he says. "I'll make us some coffee for the journey. Don't be long, my love."

Hefting my case down the stairs, Sloan quickly takes it from me. I retrieve my jacket and bag, while he continues to load our cases into the car and then returns.

"Excited?" he asks indifferently, and for the hundredth time.

Excited isn't a word I would use right now; cautious and apprehensive are definitely more appropriate. And for more reasons than one.

Cautious, because we still haven't heard anything from the police, or my father, and more so, there hasn't been any inkling about the Blacks. I'm not sure if there's something brewing in the inner circle that I'm being left out of again, but ever since Jeremy returned, Sloan and Walker have met with him numerous times.

And apprehensive, because ever since Sloan got his ring on my finger, he's been very secretive. Maybe not in the same way he has about the meetings I'm supposed to turn a blind eye to, but he's had an abundance of consultations with financial advisors and solicitors over the last few days. The only reason why I know this, is because Sophie just can't hold her own water. And it's times like these I absolutely love her for it.

I nod and smile, but his eyes narrow. He's right, I should be more excited. Today, we are finally getting our long overdue, few days away. I should be ecstatic, climbing the walls with excitement, except I'm not.

The front door shuts behind me as I make my way to the Range Rover. I pull the handle, but it doesn't open. I sigh, aware he has purposely locked it. I turn and he grabs my scarf. He then methodically drags me towards him, one handful at a time.

"Baby?" He cups my cheeks.

"It's not that I'm not excited, I'm just hesitant. Anything good never seems to last very long for us. A few days away is perfect, but we still have to come back and face an uncertain future."

He huffs, annoyed that I'm spelling out the unfortunate reality. We both know it's only a matter of time, and considering almost everything has been rosy recently, I'm not such an idiot to believe it can last much longer.

"I understand, I really do, but for the next few days, can you just forget it? For me?" I nod in agreement as I climb into the car. Settling in for the journey, the prickles on the back of my neck garner force. I rub it, curious as to why I am experiencing them again.

We exit the gates and he picks up speed, as we move deeper into the countryside.

Re-tuning the radio when the signal dies, I catch his gaze. We've been in the car for over an hour, and I'm getting anxious. He hasn't said where we're going, and I haven't asked, but I figure I will let him keep his secrets. *For now.*

"Here," he says when we stop at a set of lights.

He hands me my old phone and it starts to vibrate with my mother's number. "How many times has she rang?" I query, watching the screen fade to black.

"A few in the last day or so. Sorry, I should have told you." The morning after my father's surprise hotel visit, I lobbed the thing at him and designated him its new keeper. It was safer on my psyche for it to be in his possession rather than mine.

"No, it's fine. I probably wouldn't have answered anyway. I honestly don't know what to say to her." I bring my hand to my mouth, my eyes trained on the screen, appreciating how everything can turn to shit in the blink of an eye

"Answer it," he coaxes. "It might be important."

"And it might also be lies." I glance over when he pulls up on the side of the road and slaps on the hazards.

"Baby, I appreciate you're trying to move on, but she's still your mother. And she's sick, and that's the reason why she keeps calling." I narrow my eyes; eight months ago he wouldn't have been this forgiving.

"Is there something you want to tell me?" I ask, since there's obviously an underlying truth here that I'm not aware of.

After a moment of silent deliberation, I realise I can't keep living like this. There has to come a point where I say no, and it's already been and gone. And yes, I know I'm probably making another huge mistake, but I can't go back there. Not to that city, not to that house.

Not back to being that girl again.

I switch it off completely and slip it into my bag. Chancing a look at Sloan, he doesn't appear too happy with my choice, but it's tough. It's done.

I stare blankly ahead and turn up the radio as he finally admits defeat and moves off.

Passing through two stone pillars, my eyes delight at the surrounding scenery. Everything is covered with a glimmer of sunlight, making it look very picturesque.

"This is beautiful," I gasp, as the hotel finally comes into view, spanning out in front of us. Finally, the excitement I wasn't feeling starts to come out. Sloan smiles when our eyes catch.

"Hmm, thought you'd like it."

"Have you been here before?" I query, then wish I hadn't. I really don't want to know how many times he has tested out the mattresses. Especially if it involved a certain redhead who can't seem to stay out of my life.

"A few times. Personal business." He grins slyly. "Trust me."

"I'm going to stop trusting you one of these days! You know I don't like surprises," I mutter.

"You'll like this one."

Ignoring his innuendo, I gaze in awe at the beautiful manicured gardens, set in the expanse of land housing this pristine place. Getting out of the car, a porter approaches.

"Good afternoon, Mr Foster," the smart, suited man greets him.

I walk towards them, and my eyes work up from his expensive shoes, to his custom-fitted suit and the silk tie gracing his neck. This isn't no porter I've ever seen before. He sure as hell isn't dressed like the ones at the hotel, and that definitely is a place where anything less than perfection is not tolerated.

"Is everything ready?" Sloan asks, approaching.

"Yes, sir." The man holds out his hand. "I hope your stay will be very memorable, Miss Petersen." He smiles broadly, looking extremely pleased with himself.

Taking his hand, I bristle and quickly slip mine away. He doesn't notice, since Sloan has, and he beckons him forward in quiet conversation. I linger behind, still overly enthused by the place.

"My love?" Sloan calls from the entrance, and I hurry over. Positioning my hand close to his chest, he leads us into the beautiful reception area.

Dark wood fixtures and two winding staircases dominate the space. Lingering close to his side, my attention is captured when two women exit the ballroom and glance over at us. Their smiles are radiant, and one nods at me. Watching them walk away, I'm drawn to the room and slowly move with intrigue.

"All in good time, my gorgeous girl," Sloan says, pulling me back.

"But..." I have no idea what I want to say, but whatever is happening inside that room definitely has something to do with us.

Sloan's finger covers my mouth. No words are expressed, and I allow him to have the upper hand in silencing me.

"I trust you," I whisper. Staring right into the depths of my soul, his hand massages away my curiosity, although not entirely.

I clutch the key card as I step into the lift. Holding me to the point of cutting off my circulation, Sloan runs his hand through my hair, until we stop on the second floor. Slowly walking down the corridor, he pauses at the last door.

"Honeymoon suite?" I query in confusion.

"A little premature, maybe." He laughs and swipes the card through the lock.

Investigating the suite, it isn't very dissimilar to the hotel. Clearly, the ongoing theme with these overpriced places is opulence and grandeur. Whether or not you get your money's worth is another matter entirely.

"Let's go and explore."

Sloan presses down my shoulders until I'm sitting, then he pulls off my boots and replaces them with my trainers.

"Always one step ahead," I state, as he pulls the laces tight.

"You have no idea."

The hotel appears through the trees as I run through the woods. Sloan jogs behind me, trying to catch up.

This afternoon has been one of the best of my life. After exploring the trails that captured my attention, he led me into a little churchyard, housing a picturesque chapel. Walking around the building, it was everything we had described; small, intimate, and set in serenity.

I've made a mental note to tell him, because all he has done for the majority of the afternoon is apologise for being monopolised by work. His phone has been ringing. *A lot.* Each time I told him to leave it, he refused. I've heard *'it's important'* far too many times to believe it really is.

When we enter the foyer, I feel inexplicably light on my feet, if not a little exhausted.

"I want to show you something."

Sloan tugs at my hands and guides me towards the mystery room. Stepping inside with hesitation, everything looks magnificent. Ivory material drapes the high windows, and the tables and chairs are covered with ivory and midnight blue silk.

Unable to vocalise what's running riotously through my head, I continue to walk around the room. There isn't a thing I miss, and the one thing I definitely can't miss is the immaculate monstrosity of a cake I had admired in that bloody book. His chuckle breaks free when I touch the cartoon effigies of the bride and groom.

Oh, my God...

This is our wedding.

This is where we're going to be married.

"Say something," he says behind me, his tone undeniably worried. Ignoring him, allowing myself another minute to absorb all this, I finger the little statues again.

"I'm getting married today!" Squealing out in happiness, I jump into his arms and laugh.

"No, *we're* getting married today!" He spins me around; his eyes full of pride. Kissing him repeatedly, I pull back.

"How did you manage this so quickly?" I ask incredulously. Witnessing his blasé demeanour and the shrug of his shoulders, another thought crosses me. "Oh no, you didn't! What poor couple did you buy off in order for them to give up their dream today?" A loud laugh rumbles from deep within him.

"Easily and nobody. I've had this booked for a very long time, hence my meetings here," he says confidently. His fingers massage my cheeks, and he stares at me with nothing but undivided love.

"And if I'd have stayed up north?"

He considers his response momentarily, then smiles. "I'd have thrown your arse in the Aston and drove you here kicking and screaming."

"A foregone conclusion," I murmur.

He nods slowly. "This was always the final conclusion. The ultimate dream. For nine, long goddamn years."

Shifting in his tight hold, I do another glance around the room.

"I can't wait to marry you, but are you sure you really want to marry me? I come with a lot of baggage and not very much to offer."

"I wouldn't have you any other way." He carries me towards the door and drops me down. "I shall meet you at the chapel in an hour, Ms Petersen."

I lean back, not sure I've just heard right. "What?"

"*That's* where we'll be married."

"How did you know I'd love it?"

"Because I know you. And I can read you like a book, even when you think I'm not looking."

"Sloan..." I start, not quite sure what to say. Yes, I really, desperately, want to be his wife, but not like this. Not hidden away where no one can see it.

"No, my love. I want to wake up in the morning and know that you are truly mine. I want to make love to my wife and never stop making love to her. Nine years and counting, and I refuse to wait any longer." I rest my head on his shoulder, completely overwhelmed.

"This is crazy. They will kill us. Marie will kill you!"

He shrugs again, still unconcerned. "I'll take my chances."

He shuffles us into the lift, and I coil around him. I smile to myself, realising this will be the last time I'll hold him as a single woman.

Entering our suite, I gasp when I see Charlie and Sophie standing there with beaming smiles.

"Don't be too long, Ms Petersen." He winks and then he's gone.

"Step to it, Kara, we only have fifty-five minutes. Shower, now!" Charlie stuffs a couple of towels into my arms and pushes me towards the bathroom.

Under the water, I start to cry, thinking of all the amazing moments in my life so far. My head lulls against the tiles, Samantha filling my thoughts. How I wish things could have been different between us. That she could be present, watching the best day of my life. Although that will never be.

And my mother. She will never get to see this day, either. And regardless of what I may say, I would love to have her here. To have one happy memory that we can share together.

The banging on the door demists my provocation. "I'll be five minutes!" I shout, praying they don't barge in and drag me out. Although I wouldn't be surprised if they did.

"We haven't got five minutes!" Charlie shouts back. I huff and quickly rinse my hair. Making fast work of drying off and brushing my teeth, I step out.

Loitering in the doorway, Sophie and Charlie are facing off, each trying to best the other.

"She's wearing it up!" Charlie says, her eyes wild and determined.

"No, she isn't! She was self-conscious enough when it was his birthday. She won't want them on her wedding pictures!"

"But it looks more elegant up!"

I scrub my hands over my face and stare at the ceiling, hoping some divine intervention will assist me. *Wishful thinking.*

"Please, can you both just shut up? This is my surprise wedding, have some respect for Sloan's wishes!" They titter between themselves, until Sophie points to the dressing table chair. I stomp over, my head already starting to feel a burgeoning migraine.

In the reflection, Charlie is digging around in her vanity case, until she pulls out what she needs and sits in front of me. Twisting the chair around, she gets comfortable.

"Close your eyes," she says softly, with an eyeliner poised in her hand. Dropping my lids, I attempt to relax and ignore the tugging on my hair behind me.

"You better not be asleep!" Sophie's stern voice invades my daydreaming.

"No, I'm awake," I reply, sounding sleepy even to my ears. I look in the mirror with a startled expression. "I forgot how good you are at this," I compliment Charlie, who looks impressed with herself. I gaze in awe at the scars that are barely visible - unless you know they are there. "Thank you," I whisper tearfully, looking at them both in the mirror.

"Don't cry!" Sophie says.

I casually look around the room and a certain sense of horror fills me. "Please tell me I have a dress?"

Charlie's hands fix atop my shoulders, and she turns me to the door with the white dress bag hanging on it. "We came fully prepared for this event."

Running my hand over the zip, the fabric spills from the opening. Carefully removing it, I smile. Strapless, fitted, and full length. And thankfully, not a bloody sequin in sight. It's exactly what I asked for; simple, elegant – and no layers.

As I glance over my shoulder, they both smile at me with watery eyes.

"Erm...we have twenty-three minutes," Charlie says, verging on breaking down. Sophie approaches and holds the lingerie I had bought with Marie.

"Hurry," she says, passing them to me.

Needing a moment alone, I rush into the bathroom and slip into the underwear and then the dress. A knock on the door startles me, and I hastily gather the front. Marie enters, looking magnificent in *that* cream suit. Always the perfectionist, her hair doesn't have a strand out of place, whilst her smoky eyes and pale lips complement her colouring beautifully.

"Thought you might need a hand," she says, zipping me up. She delicately touches my hair, while her eyes work my chest, appraising the excellent job that has been done.

She leads me back into the bedroom and opens her palm to reveal my diamonds studs. Putting them in my ears, she motions for the girls to join us.

"You need something old," Sophie says.

Charlie gives her a glorious smile. "No, that's already sorted." She shares a look with Marie, who turns her attention back to me.

"Something new." She takes a box from Charlie, revealing a silver headband, and slides it into my hair. "This is from the three of us."

"Something borrowed," Charlie chimes in again, removing the locket from her neck. Opening it, it is of her and Sloan when they were kids, in the arms of their mother. I study it with sad eyes, wondering what she will think when she hears her only son has gotten married, and she's not even here.

"And something blue!" Sophie grins coyly and tosses a small gift bag at me. I open it and almost have a heart attack.

"No..." I shake my head.

"Yes, he'll love it!"

Taking the bag from me, Marie's eyes reciprocate mine as she removes the innocuous item. "I think you two need to get ready. Quickly!" She turns back to me and shakes her head.

"You look stunning," I comment, sliding the nude heels over my feet.

"And you look like an angel, my girl."

I stare in the mirror; between the amazing talents of the two women, now zipping each other up, my appearance is astounding.

My make-up is neutral, and my hair is intricately styled. Even though I'm exposing more skin than I should be comfortable with, I feel beautiful. Deserving of this life-changing moment.

"Do you think he'll like it?"

Charlie snorts. "Kara, of course he's going to like it! He chose it - all of it! The dress, the shoes, he bought them last year, along with that blue gown. He made me swear never to tell you. This isn't something that was spur of the moment, this has been in the offing for a long time."

"You look beautiful, babe." Sophie then wraps her arms around me and whispers in my ear. I gasp at her vastly crude, and somewhat inappropriate words, but let them go, because I definitely am going to do just that.

"Well, we look good!"

"That we do," Charlie affirms, bringing up her phone up in front of us and taking a picture.

Chapter 30

WALKING THROUGH THE hotel, Devlin is waiting at the entrance. He tugs his tie, looking extremely different in his full morning suit - complete with earplugs that match the colour of the waistcoat. Grinning, he leans down and kisses my cheek.

"He's already on the verge of having a premature heart attack. Now, just get in there and get a ring on it!"

I laugh and slide into the car.

I stare into the distance as we careen through the early evening darkness. Marie strokes my hand the entire journey. Clearly, she thinks I need reassuring, but seriously, I've never been more certain of anything in my entire life.

Pulling up outside, the sun is setting through the trees. Ascending the stone steps, each one carries me closer and closer towards a future I plan to experience to the full. The atmospheric lighting twinkles in the open doorway of the small, intimate chapel, and I halt when a thought slaps my psyche.

"I don't know what to do!" Panic overcomes me. Marie shifts, probably thinking I'm having second thoughts. "No, I mean, normally you have a rehearsal or two, right? Well, I don't know what I'm supposed to do!"

She laughs. "Honey, you put one foot in front of the other, and you don't stop until you get to the front. The vicar will guide you through what you need to say. Stop worrying!"

And I do, until another thought sticks in there.

"Who's giving me away?"

"I am," she says proudly. "And I wouldn't give you to anyone else." Leading us away from prying ears, she stops near an old, redundant fountain and smiles. "You grew up to be strong and smart, and extremely beautiful, inside and out. You're both very lucky to have found each other, not everyone is blessed with a love like yours."

"Marie?" I query, as her expression twists sombrely. I slide my thumb over her cheek as she tries to avoid my stare.

"Now," she says teary, removing my engagement ring. "Let's not keep him waiting any longer." She motions to Jake, who let's go of

Charlie, and pushes open the old double doors and the procession starts to play.

Marie fusses with my dress for the final time. She then holds out her hand and Sophie puts a large bouquet into it. Taking them from her, we link arms as we start the last journey of Kara Petersen.

Walking the short distance through the chapel, my breath lodges in my throat as Sloan stands at the end, waiting for me. All dressed in traditional morning suits, he is flanked by Walker and Stuart. He stares at me ardently, until Stuart delicately nudges him and they grin at each other. Walker, ever the cool one, rolls his eyes and smiles.

Breathing out, needing to ground myself thoroughly, I smile at everyone present. As already discussed, intimacy is the key here.

To my left, Gloria and her husband, I presume, are standing with their arms linked. The way he holds her and wipes his finger over her cheek, tells me their love has also spanned a lifetime. On my right, George is looking thoroughly pleased with this evening's events, as are Tommy and Parker, who nod simultaneously when I pass.

I glance into the eyes of each person present; the majority are Sloan's colleagues, the few girls Soph and I went to college with, and a couple of the old-timers from the catering staff that I've known for years.

Reaching the front, Devlin and Nicki are both wearing identical beaming smiles, but they are not the reason why I almost trip over myself. At the head of the gathering, in between Jake and Jeremy, is a woman I didn't expect to see.

Julia Emerson.

I pick up my pace again and observe her carefully as she brings her hand to her mouth, seemingly in shock. The tears start to flood my eyes, and a little whimper escapes me.

"I'm sorry I didn't tell you, but she wanted to be here," Marie whispers.

Letting me go, I take the last couple of feet solo, until my hand entwines around Sloan's and he turns me to face him. Cupping my cheeks, his eyes burn with passion and pride.

"You look beautiful. I never want today to end, but there's something we must do first." He turns me around to the front.

The vicar smiles as he welcomes the congregation. The traditional sermon begins, and I lose myself in midnight blues.

Listening to the calming voice of the man speaking, I barely register the moment he asks if there is any reason why we may not lawfully marry. Sloan and I look around simultaneously, letting out a combined sigh of relief when the moment passes without event.

Everything is a blur, up until Sloan lifts my left hand and smiles. "I, Sloan Oliver Foster, take you, Kara Petersen, to be my wife. To have and to hold... For better, for worse... In sickness and in health... I make this vow."

Tears of happiness form in my eyes and my heart feels inexplicably heavy with joy. My body quivers when it's my turn, and my hand shakes lifting his. Taking a breath, I focus on the only light in the room – the one in front of me.

"I, Kara Petersen, take you, Sloan Oliver Foster, to be my husband. To have and to hold... For richer, for poorer... Till death us do part... I make this vow."

Strong fingers tangle in mine, while I listen to the vicar speak of vows that are binding and forever. Upon requesting the rings, a shuffle behind me resounds in the quiet. Sloan's mother grins beautifully and passes over two very plain, gold bands. These are the something old that Marie and Charlie were exchanging knowing glances about earlier.

Sloan positions it and repeats the vows. My mouth is dry as I take what was his father's ring and slide it onto his finger. Inhaling an unobtrusive breath, I say the words, my heart full of love and pride.

"You may now kiss your bride," the vicar eventually says.

Sloan grins at him and tugs me closer. With the congratulatory applaud rising in the small congregation, he wraps his arms around me and bequeaths me with a kiss that should not be seen in public. Cradling my back, he lowers me, and I acquiesce easily, uncaring in my happiness that everyone is present and, judging by the raucousness filling the building, vocally loving every minute of it.

His arms hold me securely while he keeps me tipped back at his very loving mercy. Finally lifting me up, he strokes his hand over my hair and down the back of my neck.

We follow the vicar into a small side room, and I gather up my dress as he slides over the register. I stare down at my name - this is the last time I will sign as Kara Petersen. Passing the pen to Sloan, he quickly signs and pulls me up.

Leading us out, flashes go off consistently, and I laugh, rejoicing in this incredible man who has given me so much to look forward to.

"No regrets?"

"No," I whisper, and slide my hands under his coat. I lean my head against his chest, listening carefully to his content heartbeat.

The clearing of a feminine throat draws us apart, and Julia fills my vision. Reaching out her arm, I voluntarily walk into it. Her touch, so much like her son's, it feels abnormally natural to have her - a stranger - this close.

"You look beautiful. My son is very lucky to have you." She wraps her arm around me and walks out of the chapel with us.

Outside, evening cloaks itself around everything; the world duskier now than it was when we set foot inside. Holding my door open, Jeremy approaches and puts a protective arm around Julia's shoulder. I smile, thankful I choose not to throw him under the proverbial bus.

"We'll see you shortly, my love," his mother says, using the same tone Sloan does on me.

I hold up my dress to get in the car. I place my hands on my lap and glance to my side, as Sloan lifts his coat-tails and sits.

"Now I know where that comes from."

"That you do, *my love*." No sooner have the words left his mouth, my legs are tugged onto his lap, and he slides me over. "Now, *my love*, would you like to get a little lost on the way to our reception?" His brows wiggle up and down, and I bite my lip, wanting to stay lost in this moment forever.

"Beautiful, and finally, irrevocably mine." Unravelling my hair with his hand, running it through the strands, which have grown out in the last few months, he gazes. "Kiss me, Mrs Foster."

With a smile I can't hide, I slide my hand across his face. He gently holds my wrist and kisses the inside, before taking each finger and pressing the pads to his lips. The car starts and, as brazen as he can sometimes be, he diverts my attention by peppering me with kisses and nips, until he reaches my chest.

I close my eyes, delighting in the fact my life has just become whole; completed in ways I have dreamed about for as long as I can remember.

Driving through the hotel's pillared entrance, I lovingly twist my wedding band with my thumb. Sloan, enthralled by my action, raises my hand up.

"This was my mother's wedding ring. It's been passed down my father's line. One day, I'll be giving it to our son when he gets married."

"Son? I want daughters."

"No, you clearly want me in prison!" he laughs, while I let out a little yawn.

"Tired?" I nod with a sound of confirmation. "Well, as soon as the clock strikes midnight, we're gone." He carries me out of the car and into the hotel.

We stop just outside the room; the party coming from inside is loud. Far too loud for our intimate gathering. Pushing open the door, the other hotel guests are mingling around inside, unsure of what kind of celebration this is, but clearly enjoying themselves regardless.

"Better still, let's get out of here now." He lifts my hand, kissing my ring.

"Isn't it tradition to cut the cake and throw the bouquet?"

He shrugs. "Yes, but we don't follow tradition." I tilt a brow. "But if you must," he says, jogging us into the room and picking up a knife along the way.

A squeal resounds behind us, and Charlie stands there, hands on hips, as Sloan cuts off a large slab of cake.

"What?" he challenges her. "Grab that bottle of champagne, baby. Actually, I believe we agreed there would be lots – grab two!"

I snatch up the bottles from the table, but he eyes me suspiciously as I spot Marie. Approaching her, she and Walker look like the perfect couple, complementing each other beautifully – his rough to her smooth.

"Oh, you're here! We need to... What's the matter, honey?" she asks when I pass her the bouquet. "Oh crap, are we throwing it now?"

I shake my head. "I want you to have these because you deserve to be as happy as I am."

And on that note, Sloan drags me away. "Goodnight. And keep everyone away from our room!"

"No, you can't do that!" Marie says exasperatedly.

"Our wedding, our rules!"

"But we need to celebrate properly!"

"Oh, we will!" Sloan shouts back, causing Walker to roar out in laughter.

Sloan carries me and our supplies out of the ballroom. He bypasses the lifts and takes the stairs instead. Kicking open the door, he removes the bottles from my hands and puts them on the bedside table. Unwrapping the cake, he holds it up for me to take a bite.

"Delicious," I purr; my mouth full. Tipping my chin, he kisses me and licks the inside of my cheek.

"Agreed. Kara and cake, definitely the best combination known to man." A delightful, anticipatory shiver spans the length of my spine, as he slowly turns me around.

"Tell me what you want, Mrs Foster," he whispers against my neck. His hands run up my thighs, over my hips, and languish at my waist. There's so much that I want, but I've got the ultimate gift. I've got him.

"Still beautiful," he murmurs, moving his hands until they sit perfectly over my breasts. Clenching his palms a little, he tongues the column of my neck. "Say the words," he urges again, and his hands slide from my chest to my back.

"I…I…" I lose my voice the second the zip unfastening resounds alongside our already erratic breathing. Still mute, I breathe out when he lowers the fabric down my body, until he's lifting one leg and then the other.

Turning me around, I stare into his lust-filled eyes. Taking in my lingerie, they expand when he sees the God-awful *thing* Sophie insisted he would love.

He drops to his knees and he inspects closely, before tugging a finger underneath the midnight blue fabric that is a very embarrassing addition to my thigh.

"I love it. Now," he rises and steps back, wondering where to start. "What do you want me to do to you?"

I bite my lip, wondering if I should say what I really want. Would it be wrong to request such a thing on one's wedding night? To hell with it! There are plenty of things I've asked for, and this shall be no different – only that he's now most definitely my husband, and there should be no shame between us.

"I want…I want you to make love to me until the sun rises." Suddenly more brazen than ever, I grab the lapels of his coat and yank him closer. "And I want you to fuck me like a good husband should!" I throw my hands over my face, disbelieving I've actually just said those words to him. I'll kill Soph for planting them in my head.

Parting my hands, his smile stretches from ear to ear, and he grabs his tie and pulls it off swiftly. "I think I might be able to manage that!"

I push off his coat, and he quickly removes his waistcoat and shirt. My tongue darts out and strokes my bottom lip. Gripping my head, he stalls a moment, before invading my mouth.

He tugs at my legs, and I curl them around his hips as carries me to the bed. Laying us down, he holds my hands in his above my head and kisses his way down to my chest. Locating the front clasp, he carefully removes my bra and holds it up.

"See, I can be patient."

Massaging one breast with his palm, his mouth works wonders over my sensitive areola. Circling his thumb over my other hardened peak, making it so stiff it is starting to feel a little uncomfortable, he grins. "More?"

I agree furiously, my mouth dropping open, needing more oxygen. Throwing my hands down, I grip his shoulders as he moves.

"Lower," I request breathlessly.

He kneads my stomach, and possessively laves my belly button. He then skims down my back, until both hands are separating my cheeks. I'm too lost in rapture to watch him, and I thrust my hips in invitation. His hard chest rubs against my core, and I sigh out, my body preparing for the most amazing invasion and release.

"Baby, I'm sorry," he says ruefully, and I instantly lift up.

"For what?" The sound of tearing fabric kills the silence. "You're not patient enough!" I giggle.

His hooded blues smoulder. "I've been patient for nine years, it's overrated! Now, what do you want first, the loving or the fucking?" My legs spasm hard, and he grins. "Fucking, it is."

Cradling him between my thighs, his nose skims over my flesh. Long minutes pass by, with only his breathing and my perceptible anticipation, then he slides his tongue inside, circling, preparing me for him. He plunges in and out relentlessly until I'm mindless and boneless. Continuing his ministrations, he holds up my lower back as he moves away, a glimmer of moisture on his lips.

On his knees, he drags me further down the bed, until our centres align perfectly. Slowly, he slides inside, little by little, before he is consuming me entirely. Taking a moment, he admires me from above, before tightening his hold on my hips and finding his rhythm.

Thrusting hard into me, my back arches in provocation. His skin sliding against mine; our bodies touching, connecting, is enough to unravel me spectacularly. The sound of skin upon skin resounds beautifully. Growling his satisfaction, he fills me to the hilt, then retreats. His pelvis slams against mine and I find myself lifting higher; his body the catalyst to take me over the edge. My strangled moan fills the room shamelessly when the first wave of ecstasy compels and catapults me to an invisible high.

His hips move harder, and I rock against him as he finally gives me what I asked for - he's fucking his wife like a good husband should. I can honestly say, as much as it is still unlike me, I absolutely love it.

"Fuck! I love you," he says, between grunts and hisses. "I love this face." He kisses my lips, transferring the last remnants of my arousal. "I love this neck." His teeth nibble delicately. "I love these tits." His hands leave my back and squeeze my breasts. "And I love the way you join so perfectly with me."

Finally, he lowers his hand down between us and rubs my flesh, assisting my impending explosion. Crying out, I tighten my legs and arch my back higher. His penetration continues furiously, feeling every solid inch of him, harder and deeper. He drops his forehead to mine and stares deep into my eyes.

"I love you, too. More than living, more than breathing, more than anything else in this world," I whisper, catching my breath.

His lips crash against mine, while he manipulates my leg over his shoulder. Engorging inside me, I whimper when he growls and lunges sharply, hitting my hidden places. Invisible lights blind me – it's almost like I'm having an out-of-body experience.

"Oh, fuck! Come for me, baby."

And as always, I do.

"Sloan!" I convulse around him. Lifting me, creating a stretch that is both pleasure and pain, he rotates his pelvis, sliding deeper, harder. "Don't stop!" I beg, earning a displeased grunt.

The push and pull of our connection eases down, and I stare up at him, palming his perspired face.

"That's enough fucking," he says, out of breath. "Time for the loving."

Easing me back down, he kisses me, before adjusting my thighs and pressing my knees further apart. True to his word, he penetrates me beautifully, sliding in and out with such reverence, I can feel the tears cloud my eyes. Pulling him close, cheek to cheek, he whispers in my ear. Words of adoration and love; words of always and forever.

The words he left me in phone messages.

Moving fluidly, he entwines my legs around him. Carefully positioning his hands on either side of my head, my eyes flutter, both from happiness and overexertion.

I concentrate on the touch of his lips to my collarbone, the playful tug of his teeth on my impossibly hard nipples, and the movement of his hand, drifting down my stomach.

Enraptured by him; his messy ebony hair, his penetrating midnight blues, to the strong jawline and the fullness of his lips. Finally, he really is mine. He always has been, but now it feels complete.

My nails dig into his shoulders, while he continues to claim me as his wife, touching parts of me that no one else ever will. It feels like forever of just staring at him, concentrating on his eyes, the crease of his brow, the perspiration forming in beads, until he swells again, and the heat flows from the inside out.

Laying on top of me, he constantly strokes my forehead. I make no comment because this moment is perfect. The way it should always be.

Delicately touching me for the last time, he slides out. A little sigh of distress leaves my throat, and he rolls us over. His hand slides over my thigh, and he snaps the flouncy fabric.

"Remind me to thank Miss Chatty at some point."

"How did you guess?" I caress my fingers up and down his chest, kissing patches in between.

"I didn't; she told me. She said there would be a surprise under the dress that I had to remove with my teeth." He flips us over, glides his hands down my leg and kisses my inner thigh. "Ready, Mrs Foster?"

"Do your worst!"

The playful snap of elastic indicates he plans on doing just that.

Chapter 31

THE HOUSE IS a welcome sight when we finally pull up outside. Excitement ripples through me that I'm finally home. I grin, finding difficulty hiding the smile that has been permanently etched on my face from the moment I said, '*I will*'.

Jumping out of the car, I grab my dress bag from the back and fold it over my arm. As I close the door, my feet leave the ground, and I'm being swung around. Sloan's unruly hair blows gently in the breeze, and I rub my fingers through his inky strands.

"Put me down!" I admonish pathetically, because there's no other place I'd rather be. I hold on tight as he advances towards the door, all the while his lips glide over my neck.

"Would you deny me the tradition of carrying you over the threshold?"

Sliding my fingers around his nape, I coax him closer. "We don't follow tradition, remember?"

"No, but this tradition is an exception to the rule. I want to carry my new bride over the threshold." He kisses my forehead. "And up the stairs." He moves to my cheek. "I want to kiss and feel every part of her." He reaches my nose. "And never, ever, stop." He speaks against my mouth; his tongue seeking entry. A blossoming sensation causes the butterflies to seek flight in my belly.

I fall into the embrace and reach for the handle. I gasp when it opens in my palm. Jerking abruptly, I can feel the fear in my expression, but Sloan's eyes glint playfully.

"And unfortunately, all the wicked things I have in mind will have to wait, because we have a guest." Unravelling my legs, he nips my neck and puts them back into position. "Tradition, my love." He kicks the door back and carries me inside. Removing my bag from in between us, he hangs it on the bannister and continues down the hallway into the kitchen.

Entering, the place looks pristine. Sloan's mother, Julia, and a very smart, suited man are sat laughing.

"Hello, my darling!" she greets her son, who looks as confused as I do. "You remember Hugh?" She points to the man, who hurriedly drops his mug and holds out his hand.

Sloan's brow creases as he judges which hand to hold out. Making the decision for him, I squeeze his shoulder before sliding my legs down. Leaving the trio alone, I grab my dress bag from the bannister.

Entering into the bedroom, I grin when I see there are already pictures of the wedding scattered around. I drop my handbag, then move into the dressing room to hang my dress. For some inexplicable reason, everything feels different. This is no longer just my boyfriend's house, and truthfully, it never has been.

The door creaks open, and Julia enters. Stopping at the island, she picks up the bracelet and sighs.

"When I left England all those years ago, it was a hard thing as a mother to take one child and leave the other behind. I did it because Sloan had already been accepted into Manchester, and that's where he wanted to go. He's always been so sure of what he wants." She grins. "He gets that from John, you know. He's pretty much the only father figure he has ever known. He lost his dad young."

"You took a risk coming here, but it means a lot to have your blessing." I walk towards her and sit down against the island. She joins me, hesitating whether to take my hand. I tentatively touch my fingers to hers, and she digs into her pocket.

"I did, but it was worth it. I've waited a long time to see my son finally walk down the aisle with the woman he loves. Here," she says, passing me a pair of tiny hoop earrings. "He bought these for me when he was three. Well, actually his dad bought them, but Sloan picked them out. He was a very proud toddler when he presented them to me…along with the half-eaten, burnt cake!" I laugh. "May I?" she asks, and I nod and swipe my hair back. Her touch is invoking and simultaneously soothing.

"There are some papers that you need to sign downstairs. Come on, before my son gets annoyed that he hasn't seen his beautiful wife for five minutes. He can be a tad overbearing, you know. Something else he gets from John!"

As I follow his mother into the kitchen, Sloan's face instantly turns from borderline unimpressed to ecstatic.

Sat at the dining table, Hugh places down document after document. Each comes with its own legal explanation that I don't understand. The door opens, and I glance up to see Stuart in his scrubs.

"This better be good, Foster! I've been on duty for thirteen hours – it's seriously unlucky for some! Hi, Julia," he says, kissing her cheek, and picking up Sloan's mug and downing the remaining coffee.

"It's very good, Doc. We need an independent, trustworthy witness, and they don't come more independent or trustworthy than you. Besides, everyone else is busy." Sloan picks up an agreement of some description and studies it.

"So, if you just read through and sign here." Hugh points to the execution page. "And here," he says again, pointing.

"I'm sorry, but what am I signing? A prenup?"

Although I know, without a shadow of a doubt, Sloan would *never* make me sign anything that would be detrimental to my future, it will take me hours to read these properly.

Hugh laughs. "No. Mr Foster is signing over fifty per cent of his estate to you."

"*What?*" I ask, a sickly regurgitation bubbling in my stomach. "I thought it was all your mother's?"

Sloan comes and sits next to me. "I lied! As my wife, you are now a rightful owner of everything. The business, hotels, clubs; everything."

My eyes widen, it's a lot to take in. Pen to paper, my hand moves. Sometime later, experiencing what I fear may be Carpal Tunnel setting in, I mark the last one. Looking at it, I bite my cheek and grin.

"What?" Sloan asks.

I stare up at my beautiful, empathic man. "Signing Mrs Foster is another first. The best first."

With a cocky swagger, he perches himself beside me. "The best and last." Taking the pen, he scrolls his signature over the page. Handing it over to Stuart, he countersigns, then leaves the room with a goodbye.

"Now, how about we get rid of these three and recommence our honeymoon?" He looks up to the ceiling.

"How about you exercise that thing called self-control?" his mother's voice breaks the sexual tension instantly. "Are you done?" she asks from the doorway.

"Apparently so!" he answers, unimpressed.

"Good. I thought I would take my new daughter out today. Is that okay with you?"

"Fine, but you take-"

"Devlin's on his way over."

Sliding into my jacket, Hugh's car disappears up the driveway, passing Dev's. He climbs out and opens his arms wide for my mother-in-law.

"Beautiful women just gravitate towards me!" Dev exclaims, with a sloppy kiss on her cheek.

"Hmm, like flies on shit!" Sloan mutters, going back inside.

Julia laughs and shakes her head, a hint of Charlie's playfulness coming through. Just like Soph, she's so much like her mother, it's frightening. Going back inside for my bag, Devlin follows.

"What did the shady solicitor want?" he asks sarcastically. He winks at me and moves after Sloan down the hallway.

"I signed over half of everything."

"Shit! No wonder she looks ready to keel over. Wait, does that mean she owns…a third of WS?" Sloan's grin stretches from ear to ear. "Does my uncle know this?" Sloan shakes his head. Devlin, all smiles, crosses his arms over his chest. "You've just become my new best friend, little lady!"

"You're so fickle!" I say with a laugh, as he shuffles us out of the door. Turning back, Sloan is holding either side of the frame.

"After you're done, make sure you deposit my mother at John's. I'm going to make a long list of things I really," he grabs my jacket, "really, want to do to you."

"I'll see what I can do." Letting go, I jog over to the car and sit in the back.

Julia's brow furrows, studying my tum. "Hmm, maybe I'll be a relatively young granny after all."

"I'm not pregnant!" I rush out, my cheeks burning.

"No, but if my son gets his way, you will be." She grips my hand, and for once, I'm more concerned that I'll be chasing after dark-haired, blue-eyed children who will tell me no, sooner rather than later.

Sitting in The Savoy, I look around impressed, my other wish finally being fulfilled.

As I sat in the car, my face crimson from the assumption I will be with child imminently, I thought I would end up in some swanky department store, flexing the unlimited plastic. Instead, I've spent the afternoon walking around the Victoria and Albert, absorbing history in the exhibitions on display.

Waiting for Julia to return, I flip through the handful of leaflets I have collected. Devlin slumps into a seat at an adjacent table with his iPad and a stack of sandwiches and cakes in front of him.

"Room for two more?" Looking up, Marie is suited, booted and looking like butter wouldn't melt. Charlie smiles, dressed more casual in skinny jeans and a long sweater. Julia approaches, and Charlie wraps herself around her mother. A spike of jealousy stabs furiously at my heart, and Marie's hand squeezes mine.

Afternoon tea and sympathy is definitely on the menu.

"So, how long have you and John been seeing each other?" Julia asks Marie. Charlie and I instantly snap our heads up. This is interesting, because it's something she has never discussed before.

"Oh," she starts, looking at me cautiously. Whereas I, on the other hand, am wearing a big smile, waiting for the truth. "A while." Her voice trembles and I stroke her hand. Taking a long draw of her water, she turns the ring on my finger.

"How's married life treating you, honey?" she asks, diverting the focus from herself.

It has been three days since my surprise nuptials. Ideally, any normal couple would be on honeymoon in some exotic location, but since I don't have a passport - much to my husband's shock, because let's face it, the eighty-something pounds was better spent elsewhere when I was still living with Sam - we are still in good old Blighty. Although the two days I spent learning the exact thread count of the hotel sheets is ranking high on my best memory list.

"Amazing," I say, lost in the beautiful daydream of yesterday.

"Oh, she's away with the fairies again!" Charlie pipes up in a giggle. Pouring four glasses of champagne, she raises her glass. "To amazing!"

The words chime out, and I take a sip, feeling my hip buzz. Inconspicuously retrieving my mobile, a recording of the bedroom plays - currently decorated with flowers and candles. Rubbing my legs together, the inner need to be consumed by him is the overarching force dominating every cell under my skin.

"Do you think you'll ever get married again, Marie?" Taken aback, she almost chokes from Julia's good-natured intrusiveness. Clearly, another trait both of her children have inherited from her. "I'm sorry, I shouldn't be asking, but he clearly loves you."

"And I love him. But after being burned once, I don't know."

Julia puts down her tea and smiles at her counterpart. "After John's short-lived marriage, I never thought he'd meet anyone again. I mean, he was a bit of ladies' man back then, although he never brought it home with him. But as the kids got older, especially Sloan, he stopped. I guess he just wanted to make the right impression on a boy he considered to be his son."

Marie smiles sadly, hiding her truth under the guise she has formed perfectly. It's her defence mechanism. A way to conceal the pain that she has never imparted, not to me, probably not to John, either.

"I can't wait for Jake to ask me! He's getting down on his knee and everything. And if he doesn't, I'm saying no! I want big and memorable!" Charlie exclaims.

My hip buzzes again, but this time, Julia snatches the phone from me. "He's getting impatient. Let's go before he sends out back up."

Outside, George is stood beside the limo, holding the door open. Julia moves first, until he clears his throat.

"I'm sorry, Ms Emerson, but I'm here for Mrs Foster." Embarrassed, I look at my mother-in-law, who drops her head to one side.

"He wants me out of the way, doesn't he?" I nod nervously, and she gives me a sly grin. "You tell him, that even though I want green-eyed babies, I don't want them in nine months. Let me enjoy New York society before I have to come back and wade in sick and dirty nappies!" She turns, her hair flowing in the wind, causing every older man – and some younger – to observe her beauty.

The car proceeds through the traffic, and I twist my rings in contemplation. I yawn; my tiredness is overpowering. Dozing off, I rest my hand on my stomach, wondering. Although I'm still vigilant in taking my pills, I can't wait for the day I can create life with him. My body relaxes further, and the ultimate dream takes over.

"Wake up, baby." Sloan's voice drifts from inside the dream; hollow and echoing. His palm gently glides over my cheek; his thumb pressing my lips.

A soft, operatic voice filters through as cold water touches my feet. I yelp, my eyes darting open. The pool room is lit atmospherically, tea lights creating an intimate ambience.

Linking my fingers behind his neck, he walks us down the steps into the water, and I fall deeper into his midnight blues.

"I thought we would be upstairs," I murmur, stroking his five o'clock shadow.

"And we will be," he replies, laying me back to float on the surface. Laughing, I swipe my arms out, swimming further from him. With the water up to his chest, he paddles, before he shrugs his shoulders and comes after me.

Gripping the edge at the other side, his large hand secures over my stomach. "Hold tight." Dipping my fingers into the drainage grill, my back tenses while his hand drifts down my abdomen, over my pubic bone and finally over my clit. My head instinctively falls back onto his shoulder.

"Perfect," he compliments.

Pulling my hips back and parting my legs further, he reaches deep inside, rubbing his erection between my cheeks. I turn my head; his kiss is dominant, taking what he wants, but leaving just enough for me to want more.

"Good girl," he says approvingly. His fingers slide deeper, stretching me out perfectly.

Straightening my arms, I push back and look up at the ceiling. My back arches and my breasts peak out at the surface. Joining our lips in half a kiss, I exhale, needing more air.

"Baby..." I whimper, ready to cry out. His hand pumps at my core furiously, the heel gliding over my front.

"Not yet," he says, and I groan, not knowing if I can hold on.

He turns me around, and I wrap my legs around him, moving my lower half, rubbing my already sensitive flesh against his.

"Patience-"

"Isn't a virtue!" I finish.

I push off the side, and he moves us back to the shallow end. Moments later, my back glides up the slant. He parts my knees, admiring me uncomfortably before he slams himself inside. I gasp out, my moan filling the room, drowning out the aria.

Caging his hands above me, his favourite figure of eight motion drives me over the edge. My cry is constant; everything south is tingling beyond belief.

The water laps at my feet when he carefully turns us over, and he runs his hands up my sides, assisting to help me sit tall above him.

"Fuck me, baby."

Entwining my hands in his, he drags them over his head. Bracing myself, I rotate my hips and tighten my muscles, loving the way he hisses in response. He expands inside me and sucks a nipple into his mouth. His groan against my flesh creates a new kind of music in the room; one that is of pure, endless passion.

Flopping my head to his chest, I kiss a slow line up the middle. Leaving our arms outstretched, I twist his ring. He copies my action, smiling beneath me.

"Are you ready for round two, my gorgeous girl?"

I nod continually. "And three, and four."

Clambering out of the pool, he cradles me in his arms. A trail of water follows us upstairs into the bedroom, which is also still softly lit.

"You've been busy."

"Indeed. And in a minute, you will be, too."

Laying me down, he smirks beautifully. Progressing further down my front, he pushes my knees apart and brushes his finger over my core. I lift up as his eyes darken.

"Did I ever mention how much I love to taste my wife?"

Watching his head lower again, my eyes find the ceiling, while my fingers find the sheets, and he proceeds to show me just how much.

Chapter 32

MY EYES ACHE from the amount of time I have spent staring at the screen today. The tap of my pen drowns out the rare silence as I try to reconcile the invoices that Walker tossed at me this morning and then left for a meeting with a new contractor.

My phone starts ringing on the other side of the desk. After nearly an hour of playing phone tennis with Sloan, and his innuendos of how lonely his office is, I flipped it over, refusing to yield. He isn't helping my concentration in the slightest.

The wretched device continues to ring and, unable to avoid him much longer, I shake my head when his text comes through.

Opening the message, I splutter when a snap of his wedding band appears, with the words 'you vowed to honour me'.

Honour, my arse!

If he thinks I'm driving myself across the city just so he can test out the strength of my knicker elastic, and the sturdiness of his boardroom table again, he has another thing coming. Not to mention, I've spent more time naked than dressed lately, and I probably am going to end up both pregnant and suffering a severe case of cystitis at this rate.

Still staring at the message, I smile. It has been exactly two weeks since our impromptu, intimate ceremony. In that time, he has become very inventive in bringing our vows to life. The words have repeatedly been reaffirmed in the heat of passion.

And a lot of champagne has been consumed in the process.

Staring at my own ring, I've experienced every emotive sensation it represents between us. A union for life – a promise of forever. It's even more significant since this was his father's ring; a promise to his mother before fate intervened and proved supreme.

A tear comes to my eye as the unimaginable idea of not having him hits me. The loneliness I felt in the time we were shamelessly torn apart, and again, when I took it upon myself to preserve whatever dignity I still carried, it never felt like this.

A life without him in it is indescribable.

And soul-destroying.

Replying with a simple capitalised *no*, I put it back down and finish inputting the figures in the rare silence.

Gratefully, the guys have pretty much left me alone these last few weeks. Not only am I finally settling into the old routine of work every day, plus the constant presence of either Devlin or Tommy darkening my shadow, I have also gotten to know Julia - or Jules - very well.

I would be lying if I said it wasn't hard to see with her every day, knowing she was already up to speed with all the trauma that has pierced my short life sporadically, but unfortunately, she is also plagued by that hurt, too. Not only for me, but for her own daughter.

As we said goodbye at the airport, she took me in her arms and apologised for her part in keeping Sloan away from me. Naturally, I smiled respectfully, but it's water under the bridge now. Whilst I want to remember the good times, I'm slowly learning to compartmentalise the bad and store them away indefinitely again.

I admit, the urge to ask Sloan to speak of those lost years is truly tempting. Walker once promised he would tell me, and I pushed aside the idea of approaching him with the overdue request. It wasn't right to be asking such things while she was still here, but now that she has flown back to New York – with an open offer of extended visitation – the idea isn't so unpalatable.

Picking up the next invoice, my phone starts again. I huff out, pissed off that with all his distraction, a job which should have taken me only an hour or so has taken almost triple the amount of time.

The infernal noise stops, and I turn it off completely. My fingers run over the keyboard at speed as I finish inputting the figures. The skies outside have darkened, and a flash of lightning illuminates as the rain beats against the window.

Rolling back on my chair, I pull down the blinds but am spooked by the dark shadow lingering outside. A shudder runs through me, because today I've been left completely alone. Even Tommy is out. Squinting, I can't make out the shadow too well, but the prickles on my neck cause my blood to freeze over and a chill to erupt.

I grab my phone. With my finger over the 'nine', the office line starts to ring. "Good afternoon, Walker Security," I answer, still watching the hooded figure walking a pothole into the pavement.

"Hey, honey. We're on our way back. See you in twenty," Walker says.

"Okay," I reply nervously. The silence on the other end is deafening, until he breathes hard.

"Kara?"

"Erm... I'm fine, but someone is loitering outside."

A hiss sounds through my eardrum, realising I've just ignited the catalyst. Again, another harsh breath bounces down the line, and I hold firm, refusing to give the unknown credence.

"Stay inside. I'll deal with it when we get there."

He hangs up, and I stare down at the steel fencing, watching the camera move under the live feed. The unfortunate thing about this location, is the fact that every walk of life comes here, since it's also peppered with ageing office blocks, builder's merchants, and the salvage yard around the corner. Whoever it is might just be an innocent bystander, lost in the maze of small streets. Then again, it might be someone who preys on the innocent, someone I dare not give life to again.

Squeezing my eyes, appreciating the reality that I've foolishly closed the lid on, I jump when the phone rings again. Grabbing it for the second time, I bring it to my ear.

"John, I'm fine."

"Hi, Kara," Stuart greets from the other end. His tone is lacking, and the already terrified sensations tearing at my insides deepen.

"Stuart..." I break down before he has even said the words.

It's finally happened.

"Kara, I'm sorry..." His voice trails off while I slouch to the floor.

She didn't make it.

I just started my shift.

I'm very sorry.

My body shakes uncontrollably as the reality hits me like a ball and chain. I always knew this was the way it would end for her - one way or another - but there was always hope. Hope that was fragile and unobtainable, but still *hope.*

"Can I see her?" I pray he says yes. The last memory I have of her will not be in the goddamn morgue. Forgetting everything that has brought us to this moment, the things that have been said and done over the last twenty years, I refuse to have that final memory of her etched in my mind should I think of her in the future, because I know I shall. Her memory will be a permanent fixture in my shattered heart.

"Of course."

"Thank you," I reply and take a deep breath, preparing myself for the obliteration that will shortly be mine. "I'll be there as soon as I can."

Hanging up, I dial Walker's number, but it's engaged. As my bad luck would have it, after trying the other four numbers of the men who have seemingly vanished off the face of the earth, I succumb and ring the last.

"Good afternoon, Emerson and Foster, Sophie Morgan speaking." I press my lips together at her cheery greeting. Unable to formulate the right words, when her relationship with Sam was always one of mutual hate, I hang up. Grabbing my belongings, I run out of the room and down the stairs.

Throwing myself into the Evoque and locking the doors, I wait at the gates as I tap in the code. I study the street; whoever was waiting with suspicious intent has apparently gone. Again, it's a false sense of security that is bringing me little comfort, but it's still comfort, no less.

I fight back the tears as I begin my final journey to see the woman who consoled me when I was broken. She who assured me everything would get better. She who enabled me to create this life for myself, both the good and the bad.

And she, who will, in time, become just another faded memory, tucked away in the outer reaches of my already damaged, corrupt mind.

The sound of my terrified steps reverberates through the corridors. Trying to hold off the unavoidable for as long as possible, I have purposely taken the long way to Sam's room.

Approaching the ward, the nurses on duty instantly stare down, or find something to keep themselves occupied. Their sincere expressions are lost on me because I lost her the moment I opened my front door and the bastard Kray wannabe was sitting in my living room. Whether this was the final intention in his unknown game at that point, who knows, but nonetheless, she was on borrowed time the day she crossed his path.

It's a grave thought, but I am, too. Always will be.

"Kara?"

Pivoting on my heels, my hands cover my mouth, and I feel my knees give way from the rest of my body. Stuart grabs me before I hit the deck completely.

"Let it out," he urges, pinning me against him, not allowing me to lose control alone.

I cry irrepressibly, the weight of the last two decades bearing down on me, until I feel it will pull me under and never give me the freedom to breathe. Gripping Stuart's back, I sob out every tear imaginable, remembering every moment unimaginable.

With my eyes closed, raw from mourning, I step back. Dragging my sleeve over my face, my legs move. One step, two, three, and before I know it, the door of damnation is looming in front of me. Taunting me, provoking me, inadvertently showing me I have led her to this place. A place that will also hold me, and in the darkness consume me.

The silence is thick, deathly, when I step inside. As Stuart flicks on the light, I jolt, attempting to shuffle myself back out. I can't do this. I can't sit here, speaking words I know she will definitely never hear. Stuart, already anticipating my action, blocks my escape.

"We once talked about chances. This is the last chance you will get to see her properly. The next time you talk to her, it will be to her gravestone."

Nodding, although not quite sure what I am nodding at, I suck it up, because he's right. Slowly converging upon her lifeless form, I reach out and stroke her face gently. She still feels warm but gone are the mass tangle of tubes and machinery assisting to preserve life.

Now, it's just her.

Just Samantha.

Lurching back, my tears fall, and my body shakes as I try to convey comprehensible speech. Stuart grips my shoulders and moves me around to sit in the chair.

"Last chance, honey." I look up him with sad eyes, and he quickly leaves the room. I stare at the door for a long time. What can I say to her that I haven't already? Would she hear it, wherever her soul may roam now? Would she even care if she could?

I carefully trail my fingertips up her arm. It's a bizarre sight, seeing her like this, knowing she has finally gone, and yet staring at her, she could just be sleeping.

"I love you." And I really do.

These are the only words that will ever mean anything. Setting aside the tumultuous events that we would all prefer to forget, I never stopped loving her. I may have told Sloan that in another time I would've washed my hands of her, but we both know they were just words to pacify him. Because in truth, I never could. That's why I endured her antics year after year, lagging behind, picking up the pieces. Praying it would get better.

We would always be two halves of a broken soul. Just like my past binds me to him, it also tethers me to her. Bound together through a childhood of betrayal by those that were meant to give us life and protect us from harm.

Touching her wrist, I wrap my hand around the bracelet and lay my head on the bed. Re-enacting the solitude I felt performing this previously, my brain stops running wild, and harmony flows through me.

A small curve tugs at my lips, my mind drawing out years-old memories. The girl whose blonde pigtails flailed out when she would run towards me, arms wide open. To the girl who sat beside me, hiding her own bruises and pain when I needed someone to care.

"Kara?"

I lift my heavy head; the life inside me has all but drained away. My eyes are sore and tired, but my memories are alive, firing up everything I had forgotten.

"John's looking for you. Did you tell anyone you were coming here?" Stuart asks.

"No. I tried calling them all, but no one answered." Standing, feeling every muscle silently protest, I roll my shoulders and feel the knot in them tighten.

He picks up the clipboard from the end of the bed and pulls off the forms I had signed. The tearing of the paper is louder than it should be, and he stuffs them into his pocket.

"At least take some solace that you didn't have to make this decision. You didn't put the final nail in the coffin, that bastard did."

"But I helped. Either way, I'm responsible for her lying here." He doesn't respond but looks away with unambiguous guilt. "All the arguments we've had, the lies, the days I could've wrung her neck, it doesn't matter now. Still, this is my fault."

"Here." He leans over and unfastens the bracelet - my last gift to her - and passes it to me. "You can request the funeral home to put it back on if you want her buried in it."

Buried.

The word is so final, but I'm deceiving myself, because this door had closed the moment she opened hers to Deacon for the last time. But in doing so, she will finally experience the peace in death that she would never have in life.

The door opens again and an orderly enters, bowing his head in respect. Stuart, ever the professional and still compassionate friend, holds me while the man drapes the sheet over her body completely, signalling her final destination.

Unable to take much more, I run from the room. The corridors are a never-ending maze of clinical brightness, and I feel the minuscule contents of my stomach roil with the acid. Reaching the entrance, I double over the nearest bin and throw up. The retching leaves my body worn out, but I can't stop. The waters rush my mouth again, and the need to purge every fucked-up past decision is the only choice I have left.

The air dispels my lungs in deep pants, and I carefully straighten myself, my stomach still experiencing the waves of culpability churning inside.

Inside the car, I slam my head against the rest repeatedly, and finally, I let it out. A heart-wrenching scream emits the confines of my throat.

Lost inside my own heartbreak, I tilt my head as raindrops hit the windscreen. The prickles on my neck heighten and suddenly, a raw sensation burns. Turning the ignition and activating the wipers, a few hundred yards across the diminishing light of the car park, is the same figure from outside the office. He starts to walk towards me, and I wonder what I should do.

I find my phone, switch it back on and dial. Marie answers in seconds. "Hi, honey."

"It's done, she's gone," I say in a defeated tone and end it.

My eyes remain fixed straight ahead, until a thud bangs on my window. I jolt as my father appears in my peripheral vision, standing in the rain, soaked to the bone. Looking between him and the hooded figure, I know this can't be coincidence. In the corner of my eye, Ian's hand reaches up to the glass. My finger lingers on the button, and I lower it a fraction. I remain silent, because there's nothing left for us to say to each other.

"Kara?"

"How did you find me here?" I whisper sadly.

"I followed you. I'm sorry about Sam." I shoot daggers at him as the tips of his fingers curl around the glass. Slamming my hand on the wheel, my hatred answers for me.

"What more do you want?"

"Kara, please. I'm sorry. I've fucked up everything," he whimpers.

"You've got your money, so just leave and never come back!"

Dropping his hand, he shuffles almost lifelessly across the tarmac, until his silhouette disappears into the night.

Finally, I have closure.

My phone starts to ring again, and I rotate it in my palm. All the while the now familiar figure beckons closer and closer, then the metal reverberates from his hands slamming down on the bonnet. The hoodie conceals him, but I know. Lifting his head, he stares cruelly.

Deacon.

He wipes the rain from his brow; his evil grin fixes firmly across his face. My anger, steadily rising, is prepared to break free and damn the fucking consequences. I rock my foot on the pedal, the car pulling against the strength of the handbrake, desperate to lurch forward at speed.

Slowly, methodically, he walks around to my window. The muscles in my neck pull taut, and I shift my eyes. Blowing me a kiss, he mouths the word *soon* again. Watching him walk away, I don't doubt him for a second.

Soon will come full circle.

And so will I.

Pressing my head to the steering wheel, my anguish fills the car. My mother, my father, Samantha, and now the future that is guaranteed to be torn away from me again. Wiping my eyes, I acknowledge the sound of ringing.

"Hi," I answer timidly.

"Baby, stay where you are. Parker's on his way over to get you. I need to make sure you're okay," Sloan says with concern.

Salty tears continue to sting my eyes, because whilst I have just got closure on one aspect of my life, the door has fully opened again on another.

"No, there's something I need to do first. I'll see you at home."

"Kara? Kara!" I hang up, because I can't listen to him console me over the death of a woman he openly despises. And also, over the fact that his enemy has just walked from the darkness back into my light again.

I exit the car park and drive to the one place I hate, because within its walls is the only person who will give me the truth.

Slipping out of the car, I study the area as I make my way down the alley. Glancing back, right now I'm being foolish, taking unnecessary risks that could result in dire consequences again.

I slap my hand on the bell and wait for him to open the door. Its unlocking is my undoing, and I fall into him as soon as I see him. No words are spoken as he hustles me inside and bolts the door. He keeps me close as he guides us through the back corridors, up a flight of stairs, and into an office.

Finally letting me go, I wipe my eyes and nose, and glance around. Jeremy motions towards the sofa under a window that overlooks the entire club.

"Kara?"

I shake my head. "Sam...she... She died today."

"Oh, shit, I'm sorry," he replies. "I tried to help her, you know." Staring into his eyes, I know he's speaking the truth, except his words fell the same way mine did – on deaf ears.

"My father was at the hospital, asking for forgiveness... I hate him so much. Him and my mother!"

Jeremy sighs, moves closer, and wraps his arm around my shoulder. "It's too little, too late, but that's the pain talking. We both know you don't hate her. To say it means you hate a part of yourself," he murmurs.

"It's all my fault." Drying my face, I know I have to tell him about my other visitor. "Deacon was there, too," I whisper.

He instantly drops me, then moves to the desk and snatches up his phone.

"No, please don't."

"Kara..."

"I just want to close my eyes and forget. Just for a while." Curling up on the sofa, he drapes a throw over me, and I hold it closer, desperate to feel safe in the cold, harsh reality that has finally come to pass.

"I'm guessing the money's already gone then?" Walker mutters.

"How long has she been out?" Sloan asks tenderly.

"Not long. I've no idea what's going on in her head, but she's blaming herself."

Sloan's sigh fills my ears. "She always will. That will never stop."

"That's not all. Deacon was there."

"At the hospital?"

"Apparently. She needs to call the police, and get it followed it up," Jeremy's voice trails off.

"No, I know what to do. I know exactly who to call."

"John, don't."

"No? Have you forgotten what the Blacks did to you? How addicted you were? Forgotten how you got that scar? No, I didn't fucking think so. You want her forgiveness, you fucking back me, sunshine!"

"Sloan, do you want to talk some sense into this arsehole?"

"No, because the police don't seem to give a fuck. She will never live a full life until he's gone. John, do whatever it takes."

Rubbing my eyes as they continue to speak around me, soft touches stroke over my face, and I focus intently as Sloan fills my sight.

"Hey, my love." I cautiously shuffle away, until a few feet separate us on the sofa. "Baby, talk to me."

He looks tortured as I wrap my arms around my knees and rock, consoling myself. I can't help it, because I know whatever leaves my mouth will not affect him in the slightest. Yes, he will spare a thought for me, but he won't give a toss about her.

I laugh loudly. The sound is terrifying, even to myself. "She's gone, you got what you wanted. She's not a threat anymore."

He stands, a look of *what the fuck* spreads across his face as he palms his chin. "That's a little fucking low!"

"It's true, isn't it?" I reply, taking in Walker's hardened stance and Jeremy's sympathetic gaze. Yes, it is, and I've known it from the moment he knocked on my old front door and that day's naked conquest answered.

"Baby, I didn't want her dead!"

I shrug off the throw and rush towards the door. Running down the stairs into the VIP, Marie spins around, and Stuart grabs her when she tries to get to me.

"Kara…"

"No!" I scream at her. "Stop lying to me!" Looking up at the office window, Sloan fills the pane perfectly. "I did a really shitty fucking thing in leaving, but none of you went to see her!"

"I did see her!" Marie screams back, breaking free of Stuart. Breathing hard in my face, the fire on my cheek registers her sharp slap. I move away in shock, but notice Stuart looking up with a nod. I turn my attention back to Marie, who is like a bull to my red rag at the moment.

"Once! You. Went. Once!" I scream. I'm losing it completely, and I don't know if I can claw myself back from this. "I fucking hate all of you!" I rip off my rings and throw them on the floor.

"Kara?" Stuart's voice drones out behind me. I turn just in time to see the reflection bounce off the needle before Marie rushes to my front and my knees collapse beneath me. "Ease down," he says, holding me, as my vision fragments and liquid calm subdues me into tranquillity.

"Urgh."

I roll over and slam my arm hard over my face, causing my nose to sting in the process. Looking around, I'm alone in the suite bedroom. Tugging up the duvet, I fold it around myself and shuffle onto the landing and down the stairs.

"Hey, how are you feeling?" Stuart asks when he sees me hanging back in the doorway.

Sloan looks ashen, knowing that he allowed his friend to sedate me to keep me calm. I don't blame him, because if I had been allowed free rein, there's no telling what I might have done.

Then it hits me. My hand. I look down, seeing my rings are back where they rightfully belong.

"A bit groggy."

Sloan makes a move to get up, and I stop my pacing. Identifying my reluctance, he downs the last of the wine he is holding. Marie and Walker watch studiously as I position myself in the living room.

"The nausea will subside shortly. I didn't give you much; just enough for you to rest."

"Just enough to put me down like a dog, more like." I bite my tongue before anything else can roll of it that I don't really mean. I should be grateful they love me enough to put me first when the world implodes spectacularly.

Without further hesitation, I pace towards Sloan, nudging his ankles with my feet. He parts his legs, and I sit on the floor between them and curl my arm around his calf. I strain my neck to look into his eyes, but he reaches down and lifts me onto the sofa.

"I'm sorry."

"So am I," he replies sincerely.

Dropping my head in his lap, my heart thunders inside my chest when I lock eyes with Marie. Sadly, I know it doesn't matter what I say, because the damage has been done. It's evident in her eyes that something in our relationship has now changed.

"Please don't hate me," I murmur.

Her perfect features sadden further, and she instantly stands. "I'll wait in the foyer," she says, quickly grabbing her things.

"I'll walk you down." Stuart takes her hand. "Goodnight."

I sit up as Walker approaches and grips my chin firmly. "It's a hard thing to love someone so much only to have it thrown back in your face. Tomorrow, you apologise. I mean it. You do whatever it takes to make this right. Understand?" He grits his teeth, and I nod my head in disgust. Disgust that I have just fractured a small part of my relationship with the only person ever to show me any kind of affection for such a long time in my life.

I open my mouth to say I will, but nothing comes out. The door shuts, and I break down, weeping into the duvet.

"Let's go to bed. You'll feel better in the morning."

Clenching his shoulder in my fist, I squeeze tight. Except I won't feel better come morning, because nothing will change.

Marie will still be pissed at me, my mother will still be sick, my father and Deacon will still be roaming the city, and Sam will still be dead.

Nothing changes.

Chapter 33

CLUTCHING THE SOLITARY red rose to my chest, black coats flail in the wind. I avert my eyes to Marie, who stares gravely while the vicar conducts his sermon.

It has been six days since my mental breakdown at the club. Five days since I grovelled and made it right. And four days since she said I was right to be angry. And that is the real crux of the problem because I have no right to be incensed at her. I, too, didn't give a second thought of the woman in the gasket until it was too late.

In between then and now, Sloan has singlehandedly organised the funeral. From the stone to the flowers, he did it all – and he paid for it all, too. His one and only gift to her. But I would have given my last breath for anything other than his financial recompense.

I stare into the hollow hole as her place of eternal rest is slowly lowered. Dropping the rose into the grave, I finally raise my head. Jake and Charlie, followed closely by Sophie and Stuart, start to walk away. Tommy, Jeremy and Parker follow by example.

Looking at the rest of the mourners, people she had worked with, paying their last respects - if that's what they are really here for - there is no sign of her parents. Sloan called them, much to their disinterest. He even offered to pay for their travel and accommodation, but still no show. Why he even bothered was an effort squandered. I knew they wouldn't come. Sam was to them what I was to my own father; a hindrance, a burden. Just like me, she was neither wanted nor needed.

"Are you ready to leave?" Sloan asks gently. He raises my hand, and the glimmer of our rings reflects under the sun. For better, for worse, in sickness and in health, till death us do part. All of the above and more is what we have experienced in our time together.

Gripping his hand, I walk with an empty heart, shrouded in loss, out of the cemetery towards the car. Staring out of the window, I watch the world drift by.

"Do you mind if we go to the office? There are some documents I need to collect." His hand curls tightly around mine, and I agree because any change of scenery is welcome right now.

Outside the office, Sloan climbs out and reaches in for me. "The Aston's in the basement, thank you, George," he says, as the man pats his shoulder and departs immediately.

Heading into the building, Sloan's grip never falters as we board the first lift. My stomach feels empty, until the doors ping open and a deathly silence greets us. Something feels off. I peer into the empty rooms, and a sense of foreboding lingers inside my heart of something waiting.

Inside his office, I sit at his desk while he retrieves various documents from the cabinet. Crouching down on his knees, he tilts my chin and strokes it. He is about to say something when Walker and Jake storm in.

"We've got a problem." Walker looks between us, his age lines more prominent than usual. "Franklin Black is outside your house."

Sloan's fist thumps down on the desk, and he lets out an angry huff. "Well, let's not keep the old bastard waiting, shall we?"

"Sloan..." I say in a panic.

"Don't worry, he'll be gone shortly. Right, let's get this shit sorted once and for all. I want him gone." He presses his hand into my lower back and guides me to the door. "John, have you got it?"

"Yeah, I've got it alright." He pats a large bag over his shoulder. "The others are on their way over after they drop everyone off."

Sloan turns and holds me, but that look of undeniable concern is etched over his forehead. "Don't let him provoke you." I nod, because his words are easy to say, maybe not so easy to convey.

A crack of thunder and lightning darkens the sky above as we speed out of the city. A storm in a teacup is brewing overhead, ready to burn at any moment.

When we up outside, Tommy and Parker are already waiting, each astride a motorbike. Walker's Range Rover idles behind us, and the black Mercedes of Franklin Black is blocking the gates.

Sloan climbs out and strides over with purpose. Smashing his fist against the window, it lowers. Franklin's expression of glee is evident, even from my obscured view.

"Move your fucking car!" Sloan's face is unrecognisable. The look plaguing him is one I've never witnessed. He folds his arms and steps back, while Franklin does as wisely advised.

Tearing open the car door, Sloan slams it shut behind him, and I cower. He turns, sensing my fear before he has even seen it compel me.

"Remember what I said."

Before I can reply, he slams his foot down and speeds down the driveway. He breaks harshly, climbs out, then lifts me over the handbrake. Heading straight into the office, Walker and Jake are two steps behind. The three of them move to the safe and Walker drops down the ominous holdall, while Jake plucks out three guns and starts loading them.

Realising I'm watching with morbid curiosity, he gives me a pained look. Without so much as an explanation, Sloan snatches up one of the guns and slides it into the back of his trousers. Walker does the same, then checks the other firearm concealed at his side.

Seconds later, the doorbell rings.

I shift from one foot to the other, watching in astonishment as Frankie Black saunters down the hallway, surveying his former marital home. His eyes narrow, obviously revisiting days gone by. Days when he wasn't known as a thug and supplier of illegal narcotics, instead they were his glory days. The only time in his miserable life that his short, ill-fated union granted him money and status.

Approaching slowly, he runs his hand down my face, and I freeze.

"Get the fuck away from my wife, Black!" Sloan shouts, moving from his position in the living room.

Franklin spins round, thoroughly surprised. "Wife? Well, well, little sweets, isn't this an interesting turn of events. One that benefits me more than it will you. But there's plenty of time to discuss that later. Will a turn around the gardens and a lap of the pool be permitted?" He glimpses over at his ex-stepson mockingly.

Yes, he is ready to taunt.

"You know what I liked about you, little Petersen? You always knew when to stay hidden." He reaches for my top and I back away. A shuffle behind me indicates someone else's displeasure of the bastard touching me again. "I'd like to say I feel sympathetic, but if you'd have stayed hidden, you wouldn't be suffering now. You did this to yourself."

"Don't fucking touch her!" Sloan roars again and pulls me into his side. Insolently, Franklin ignores him and pitches his black gaze on me.

"I would like to say I approve of your betrothed, sweets, but sadly, I do not. There's no excuse to marry a bastard, regardless of how filthy rich he is. Just ensure that when your divorce papers come through, you get what's yours. Which leads us nicely to the reason why I'm gracing you with my presence."

"I won't warn you again. You stay the fuck away from my wife, my sister and my mother!" Sloan's hands fist at his sides. His eyes are wide, venomous.

Franklin faces him head-on, and it's clear the man really doesn't have any cares in the world. "I don't want your mother, son."

"I'm not your fucking son!"

"True, but since I'm the only father you've ever had, you should be grateful, son." Franklin, thoroughly enjoying seeing Sloan lose it, rubs his hands together.

"No, my father is dead. You're just the evil fucker she married on the rebound."

"Yes, well, maybe I should've taken care of it when she told me she was pregnant. You think so highly of me, I'm disappointed."

Turning to Walker, who has one hand behind his back and the other in his pocket, he shakes his head. My body tightens, and I brace myself for more mudslinging.

"Enough of this shit, you give me what I came for!"

Sloan cradles his chin with his thumb and forefinger, a mocking laugh fills the room as he stands up to the man who has destroyed everything, in one way or another.

"I'll give you your fucking blood money, but you make sure you get as far away from here as possible!"

Franklin's jaw grinds, and he looks at me, an arrogant smile flashing over his face. "Fine. Two should do it."

"Done. But if you come back here again, I will personally bury you."

Franklin's booming laugh erupts, and he moves in front of Jake, who has got his gun out, and Walker, who is clearly holding back whatever he really wants to do with his.

"Mr Walker! I should have known you wouldn't be too far behind, holding his hand, guiding him through life!" He stops and looks back. "Little Sloan, all money and power, but stop making empty threats, boy."

"Oh, they're not empty. I once questioned whether or not I could kill a man in cold blood, and when I look into your eyes and see those of your bastard son, I will gladly do time for you both." Sloan's eyes are dark, the blackest I have ever seen, and the underlying truth is, the threat isn't empty.

"I think our conversation here is done. Have the money transferred to this account. As soon as it lands, I promise you'll never see me again."

"And Deacon?" Jake asks from the other side of the room. "You better make sure he disappears, too. Because if you don't, the next time you see him, he'll be in a fucking box in pieces. Even if I have to do it myself."

"Well, at least one of you has big balls! I think I might have to congratulate my daughter on such a good choice. You could take heed of her, Kara. However, I've not seen him for…nearly a year." He turns with a knowing glare. I shake my head at the memory and leave the room.

I halt in the hallway; Tommy and Parker are waiting outside the door, both holding guns. Seeing the way they all carry them with such ease is comforting, and it really shouldn't be.

"And Ian Petersen?" Sloan asks coyly, needing some verification as to what my father's true intentions are. Franklin chortles, and I stop at the top of the stairs.

"Up until a fortnight ago, I also hadn't seen him in nearly a year, either. You can imagine my surprise when he showed up on my doorstep, stuffed two grand in my hand, bought a bag of blow and then left." I grip my hand over my chest, realising what I finally have to do.

Sat in the spare room, toying with my old mobile, sometime later the front door slams. Standing at the window, I watch as Franklin climbs into his car with a smug grin of finality. The wheels crunch on the gravel before it disappears into the countryside.

Two ghosts have been laid to rest today.

Two down, two to go.

"Baby?" Sloan calls out from downstairs.

I look at the door; I really don't want to go back down there. Taking a deep breath, I make my way downstairs, but the living room is now empty. Entering the office, Sloan and Walker are sat in front of the computer, along with Jeremy.

"Hey, come here." Sloan pats his knee, and I perch myself on it. He strokes my face, knowing today was hard enough already without this to put the cherry on top. "Baby, the bastard said something-"

"I heard him." I stare into his eyes and become lost - more than I already am. Lost in love with him, lost in my heart with him. Lost in my own head with only myself.

"Done!" Walker spits out and pushes the keyboard aside. He turns and stares at us, a sad expression when it should be one of elation, considering Franklin Black has finally gone.

For now, at least.

Looking at the others in the room, Tommy clenches his fist and rotates it. I look back at Sloan, who is still holding me tight, but his resigned look builds.

"Baby, I just need to get out of here for a while." He kisses me, and I cling to him until I know I have to let him go.

"Be safe, all of you." I kiss him again. "I love you."

"And I you." Then he is gone.

Minutes later, the reverberation of bikes revving outside dominates the silence.

Twitching the curtain, Sloan, now dressed in jeans, boots and leather jacket, mounts his bike, then the five of them plough up the driveway.

"Do you think he'll come back?" I ask, wondering if Walker is prepared to answer that loaded question.

"Don't worry, honey, he's been riding with them for years."

I chuckle pathetically. "No, he'll always come back to me. I meant Franklin." I turn around and perch on the windowsill.

"No. He's finally got what he wanted." He leans on the desk directly in front of me. "He'll take the money and disappear. It means things around here will change, though."

"Like what?"

"Well, Jules won't have to hide away anymore, for starters. I'm sorry you had to find out the way you did."

I breathe out. "I understand. I can only imagine what they must have lived through."

He pushes off the desk and starts to walk out of the office.

"John?" He looks over his shoulder at me. "The last time Franklin made an appearance, Sloan asked me to ask you about how you met his mum. I'm calling it in."

Reluctance streaks across his face. "Go and grab whatever you need. I'm sure you or the kid won't want to be here tonight."

Trudging away, I pause in front of him. Reaching up, I gently kiss his cheek.

"Thank you."

Chapter 34

THE ATMOSPHERE IS dense, as we drive through the damp, grey streets. Pulling up outside the hotel, Walker throws his keys at the porter.

I grip my bag and proceed through the foyer. Pressing the lift button, I slide into the back corner when it arrives and start my silent countdown.

Trepidation overcomes me when we step into the suite. Leaving Walker to engage the security system, I head into the kitchen and drop my bag on the island.

"Grab a couple of glasses," he says, walking out with a bottle of wine.

As I enter Sloan's office, he strides over to the cabinet and drags out some files – the ones I had found ages ago. He turns in my direction, his expression tormented by guilt. Sitting down, I pick up the picture of Sloan and Charlie together as kids.

"Why did he do this to us?" I mutter rhetorically, undecided as to whom I'm referring to.

"I don't know, honey. That's the truth." He approaches and drops down the files.

I cover my mouth, debating whether or not I want to see what lurks inside. I guess part of me still believes the less I know, the safer I will be. But even I know that isn't true anymore. The walls I had built around myself were never going to be strong enough to keep out the real perpetrators of pain.

"Open them," he whispers.

"Am I going to like what I find?" He shakes his head remorsefully.

I pick one up and pull out the documents. The first thing I see is a picture of my teenage self, and I stare at it in disbelief. I'd forgotten just how fragile I looked back then. It's a wonder social services didn't come and take me into care sooner. I drop the picture and pick up the next document. It's the missing person's report from Manchester Police. Reading it, tears sting my eyes.

"It's not wrong, is it?"

"What's that?"

"When kids go missing and end up walking the streets of London. You don't realise it at the time, but if you make it through, you're one of the lucky ones."

My hand shakes as I reach for the next file. He beats me to it and spreads the contents over the desk. My eyes work over each piece; they depict my life from fifteen to only a few years ago. I'm astonished; I had never seen anyone taking these pictures. Then again, I'd spent so much time in my own head, some days I was lucky if I could see beyond my own outstretched arm.

Walker watches me absorb it all. "Does Marie have a file, too?" I ask, and he grins, rubs his jaw and leans back.

"I was twenty-two when I first met Jules. A friend of mine, Dominic Archer, worked in security, installing systems, personal security, that kind of thing. He said the gig was fairly easy, and the money was good. I hadn't been out of the army long, and I was finding it hard adjusting back into normal society. I had a few jobs on and off, door work, serving court papers, but nothing was really concrete, so eventually, I agreed. One day, a woman called the office, inquiring about what type of services we carried out. I was intrigued when she said money wasn't an issue, and so I invited her over for a chat. I expected some wealthy socialite to come in, requesting a guard to man her electric gates day and night. My dealings with the wealthy always made me believe they had disillusions of grandeur, but the woman who turned up on the doorstep was far from disillusioned."

He reaches over, unscrews the bottle and pours two small glasses.

"She stood there in a large hat, a full-length mac and a pair of dark sunglasses. It was the middle of a rare, hot summer. I thought it was a joke, until she hobbled up to the office and removed them. I was speechless. Her eyes were swollen, her nose was broken, and she could barely speak her own name. We sat for hours whilst she spoke slowly of her husband who would beat her senseless over something of insignificance."

I take a long sip as the door creaks, and Sloan quietly slips inside. A strong smell of petrol emanates from him. He sits on the sofa, emotionless and passive, and I brace my hands tight on the desk just so I don't go to him for comfort.

"Jules spoke of the times her husband would disappear for days on end. How her friends would comment on seeing him in the casinos, gambling with different women. She always brushed it off, but confessed she would be happy if he left. Except, every time she raised the subject of divorce, he got violent."

He picks up a framed picture of a young Charlie and her mother, deep in thought.

"The next day, I went along to the house. Needless to say, I was impressed. I remember looking up at the gates, realising even the wealthy got dealt a shitty hand from time to time. I stood there, ringing the bell, then two terrified kids came running up the driveway. Sloan was twelve and Charlie was eight. Seeing the looks on their faces, and the faded bruises peeking through the sleeves of their t-shirts, it changed me. It was at that moment I knew I would never turn away from them. And I never have."

I stare, seeing him trying his best to disguise his emotions. I blink, also trying to hide mine.

"How did Frankie take to you?" I query.

"He didn't. He came home the same night, demanded cash, but left empty-handed. Of course, it was never going to be that easy. Not long after, Jules was diagnosed and was booked in to start immediate chemo. Frankie took advantage of the situation and dragged it out as long as he could. It took months for him to sign the divorce papers. All the while Jules was still recovering and still raising his bastard spawn, or rather trying to keep him under control, since Franklin let him run riot. Even his own mother didn't want him. About a year later, he picked up Deacon, and we never saw him again. Not even when Deacon attacked Charlie."

"And I'm the one who brought them back."

"No, it was only a matter of time." He looks at Sloan with an expression of pure guilt. "Before Jules left for New York, I made a promise that I would always look after them, and that's what I've done ever since." His voice starts to break, and I understand why they concealed her.

Sloan slowly approaches and picks up the eight-year-old photo of me. "This was always my favourite," he says with a sad smile. Walker stands and squeezes his shoulder.

"I'm going to take Marie out for dinner. I'll see you both tomorrow."

I pull his arm. "You're a good man, John Walker." He smiles and finds his way out.

Sloan looks over the documents and then to me. "This is all of it. Every piece of information I had him collecting on you over the years. There were times I would sit here and just look at you, wondering what you were doing, who you were with. There was one time when we came back to the hotel, and there were two homeless girls outside.

John looked like he'd seen a ghost. I glanced back at the brunette, remembering the last time I saw you. Unknown to me at the time, I didn't need to remember, because it was you."

"I remember."

And I do. The way Stacy and I had planned to get a free meal for the night. But I got something better - I got a mother and a few invisible guardian angels.

"I remember being stood by the board outside. I remember seeing a vehicle pull up. That's also the day I became Marie's."

"Do you remember the next time?" he asks softly, trailing his fingers up and down my arm. I shake my head, wondering what he is referring to.

"A few years ago, I was in a restaurant with Christy…" He quickly peeks at me.

"It's okay to talk about her." I give him a small smile, wanting him to continue.

"We had the same old argument again; why didn't I want to commit. I had been *seeing* her, on and off, for years. I never loved her, because my heart belonged to someone else." He raises his eyebrows, and I smile shyly. "She stormed off outside. I was ready to start shouting at her, but a woman stepped in my path. She put her hands on my chest, and I was finally looking at the face that had haunted me for six years."

I let my head fall back and look up at the ceiling. "Over the years, only three people have ever managed to make me feel calm; the man who saved me, the one on the street, and finally, you. And you were all one in the same." I shake my head, not quite believing that chance had brought us together on numerous occasions.

He picks me up and sits us back down. "Well, I did turn fate in my favour a few times. That, and John and the boys following you occasionally assisted," he says with a grin.

"Things could have been so different," I murmur rhetorically. "How did you get the police and social services reports?" I ask, thumbing through the documents, reading the dossiers of abuse and pain.

"John has some contacts up in Manchester."

I skim over the hospital report, while my hand instantly rubs the scar on my thigh. My lids flutter, remembering the bloodied knife tip, the punch to my face, and my hands being tethered above my head. For a moment, I relive the kicking and screaming until I was no more.

Collecting up the pictures and putting them in order, I hold them tightly. "I don't recognise her anymore. She isn't who I am now."

"No. This girl is gone. She left the night you marched into this suite with intent. She left the day you came back."

"I want to go home."

He lifts me up and carries me into the bedroom. Tightening my legs around him, my back gently touches the wall behind us. His hand presses my chest, directly over my beating heart.

"You are home," he whispers, turning to the bed.

Chapter 35

SIPPING MY JUICE, my phone starts to ring. Stretching over the worktop, my mum's name highlights the screen. It has been weeks since I last saw Ian, and I still haven't found it in my heart to call her. I'm still in that place of mourning, but I'm not entirely sure why until I talk to her. The sound dies away, and a single beep indicates a new voicemail.

Sloan, oblivious to anything happening around him, rushes by collecting up what he needs for today's board meeting. I watch intently, needing something else to fix my attention on, while he thumbs through a stack of papers. He stuffs them into his bag and swings it over his shoulder.

"Busy day?" I query.

He smiles, pinching his nose. "Hmm, the headache is starting already. Hopefully, they won't squabble for five hours this time. What are you planning on doing? John said you asked for today off."

"Going out with Marie," I reply far too quickly. Turning to my old phone, sat innocuously on the worktop, I know precisely what I'm doing today. I'm finding my courage.

"Got everything you need?" he asks, kissing my nose. "Walk me out?"

I smile. "Of course."

I gather up my things and slide into my jacket, as I make my way into the private foyer and press the lift button. The doors open seconds later, and I step inside. Counting in my head, the ground floor can't come quick enough.

Striding across the immaculate marble, my steps resound in my ears, and guilt overcomes me as James' head whips up. He nods, but unfortunately, neither of us will forget the night of the ball and the truths that finally saw the light of day.

With one foot in front of the other, George is plodding up and down on the pavement outside. Sloan opens the limo door and throws his bag into the back; the same moment Devlin's convertible pulls up behind.

"Come here," he requests. I tug on the back of his waistcoat, and he leaves me with far too tempting a kiss before grinning and getting into the car.

I watch the limo disappear into the sea of vehicles heading deeper into the city. Turning my back on the street, a prickle of awareness runs from my nape to my tailbone. I rub my arms, then twirl around, unable to see anything - *or anyone* - that has caused it to become apparent.

Still apprehensive, I slip into the BMW and strap up. Craning my head, two drivers opposite shout and gesture obscenely at each other. I lock my door - although futile with the top down - and grin as the 'arsehole' and 'wanker' continue, uncaring of the drivers blaring their horns behind them. Devlin edges out into the madness, as my phone rings from the dash.

"Hey, it's me," Charlie says before I can even say hello. "What are you doing for lunch today?"

"Erm, I don't know. I'm on my way over to Marie's," I lie. Well, technically I am, but after something else that is more pressing and long overdue.

"Well, we'll be in The Swan about twelve-thirty, if you fancy it? Or if his highness lets you. Hopefully, I'll see you later." She hangs up, sounding far too cheery, whilst I'm on edge.

"Are you sure you still want to do this?" Dev asks.

"I'm sure," I respond, half-heartedly.

"You haven't told him, have you?"

I shake my head as Dev pops on his sunglasses and sighs. I know he hates being part of my deceptions, but this is a deception of the best kind. The kind that will eventually ensure I can sleep easy again. *One day.*

We stop outside the building, and I glance over at Sloan's office. What are the chances he might actually be looking down on the street right now? I scrunch my face up, pushing the ridiculous notion aside, then step out.

Pressing the bell, I wait for the inevitable.

"Hello?" Margaret's voice comes over the intercom.

"Hi, it's Kara Foster." She doesn't respond, but the latch releases. Taking the steps two at a time, I push the reception door open.

"Long time, no see!" Margaret says, approaching. I hesitate, then take her hand. She turns my palm, admiring my ring. "I heard a little rumour. Congratulations!" I'm about to reply when the buzzer rings again, and she mutters and goes to answer.

"Hello?"

There is an unwelcome pause until someone answers.

"Erm, hi?" Dev's static voice fills the room. Margaret raises a brow, and I laugh.

"It's Devlin. He's with me. Is it okay if he waits?" Margaret sighs in relief and lets him in. Minutes later, Dev lurks in the doorway, looking around, thoroughly uncomfortable. He passes me a caramel latte, glancing between the few chairs and the exit.

"You can wait, dear. Would you like some biscuits?" Margaret asks him, and his face lights up like Christmas.

Taking the seat next to him, he's all charm when she returns with chocolate digestives and coconut rings. I turn when he nudges my side. "When are we coming here again?" I chortle; he's so cheap. A few treats and he's anyone's.

"I'll see you both in a couple of weeks," David says, holding his office door open, as a teenage girl and her mother step out. I rise as the girl makes eye contact with me, and sadly, I recognise that look. That gaunt, vacant, lifeless stare. I identified it in myself so many times growing up. It breaks my heart to witness it again in another so young.

The girl stops in front of me, not knowing which way to walk. I stand aside to allow her to pass, but watch in horror when she trails her sight to my wrist, the one bare, showing the infliction I've suffered. She takes a breath and smiles sadly. Watching her back trudge towards Margaret, I hope one day she finds her own protector. The same way I have.

"Kara?" David's voice echoes around the small space. Picking up my handbag and jacket, I slowly step into his office.

I look around, somewhat satisfied that nothing has changed. Sitting in what had become my usual seat, I take a sip of coffee and put it down.

"I didn't expect to see you today," David comments. I take a breath, ready to speak words I haven't properly formulated.

"No, I-I-" I stop the instant the stutter takes hold. "It was never my intention to come back. To sit and speak of things that cause me to regress. Truthfully, I guess when I called, I was kind of hoping you'd be full up, but low and behold..." I murmur. He presses his hands together, deep in thought.

"Well, I'm glad you did. It takes courage to walk through my door. So, now you're finally here again, what shall we talk about today?" he queries with a kind smile. I sit back and fold my arms.

"Is it possible to completely forgive someone who saved you, but had inadvertently forsaken you?" It's the first thing out of my mouth, but it's the one thought that has plagued me repeatedly.

Since the wedding and Sam's death, I keep wondering if I have what it takes to turn Jeremy over to the police. As the weeks and months have passed by, I keep wondering if it's a mistake. I know he should be brought to book to answer for his crimes, but ever since he finally confessed and the reasons behind them, I don't know if I can.

"In what context?"

"A friend," I confess shamefully. "A good friend. Someone who is suffering my past alongside me."

"It's not a question of possibilities, more a question of whether or not you can."

"That's what I thought." I pick up my coffee and take another sip.

Sensing I am slipping back into my head, David leans forward. "Tell me what has happened in your life since we last spoke."

I shuffle in the seat, uneasy, wary of divulging too much. But as previously mentioned, inside these walls, unless you are a minor, everything is confidential.

"I don't know where to start," I mumble.

"Why did you decide not to come back, Kara?"

Sighing heavily, I rub my temple. "The last time I left this office, I saw a man I hadn't seen in years. A man who proved that life turns in circles and eventually, we all come back to the beginning." Staring at the bookshelf behind him, I mumble my way through a year of confessions; nightmares I want to keep boxed and sealed forever.

"I've never felt so ashamed the way I did when the officer looked at me. I made Sloan and Charlotte relive it when I knew they didn't want to. But in hindsight, my tears and truth were in vain, because I haven't heard anything from the police in ages. And honestly, I didn't expect anything more. I mean, why would they? It's taken me nearly a decade to report it."

Heat runs through my veins like a fire inside is burning out of control. A lone tear drips onto my hand, and I glance down as it stains my skin, almost drying upon contact.

"Kara?" David's voice sounds distant, while the blood rushes to my ears. Suddenly, it feels like the walls are closing in, and I drag my jacket on and sling my bag over my shoulder.

"I need some air." I run to the door and rip it open. Closing it behind me, I tug at my top and slouch against the wall.

"You okay?" Dev asks, concerned, as the door opens beside me.

"Fine," I reply. I'm not, but it's as good as it's going to get.

I straighten up and approach Margaret, who holds out a glass of water. Taking it from her, I down it in one.

David approaches and hesitates. "Kara, as one of my patients, I can call the police and ask them to follow up your statement."

I nod. "I'd appreciate that."

He flips through his appointment book, but stops after a few pages and gauges me. "Shall we say the same time next week?"

"Actually, have you got one earlier?"

He rubs his chin and smiles. "Nine?"

"Thank you," I reply. Nine is definitely better, because it means Sloan can drop me here first – when I finally tell him. I take the appointment card and slip it into my purse. Devlin grips my hand and leads me out of the office.

"Do you think John will mind if I'm late next week?"

He chuckles. "No, of course not."

Pacing down the stairs, my bag sings at me. "Dev, wait a minute," I say, digging around inside for my mobile. Lifting it out, my father's name appears on the screen. Like every other constant in my life, I knew he couldn't stay hidden forever. I reject the call, follow Devlin onto the street and into a deli shop. Standing at the counter, waiting to be served, my phone rings out loud again, much to the annoyance of the other customers.

"Yes?" I hiss, as quietly as I can, seeing the bastard's name again.

"Miss Petersen?" A man asks - a man who isn't my father. The lady behind the serve over gives me a pointed glare, silently furious that I'm holding up her queue.

"Sorry, one moment. Ham and cheese on white, please." I request my usual. "Sorry, who is this?"

"I'm Detective Michael Bradshaw. Greater Manchester Police."

I swallow audibly and bring my hand to my mouth, my eyes starting to water and my knees already failing to hold me upright.

"I'm very sorry, Miss Peter-"

"Mrs Foster," I interrupt, prolonging the inevitable. I can feel my body begin to harden. There was so much that I needed to say to her that I never did. So much I had to tell her, but now never will. If I had known this is how it would end, I would never-

"I'm sorry, Mrs Foster, but your father was found dead a few nights ago."

My mouth falls open, and I lift my eyes to the menu board and swallow back the bile.

"What? Where?"

"He was found overdosed in his car at the services just outside the city on the M62. Can you tell me the last time you saw him, Mrs Foster?"

I swallow hard, not wanting to admit our part in the proceedings of his death. Sloan's good - albeit good riddance - gesture, is clearly the unknown defining factor here. And sadly, I know I will have to own it, because it will be seen as suspicious as to how he afforded such a substance with so little legal income.

"I saw him briefly a few months ago when he turned up at our hotel."

"*Your hotel?*" the detective queries.

I breathe out, already sensing everything ready to lose the battle to stay whole and strong. "My husband owns a chain of hotels. My father showed up, and my husband gave him money..."

And of course, we both knew we wouldn't see him again until said money ran out and then he would be back, knowing exactly what leverage to use to milk the human cash machine whenever the need arose.

"Well, that answers my next question. He was found with a large amount of cash and substance on his person. Your mother has been informed of her husband's death. I believe there were separated."

"Yes," I murmur. My mind is reeling, and for some reason, my heart is breaking. Jeremy, astute in his observations through the life he has lived, was right. He was right when he said to say I hate my mother means I hate a part of myself. Because right now, she's all I can think about.

"That's three pounds, please," the woman interrupts, lobbing my sandwich on the counter.

Still listening to the detective, as he tells me he will need to see me at some point, either here or there, I fail to absorb his words. The last thing I hear is 'I'm very sorry', and he hangs up.

Bustling through the long queue of people and running out of the shop, the woman calls out to me. Outside, the fresh air stabs me like knives, and I slam my back against the brick wall. My heart breaks, realising what Sloan and I have inadvertently done.

My mind unravels; wondering what life has left to throw at me. I straighten myself up, then walk numbly towards Sloan's office.

"Kara?" Dev shouts, and I stop and turn.

"My father OD'ed, Dev. He did it using the money that Sloan gave him the night of the function."

He scrubs his hand down his face and grabs the back of his head. "Oh fuck! Go inside; I'll call John." Embracing me momentarily and kissing my forehead, all I feel is cold.

I wander aimlessly through the foyer, until a guard rounds the reception desk and smiles. "Good afternoon, Mrs Foster."

I mumble hello, and continue to trudge calmly, studying my reflection cast on the marble floor. My stomach squeezes as I board the lift.

"One, two, three," I murmur, grasping my belly, trying my hardest to keep the minuscule contents from making a return trip.

My steps echo in the deserted corridor, and I realise Soph and Gloria are probably at lunch. Pushing back the door, Sloan's office is empty. I deposit my bag on his desk, when the sound of his voice floats in. I pace towards the boardroom and pause at the panes of glass.

Touching my pads to the coldness, once again, he is conducting a meeting. So reminiscent of the night I returned, but this time, I shall not be running. This time, I have nothing left worthy of preservation, only his love.

I press my forehead against the glass, ready to turn, when I open my eyes and see his finger in front of me on the other side, pointing up. Lifting my head, his hand presses against the glass, but his look of concern is prevalent. I step back and mouth '*I love you*' and point to his office. He nods and turns back to his colleagues.

I rub my chilled limbs, then pick up his spare suit jacket and slip into it. Inhaling the lapels, absorbing his scent, I drag down the throw from the top of the sofa, curl up and close my eyes.

My father's voice irritates, as my mind tears down the walls and transports me back to the day the wheel started to turn again.

Falling into the darkness, a frail and weathered man walks towards me. He circles, like a predator toying with its prey, ready to strike and kill for survival.

His survival, not mine.

With a smirk on his face, he leans in. The noxious smell of spirits is so real, I can almost taste it.

"Well, you finally did it, sweets," he says gleefully. "I always said you would."

"Did what?" I whisper, terrified in my nightmare.

"You finally fucking killed me!" His chuckle is maniacal as he turns and walks away, fading into the impenetrable blackness.

Bracing my hands over my head, I breathe deep and expel the pain in a heart rendering scream.

"Did you know?" Sloan's low rubble drowns my silence, while soft fingertips massage my forehead.

"I swear I'd literally just found out," Walker replies. "Dominic called me about half an hour before Dev did."

I shuffle against the strong, familiar thighs under me, and rub my eyes. "Where am I?"

"Hey, my love." Staring up, I find the comfort inside Sloan's blues. I shift, causing the seat belt to strain painfully across my chest. Unclipping it, he sits me on his lap and brings it back over us.

"Safety is paramount," I whisper.

"Everything to do with you is paramount."

I stretch my neck back and rest my head on his shoulder. "I'm sorry I disturbed your meeting." I outline his jaw with my finger and stare out of the window, thankful we're almost home. The farmers' fields paint the landscape for miles, and the buzz of electricity and metal intermingles with the sound of the tractors tending the crops as Max opens the gates.

Inside the house, I slowly walk upstairs. Midway, I look back, and Walker has his hand on Sloan's shoulder. I smile, grateful, because I need time to process today alone.

Pushing open the door to the spare bedroom that still resembles a charity shop, I look around, trying to remember where I had seen it last.

I drop to my knees, upend the box, and tip everything out. Tears cloud my eyes as I stare at my mum's picture. Moving my thumb over her face, I curl up and allow the truth to annihilate me.

The creak of the floorboard outside resounds. Opening the door, Sloan is sitting on the floor in his three-piece, knees bent, hands in prayer at his face. He smiles. It's forced and unforgiving, but it's there all the same. He holds his arms open, and I crawl into them. Pressing my head against his chest, I grip his biceps tight and fall back into the memory of the last time I ever saw my mother.

"I got a phone call."

"Baby, I-" I'm aware he already knows, but I need to say this.

"I need to go back to Manchester."

Chapter 36

THE MILES OF motorway flash by as Walker presses harder on the accelerator. The precipitation-laden skies guide our passage back to the place where my nightmares began. The day has gradually darkened, and we are now driving into the storm.

The tension emanating is befitting the journey – it's one none of us wants to make for very different reasons.

Marie turns from the front seat, where she has sat quietly since getting in. Her expression is one of apprehension, and I hold her gaze, needing to remain strong. She's conflicted. She hasn't said it; she doesn't need to. I can't imagine what she must be thinking, knowing today she is finally going to come face to face with the woman who couldn't protect me.

These last few days, I've been starting to see my life in a different light. Married, content, and knowing one day I will be carrying my own child, I understand Marie's unspoken fury. Because, I too, would never allow anyone to hurt my flesh and blood. I would kill before I allowed to be done to my child what my father had allowed being done to me.

Clearing my head, the sign for the M6 North passes at half-mile intervals, and we finally take the last slip road off.

Walker gives out a loud sigh and fiddles with the radio for the umpteenth time. He isn't happy about today's road trip either, but they will all have to live with it. Because for all the wrongs that I've done, I'm determined to do something right at long last.

I will not let my mother suffer alone, not the way I once had. I appreciate they might not think she deserves my forgiveness, but I do. I won't go to my grave one day wondering *what if*. Deep down, I love her. I always have. She just wasn't given a chance to do what should have come naturally. She's spineless, but I can never hate her. To say no, can sometimes be the hardest thing in the world. To be the best you can, to please everyone. No, I can never hate her, regardless of how many times I may say it. But at the same time, I know this is the last time I might see her.

Driving deeper into the city, my heart skips a beat sporadically, waiting for the unknown to materialise. Staring into the distance, I remember all too well the devastation that was given life here. The pain that can never be erased. The heartbreak that can never be repaired.

I remember.

A sick feeling regurgitates in my stomach, instigating a churning sensation. Sloan's hand gently covers mine, and I turn to him, unable to say words that he will never believe.

"We'll be there soon," he says quietly, stroking my cheek.

I don't respond, because the place we are heading is a place I never wanted to see again. It existed now only in my nightmares. Closing my eyes, I fight back the heartache and pretend to be asleep. Assailed by my memories, my mind draws out the past again.

Sitting on top of the stairs, I hug ted close to my chest. My mum and dad have been arguing for ages, and I hate the sound. It scares me, but not as much as the man who comes to our house. Uncle Frankie. I don't like him. He's why my mother cries. He's why my father doesn't want me.

Dragging ted back into the bedroom by his bad arm, I stand in front of my bookcase. I point at each book and pull out my favourite, The Snow Queen, and sit cross-legged on my bed. Sammy sometimes reads this with me, but she's in trouble today, so she isn't allowed to play with me. Her daddy said so.

The shouting is still loud, until my mum wails. The last time she did that, she had a poorly eye the next day.

A door slams and someone runs up the stairs. Unable to read and listen, I scramble down, grab my torch and ted, and open the cubbyhole door. Returning for my book, my door opens, and my mum is holding her face. She picks me up, and I struggle in her arms, hurt that she's crying. I want to tell her that I love her, but instead, I kiss her tears away. She smiles, sniffing my hair and takes the book.

Dropping me on the bed, she brings back ted and sits me on her lap. I hug him tight and read the first line. Smiling up at her, she kisses my nose.

"You're a clever girl, baby. God, I'm so sorry, and I love you, so, so much."

"I love you, too, Mummy." I wipe her eyes again, and she holds me close as her voice fills the room.

"We're here," Walker speaks up, and I look up to see him and Marie getting out simultaneously.

I rub my damp eyes, remembering a moment I had buried. My mother loved me. There are so many moments that I'd forgotten, but it doesn't matter, because she loved me.

Always has; always would.

Hands encase my face, and Sloan turns me to him. "You were murmuring."

"My mum used to read to me," I say at his curious expression.

He smiles, but I don't understand. "I know she did. She told me." And yet again more secrets. "I always said I would never come back here, unless it was life or death. The day of the ball, this is where we were."

"Why?"

"I wanted permission to marry her daughter. It was the right thing to do."

"You didn't have to do that," I whisper. Depressing my seat belt, he lifts me over his lap.

"Baby, I did, because I never want you to live with regret. You're my wife, my equal in all things. And when you're hurting, so am I."

"But you despise her."

"Initially..." He stops and nods at Walker, who has just tapped on the window. He looks uncertain, and I wait for him to speak whatever it is that's going to upset me.

"I invited her to the wedding, but she refused. She didn't say why." He picks up the bag that has been nested to his side the whole journey. Unzipping it, he holds up a silver frame. A moment to remember – our perfect day.

"Thank you," I say earnestly. Gently lifting me, like I'm the most precious thing in the world, we get out of the car.

A brisk, northerly wind whistles through the trees and I shiver as it wraps around my bare legs. Yet it isn't the cold playing havoc with my senses, it's the thought of finally seeing her again. Speaking is one thing but seeing is completely different – especially since I've avoided both for so long.

I dig my nails into his palm, probably to the point of pain, as a soothing noise escapes his throat. Passing through the stone gateway, this is the second time in as long that we've had to grace one of these places. And the second time Sloan has reluctantly dug deep into his pockets without request or protest.

I focus blankly ahead as we walk through the silent graveyard, finally reaching the lone figure standing outside the church doors.

Dressed head to toe in black, playing the part of the grieving widow, is my mother. The weak-willed woman who has never carried any sort of fight within her. Who allowed herself to be swallowed by the caustic existence that *he* cocooned us inside of. A woman, who, like me, was bought and sold to keep the peace. Two completely different scenarios, but exactly the same outcome; it bought our compliance and silence. It ensured we diminished in the dark.

But finally, that darkness is fading.

I approach with apprehension, as a glimmer of light cuts through the trees, revealing her true appearance. Gone is the attractive woman I remember from my childhood, the woman who I look like in so many ways. Now, her complexion is dull, defeated by the life she has lived and the pain that has plagued it for as long as we both can remember. Standing in front of me is a woman who has lived a life of destitution and horror.

I move closer, one step at a time. Unable to restrain my heartache, I drop my bag and start to turn. My pathetic, half-willed attempt at escape is cut short, when Sloan grabs my arm and refuses my emancipation. Leaning against him, my hand splayed over his chest, he rocks me.

"I can't do this," I whimper. Truthfully, each time I think I'm resilient, my mentality proves I'm still weak.

I inhale deeply, facing the stone wall, until the church bells toll overhead. Wiping my eyes, I turn, smooth down my black ensemble, and do the walk I never thought I would.

Rounding the corner of the building, I push the door back and watch in disbelief as Marie quietly talks to the woman I haven't seen in nine years.

Lorraine looks apprehensive as she slowly lifts her hand. Looking between Walker and Sloan, who is bizarrely at ease, I slowly take it, then wish I hadn't as the unmistakable burn flares up. Clenching my fingers, I tolerate it.

"Hi," she breathes out.

"Hi…Mum," I reply, the word foreign on my tongue. Her eyes glaze over, and she starts to sob. "Please don't cry." It's the first thing that comes into my head. I lean forward and run my hand down her face. The tingle under my tips is evident. Noticing my discomfort, she moves back.

Minutes later, the vicar enters and closes the doors. As expected, we are the only mourners. Walker and Marie sit together in a pew a couple of rows back, and Sloan and I take the one in front. My mother, clearly uncomfortable, sits on the opposite side.

Alone.

Tears nip my eyes unforgivingly, and I turn to Sloan, who looks partially ashamed and nods. Approaching her, she smiles and moves over.

In my peripheral vision, her hand fidgets restlessly on her knee. I can already feel my skin itch incessantly, but resist the temptation to flee when I slowly touch my fingers upon hers.

Sitting here, feeling her hand curl around mine, experiencing a sensation like a naked flame has been lit underneath it, I will allow her this small invitation to finally play the parent. After all that has been said and done, she's still the woman who brought me into this world.

I glance around the interior, and my eyes meet Marie's. A jealous streak flashes over them, but she has nothing to be fearful of, because we both know if it wasn't for her love, I wouldn't be here today. I wouldn't be sat in this pew, holding my mother's hand, half-listening to the vicar speak of a man who deserves to be six feet under.

I study the good man of the cloth as he describes a loving father I don't recognise. It's hardly surprising, because this eulogy was never going to be the horrible truth. Hardening my own emotions, I block out the spoken lies filling the small church.

With a gentle tap on the back of my hand, I look into my mother's eyes – also my eyes. She's wearing a curious expression of relief, and I follow her gaze straight ahead. Tightening my fingers in hers, the coffin mocks us from only a few feet away. And although solace should never be found in days like today, that box marks the end. And it ensures he can never hurt me, or her, again.

Standing with my arms crossed, the soil is deposited back into the earth as the coffin is interred. Two defining emotions are waging a war inside me.

Guilt and relief.

Glancing over my shoulder, my mother is standing in between the men, clearly nervous under their watchful gaze. I give her a small smile, and she hesitantly walks over the spongy grass, until she's by my side.

"You didn't have to come today," she says quietly.

I tilt my brow. "We both know I did. Closure doesn't come more final than this," I reply, as the trio stop behind us. "Can we be left alone for a while?" I ask, a part of me knowing I should never have to request permission to speak to my own mother privately. Sloan starts to move, but I shake my head; I want him to stay, because this has also been his life for years.

We move back into the church, and Sloan closes the doors behind us. He sits a few feet away, pretending not to listen. Digging into the bag, I pull out the wedding picture of us and hold it out to her. The sun floods through the stained glass and highlights the auburn tones in her greying brown hair. Watching her study the picture with tears of happiness, brings me a new, inner peace.

"I would've liked for you to have come," I say honestly. In retrospect, my only real regret, one I didn't want to voice, but by all accounts, Sloan already knew, is that my mother was absent. I know I should just walk away from her after all the things that went on under her roof, but I can't. I love her, and seeing her again after nearly a decade of carrying the pain of the last time we spoke, I feel it more than ever.

"You're so beautiful. So grown-up." She runs her fingers over the frame and glances at Sloan.

"Nine years does that," I reply playfully, hoping she doesn't think I'm being sarcastic or rude.

"I've missed out on so much. I'll never forgive myself."

I mouth *no*. I don't want to keep living in the past. I have a future to look forward to now, and I would like her to be in it, in some shape or form – just not in this city.

A deep throat clears, and Sloan steps forward.

"This is my husband, Sloan," I say proudly, loving his smiling cheeks.

"I know, we've met."

"It's nice to see you again, Mrs Petersen."

She pats the other side of the pew for him to sit, and he drops and takes her hand. "He's a good man, Kara," she croaks out.

"He is."

"Thank you, for everything. For loving my daughter...for giving her everything I never-" she stops abruptly, and Sloan and I exchange a glance, realising how difficult this is.

"You don't have to explain, I remember." I remember the sound of my mother's tears far too well. It's right up there with the sound of my own.

"I love you, so much," she says, just as a knock comes to the door and Walker pushes it open.

"I think you've overstayed your welcome," he says, jerking his head to the people waiting behind him.

Back outside, my eyes work over the multitude of gravestones in the peaceful cemetery.

"Are you okay, honey?" Marie asks quietly behind me.

"I'm fine, surprisingly. Are you?" I query, wondering what the woman who saved me thinks of the woman who birthed me. She doesn't respond, and Sloan's perfectly timed reappearance is a blessing. I can't have my heart secretly breaking for two women today.

"I'm not entirely impressed, but she gave me you, so I'll make an effort. John and I were talking about taking her for a late lunch somewhere. Is that okay?" I nod and fall into her embrace.

"I love you, and thank you," I whisper. She kisses my cheek, then goes to have a word with Lorraine about this afternoon's pre-made arrangements.

"Let's go check into the hotel, my love." Sloan entwines our fingers, and I tug his firmly. He rubs his chin with his thumb and forefinger, bestowing me with a curious expression.

"I'd like to go home," I say, my mind resolute.

"We'll only be here a few more days."

I sigh; I knew he wouldn't understand. "No, I meant my childhood home." His stance instantly hardens. "Please," I whisper when he refuses to meet my gaze.

He finally agrees under duress, but the silence is thick. I know he thinks I've lost my mind, and maybe I have, but seriously, I just want complete closure. I want to be able to walk away from that house and finally let it go. It's a beautiful theory that will probably never be true, but I have to put my faith in something.

The air is tense; tangible, and growing around us as Walker speaks to my mother. She digs into her bag for the keys and brings them over. Clamping them in my palm, her look of shame is undisguisable.

"Thank you," I whisper, and then hesitantly lean in to kiss her. The fire flares a little, but instantly dies when she moves away, clearly as uncomfortable as I am.

"We'll get a taxi to the hotel. Be careful, kid," Walker says.

"Always," he replies, still looking at me.

Driving through the maze of streets, Sloan knows precisely where he's going. I didn't see the need to guide him because he has been here before.

Eventually, the place of my obliteration comes into view, and his eyes turn to slits, undoubtedly seeing things that no longer exist.

"That night's already coming back to haunt me," he says gravely.

I stare at the house; it looks exactly the same. The overgrown garden, the door in need of a fresh coat of paint, the windows of which the curtains have seen better days. Acid surges in my gut, and suddenly this wasn't such a good idea. I don't want to be here, and I don't want Sloan to step inside again.

He gets out of the car, but instructs me to wait as he looks up and down the street with concern. Opening my door, he helps me out and holds me close. Walking up the garden path, the fear is tangible inside my chest.

The moment I slip the key into the lock, my hesitation proves dominant. Sensing my distress, his arms come around my front, and I grasp them hard. Fear ripples through the air; the ghostly sound of long-gone tears carry over the atmosphere.

Walking through the small rooms, I make myself remember. Again, everything is exactly as it was when I left for the last time. The same wallpaper peeling at the corners, the same furniture occupying the living room, and the same carpets in desperate need of replacing. I feel ashamed; sad for my mother, because my father preferred to drink away whatever little money they had than allow her to make this house a home.

A small smile plays on my lips when I see the picture of myself on a shelf, still only a toddler. Dirty face, pigtails, missing tooth, dungarees and all. I reach up to grab it, but Sloan already has his hand on it. He grins, studying it reverently before he starts to look around for more. I watch intrigued as he picks up various ones - me alone, then my mum and me - and holds them firmly. His expression changes when he sees the wedding picture of my parents. They look happy, only young, with the world at their feet to experience together, a bit like we are now.

It didn't take long for it to turn to shit.

He lifts it down and puts it on top of the stack. Cocking my head, he shrugs his shoulders.

"Well, I thought I would get them copied while we're here. They're your memories, and they deserve to be seen in our home. I'll understand if you don't want this one." He holds up my parents' wedding picture.

"It wasn't always bad. They're few and far between, but I do have *some* good memories here."

He smiles sadly and strokes my cheek, his eyes flitting up the stairs. I share his growing expression of concern because aside from clearing out what I took when I fled, my last real night in that room, he was there with me.

"Hold my hand," I whisper, but his palm is already caressing mine. Tipping my chin up, he kisses me.

"I'll never let it go."

The steps creak under us, and I take a deep breath at the top of the landing, my hand taut on the bannister. I don't know which way to turn, but I know there's only one option.

Entering my old bedroom, my mind instantly takes me back a decade. The walls are still pink and white, devoid of any personality. Gliding my hand over the duvet – the only thing that has changed – my eyes shift to the headboard, pinpointing the faint ligature marks where the bastard had me tied down while I thrashed in vain. Salty tears sting my eyes, and I drop my head.

"Hey, it's over," Sloan says, attempting to console me, but he's wrong.

"No, it's not. It never will be, not until…" I wrap myself around him, unable to complete the prophetic statement of truth.

Slowly lifting my head from his shoulder, I swallow back the bile surging up my throat. His phone starts to chime, and he takes the call and steps outside. Listening to him discuss business with Sophie, I presume, is calming.

As I inch closer to the cubbyhole door, I don't know why I'm so fearful. Except, inside this house, this room, I have plenty to fear. In my heart, I'll always associate this place with pain.

I rotate in a perfect, but awkward circle, then drop to the floor and curl my knees up to my chest. Resting my head against the wall, the images assault me, one after another, and I cry for the little girl who sought protection in this box but never stood a chance.

"Hey," Sloan says from the doorway, and I wipe my eyes quickly. He gauges the tight space, pulls me up, and slides down the wall. Sitting on his lap, squashed together, I lull my head back.

"You know the real reason I don't like you begging?" I shake my head. "Because the night I first entered this room, you begged me not to hurt you, like he hurt you." The silence is strained until he speaks again. "Tell me about a good memory," he says, nuzzling my neck.

Holding him, while he kisses a multitude of shapes over my skin, I recant the sparse good times. And end it with the very best one.

The night he saved me from the darkness and brought me into the light.

Chapter 37

MY EYES ROAM the small hallway as I move from the kitchen to the living room. It has been two days since I sat upstairs with Sloan, attempting to gain supremacy over my personal demons. The reasons why I always feared this house, or more specifically, the cubbyhole, no longer exist here. It's just bricks and mortar now, but being here still causes a sickness inside that cannot be cured.

Stopping outside the door, wondering how I'm going to juggle opening it, I'm halted by my mother's sound of happiness. It's been a long time since I've heard her laugh in this house. It makes me feel guilty, because I know a return visit is out of the question. And it's something we have both avoided discussing since I set foot in the hotel the day of the funeral and really talked to her for the first time in nearly a decade.

With three hot mugs close to my chest, I depress the handle with my elbow and walk backwards into the living room. Turning, I'm lucky I don't burn myself when I see my mum still laughing, as Marie pulls out pictures - age fifteen plus - from the bag of tricks Sloan has brought with him.

"Hi," I murmur, hearing the surprise in my tone at witnessing them so relaxed after only a couple of days.

"Hey, honey. Your mum and I were just talking about you."

"Huh." I place down the drinks and take a seat.

"Baby, don't be paranoid."

I discreetly glance at Marie, judging her take on my mother's endearment. Her expression is passive. And fake. Letting it go, I sip my coffee and watch them interact together. It's a strange thing to see the two women who have played a part in my upbringing sit and talk. To an outsider, they seem like old friends catching up.

My mother's eyes capture mine, and she saddens. "What's wrong, Kara?"

"I'm sorry I never called you," I whisper. "After reading the hospital letter, I didn't know what to say."

"Baby, I never expected you to. Every time I called, a part of me was glad you never answered. I didn't know what to say either." She turns away and sips her tea.

"Mum?" She looks up inquisitively. "I think you already realise, but I can't come back here again." Her eyes close, because she clearly doesn't want me to leave, and I clearly cannot stay...or return.

She sighs. "No, me neither. The council have given me a month to clear it out."

"So, you're not living back here?"

She shakes her head. "No, I'm living in Warrington now. I have been since we last spoke."

"Who do you know in Warrington?"

"No one, but I just wanted a fresh start. I went to a women's refuge, they sorted me out somewhere to live, and I've changed back to my maiden name. I'm also working now, too. It's only shop work. It's not brilliant, but it's a start."

"That's really good. What about the letter?"

"I'm fine, honestly. The doctors referred me to the hospital after they found some abnormal cells in a smear test last year. That's the letter you saw. My results came back clear. I'm fortunate it was just a scare."

"Do you have to go back for further testing in the future?" Marie asks her.

Zoning out their voices, I stare up at the pictures on the wall, the ones I remember so vividly from a decade ago. Touching my fingers to my chest, a weight has been lifted by hearing her truth. I shouldn't feel so happy, but I do.

The conversation switches, and I'm glad Marie is making an effort like she promised she would. I only hope she knows that she will never be replaced in my life. She will always be my mother. She will be the one I seek guidance from, and the one I shall always run to.

I listen intently while they swap stories of me at various different stages of my life. I roll my eyes as my mum talks about my abysmal makeovers on my old dolls and my tea parties with ted, to Marie's amusement at shopping for dance dresses and forced employment.

My attention is snagged when my mother asks how we met. Sharing a look with Marie, I nod. As much as it's going to hurt her, she needs to know what I lived through. She needs to know the life I sustained that made me determined to survive.

Listening to Marie dredge up the past articulately, I pretend to stare out of the window. I flinch the instant my mum's sobs fill the gaping hole of sound. Yet there is nothing I can say because I'm one of the lucky ones.

I glance back at them; Marie's icy stare and my mum's green glare induce shivers. Had Marie not busted me, I wouldn't be here today. We all know how it would've ended for me; pimped out, broken. Possibly dead. Far worse off than I ever was here – if that's even possible.

Turning back to Lorraine, I am her daughter in every way. I see myself in her when she laughs or when she's sad. I share so much of her genealogy, it's like looking in the mirror. The only thing I don't share is her ability to turn a blind eye.

Picking up the wedding picture, she runs her thumb over Sloan's face. "He really loves you. I didn't realise who he was when he called and asked to see me. It wasn't until he spoke about that night... He saved you, more than I ever could." She can't bring herself to speak the truth, and I won't press the issue because I don't want to relive it.

"Why didn't you come to the wedding?"

She sniffs and begins to wipe her eye.

"Lorraine?" Marie asks.

"Because no one really wanted me there."

I shake my head. "That's not true."

"It is. He invited me because he felt obliged to. I'm not stupid."

The room falls into silence, and my eyes meet Marie's, seeing the unspoken truth. She's the first to break contact, proving my mother's words correct and just. Regardless, nothing changes for me, I still would've liked for her to have been there.

The conversation picks up again, taking away the air of hostility. Sipping my coffee, my phone vibrates, and Sloan tells me he will meet us at the hotel later. I haven't asked what he's been up to, and I think it's better not to know. This city holds too much animosity for both of us. I can honestly say, hand on my heart, that I can't wait to leave. But after all these years, I finally deserve to know the truth.

"Why did you let him..." My voice is a ghostly whisper carrying over the tension. Marie grips my hand as I dare to ask the question we have all avoided.

My mum lets out a heavy sigh and places down her mug. "I was the worst type of mother, Kara. I cowered in a corner and did as I was told. I allowed him to take the money and leave us practically starving most days. I was too frightened to say no. For a time, it was okay, until Franklin came back. That's when everything went downhill. I tried to say no. I used to take you to the park and that way we had somewhere to escape to. The times I had packed up our stuff and tried to leave, Ian would beat me. One of the worst times was one Christmas Eve. Looking back, I should have taken the doctor up on his offer of finding us a safe house."

I wipe my cheeks as I remember the story I recanted to Marie. I turn to her, seeing her eyes glassy again. Listening to my mum continue, I realise why Sloan isn't as enraged as he should be – her life was partially reminiscent of his mother's.

"I was terrified of my own shadow. After you left, I just wanted to die. I had nothing, and I had only myself to blame for it. I know I shouldn't say it, and I should be sad that he's dead, but a part of me isn't. After the initial shock when the police called me, I felt relieved, like I could finally breathe again. You know?" I nod, knowing exactly how she feels.

"It doesn't make you a bad person, because I do, too."

"I'm glad you found someone who gave you a good life." She turns to Marie. "Thank you."

Marie smiles through her tears and holds my mother's hand. Lorraine repeatedly thanks her, and I don't know if my shattered heart can take much more.

"Let's not dwell on the past," Marie says, stroking her hand.

Sniffing back, my mum musters a smile. "Tell me something good. Tell me about everything I've missed over the years."

And for the next few hours, that's exactly what I do.

I grip Marie's hand as we get out of the taxi and walk inside. Heading straight to the hotel bar, I flop down into a tub chair and gaze out of the window. The sun is punching through the dark clouds covering the sky.

Marie returns moments later carrying a bottle of wine. She remains silent while pouring two glasses. Studying her, and how her demeanour has lightened somewhat, my mum's earlier confession is leading me to believe things I hope are unsubstantiated.

"Is what she said true?"

Marie looks at me inquisitively. Whether it is because she is also going to have to confess things that are unfounded, I don't know.

"Kara-"

"Please."

She nods and picks up her glass. "He did invite her. Admittedly, John wasn't keen, but Sloan was adamant that he wanted her there, not just for you, but for him. He never wanted you to look back and make-believe."

I take a long draw from the glass and relax back, insofar as I can. "And what about you? Would you have been happy to see her there?"

She sighs and turns away. "The day of the ball, I knew they were coming up here to see her. A couple of days beforehand, when Sloan said he was going to call and invite her, I confess I was insanely jealous because I thought I would lose you."

Shuffling my chair closer, I grip her hands. "What you did for me... I can never repay you for. And there are no words I can say to express my gratitude. You will always be my mother, regardless. I hope you know that."

"I do, honey, but it hurts so much, knowing what happened to you. In truth, Lorraine had lost you years before you ran away. By coming back here, you've given her a second chance. I never thought I'd say this, but take it with both hands and never let go. Sometimes you don't realise just how lucky you are." Her eyes drift over the table, and sadness overwhelms them. A part of me wonders if she is referring to herself or me.

I'm saved a response when a couple of women on the next table over grin salaciously. Seeing what has them engrossed, our men stride confidently into the bar. Sloan drops down a bag, picks me up and deposits himself in the seat, dragging me back down. He snatches up my glass and downs it in one.

"How's your mum?"

"She's fine. We talked and agreed to make more of an effort. Although I don't know how she'll feel about coming down to London. Or how I feel about going to Warrington."

"Warrington? What's in Warrington?" Walker asks.

I shrug my shoulders. "A fresh start, apparently."

"That's good. What about the house here?" Sloan enquires.

"The council want it clear within a month. She's donating the majority of the stuff and just taking the little things; pictures, photo albums, things like that."

He then motions for the waitress working the room, and she takes his request for the best bottle of red they have. Minutes later, she returns and places his choice on the table. Sloan tips her very generously, and her face lights up as she scurries away.

"What's this for?" I ask, glancing at Marie and Walker, who sense they are unwanted and get up.

"We'll go get something to eat. Come on, angel."

Marie kisses me goodbye, then wraps herself around him as they head off.

A nervous shiver creeps up every cell, and I shift in his lap. "What's in the bag?" I query suspiciously. There can only be so many pieces in there, and none will be fit to be seen in public.

"Just a little something I picked up. I thought I would have someone model them for me. Maybe I'll ask one of those women…"

I throw my head back and laugh. My outburst raises a few brows, and the women at the other table throw me a few glances of disdain. Standing, I grab my kid's hand and the bottle, then drag him up.

I slide the key card through the lock; the room is light and inviting, holding an air of excitement. Walking backwards slowly, he digs into the bag and pulls out a few scraps of flimsy fabric. Crooking his finger, I meet him in the middle, and he unbuttons my chiffon blouse. I roll my eyes and shrug out of it, while he quickly strips me bare.

"Isn't it a bit pointless to go through all this when I'm already naked?"

"Definitely not."

Ripping the tags and hygiene strip off the knickers, he holds them at my feet. Sliding them up my thighs, he snaps the elastic at my hips, running his fingers down the front to straighten the fabric.

He slowly stands and holds the bra out in front of me. I lift my arms as he slides the straps over my shoulders. Fastening the back, his hand moves in between my flesh and the fabric, and he carefully positions my already aching breasts. He repeats the action with the other side, then steps back. With his chin resting on his fist, he treads a slow circle around me, ensuring his flesh skims mine.

"Close your eyes, my love." His hand presses my stomach, and I lower my lids. Long minutes pass by, until he touches my foot, making me jump. "Easy," he says, placing my hand on his shoulder. I grip it tight, as silky fabric is pulled over my toes, all the way up until he is positioning the lace hem over my thigh. "Beautiful."

Inhaling, I swallow, moistening my parched mouth and throat. "Sloan," I whimper.

"I've got you," he replies, a smirk in his tone.

326

His hand's stroke up and down my other leg, until he covers it with the remaining stocking. He lifts me up, and the softness of the duvet touches upon my back.

"Open your eyes, baby."

I turn and see him lying next to me, shirtless, beautiful. *Mine.* His fingers toy with my hair, then explore my flesh, until they are on my abdomen. His eyes are dark and brooding, as he draws random patterns over my stomach.

"Touch yourself for me." Hesitant, still unsure of being on display like this, I perform his request.

Watching me, he deftly removes his jeans and shorts, and they clunk on the floor. He pushes down on the inside of my knees, parting my legs further. Feeling the tug of ecstasy, I work my fingers harder and close my eyes, willing myself to give him what is his.

Positioning himself between my thighs, I cradle him as his fingers seize my hips, and rake up my sides. Brushing my satin covered breasts with his thumbs, my nipples harden further in immediate response. My back arches under his dexterous tongue that is licking a long line from my collarbone to my belly button. My breathing spikes as he progresses further down to my centre. Dragging the flimsy fabric aside, he holds one hip firmly, continuing to demonstrate his ability. I grab the sheet, while each lick and tug on my folds causes me to press further into him. Unable to take much more, my body starts to peak beautifully.

"Not yet," he murmurs. He takes my other hand and wraps it around his length. "Put me inside you, baby." I guide him, until his tip presses into my opening, and I sigh out at the exquisite sensation of him filling me.

"Ready, naked, and definitely all mine," he says, sucking my moist fingers.

"Please," I whimper, ready to beg for release.

Sitting us up, his knees press into my buttocks, pushing him so hard, I can feel it extraordinarily deep. Sliding my legs around his hips, he takes a firm hold of my waist. His thumbs rub my hip bones as his fingers press into my lower back.

My hands grip his biceps, finding leverage. Writhing against him, impaled perfectly, I scream out his name as my orgasm shatters all coherent thought and reason. Plunging me up and down, never losing momentum, the seriousness of his expression mixed with his action is questionable, but I know he's making a statement with every thrust.

Roaring out my name, he quickly lifts me, and my lips meet his, tasting myself on him. Pillaging my mouth, he speaks hoarsely. "Turn over."

On my hands and knees, he gently spreads my legs. What I expect him to do is the complete opposite of what he actually does, when he presses a couple of fingers into my wet heat, using his hand on my hip to rock me back and forth. Withdrawing, he slides back into my core, while desire continues to fire every nerve ending.

"How do you feel, my love?"

I look over my shoulder with a smile. "I feel...amazing." I drop my head down, close my eyes and revel. Thrusting gently, his hand snakes up my thigh, until he is massaging my already sensitive flesh. My head drops; I'm boneless and ready to succumb to passion.

"Come for me, baby. I've got you."

He leans over my back, kissing softly up my spine. My breathing deepens until the quickening is unavoidable and I call out in time with him. Slamming my hand on the headboard, he lifts my chin and turns me to look at him again. Pushing into me one last time, ensuring I'm satisfied, he finally slows. Carefully withdrawing, he rolls onto his back and lays me over his chest. Kissing my face, his eyes soften.

"You're the best thing that has ever happened to me. John once asked me when it stops. I told him when you had my name, my ring on your finger and..."

"And what?" I whisper.

"And when you had my child in your belly." His thumb strokes the side of my tum for emphasis. "I don't mean right now, but one day."

Tucking my head into his neck, I kiss his jaw. "I want one day, too."

Chapter 38

SLAPPING THE SKILFUL, sneaky palms away, I hurry out of the shower, flustered and feeling dirtier than when I got in. Everything was going swimmingly, until *he* stepped inside. I chortle because his mother was absolutely right. At this rate, I *will* be pregnant by Christmas.

Picking up my pills from the vanity, I reassure myself there isn't going to be a welcome surprise anytime soon. Dropping them down, I wrap myself in a towel, while his arm snakes around my middle.

"No! You've already made us late!"

"Ten more minutes isn't going to hurt then!" He picks up the blister strip and winks. "Shall we flush these and practice making babies?" His brow wiggles mischievously.

"Don't we practice that enough already?" I reply flippantly.

Holding my hands away from my body, he walks me back into the dressing room. My lower back presses against the island, and he smiles against my lips. His eyes flick down to his Rolex, and he pulls back abruptly.

"Oh, shit. We're going to be really late!" He turns and strides his naked self to his side of the room.

As always, I shamelessly watch him move, or more precisely, the way his backside moves, the muscles flexing hypnotically under his skin. Staring, completely lost in love with all sides of this amazing man, the sharp snap of fingers halts my daydreaming.

"The show from the front is pretty damn good, too," he says, biassed in his own conceited opinion, but he really isn't wrong. Playfully, he points me to my side, and I shuffle over. I'm getting better at that these days; doing as instructed.

In front of the full-length mirror, I quickly dry my hair and tie it up in a low, messy bun. Slicking on a minimal amount of make-up, I give myself kudos for personal presentation. The good old war paint is also something else I'm getting better at, too.

I browse through the rails and pick out a long black top. Grabbing a pair of skinny grey jeans and navy underwear set from the drawer behind me, I quickly slip into them. Pulling down the hem, the top skims my bum and exposes my arms, but sits high on my chest, ensuring it definitely covers my now silver markings.

Perusing the shoes, I grab the first pair he ever bought me. These are the ones I pull out more often than not. A, because they are actually comfortable – through constant wear; and B, because of the meaning behind them – I was never a quick shag just to pass the time.

I was never a quick *anything* just to pass the time.

His throat clears, and I pull a face. "What now?" I ask innocently, holding the heels.

"I don't like *them!*" I turn to find him pointing, his shirt in hand.

"Huh," I huff, looking at the shoes. "You bought them!"

"Not the bloody shoes, the jeans!"

"Your club allows jeans!"

"Well, tonight, I'm changing that!"

My mouth falls open. "So, you're going to make everyone already there walk around naked from the arse down?"

"Very funny, smart-arse Foster! No jeans for you is the new rule!" He waits, hands on hips because he knows that he's vying for it. And I know he wants it.

Sauntering over to him, his messy damp hair shines under the walk-in lights. His eyes narrow as I reach up and kiss his cheek.

"And what would you have me wear tonight?" I ask coyly, walking my fingers up his gorgeous chest.

He grins wolfishly. "The same thing I have you wear most nights – nothing." He drops the shirt to the floor and tugs on my waistband.

"Fine!" I concede with a grin. I start to remove the offending denim and flutter my lashes. I know exactly how to get my way in this disagreement. "I'll wear one of those nice, short skirts over there." I point to the rail of *belts* – definitely a Charlie buy at some point. "And when I have to lean over the bar, and I inadvertently show my bum to the world because I'm too short, you can't complain. Now," I smile broadly, "which one would you like me to wear?" Chewing my bottom lip, I wait for his answer.

"Okay, I'll give you that. Keep the jeans on," he replies, almost pained, and starts to fasten them back up.

"That's what I thought." I attempt to walk away, but he drags me back. Pressing me into his front, his hand drifting down my abdomen, he sucks my bottom lip brusquely.

"But tonight, I'm ripping the fuckers off!"

"I'd be disappointed with anything less!"

Finally dressed, we leave the room, and he flicks the light off on the way out. The landline starts to ring, and we both ignore it as I reach the bottom first, a shoe in either hand. Sliding into them, I skip into the kitchen for my bag and pull out my phone. Ready to inform Sophie and Charlie that we are finally on our way, I notice a few private missed calls. I shrug it off, because I know from personal experience that call centres have staff working all hours. Silencing it, I slip it into my pocket and put on my jacket.

Evening is setting in in the twilight as I leave Sloan to lock the door, and I quickly move towards the car. Sitting in the limo, the privacy glass is down, and George looks tired. As soon as Sloan gets in, the glass rises and his warm hand massages my knee.

"Yep, I'm definitely not liking these!"

The lights flash around the vast, matt black space, as I lean over the metal and glass railing enclosing the VIP. The beams strewn across the dance floor below, creating a pool of vibrant colour. I bend further, resting my cheek on my hand, already feeling somewhat tired – and maybe a little inebriated, in my quest to find Dutch courage to come here tonight.

My eyes delight in my husband, who is twirling his little sister around like a pirouetting ballerina, much to Jake's annoyance, which I'm positive is borne from her flirty little skirt that is striking its own pose – and gaining her quite a bit of male attention.

I glance back to the bodies packing out the club - wall to wall and bar to bar - and people watch. Sophie and Leanne – whom I haven't seen since I last graced this place for a night of not so good fun - dance together in the crowd below with Nicki, who they have finally managed to prise away from an amorous Devlin.

As the music changes, their arms reach up to the sky, until they see me and start to motion me down. I shake my head; this still isn't my thing. Probably never will be. Swaying on the spot, unable to stop my limbs from reacting, I concede defeat. Tonight, I will allow myself another night to forget, a night to remember I'm still young. Hand on the rail, I make my way down to them.

A weak prickle flares inside when Leanne wraps her arms around me. The sloppy kiss to my cheek is far too much closeness I can handle, and I laugh, pushing her back gently. She doesn't see my disapproval, since some random guy takes her fancy and they move together, deeper onto the floor.

Sophie's head bobs to the beat; her arms and shoulders moving all over the place. Knowing I hate this, she guides us to a less congested area. Twirling around together, not trying to impress or giving a damn about anyone else, feels freeing.

The songs change intermittently, one blending fluidly into another, creating a cacophony of sound to match the energy emitting every person present.

Wiping my hot brow, I point towards the bar. She nods, makes a drinking expression and laughs, before continuing to dance alone, since Nicki has abandoned us.

On my way over, Stuart, free of his scrubs and everything else that gives away his profession, occupies my vacant spot. Still looking over my shoulder at my best friend and the man she clearly loves, my feet find the bar.

Tapping my foot impatiently, I wait. Until waiting becomes a fool's game, and no amount of waving my money is going to get me noticed.

"Excuse me?" I call out to the man being hollered at by thirty different voices. Standing at the end, aware I will never be served, gives me time to reflect. This is the first time in a while that I've felt free, liberated. I smile to myself as I glance down at my rings. Lost in my reverie, someone nudges my shoulder. I gasp, ready to slap whoever has just touched me, when Jeremy's scarred cheek fills my vision.

"What can I get you?"

I glance over the bottles and grin. His deep tones mock me as I give him my unconventional request - one that's never going to materialise, of course.

Seconds later, a familiar presence stands behind me. His large hand reaches up my front, causing my nipples to pay attention. His touch is an extension of my own, and I instinctively lean back. Warm breath glides over my neck, and the fine hairs stand on end – for all the best, most amazing reasons.

"I've got you, baby," my beloved kid whispers, before slapping his mate on the back in jest and walking behind the bar.

"A triple vodka and a double rum – in the same glass - for your lady, and I'll have another," Jeremy says, holding up his empty ale bottle.

"Sorry, sir, you-" The barman stops mid-sentence, realising his mistake. Sloan coolly waves him off and proceeds to sort out our drinks.

Sliding the glass in front of me, he rests his elbows on the bar and glides his finger from my temple to my chest, wiggling it at the neckline.

"Your triple vodka and double rum – in the same glass," he says proudly. I look down, totally unimpressed with the lemonade in front of me. I pass him my twenty while Jeremy roars out laughing and picks up his bottle, before becoming lost in the den of shadowed people.

"I only take payment in kind," Sloan says, coming around to me. "Preferably from my beautiful, lucid wife."

Picking up my glass, I grab his other arm and bring it around my belly. Making our way through the sea of people, it's clear this place has a regular clientele as many of them greet him.

"Dance with me," he whispers, nipping my earlobe. I glance back at the dance floor, hoping there is a miracle opening. As expected, it's still wall to wall. "That's not the kind of dance I'm talking about."

I follow his line of sight, and my eyes skim over the VIP. While the dance floor there is empty, the sofa looks far too inviting to my weary legs right now. His unambiguous desire is all too revealing, and he smiles, clearly wanting to do something else and starts to guide me towards the stairs that lead up to the office.

"No," I whisper, watching his grin morph into a sulk. He's wishful thinking if whatever he's concocting inside his head is going to transpire here.

Not a chance in bloody hell! I'm not one of those girls!

Standing my ground on the third step up, perfectly aligned with him, he grips my hips, pressing our bodies together. He hardens between us and looks down, a naughty gleam twinkles in his eye.

"No? Well, I think this little disagreement calls for some very agreeable make up sex. Besides, we still have...fuck it, I don't know, ten days to make up for?"

I laugh in amazement. "You can't remember, but I think our wedding now supersedes it."

"Fine. I'll just fuck you later like a good husband should!" Leaning in to kiss me, his pheromones both intoxicate and intrigue. Later cannot come soon enough.

"There you both are!" Marie says from behind us, obviously having just heard everything. Sloan grips my shoulders and rolls his eyes, moving aside to reveal her.

With her hands on her hips, her curious but understanding expression says it all. She knows she's interrupting, and she really doesn't care. I laugh when she pushes him away and drags me back down the stairs.

"Right, aside from what I know you'll be doing when you leave here tonight, we need to talk about tomorrow," she says. Following her to the bar, I climb onto a stool.

Tomorrow, Sloan has kindly offered this place out for a party for one of the city's many children's homes. I haven't enquired as to why, but he seems to be doing more for the local area from his own pocket lately, rather than asking his wealthy colleagues to dip into theirs.

"Where's John?" I look around, realising I haven't seen him tonight. Or Tommy or Parker, for that fact.

"Oh, he's got business in Peterborough," she replies, pulling out the attendee list.

"He goes there often," I mutter, sipping my pop.

"Yes, I know," she huffs and lifts her eyes to mine. "My ex lives in Peterborough, honey."

I almost choke before the last word is out there. "You don't think?"

"I don't know. I've never told him, but it wouldn't surprise me. Anyway, tomorrow…" She goes off on a tangent, and I stare at her, wondering what really lies beneath the perfected façade.

"Any questions?" I shake my head because I don't have a clue what she's been telling me for the last twenty minutes. "Good, I'll meet you at the office about nine."

"Why so early?"

"Well, we need to pick up the stuff."

"Doesn't it normally get brought over?" I ask surprised.

"Kara, we're getting it all at a cut-price. We can't expect them to do everything." She collects up the papers and slides them back into the wallet.

Climbing off the stool, my bladder screams at me. Heading towards the ladies, Sloan stops me. "Not now!" I half-shout, and he laughs and stands aside.

Hands under the dryer, my phone vibrates against my backside. Rubbing my palms down my thighs, I pull it out to find the caller has rung off. Again, it's a private number. I furrow my brow. That's three calls in as many hours. Heading out, it beeps singularly. Sloan is still outside the door, laughing and chatting with Jeremy and Stuart, as Sophie darts past me.

"Sorry, chick!" I hold my hands up, because who am I to get in her way.

"Can I use the office?"

"Sure, what's up?" Jeremy asks.

"A private number has been calling, and someone finally left a message." Marching up the stairs, I keep the phone to my ear as the man speaks. I stop when Jeremy opens the door, not quite believing what I'm hearing.

I dash to the desk, take down the number and dial it back. Sloan looks curious - he's not going to be when he finds out.

"Baby?" I wave him off the moment the man finally answers.

"Hi, this is Kara Petersen. You left a message for me."

"Evening, Miss Petersen, I'm Detective Daniel Roberts. You spoke to a colleague of mine a few months back about an unreported rape nine years ago. I've been trying to contact you, but there was no answer." He's the missed calls then.

"Yes," I confirm, reluctant to rehash it again. Especially since his lovely colleague didn't seem interested in the slightest, and I broke my fucking heart and spirit telling it to him.

"Sorry for the lateness of my call, but are you able to come down to the station?"

I look up at Sloan. "No, my husband and I have an engagement this evening."

"Oh, congratulations."

"Thank you. I'm sorry, but why are you calling me? I haven't heard anything in months."

He sighs over the phone. "A woman was attacked last night. She was also raped." I bristle; I know precisely where this call is going.

"A-and what does this have to do with m-me?" The stutter of inconvenience breaks through the barrier. But it's always the same because I know.

Sloan and Jeremy's attention is piqued, and they edge closer, looking between each other with morbid curiosity, possibly realising what is being discussed.

"She claims she was attacked by a man named Deacon Black at the club she works in. We picked him up this morning and are currently holding him pending investigation. The woman identified him, but she's currently refusing to talk. Due to the statement you made, I'd really like you to come down and ID him."

I breathe out harshly. "What? No... I don't think I-I-"

"I'm sorry, I'm not making myself clear. He'll be in a line-up. He won't know you're there."

I inhale in shock, because he will know.

"Do you mind holding for a minute?" I don't wait for his response and put my palm over the mouthpiece.

"Baby, what's wrong?" Sloan asks, full of worry, grabbing my face.

"They've arrested him. Deacon. He attacked a woman..." Sloan immediately takes the phone from me. I turn, hugging myself, and Jeremy holds out his hand, but I step away.

Walking towards the window, lights bounce off the club walls as Sloan continues to speak to the man. I study each person below, wondering if anyone down there can assimilate with me.

"How long can you hold him?"

The bile in my stomach rises, threatening to make its way up my throat. Slumping onto the sofa, I rock silently because it's finally becoming real.

There are so many questions that I need to ask. Such as, if they do charge him, will they release him on bail? If the CPS find it worthy of its day in court, will I be expected to stand in front of him and give evidence, while being picked apart by whatever shady bastard barrister he can afford?

There are far too many 'ifs' at the moment, and I stand again and pace, my nerves shot to shit and my mentality is on the verge of falling apart.

"That's fine. We'll be there around two tomorrow." Sloan gives him his office and mobile numbers, then hangs up. Rushing over to me, I hold my hand up pathetically. "Baby, don't. They can hold him for twenty-four hours without charge. It's almost over, there's no way he'll get bail."

"You don't know that," I counter, my unshed tears resound in my voice.

"Shush." Wiping my eyes with his thumbs, he removes his jacket and puts it on me. "This time tomorrow, he'll commence rotting in hell at her Majesty's pleasure for a very long time."

Hiding the tumultuous emotions stampeding inside, I take a deep breath, trying to appease myself with words that may not come true.

And this is another constant in my life, the newest addition to the long list of errors that I should have done something about after the event. Because if I had, my confession might have been taken seriously, rather than sweep under the rug. Only to be thought of

336

when the current victim will not say a word against him, and desperation lingers.

Sloan's phone rings and he answers, showing me his back. I pick up bits here and there, and guess it's John on the other end.

My mind is caught up in the past, and what may possibly be thrown at me in the future. It's also numb because if I do what's expected of me, I will be destroying a good man's life.

Jeremy's.

Turning my attention to the figure we have both forgotten about, he looks pitiful. It's the forsaken expression that breaks my heart, because this time tomorrow, he too, might be in a cell.

Capturing his gaze, we're both abundantly aware Deacon will not go down alone. He threatened to end his life once already, I doubt he will have no equivocation in describing in great detail the team effort involved in that night nine years ago. And I very much doubt the British justice system will exonerate him for being high and addicted and not knowing any different.

Maintaining my composure, I wonder if the next time I see him it will be in a prison visitors' room. Sloan moves and stands in between us both.

"Remy…" he begins.

Jeremy holds up his hand and smiles sadly. "This needs to be done. I've been running from it for nearly ten years. I'm tired of being devoured by the guilt. Of my every thought being consumed by it. I'm not running anymore. I need to be held accountable for what I did." He turns to me. "Maybe I'll get my redemption after all."

Fighting back my fear and heartbreak, I approach and kiss his scarred cheek. "You've always had it. I was just never strong enough to say it." Walking backwards, it saddens me that tomorrow, he will face his fate through his own confession.

"I need to make arrangements for certain things. I'll leave a wallet in the drawer for you to execute." He moves to the desk and pulls out various documents. "I'll be here in the morning with Marie. Goodnight, honey."

Sloan grinds his jaw, moves towards him, then leans over the desk. Whatever is said between them, I'm not privy. After a few tense minutes, Jeremy gets up from the chair and moves to hug his friend. I look away, because I feel ashamed watching, even though I shouldn't.

Walking down the stairs, Marie quickly approaches. "John's just called. Is it true?" she asks, full of panic.

Sloan nods. "Get your things, we'll take you home."

"About tomorrow, you don't have to do it," she says.

"No, I want to. I was one of those kids too once, remember?"

Hugging her, I let go grudgingly. I hold Sloan's jacket around me as he moves us through the belly of the beast and out into the night.

Staring out of the car window, the beacon of lights fades into the distance behind us. Pulling up outside Marie's, she kisses us both and climbs out. Watching her stride up the garden path, her head tilts, and her hair is highlighted from the landing light inside. She looks around; her hand on the door handle.

"Marie?" Sloan calls out.

"Nothing. I just thought I turned the light off earlier, that's all. I'll see you in the morning, honey." She steps inside and closes the door behind her. The living room illuminates, and Sloan finally closes the car door.

"I've got a really bad feeling," I confess.

"Go to sleep, baby. I've got you."

His hand strokes my forehead, soothing my inner disquiet. Resting my head on his arm, I try to relax, but I can't, because the nightmare hasn't ended – it has only just begun.

Chapter 39

"I LOVE YOU."

Maintaining my hold around his waist as we stand beside the Aston, I stare into his dark, worry charged eyes. They have carried this look since we left the club last night. It's a look that culminates every emotion he is hiding inside.

"You're shivering," he mutters.

"I'll be fine," I reply to soothe him, incapable of allowing the same to empower myself.

"Morning," Dev says on his approach, breaking the tension.

Sloan digs into his pocket and throws him the keys. "Take my car."

Devlin looks down at his hand with a vacant, judging expression. A silent look is imparted between the two, before Dev passes his own keys to a porter, climbs into the Aston and starts the engine.

"I'll pick you up at one-thirty." Sloan kisses me goodbye. I reluctantly let him go and watch while he gets into the limo.

The dark, pewter sky rumbles overhead, and I glance up at the clouds parting, exposing the sun. It creates a sharp contrast of light and dark that I will always have an affinity with.

The windscreen wipers work hard against the waves of water descending the heavens, as we sit in heavy traffic.

Fidgeting, the atmosphere feels bizarrely strained. The words lodged in my throat refuse to be heard, because later today, I wonder if I will be held solely accountable for Jeremy's actions, and his inevitable detainment. I shudder; I don't want these men to hate me for it.

Dev's hand slowly finds mine, and I turn. "We'll always love you, Kara. All of us. We have for years, even though you never knew us. The respect and admiration we have for you is-" He shakes his head, trying to find the most fitting statement and failing. "I mean, seriously, who couldn't love you when we had to stand outside in the cold and rain-"

"Point taken!" I laugh out, but my smile disintegrates with a single thought. "Do you think he'll forgive me?"

"Kara, you have nothing to be forgiven for. You were a child. You and Remy are both casualties of someone else's war, and he will always be unable to forgive himself."

"Sloan," I say numbly. Dev remains quiet and stoic, until Marie's office building is in front of us.

Opening the door, I hold my jacket over my head, and sprint towards the entrance, security card in hand. Inside, Dev shrugs out of his jacket and then helps me with mine, shaking them off as we jog up the stairs.

"Hey, baby," Dev says, as he embraces Nicki. She looks a little embarrassed at my presence, and I move quickly to Marie's office.

"Morning," I greet the empty room. Stepping back, I crane my head at the embracing twosome. "Nicki? Has she nipped out?" I ask, padding towards her, while she quickly straightens herself up.

"No, she's not arrived yet. I called the house and her mobile, but there's no answer. I figured she might've already gone to the suppliers to get the goods. Or maybe John's back early. I don't know."

"Okay," I reply, dialling Marie but not getting a response. I thumb through my phonebook, hit Jeremy's number and wait.

"Hey," he answers almost immediately. "Are you and Marie on your way over already?" I stop my slight swaying.

"No, I was actually calling to see if she was with you. She hasn't come into the office yet."

"I'm still at home. She might already be at the club; I gave her a set of keys the other day. Come and pick me up, I'm not going to be needing my car today." I open my mouth but stop, and he breathes in sharply. "Kara, I didn't mean it like that."

"I know you didn't," I whisper. "We'll be there soon."

"Okay. I'll be waiting, honey."

Putting the mobile back into my bag, Dev moves towards me. "Is she there?"

I shake my head. "No, Jeremy's still at home. We'll go pick him up and go to the club. He gave her a set of keys, apparently."

"I'll see you later, baby," Dev says to Nicki on our way out.

Standing at the passenger side, he throws me the keys. "You're driving. I need to check something."

Inside, I quickly adjust everything and feel nervous for two reasons. One, because Sloan has never introduced me to his other baby before, and two, because Marie is strangely AWOL. It's also probably not the best time for us to get acquainted since the latter is troubling me more than the former.

Setting off slowly, I obey the five miles per hour limit in the car park and advance towards Jeremy's place.

"Jake, is John back yet?" Devlin asks as we move slowly through traffic. I keep my eyes on the road and my ears on the man beside me. "No, we can't find Marie. Just find out and call me back."

A sickness rises up my gullet. A thought that isn't possible is punching its way through. The way she looked at the house last night. Something isn't right; I can feel it.

Turning the corner onto Jeremy's street, he's already at the kerb waiting for us. No sooner have I pulled up; he's opening my door. He indicates for me to get into the back, and I instantly unbuckle and slide into the ridiculously tight space.

Driving through the morning chaos, a vibration fills the car, and the men in front both check their phones. I dig into my bag to find a stream of private missed calls and a text message.

"Finally!" I exclaim, when Marie's name appears, telling me she's already at Oblivion. Holding the phone tight, I wait for any voicemails to come to through from the missed calls. They don't.

We pull up alongside Marie's Mercedes, and relief washes over me. Jeremy steps out of the car, and Dev and I follow him down the alleyway. Unlocking the door, he holds it open and enters last.

Walking through the club's back corridors, he flicks the lights on and pushes back the doors to the main floor. The beams of light shine brightly; the cavernous space is mind-blowing when empty.

"Marie?" I call out, seeing her handbag on the bar. I rotate in a circle and rub my head, wondering where she is.

"She might be in the ladies," Devlin suggests, removing his jacket, before jumping over the bar with one hand.

"Show off. I'll go have a look. Jeremy?"

"Yeah, honey?" he answers, three bottles of water in his hands.

"Can you start getting the tables and chairs down and set them out in rows? There's about fifty or so kids, so just do what you can."

He laughs and takes a swig of the bottle. "Sure."

Leaving my bag next to Marie's, I slide my phone into my pocket and head towards the toilets. The lights turn on automatically as I pass, and it's an eerie sensation to be wandering around alone in such a large and very lonely place.

My eyes work aimlessly over the spots I was verbally flayed by Christy, and I lean against the wall momentarily, thankful that that nightmare is definitely over with.

Pushing open the door, I stick my head inside. "Marie?" The facility remains silent with only my voice lingering. Checking each cubicle, they are all empty. At a loss as to where she is, I perch my backside on the row of sinks. Tightening my hands around the edge, I breathe deeply because there's going to be some long-overdue matricide when I get my hands on her.

Turning around, I brush the stray strands from my face. The fluorescent lights cause my healed scars to shine, mitigating my hidden fears. Yet, after this afternoon, those fears will be gone. Only mentally, but still gone.

"Marie?" I whisper, redialling her number again to no avail. Something definitely isn't right here.

Back on the main club floor, Jeremy and Devlin are nowhere to be seen. Hollering out their names, the reply is my own voice echoing off the walls.

I look around and up, and relief fills me when I notice the office light on. Running up the metal stairs, I throw back the door to yet another empty room. As I step inside, the fire on the back of my neck stokes to life, and I audibly shiver. I rub my arms as I approach the desk and pick up the papers that Jeremy clearly hasn't left in the drawer as advised. Sitting down, I scan over what he has written. A defeated sigh escapes me, and I shake my head.

"Jeremy," I murmur, unable to contain my meaningless guilt.

I drop them on the desk and get up to leave, but a barely audible whimper stops me. I pivot around and narrow my eyes in curiosity, until a muffled groan carries over the silence again.

Staring manically at the chair, I edge cautiously towards it. Gripping my hand on the back, I slowly turn it around. The oxygen feels like it's being sucked from my lungs, and I step back in absolute fucking horror, with both hands over my mouth.

"Oh my God!"

My pupils dilate in shock and drift down Marie's body. From the dark patches developing around her eyes and cheeks, to her cut lip, stained with dried blood, and finally the cable ties, binding her to the chair. The unforgiving plastic cuts deep, bloodying her pale skin, and her half-open eyes plead with me. A rush of blood to the head ensues, and I feel myself swaying.

Nine years comes back hauntingly, starting with the instant I was bound, limb by limb, to my own bed. Tears cloud my eyes, because today is the day I've feared since I set foot back in the city. I've never been able to escape it. I knew it then, and I know it now.

"Devlin? Jeremy?" I scream, praying they can hear me.

Dropping to my knees, I struggle with the ties, unable to get the damn things off. Every tug causes her to pre-empt a stifled moan. Eventually, admitting defeat, I cry out, frustrated and frightened.

"I can't get them off!"

Her eyes flick to the drawer, and I rip it open. I gulp when I see a small gun, amongst random bits of papers and stationery. Rummaging through, a pair of scissors glint underneath it all.

Cutting through the plastic at her ankles, she kicks off her shoes. I move to each wrist, slicing through carefully, seeing the lines of blood brandishing her skin. A mark of evil. As I bend in front of her, I hold both ends of the duct tape covering her mouth.

"I'm sorry," I whimper tearfully, then rip it off. A pained gasp escapes her throat, and she stands wearily with a slight wobble.

"God, I'm sorry. This is my fault!"

She grabs my face hard; her eyes wide with fear. "He's here! Run!"

"No!" I shake my head. I can't leave her, not like this. Not the way I was once left. Marie, finding her own strength, tugs my arms.

"Get out of here now! Run!"

"Yes, sweets, run!" Deacon's menacing lilt fills the room, and I spin around to find him leaning on the architrave, blocking our escape. I drag Marie behind me and zone out her tears, because it's the only way I will live through this again.

And I will. I will live through it.

Whereas once I was the victim, I never will be again. I'm a true survivor, and he shall never, ever, take that away from me.

"You stay away from us!" I scream at him. "Jeremy and Devlin are downstairs!"

Deacon, thoroughly amused, edges inside. "The turncoat cunt and the useless army twat are locked in the fucking cellar!" he says mockingly, reaching into his coat and pulling out his favourite weapon of choice. "You remember this, don't you?" He turns the knife in his hand and points it at me. The light reflects off the blade's surface, and something inside instantly sits up and pays attention, recognising and remembering the painful infliction that knife has caused.

"Now," he says forcefully and slams the door shut. "I wanna play another game!" He starts his predatory walk from the door.

Marie and I move as one sideways back around the desk. The world freezes; only our breathing is heard above the small clock ticking on the wall.

"Scissors." Marie's low mutter seeps into my eardrum behind me.

Glancing around the immediate space, meeting the devil's eyes, I try to remain calm. I stretch my neck in a calculated move; relieved they are where I left them on the desk.

Marie's hand on my waist tightens, and I struggle to hide the cold shiver running through me. But it isn't her, it's *him*. It's always been him.

Something digs into my back, and I bring my hand behind me. Her thumb brushes my skin, and I touch upon cold metal. Looking into the drawer, the gun is gone. I take it from her, but don't know whether or not I'll actually be able to use it. Yet there's no time to think about that, or the potential consequences if I do, as Deacon's approach becomes more determined.

"Stay where you are!" I shout pathetically, reaching out my empty hand. "I swear to God, I'll fucking kill you!"

He stops, looks curiously, and scratches the knife to his cheek. "And how do you think you're going to stop me?"

My hand shakes as I hold the gun, proving I'm no match for him. Never have been, never will be.

He lurches forward, and my finger pulls the trigger. Nothing. Fuck! I pull it repeatedly in vain until he laughs. The sound is like fingernails across a blackboard. Digging into his pocket, he throws a few bullets over the desk, and I sob, dropping the defunct weapon.

"You've got the losing hand here, bitch! And for that, you're going to fucking pay!" Running towards us, I suddenly find a renewed strength inside. Waiting until he is within reach, I pick up the scissors and dig them into his shoulder, causing him to groan out and fall backwards. Marie, also spiked by adrenaline, dashes to the door and rips it open.

"Marie?" I shout, chasing her down the stairs, my feet rumbling on the metal. "Call the police!" I quickly throw her my phone. "Tell them he's here!"

"Run!"

Behind me, I can hear her trembling voice. "My name is Marie Dawson. I'm at the Oblivion nightclub. Deacon Black is here, he's... KARA!"

Halting immediately, her piercing cry is accompanied by the sound of something thudding to the floor. I grip my chest but dare not turn back. I sprint down to the main floor and dart my head left to right. Running towards the back corridor, I scream out but receive no reply. I double over and grip my knees, since my lungs feel as though they are about to seize up.

"Devlin? Jeremy? Please, somebody, help me!" I scream, until banging captures my attention.

"Kara?" Jeremy's shout is weak.

Running down the stairs into the cellar, I unbolt the door, and he grabs me with bloodied hands.

"He's here! Marie...Oh, God..." I cry, wondering what he's done to her. "Where's Dev?" I ask the same moment my eyes drift across the floor, and a familiar black boot captures my attention.

"Dev?" I crawl towards him. Swiping my hand over his head, the bloodied makeshift tourniquet that has been fashioned from a strip of his shirt is assisting to stem the flow.

"He'll be fine, Kara, but you won't."

I drag back instantly, pulling myself as far away from him as possible. "Jeremy... No, please don't," I whimper, realising this could be yet another well-concealed deception. His expression hardens, and for a moment, everything he's led me to believe is a lie. Words fail me, and I slam my back into the wall, fearful of what is actually real.

Ignoring me, he picks up a sweeping brush, presses his foot on the head and rips off the handle. He tugs me close and shoves the car keys in my pocket.

"When we get back upstairs, I want you to run. I want you to get in the car and drive." I start to shake my head. "I mean it! You don't fucking stop!" He smashes a kiss to my forehead.

"Thank you," I say, although it's definitely the wrong time to be expressing my gratitude that he definitely hasn't sold me out again.

"Redemption, remember?" he says and pulls back. Edging out of the cellar, the constant tap of metal on the barren brick wall echoes in the long passageway.

"Kara..." Deacon's voice drifts towards us.

Holding the crude weapon, Jeremy grabs my elbow. Running through the corridors, I have no idea where I'm going. It takes all the stamina I have to keep up with him, but thankfully, he never lets me go.

Unlocking and kicking open a door, we are back in the main room. I hesitate, seeing the club entrance and the keys in my hand. I turn to Jeremy, who is silently hissing, pointing at the door. Clutching the keys securely, I prepare to run, until my eyes scan the area and I spot Marie's leg.

"Kara!" he screams, as I tear away from him and slide across the floor to get her. Cradling her in my arms, she flinches. A slow stream of blood is coming from her hairline, and I pressurise my hand over it.

"I'm sorry, I'm sorry, I'm sorry..." I repeat. Stroking her face, there's nothing I can say to make this right. She wasn't supposed to get caught up in this. She certainly wasn't meant to get hurt like this. Rocking her gently, her eyes slowly open.

"I'm okay, baby. I love you, but leave me," she whispers.

"Oh, isn't this sweet, sweets!" Deacon stands in the main doorway, hands on the wood, grinning viciously.

"You and me, bastard! Let's fucking end this!" Jeremy twirls the stick in his hand and points it at him.

"With pleasure!" Deacon replies, widening his arms in front of him welcomingly.

Jeremy runs at him, and I watch, horrified, as he smashes the stick over his shoulder. The rat bastard lumbers back but doesn't fall. Jeremy continues to thrash out at Deacon, who steps backwards, beckoning him with his hands gleefully. He strikes out again, but Deacon sidesteps it, and the stick smashes on the floor.

With a momentary advantage, Deacon lands a solid punch to his face. The sound of flesh upon flesh drowns out everything else in the ample space.

On my knees, I help Marie up. She wobbles a little but regains her footing. Looking back, Jeremy is starting to wane. Not surprising, considering his hands were already bloodied and injured to begin with.

Quickly moving towards the door, something thuds hard behind us, reverberating on the floor, and Marie screams. I turn the same instant Deacon knocks her aside and grabs my hair. Struggling with one hand, I try to push him away, but it's in vain. Like all the times before, he is too strong, and I'm wasting my energy fighting against him – but I will never stop fighting.

I fall back and cry out shrilly when my head slams against the floor. Pain shoots through my skull to my forehead. Deacon's hand connects with my cheek and nose repeatedly, until it feels like my head is ready to explode.

Fighting back the shock, my self-protection mode finally kicks in. Doing what comes naturally, I claw and scratch him, concentrating on his bleeding shoulder, desperate to be free of this evil bastard once and for all – however, that may be.

He grabs hold of my blouse and rips it down the front. Pressing the knife against my skin, I try to get him off, until another punch to my face stops me, and he drags on my hair again.

"This is so much fucking easier when you're tied up. When I'm done with you, you'll be in a fucking box! Let the cunt sit at your grave and mourn you!" I squeeze my eyes as he continually slams my head down. I'm so dazed and confused that I wither and collapse beneath him.

Deacon stands above me, and I turn onto my stomach, crawling on my front, my arms and legs weakening. I gasp out when his boot kicks into my ribs. With my body desperate to give out, the sound of hard running echoes loudly.

"Get the fuck away from her!" Jeremy roars out.

Barely able to see, he stands with his fists rounded and his face bloodied. He lunges at Deacon, and they fall over the chairs onto the floor. Jeremy, fuelled by his hatred of a past that ensures he will always live with regret, delivers punch after punch.

Weak and beaten, my eyes begin to close, and I cry out when someone grabs me. Marie runs her hand over my head and holds me close. My guilt is abominable as I take in her hair, matted with dried blood, the deepening bruising to her face, and the cuts that may permanently scar her wrists.

"Shush, baby. It'll be over soon."

Peering back with morbid fear and curiosity, Jeremy and Deacon are literally killing each other. Until Jeremy turns, and Deacon's fist catches him out. With his hands smeared crimson, Deacon beats his face to a pulp. Jeremy, unable to take much more, finally drops to his knees. Bending down in front of him with an evil grin, Deacon pulls out his knife. I slam my hand over my mouth, as he digs the blade into Jeremy's cheek and slides it down. A mirror image of the first scar; the second sign of betrayal. Jeremy's pained groan is crystal clear, and he grabs his face and drops to the floor. Deacon, rejoicing in his action, kicks the man when he's down. *Repeatedly.*

"I'll be back for you in a minute!"

Marie and I scramble away as he swaggers over. My back hits the wall, and I look on in horror as Marie stands in front of me, protecting me, forsaking herself.

"Stay away from us!" she screams.

Deacon cracks his neck from side to side and his evil grin stretches, then he backhands her. The sound of the strike is deafening. Her body hits the floor instantly, and she writhes and moans in pain.

A glimmer of light flashes over my eyes, and I stare at the knife, constantly turning in his hand. Lunging towards me, he drags me up by the neck, and my hands instantly find his when my feet leave the ground. Kicking out, the action is futile; I can already feel the life being cruelly taken from me. Squeezing my eyes, swallowing back the suffocating sensation in my lungs, the shattering of glass from somewhere makes me open my eyes.

"Take your fucking hands off her!" Devlin is limp, covered in his own blood, holding a rudimentary glass weapon. Deacon drops me, and I gasp for air, holding my neck. In my limited vision, Devlin raises the jagged crude bottle. "Come on, you son of a bitch!"

The loud smash of wood booms out. Multiple feet enter the building, and the loading of guns resonates. "Drop your weapons!"

My heart beats furiously as armed officers, lots of them, stand sentry. Finding the strength to crawl back, Deacon remains belligerent and unresponsive to the request. He reaches down, grabs my shoulder and holds up the knife.

"I said drop your weapon!" an officer screams again.

"Why?" I gasp, seeing my reflection in his dead eyes, needing to know the truth of his hatred for me.

Everything moves in slow motion, and the blade is all I can see as it comes towards me. Horror consumes me, and I close my eyes, waiting for eternal peace to finally be mine.

My mind is awash with years old images and memories. All of them. Every single person who has touched or tortured my life; my parents, Sam, the kindred runaways, to Marie, Sophie and Walker….

Sloan.

I smile as my one and only light in the darkness shines behind my eyes.

"Drop your weapon!"

Long minutes tick by, until something jolts over me and multiple shots fills the room. Sharp, sudden pain courses through me, followed by something heavy being thrown on my front. My breathing comes out in pants, exhausting my lungs until it eventually becomes shallow. Everything feels weightless, like I'm floating. Several voices speak around me, but they begin to grow distant and hollow.

"What's your name, sweetheart?"

"Kara. She's called Kara."

"Stay with me, Kara. Look at me!"

"Please don't let her die!"

Drifting deeper and deeper, I know I have nothing left to fear in this life. Its pain can't touch me anymore. But for all the bad, it gave me something good, something beautiful.

It gave me Sloan.

And he is the last thing I see, as my light finally dies.

Chapter 40

AN INTERMITTENT PULSE resounds in my ears. I slowly open my eyes, and an off-white ceiling and clinical smell greet me. Parting my lips, my tongue slides across their parched, chapped surface. Gulping, assisting in creating saliva, my dry throat feels like I have swallowed razor blades.

"Did no one think to inform us of the bastard's release?" Sloan's angry tones rise above the beeping.

A sharp pain cuts from my arm to my shoulder, when I attempt to move. Tilting my head, he is standing by the window with another man I've never seen before.

"I'd like some answers, and they better be fucking spectacular, because my wife shouldn't be lying in this bed again! Not to mention, that no less than an hour or so after you had hung up, he was in my mother-in-law's house, almost battering her to death!"

"I'm sorry, Mr Foster, but I wasn't told. At the time of my earlier calls, he was still being held. Shortly after we spoke, the woman retracted her statement. Since your wife was unable to confirm immediate identification, they had no legal ground to hold him further."

"'No legal ground'? And I suppose my wife's complaint had *no legal ground* to investigate months ago when you should have?"

"Like I said, I'm very sorry for what has happened. I'll leave now, but I'll need to speak to her when she is well enough."

"Fine, but have your superior expect a call from my solicitor, because I'm not fucking letting this go."

The man slams the door behind him and a familiar warmth covers me. I murmur and stretch, feeling like I've been hit by a lorry, although bizarrely, I feel completely refreshed. I shouldn't, given how I have ended up in the goddamn hospital again, but it's more of mental refreshed than a physical one.

"Thank God!" Sloan's exclamation is a welcome sound, and I rub my eyes fully open. He looks tired and exhausted. And he's still wearing the same suit I had picked out for him *three* mornings ago. I don't have to ask to know that he hasn't left my side again. As always, I'm more concerned for him, than I am for myself, but that is never going to change.

"Hi," I whisper.

"Hey, my love."

Stroking his face gingerly, my arm is sore and heavy. I try to sit up, but it's useless, considering one limb just isn't working. He lifts me to rest my back on the headboard and I turn to my shoulder, which is bandaged down to my elbow. Rotating it, pain seeps back in, and I wince.

"What do you remember?" he asks, touching my sore face, while his own screws up in anger.

"Deacon was at the club." My eyes drift over the sheet, while everything comes back in orderly fashion. "Marie was tied to the chair in the office. I got her out, but he was at the door. I stabbed him with the scissors, and then we ran. The corridor...the cellar... Oh, God!" I bring my hands to my neck as tears flood my eyes. "He hit me repeatedly, and he tried to strangle me. I was on the floor, and he had his knife pointed at me, but then the police came in. The last thing I remember was...pain." I touch my shoulder. "I thought I was dying," I admit. He cradles his hand on the back of my neck and rocks me.

"No, baby. It's over. It's finally over."

"Did they get him?" I ask, pulling back, ignoring the pain. "They did arrest him, didn't they? They're not letting him off again?"

He holds my head gently, although his expression is one of anger and disdain. "He's gone. They shot him. Took him straight out." His hand drifts to my shoulder. "Unfortunately, he still had the knife in his hand..."

"One final reminder," I murmur, putting my hand over his.

"One more failure," he counters.

"No. I heard you arguing with the detective," I confess. "It's not his fault, or mine, or Marie's. And it's definitely not yours." Wordlessly, he leans forward and tenderly kisses me. "How is she?"

He smiles sadly. "She's doing okay. A bit cut up, very tearful...blaming herself."

"Have you called John?"

He nods. "Yeah, he's here. Speeded down the motorway at over a hundred to get back here." He looks sheepish, and I narrow my eyes.

"He got caught, didn't he?"

"Hmm, according to Parker the officer didn't take too kindly to his language, and they told him to expect a court appearance." I roll my eyes; it's the least of his worries. "You up for a walk?"

I tentatively move my arms, and although still heavy, I think I can make it with the use of the wheelchair in the corner. "Sure, I'd like that." Reaching out for him, he bends, picks me up, and walks us out of the room.

"I can still use my legs…just!" I admonish, tucking my head into his shoulder, while he grunts his loveable disapproval. On the way through the corridors, Stuart stops us.

"And where do you think you two are going?"

"Hi, Doc. We're going for a walk, apparently."

"Sloan?"

"I'm taking her to see Rem, is that allowed?" Stuart rolls his eyes and nods.

"How are you feeling?" he asks, pulling out his light pen and shining it in my eyes.

"Fine, until someone just blinded me," I chide, annoyed that I'm now not only being carried like a child again, but also seeing blobs of light.

"You've got your sense of humour back," he says dryly, waving his hand as we continue our pace.

Holding on tight to Sloan's neck, we walk into another room. He drops me on the bed, and Jeremy turns from the window. I can't bequeath a smile seeing him cut up again.

"I'm sorry, Kara. We didn't realise he was in the building until-"

I shake my head, and he stops. "We all knew it would eventually come to this. It had to, but he's gone now."

"I've been thinking about it, and I'm still going to turn myself in to the police, tell them what I did and live with the consequences."

"No, I don't want you to." I glance at Sloan and back again. "As far as I'm concerned, it's finally over. You, inside, prolongs it. And it means my suffering continues, as will yours, and I can't live with that."

"Kara-"

"No. You've been living with the consequences of it for nine years. It's done!"

Tearful, I get off the bed and shuffle out of the room. Loitering in the corridor, Tommy and Parker move towards me, finishing in a combined run as they pick me up and swaddle me between them. Uncomfortable, I shuffle out.

"John's in with Marie. We'll take you to her," Tommy says, looking down at my hand. I take it willingly, then Parker's.

"Look who we found roaming the corridors!" Parker jokes as we enter. I stop in the doorway, absorbing the frailty of a woman who has always been my inner strength.

"Hi, honey," she says, starting to cry. John lifts up out of the chair, but I stop him, and climb onto the bed and curl up against my mother. Running my hand down her face, she hisses when I cling to her.

"Sorry," I mutter, as she kisses me.

"He was waiting in the house. He pretty much knocked me out as soon as I entered. I woke up bound and gagged."

"Did he….?"

She rapidly shakes her head. "No, baby, he didn't touch me. Not like that. I'm sorry I wasn't strong enough to fight him off, for allowing him to hurt you again."

"No, no, no, no…" I repeat until her finger covers my lips.

"I'll never forgive myself."

"And I'll never forgive myself that I brought him back here. And he finally did what I feared, and he hurt those I love." Holding her tight, she eventually drifts off.

I lift my head as the light snore blowing against my face indicates it's my time to leave. Looking up, I'm still alone with her, Walker having left some time ago.

"I love you, Mum," I murmur and kiss her cheek.

Fidgeting with the nightgown, pulling the open back shut, I trudge down the corridor. I pass by the nurse's station, and Stuart steps out and hands me some paperwork.

"So, I've been told in no uncertain terms that you *are* going home tonight." He touches my cheek with a look of disdain. I don't know if I want to look in the mirror judging his expression right now.

"Is that for my benefit or his?" I jerk my head to my room, where I presume my beloved kid and his surrogate father are waiting.

Stuart laughs and motions me to the other side of the station. I pull up a seat, sign off the discharge papers and drop the pen.

"Is Marie going to be okay?" I ask.

Cradling my chin, he studies my face while he speaks. "Physically, the rat bastard didn't do too much damage. The knock to the head is superficial, but obviously, the wrists and ankles *may* scar. Mentally, however, I don't know. Honestly, you know more about that than I do. Look, if you need anything tonight, give us a call, and I'll be right over. I'll see you later." He kisses the top of my head, picks up his stethoscope and leaves.

"Hi, Doctor Andrews said to give you these." A young nurse passes me a clean set of scrubs.

"Where are my clothes?" I ask, not that I want to see them again, but still, knickers and a bra would be nice.

"Oh, the police have taken them for forensics. He told me to tell you he wants those back in a few days - something about them being dry cleaned the rich way?" She shrugs her shoulders and laughs.

Walking back into my room, Walker, Dev, and Sloan, are huddled together. Jake is speaking into his phone by the window.

"No, Char she's fine. No, you and Soph can see her another day. No, you're not coming down here! Fine, I'll tell him, for crying out loud!"

"Hi," I greet, as the quartet of heads turn. Sloan grabs me and sits me on his lap. Walker looks me over, grave and considerate, until he's eventually appeased that I'm actually fine. Sort of.

"I'm sorry I wasn't here. I failed to keep my promise."

"There wasn't anything you could have done," Dev says, squeezing his uncle's shoulder. I stare at him, fixing on the stitches to the side of his head, remembering how I saw him, face down and unconscious. He smiles, accentuating his bruising, but other than that he seems to be in good spirits. Clearly, he hasn't spent the last few days in the hospital with the rest of us.

"He's right. If you were, he would have found another way. Don't be sorry, be thankful." He pulls back, but I keep hold of his hand. "I love you, John Walker. Thank you for making me come back, for your reassurance." His brow creases as runs his hand through his hair, inconspicuously wiping his eye.

"I love you, too, honey. I'm going back to my beloved. I'll see you soon." I watch his back disappear out of the door.

"Yeah, I better get going, too, before Doc puts me in a dress again and makes me stay this time." Devlin kisses me and then Sloan.

"Wait up, Dev. Kara, Charlie and I will see you tomorrow." Jake bends and kisses my forehead. "Warning; she said she'll be by at the crack of dawn. And I do expect breakfast with a smile!" Then the door closes softly behind him.

Twisting in Sloan's lap, he rocks us back and forth. Gently placing me down, he starts the process of undressing and redressing me. Standing up, he tugs off the gown.

"Arms up."

I lift them and grimace as pain taunts my muscles. The top drops down, and he holds the trousers at my feet. Pulling them up, his eyes meet mine. For the first time since we met, they carry a different kind of hope, the kind that tells me tomorrow is our new beginning. And it is, because we've waited almost a decade to be able to share it together.

"Let's go home, my love."

I wrap my arms around him and shuffle out of the room. Sloan drops the carrier into Stuart's arms at the nurse's station on our way out.

"Incinerate them!"

Edging down the corridors, the place comes to life inside my mind, and I relive each moment with vivid clarity.

As we walk across the car park, I run my finger over the bonnet of the Aston and slide inside. Driving through the city, the afternoon sun brightens our way.

Closing my eyes, I can finally look forward to tomorrow, and the future that finally awaits me.

"Baby, dinner's here," Sloan shouts up from downstairs.

Rummaging through the junk, I pull out the pictures that he had copied and framed when we were in Manchester, and the few I still had packed away from when I moved out of the flat. Gathering them together, I make my way downstairs.

I enter the kitchen as Sloan removes a Tupperware container from the microwave. I pull one over and remove the lid, causing the steam to billow out.

"Careful."

I pick up the one and only fork and stand poised, waiting to taste whatever he's had delivered. He pulls out a single plate and starts to spoon a little of everything onto it. Picking it up, he motions his head to the living room, and I follow, pictures in hand.

He sets the plate on the coffee table, then sits on the floor and drags me down to him. Uncorking the bottle of champagne, he pours two glasses and hands me one.

"To the future. May it finally be peaceful, but long and fraught with disagreement, and lots of make up sex!" I laugh and take a sip. I lean into him and kiss his chin while he removes the frames from my hands.

"So, where are these going to live, my love?" he asks sincerely, and I watch as he flicks through them. Me and my mother, twenty years ago. Me and Sam, three years ago. Me and Marie, two years ago. And finally, us, one year ago.

"I don't know, but I know I don't ever want to forget." I pick up the pictures of Sam and my mum. "If she had been nurturing, I would probably still be in Manchester. If Sam had stayed clean, I would never have come to the hotel. These people brought me to you, and I'm grateful for that."

He continues to look until something captures his inner thoughts. Shifting me aside, he leaves the room, and I tuck into dinner while waiting for him to return. Coming back through the door, he has two stacks of paperwork in his hands.

He kneels next to me and hands them over. I pass him the fork and read through the documents in confusion. "I don't understand."

"They're the deeds for Oblivion, and the other is for an empty building I've had for a few years. After what happened, I think it's time to start afresh. As soon as the police let us back in, I'm going to strip it out and sell it to the first bidder. It can go for pennies for all I care, I just want it gone."

"Baby, I -"

"No, that place and everything it embodies is part of a life I want to leave behind. The reason why I bought it years ago, was because it was an easy way to make money, and to find easy…"

"Women?" I finish.

"Yes," he answers sheepishly. Stroking my face, he looks at me seriously. "It became my own place to forget, just for a night at a time. I even named it as such."

"What will you do with the new place? Another club?"

He shakes his head. "No, my mother has this bright idea that I should make it into a drop-in centre."

"A drop-in centre?" I query.

"Hmm, for domestic abuse. Open to everyone, regardless of their status or how much money they have in their pocket. It makes sense, since we are all a victim, in some way or another."

Staring into his eyes, it is clear he will always see us as that. Nothing will change it, but I will never attempt to change him. Victim or not, he is my saviour.

"We're not victims anymore. We're survivors."

He stares down but doesn't respond. Leaving that hanging thickly in the air, he starts to feed me, until I'm full and tipsy, and my eyes close of their own accord.

"Sloan?" I jolt in panic, sensing my body being elevated. Meeting his midnight blues, I hold him securely as he carries me upstairs.

"Shush, I've got you, baby."

Laying me down, he rolls me over him and sighs. His hand works over my face, down my neck and then my chest. Everything feels tender under his gentle touch. I wipe a tear from my eye but can't stop them from falling.

"Don't cry. Talk to me, my love."

I press my hand to his chest, silently counting in time with his heartbeat. "I once believed tomorrow would never come. It was always a reoccurring dream that would be banished by nightmares."

"Tomorrow is the real start of forever for us. One where I want to wake up every day, kiss my wife, and thank God for everything I have. One where I want to practice making beautiful, brown-haired, green-eyed children who will love to tell me no," he says with a smile. "Tomorrow is no longer a dream."

As I hold him tight, guided by his drifting voice, my subconscious takes me back in time.

Sitting in my cubbyhole, I stroke ted and pick up my book. Flicking through the pages, I look down at my adult feet, my favourite slippers from a childhood gone by adorning them. A shadow darkens the gap under the door, and it slowly opens.

Sloan's frame blocks the light seeping inside, and he reaches out to me with a smile. I stand, take his hand, and look around as he leads us outside for the final time.

I get into the car, grip his fingers and twist his wedding band. "Are you ready to go home?"

Gazing back at the house, when I wake tomorrow, this place will still exist, but I will no longer fear the monsters, or the pain it represents because love has finally set me free.

"I am home."

Epilogue

SLACKENING MY TIE and tapping my fingers rhythmically on the desk, my frustration deepens. Why I agreed to let this meeting go ahead, on today of all days, was one of my worse decisions. I have far more important things I could be doing right now; such as kissing my wife until she's breathless, spreading her out in front of me, and seeing how many times I can make her scream in ecstasy.

Halting my wayward thoughts and adjusting myself uncomfortably in my seat, my eyes roam from left to right, studying the occupants lining the table. I pour myself another coffee and take a sip, as the arguments over today's agenda continue to flow, dampening my burgeoning need.

"I do not agree to that!"

"You don't need to because you'll be outvoted."

"Who the hell do you think you're speaking to?"

I huff out and roll my eyes while the bickering continues. Every fucking board meeting ends up the same way; unnecessary squabbling and infighting. And they all once had the cheek to berate me of my age way back when. I sure as hell didn't stamp my feet when they deemed me too young and too stupid to run a company. One that is still extremely successful and lining their pockets to no end.

"Excuse me, but I'm the fourth majority shareholder of this board!" Andy Blake bleats out to anyone who actually gives a flying fuck. Normally, this shit wouldn't fly with me, but considering who the man's connections are, I'll let him have his say. It gives him a sense of entitlement, and if that's where he finds comfort, then so be it.

Picking up the tablet, I absentmindedly scroll through the dozen or so emails requiring my attention at some point.

I gaze out of the window from the head of the table. With my elbow on the wood and my chin on my hand, my phone vibrates in front of me. Dropping my eyes down, while the grown men continue to demonstrate tantrums five-year-olds would be proud of, I grin when my wife's name glows. Tapping the text, our wedding picture fills the screen. Opening the message, another comes through, telling me what I already know:

You're late!

I glance at my Rolex; it has just gone seven. We've been in here since ten o'clock this morning, attempting to hash out yet another deal that is neither use nor ornament to any man sat at this table.

Lost in the moment, I begin to flick through the pictures on the iPad. Most are just random stuff that Kara takes, but I stop on the ones of her sleeping. The ones I took the first night she became my Mrs Foster.

I slide my finger across the screen, and pictures I had forgotten about appear. Seeing my eighteen-year-old self, with my arm flung around Stuart, I sigh. These were part of the dark years, the Black years; a time when I would bed anything just to have a moment to forget. The nameless, faceless women I sought solace in whilst unable to have she who ignited the flame and kept it alight.

Guilt consumes me while I reminisce.

It has been almost nine months since the rat bastard finally met his demise at the hands of London's finest. In the days and weeks that proceeded the event, she grew more determined to live a life outside of mine and prove that she could accomplish anything.

I can still remember the day John called and told me my wife had just quit. In the middle of the day. I sat in this very room, three clients watching on rather amused, as he cursed over my speakerphone. I, in turn, smiled, proud that she was finally taking back control.

And she's been taking it back ever since.

Now she's studying part-time. I confess the world stopped turning when she arrived home one day, prospectuses in hand, proclaiming she was going to study. After much deliberation, she finally decided upon something she was well versed in, something many have no first-hand experience of – counselling.

My hesitancy at her choice, and the fact that it would raise ghosts from the dead, was overruled. As perfectly put by John, Marie, and even my mother, who better to help others than someone who is living proof you can survive and prevail and come out stronger.

And she has.

Watching the changes develop has been astounding. Gone is the girl who stood in the shadows, waiting for life to pass by quickly. Gone is the girl who hated to be touched. In her place, is a woman who is strong, fearless, determined to be the champion of those who have suffered pain. She is determined to be a voice for the unseen.

Scraping my chair back and walking towards the window, I put the tablet down and stare at the skyline.

"Sloan?"

A grin forms when I capture the reflection of the table behind me, and the memory of Kara laid out teases me.

"Sloan?"

Turning to my side, Andy Blake is now next to me, his hands gripping the windowsill. He furrows his brows from our colleagues and then back to me. His eyes narrow and I instantly know what he wants to talk about - and it isn't the commotion still raging behind us. Continuing to stare out of the window, I wait for him to say it. When long minutes pass without so much as a sigh, I break the ice.

"Are you going to tell me you don't agree with my decision today?"

He laughs heartily. "Sloan, I'd never bet against you, you know that. But there is something..." his voice trails off. "My little Evelyn is seeing someone."

He looks at me expectantly, wanting answers I really don't want to give him. Ever since the night I announced the engagement, Remy and Evie Blake have become very close. And, as already noted that night, Daddy clearly doesn't approve. My hand tightens on the iPad while he makes his assumptions.

"It's pretty serious by all accounts. What do you know about this thug she's infatuated with?"

I grind my jaw that the two-faced bastard dares to speak such things when he forgets how he made his money. Certain elements of these men I shouldn't know, but John, ever the protective father, made it our business to be well informed. The last thing I need is the police showing up and ransacking the office and our homes for illegal dealings and suspected corruption.

"That *thug*, as you so eloquently call him, is one of the best men I've ever known. You would do well not to judge, Andrew." Using his full name, my tone harder than it was before, he rubs his chin.

"But those scars-"

"Are proof of the sacrifices he will make for those he loves. Tell me, Andrew, would you do the same?" The man shifts uncomfortably, determining his unspoken answer. He walks away, and I pull out my phone, dropping Rem a text to inform him of dark clouds that may eventually come to pass.

Finally, the room erupts into complete chaos. "Gentlemen!" I bellow, causing them to stop instantly. "Quite finished? I think it's safe to assume we will agree to disagree. For once, as the majority shareholder, I'm exercising my authority. Now, sign them!"

They all groan, pick up the agreements and sign them grudgingly. Each one throws the document back on the table, still ranting and raving as he leaves. Being the last man standing, I collect up the papers as the door opens.

"Hi," Sophie whispers, edging inside, taking them from me. "Good day?" she queries sarcastically. I laugh and shake my head.

"What are you still doing here?" I ask, knowing Doc has a big night planned for her. But unlike her, I have no trouble keeping secrets. She shrugs her shoulders the same moment the good doc walks through the door. "Hey," I greet him, as he takes his missus in his arms and winks over the top of her head.

"Ready?" he asks her.

"Sure, I just need to get my things. I'll get these copied on Monday, if that's okay?"

I nod as she leaves.

"You're really gonna do it, then?" I query, seeing the perfectly fitted suit and the sweat beads already forming.

"Call me foolish, but I really am!" he laughs, patting his pocket.

"Doc, I'd call you many things, but never that. Foolish is watching the woman you love through a lens for a decade. Just one thing?"

"What?" he asks candidly, taking a step closer.

"After she says yes, tell her to fuck you like a good wife should! She'll know what you mean." Laughing, I pat his shoulder in jest. His eyes narrow and I saunter out of the door, leaving him confused.

"Sloan?" I ignore him as I walk through the empty corridors, and board the first lift that arrives.

I slide into the Aston and pull out my phone. "Hey, baby, I'm finally on my way."

"I'll be waiting."

Pulling up to the gates, the sun is beginning to set in the distance. Glancing into the security cabin, Max quickly drops his feet from the desk and straightens himself. I wave him off, tap in the code, and wait for the gates to open.

"I'm sorry, Mr Foster," he says apologetically.

"Don't be. Go home to your wife; enjoy the evening. And take tomorrow off."

He grins. "Thanks. Have a good night."

I salute him, then speed down the driveway. Approaching the door, it swings open and sprightly feet run away. I tilt my head curiously, not seeing my light.

"Baby?" I call out.

I take the stairs two at a time, but each room I check is empty. Pushing back the dressing room door, I drop my bag on the floor, next to Kara's, and strip off my jacket. Rolling up my sleeves, I push back the main bathroom door, but am welcomed by yet another empty room. Giggles drift up from downstairs, and as I turn, I'm stopped short when my eyes skim over the vanity. Picking up the object, I smile, a sense of unconfirmed completeness overwhelms.

"Kara?"

Cutting a quick path onto the landing and dashing down the stairs, the sound of laughter floats in from outside. Dusk is beckoning, and the lights sparkle along the trail. Adjusting my tie and grabbing a bottle of champagne, I slip my phone from my trouser pocket and dial. A soft ringing chimes out through the trees and shrubs as I walk down the path. Striding into the clearing, Kara spins around from the gazebo, under which she has set out supper.

"You're late!" she says, hands on hips, with a nervous, yet beautiful smile. Cocking my head, she looks different. Not tired or... I don't know, just different.

She tiptoes across but pauses deep in thought. Studying her expression, my dick stands to attention. No amount of mental coaxing will suppress him when she's near. Still watching her, since she seems to have forgotten that I'm here, I feel in my pocket, checking it's still there, and then take matters into my own hands. *Literally.*

"Put me down!" she shrieks, as my hand swipes under her legs. Her arms disobey her reasoning when they affix firmly around my neck, and she tentatively kisses my throat. This is one of the things I love the most about her; her innocence. The way she still shies away when put in a position she's uncomfortable with. But the one thing I am glad of, is that the asexual girl who retreated within herself is definitely gone.

I drop her down on the blanket, slide the hair from her face and bring my lips to hers. It feels like forever since I last saw her. Running my hand up her front, I slowly unbutton the blouse and pull it apart.

Tentatively touching her skin, the majority of the marks that spelt out the life she has suffered are gone - courtesy of the best plastic surgeon money can buy.

"Happy anniversary," she whispers, dragging her fingers through my hair. I move into her touch, needing it to soothe me; to complete me.

"Another first," I murmur.

I pull the blouse down her arms, then feel around her back and unfasten her skirt. Sliding it down her legs, I smile at the lingerie she's wearing, realising she's outsmarted me.

"Didn't I destroy these?" I query innocently, seeing something similar from our wedding night. She laughs but doesn't answer. Carefully removing her bra, her aroused nipples stick out, just begging for attention. Squeezing the breast that is now blemish-free, I suck it into my mouth, enjoying the way her hands clench my shoulders in reciprocation. Palming her other tit, her breath quickens.

"Sloan!" she cries out.

Her small fingers find my waistcoat and she has it removed and thrown aside in seconds. Pulling me close, she teases me with an insignificant kiss, then she repeats her action with my shirt, until that too, is gone.

My hands skim down her thighs, before I gently spread her knees out and lift back to study her, wondering. Dipping my head to her apex, the blood rushes to my groin, ensuring my impossibly hard dick now has my zip imprinted on it.

"Say the words, Mrs Foster," I coax, showing her my cocky grin. She closes her eyes momentarily and sighs, before opening them with a new determination.

"Fuck me like a good husband should!"

Accepting her invitation, I hastily divest myself of my trousers and shorts and rub my rock-hard shaft up her leg. I glide my hand down her back to her arse, under the lace of her shorts and make the conscious decision not to destroy them. She gives me an impressed look and wiggles to assist. I tug them down her thighs and throw them aside, then press her knees down, opening her to me.

Dragging her forward unexpectedly, her little yelp encourages me, and I take her hand and wrap it around me, moving it slowly. Her fingertip swipes over my crown, and she brings it to her mouth. The fire in her eyes burns while she licks her finger far too seductively.

I position myself at her opening, but desire gets the better of me, and I slam into her. Grasping her back, I pull her up as her core tightens and pulsates lightly. With her arms around my shoulders, she levitates herself up and down. Holding her arse, digging my fingers into the perfect round globes, I assist and guide her up and down on my length - although I know I shouldn't be as rough if what I found upstairs contains any truth. Right now, I realise I should have looked at the fucking thing properly. But right now, my need to find release in her is far too strong.

Laying her back down, I run my hand down her leg and then bring her ankle over my shoulder. With my other hand beside her head, I thrust in unforgivingly, possibly to the point of discomfort.

Moaning out, she throws her hands to her sides, grasping the blanket and drops her other knee further down, selflessly giving me more room. She's completely open to me, I move inside her heat and wetness effortlessly. Refusing to remove my eyes from hers, I observe every flicker of emotion ripple over them.

Long minutes pass by until she arches her back and my balls feel like they are about to explode from the pressure. I latch my mouth onto her nipple and suck it between my lips. My palm cups her fleshy breast, and I give it a little squeeze as she moans into me. Grunting my satisfaction, she starts to raise her pelvis up, silently requesting more. And since I would never deny my lovely wife anything, I give her what she wants.

Repeatedly.

"Oh God!" she manages to get out, pressing into me, creating a deeper connection. Her muscles hold me in a vice-like grip, taking me over the edge with her.

"I've got you, baby. Fuck!"

The strength of the orgasm rips through me like never before. Still plunging in and out, expelling myself, she takes willingly and gives in return. Coaxing me down, her tender kisses steal my breath as she arches her back higher, drawing it out until we are both breathless and on the verge of exhaustion.

Flopping onto her, still mindful, I brush my thumb across her bottom lip. Her legs circle around my back, forcing my body to respond.

"That's one!" she says, cheekily.

I reach behind, unravel her legs, and inch down her body until my nose dips into her belly button. Breathing in her scent, my senses are alive. She even smells different. I gently massage her stomach, as I continue my descent, and my nose brushes over her swollen clit. Dragging my tongue over it, she hisses, and her thighs entrap my head. I smile to myself and flick her sensitive folds. Sucking momentarily, until I can feel the change in her again, I pull back. Her head darts up, and she gives me that begging look I absolutely despise, but tonight, I'm willing to let it go.

"Something you want to tell me?" I query, dipping my finger inside, circling it leisurely.

"Oh, that's…amazing!" she murmurs, her now sludgy green eyes still staring into mine, while I pop the offending finger into my mouth.

"*That's* what you want to tell me?"

She shakes her head quickly, and I dip mine back down, wondering what it will take for her to say two words that will change everything.

My tongue breaches her centre, and I shamelessly taste my wife, until she's calling out my name – and probably giving the neighbours something to talk about if they hear her.

While I wait for her moaning and shuddering to subside, I delicately rub her stomach. Flopping back down, I cage her under me.

"That's two!" I say, with my hand still toying with the place I always want to be. She wriggles and puts her hand over mine on her stomach.

"This makes three," she whispers nervously, chewing her lip. "I'm pregnant." My smile instantly stretches from ear to ear. Kissing her until she forces me back, she bestows me with the *look*. "You're not upset that it's too soon?" she asks, questioning the ridiculous.

"No. Never. It's perfect." I dig into my pocket and pull out the test I had found upstairs. Passing it to her, she beams and twists it around.

Stroking my hands down her face, I kiss her stomach – our unborn - another first. "I can't wait to meet you," I whisper, filled such emotion and pride, that I fear I might let down my own walls and cry. I stare at her belly, longing to see it stretch and change shape, as the life we have created together begins to grow and flourish inside her womb.

"You'll be an amazing father, just like John is to you."

I crawl back up her body as the moon starts to rise in the twilight. Picking us both up, she constantly kisses my neck as I stride through the dusky trail and back into the house.

When I lay her on the bed, admiring her already flushed complexion, she rubs her fingers through my hair and smiles. "Now, make love to me."

My hand drifts down her chest, and I thumb her nipple while I align her body to mine. I smile at her mewling and sighs, the moment I slide back inside heaven. With one hand over her belly, protecting our precious gift, I know I'll never love anything the way I've always loved her.

The moonlight seeps into the bedroom while I cradle her tenderly in my arms. Unable to stay awake any longer, her penultimate words echo, and for the first time in over fifteen years, I allow myself to remember.

"Mum's going to kill you when she sees you!" I kick the door as Charlie sticks her tongue out in response and continues to makeover her Barbie's.

Sliding down the bannister, my t-shirt sleeve catches on the end and pulls on my arm, causing the dark patches of skin to burn again.

I rub my arm as I pad into the kitchen, and my mother smiles, then quickly turns away. Walking around the island, I block her movement and touch her severely bruised face and neck, seeing the true extent of what the bastard did after he took his fists to Charlie and me two days ago.

"Fucking bastard!" I swear even though I know I'm going to be told off for foul language. But I don't care, because he is, and I was brought up not to lie.

She huffs and glares. "Sloan, what have I told you about your mouth, especially in front of your sister?"

"She's not here! She's upstairs, putting your make-up on her dolls!"

"Sloan?" she says, a firmer edge in her tone.

I throw my hands up. "Fine! Not to swear and not to lie. But I'm not because he is a fuc-" Her hand stops my wayward tongue venting further.

"Baby, I don't feel well, and I'm tired. I also have someone coming over shortly that I'd like you to meet."

I grab a carton of juice from the fridge and slap it on the marble top. "Who?"

"He's the new security guard. You know, you should have gone out with Jeremy if you're bored."

I drop my head onto the worktop, trying to be as dramatic as any twelve-year-old can be. It usually works well. I learned from an early age that if I was annoying enough, I could pretty much get my own way – that is until he showed up and brought him to live with us. Now, I spend more time locking myself in my room so that I don't have to look at the little psycho's face, or feel the brunt of his psycho father's fists after he's fed up of using my mother as a human punch bag.

"He's with Deacon," I confess. "You know I don't like him." And the reasons why I don't like him are not known to my mother. I inconspicuously touch my palm, the one he took his knife to not so long back. I never told her, because she has enough on her plate.

"Honey, you just have to learn to get on. He's part of this family, too."

"But why does he have to live here? Doesn't he have a mother?" I down my orange and slam it back down again, the same moment my chair is turned.

"Sloan, stop it! You know better than this! And no, he doesn't-"

"Mummy?"

I'm saved the lecture as Charlie runs into the room, her blonde hair knotted, and her face smeared with the black pencils she was playing with. Rocking from one foot to the other, she holds her hands behind her back. I climb off the stool and attempt to get whatever she's hiding, but she shuffles her shoulders, refusing to let me see.

"Show me your hands, Charlotte."

I grin as my mum towers over her.

"I'm sorry, Mummy," she says in a tiny voice with a guilty face, and runs to the island and slaps the broken pencils on the stool.

"Oh, Charlotte! How many times do I have to tell you to stop playing with my make-up?" Mum tells her off gently, knowing if she raises her voice too high, she will put the shrill crying of a baby to shame.

Charlie's eyes enlarge, and I wait for it. I might be twelve, but I'm not stupid. Just like I know if I pull out the fake dramatics, I will get my own way, Charlie knows if she does one of two things, she'll also get hers. Which means, she's either going to put on that face she does before she's about to cry, or she's going to go wide-eyed and innocent. Squinting my eyes, hers begin to widen, and her head tilts to the side. I gasp at my mum falling under her spell.

"This is such bulls-"

"Sloan!" my mum yells.

She stands between us, wondering which one to admonish first; me for my colourful language - which Deacon says all the time, by the way - or Charlie, for using a five-finger discount in her make-up bag. She's about to open her mouth, and we start to edge back, when the gate bell rings.

"I'll get it!" Charlie and I scream at the same time and charge to the door.

While we race up the driveway, fear gets the better of me, when a large, looming figure becomes clearer. My legs begin to stop moving, and I grip

Charlie's arm. She instantly turns to me with a frightened look on her face that I've seen far too much of the last few years.

"Who is he?" she whispers, trying to act like the big girl she desperately wants to be.

"I don't know but keep hold of my hand!"

Getting closer, he's wearing combats, big boots and a t-shirt. Removing his sunglasses, he reminds me of the men that sometimes come here with him. We round the last overgrown shrub and the man grins.

"Hi, does Julia Black live here?"

"Yeah, but who are you?" I reply cockily, trying to act older than I am. I've been practising, although it's clearly not working, since he just looks like he wants to laugh at me.

"Come here, kid." The big guy crooks his finger. I slowly glance at Charlie, who looks ready to wee herself, and step closer. Pulling my arm through the railings, he grins. "The correct answer is 'yes, sir', understand?"

I gulp back and nod furiously. I start to move my arm back, but his fingers tighten and he pulls up my sleeve.

"Who did this to you, kid?" I shrug, because we're not supposed to talk about it. "Kid?" I shake my head and he sighs. "Hey, sweetheart, come here," he says, winking at Charlie, who timidly approaches, now sucking her thumb – her nervous tell.

"Hi," she whispers. His arm slides through the railings, and he strokes her face. Dropping his hand to her sleeve, he lifts it up. His expression hardens, and he looks really angry.

"Hi, sweetheart. I'm here to see your mummy, is she in?"

Still sucking her thumb, she lowers her hand and nods. "She's in the kitchen, but she's mad at us. I wouldn't go in there, because she'll be mad at you, too."

The big man roars out laughing and shakes his head. "I'll keep that in mind. What's your name, sweetheart?"

"Charlotte Louise Black," she whispers again, still unsure.

With a thoughtful look, he winks at me. "Charlotte, you say?" She nods again, a little smile coming out. "Well, I think I'm going to call you Cheeky Charlie, is that okay?"

"I like it," she giggles. "What's your name?"

"I'm Walker. John Walker. Now that we've met, are you going to let me in?"

She flashes him the beaming smile she saves for a select few and runs over to the control panel. Tapping in the code, the gates creak open, and he hesitantly enters. His eyes roam over the garden – well, what you can see of *it since he refuses to have anyone come out and preen it – and up to the rusted security cameras that work when they choose.*

"Wow, this is big," he says to Charlie, who shuffles into his side and tugs his hand, much to his - and my - surprise. I meet his eyes while he holds her hand securely, and for the first time in forever, I suddenly feel safe.

"We have a secret garden and a pool, too. Can you swim?" Her eyes are wide and hopeful since we aren't allowed in there without an adult.

"Erm…"

He looks taken aback, and I conceal my laugh as Charlie waits for his answer, although she doesn't wait long enough. Now bored, she sprints down the driveway and slips on the loose gravel, but picks herself back up instantly. I look up at the big guy, who shakes his head.

"Is she always like that?" I nod continually. He's seen nothing yet. "What's your name, kid?"

"Sloan," I reply, in my best manly voice.

"Sloan, what?"

"Sloan Oliver Foster." He raises his brows, and I sigh. "Sir," I aa, and he smiles.

"Better. You want something in life, you fight for it, including being treated with respect. Manners don't cost anything. Remember that, kid."

Walking down the driveway, his eyes look up and around, scoping the place out. I really do hope my mother knows him, because if not, we might not have a house left.

"Where did you and your sister get the bruises, kid?" I halt and look up at him, terrified of telling him the truth, but equally terrified of lying to protect the bastard.

"Franklin," I whisper, purging myself.

"Your dad?"

I shake my head. "No, he's Charlie's dad. My dad is dead."

Walker gets down to my height and runs his hand over my face. "I swear he'll never touch you again, son."

Staring into his eyes, I see the truth in his words, but unbeknown to me at the time, the bastard never did.

"I'll leave when I get my fucking money and not a moment sooner! And you, you fucking cunt, can get out of my way!" Franklin's voice booms out from downstairs.

Picking up my CD player, I slip my headphones on, letting the music drown out the pain and arguing. A reverberation rips through the house, and I run to the window, as Franklin's car speeds up the driveway. I edge closer to my door, and open it a fraction, listening to my mum and Walker talk.

"When do you expect him back?" Walker asks.

"I don't know. Deacon's still here, he can't just leave him."

"I think you'll find men like him do. What's the boy like?"

"Deacon? He's...he's cold, almost like he hates everything."

"What about his mother? Does she have anything to do with him?"

"No, she abandoned him years ago. I try my best with him, but it's hard since Franklin lets him do whatever he pleases. Each time I try to show some control, he throws it back in my face. Sometimes I think he blames me, you know?"

Walker murmurs, and I start to close my door until my mum speaks again.

"John, I know we don't really know each other, and I'm asking a lot, but I'd really appreciate it if you would accept the job. The kids really need someone they can trust, now more than ever."

I shut my door with a smile, realising John Walker might be coming around more often. Who knows, he might even be good for my mum.

Tapping my pen, doing the homework I said I had completed two days ago but hadn't for obvious reasons, the headphones are ripped from my ears. I spin around to find Deacon standing behind me. One fist is clenched, while the other holds his precious knife – a gift from his dad.

"Get out of my room!" I drag the headphones back off of him and throw them down. Edging closer, he grins. His shadow covers me entirely; being three inches taller and a year older.

"My dad's left because of your bitch of a mother. I hate her, and I hate that whiny little bitch of a sister, too!"

"Get out!" I hiss again, although I'm secretly terrified watching his hand tighten on the handle.

"I hate all of you. I will take away everything you love, and I will hurt it and damage it, and every time you see it, you will see me!"

Jolting upright, I gasp and instantly turn to Kara. The sweat rolls down my back while my lungs breathe hard. Tugging her close, his words ripple around my head. Her hand comes over her stomach, and she holds it, sub-consciously protecting the life growing inside. I lean over, kiss her cheek and her covered belly, then slide out of bed.

Digging into the safe, I drag out the files and stare at them. Calling the only man I know who will possibly be awake at this ungodly hour, I pluck the matches out of the drawer and make my way outside.

With the first file empty and its contents burning, the gate latch clicks.

"Hey," John says on his approach. I glance back from my stance in front of the fire pit and take the beer he has brought out.

"Thanks." I open the second wallet and skim through the documents. Dropping them into the flames, one after another, it feels like a weight is being lifted as each one burns.

"I was wondering how long it would be before you got rid of them," he says, scraping a chair over the patio and slumping into it. I don't respond, because we both know this is long overdue. Some ten years overdue. I swallow a mouthful of beer watching history go up in smoke.

"How's Marie?" I ask, turning to him. He smiles disingenuously and shakes his head.

"Better. The nightmares have subsided, but I don't know, I can't place my finger on it. It's something else."

"Have you asked her?"

He laughs. "Do you think she'd tell me if I did? That woman's locked up tighter than the Crown Jewels! I'm sure she'll tell me when she's ready."

"So, you've not had Dominic look into her past?" I query, knowing full well he probably has. He knocks back the bottle, shuffling uncomfortably. "John?"

"He's done some digging. An ex-husband in Peterborough but nothing else comes up. And trust me, he's tried. Whatever she's hiding…" Shaking his head, he polishes off the beer and then picks up another. "Why did you call me over anyway?"

I shrug, not wanting to tell him, but know I shall. "Do you remember the day we first met?"

"Oh, yeah! I remember that cocky little kid you used to be. Still are in some ways. Why do you ask?"

I toss the empty wallet into the fire, then slouch in the chair and stare at the flames, concentrating on the crackle.

"I had a nightmare, John. I never told you, but that night, after Franklin left, Deacon came into my room, and he pointed his knife at me. He told me he would destroy everything I loved. I never mentioned it, because at the time I thought it was just talk. You remember what he was like. But he did everything he said he would. I don't have the heart to tell her. I finally have everything I've ever wanted, and a few simple words could tear it apart." The tears behind my eyes sting, because regardless of how many times my mother taught us not to lie, there are times that I must, and this is one of them.

"Kara already knows this, kid."

"John, she was never his obsession. We both know he would never have gone after her again if I hadn't pursued her. This is all me."

"No, don't do this to yourself again."

"I know, but I... I just want to be honest. I love her so much, the thought of losing her..." I blow out calmly.

John stands and motions me up. With his hands firmly on my head, he stares straight into my eyes. "Something you want to tell me?"

"She's pregnant," I whisper.

He laughs, and his broad, beaming smile says so much more than words ever will. "I once asked you when it would be enough. You told me when she had your name, your ring on her finger, and your child inside her. In my opinion, enough is finally here, but has it been worth the decade of suffering you've had to endure to get here?"

I nod my head as I answer. "Yeah, it's been worth it. Every time she questioned, every time she attempted to push me away. Trust me, she's worth it. There's nothing I wouldn't do if she asked me."

"Good. And just to reiterate, I was wrong."

I slap my hand on his back. Over the years, he has frequently apologised for forcing me to leave her behind. Looking back now, I see why he and my mother did it. It made me more determined.

"I love you like you're my son, and I'm proud of you, kid. I know I don't say it enough, but I am. And your father would be, too. The things I've done over the years; it was always with your best interests in mind. Kara will always be the one thing I'm not proud of, but I'm proud that you never gave up. Your love for her was always the driving force behind everything you did. I'm happy to call you my son and her my daughter."

I smile, embracing the man I look upon as my father. "You taught me how to shave, how to talk to girls, how to use condoms," I laugh, remembering the multitude of fruit he had me practice on whenever my mother was out. "But the one thing you didn't teach me was how to deal with love. The pain of it, the joy of it, the amazement of it."

"At the time, it wasn't something I was particularly proficient in!" he laughs, fixing his studious gaze on me.

The French doors open and Kara steps out, rubbing her sleepy eyes. "Hey," she whispers, and wraps the robe tighter around her waist. John lets me go, and I meet her somewhere in the middle. She grins at me and holds her belly inconspicuously.

John clears his throat and grins. "Congratulations, Mum," he says, kissing her cheek.

She smiles. "Thank you, grandad."

"Right then, I'm off. I'll see you both later."

Watching him walk away, the gate latch clicks. Turning back to my love, her fingers glide over the last file, and she looks at me with silent request. I nod as she pulls out the documents, skim reads them again like she did the last time, then one by one, she drops them on the fire.

"It's almost cleansing, isn't it?"

I nod; she's not wrong. The early morning sun starts to rise in the distance, and I tug her onto my lap. Brushing back her hair, she's luminous. Although it's far too early for any real noticeable changes, she definitely looks different.

"What are you thinking about?" Her voice cuts through my procrastinating, and I realise I've been lamenting for far too long.

"Just admiring how beautiful my wife is in her present, growing condition. I have to say, pregnancy suits you."

She cocks her brows in suspicion. "Don't be getting any ideas, I still have to push this one out first. Besides, if I'm too traumatised by the end of it, I may decide I don't want anymore. That coil might become very attractive in the future!"

"I love you so much."

"And I, you," she says, reaching up to kiss me. She snuggles into me, and I put a protective hand over our baby, hoping I have what it takes to be the amazing father that John was to me.

Six months later…

"That's the last of them, Sloan," Gloria says as she sets down the bundle of files.

Today, Sophie has decided to take the day off to spend it with Kara before our imminent arrival makes an appearance. After much coercing, and the fact I actually like having her out of control tongue in the office on days like today, I yielded.

"You're too kind, Gloria," I deadpan.

She laughs and makes her way to the door. "Shall I get the lovely Spencer's some more coffee? Looks like they need it." I nod and smile.

Skimming through the financial documents, it's a wonder the man is still afloat. I collect them up, then stride down the corridor, into the boardroom. Christy's eyes light up, but instantly diminish when she spies my wedding band. Glancing down at it, I grin, unable to rein it in.

"Hello, Mr Spencer, Mrs Spencer," I say, a little too cheery, greeting her forlorn looking parents. Mr Spencer scrunches his nose up – entirely expected - but his wife is more than accommodating.

"I hear you are soon to be a father. Congratulations, Sloan," she says, completely disinterested, gripping her daughter's hand. There was a time, long ago, when she thought it would be her daughter bearing my children. She thought wrong.

"Yes, thank you. My wife is due shortly." I smile, wanting to be hospitable.

"Do you know what you're having yet?"

My smile grows wider. After much debating – because I needed to know whether I would be chasing horny boys away from our house in years to come - Kara relented and allowed Doc to tell us the sex.

"A boy," I grin.

"Oh, that's gre-"

"Caroline, no disrespect, but we are not here to talk about his impending fatherhood!" Mr Spencer hisses out. I grind my jaw incessantly, thinking up ways to make him suffer if he dares to undermine me again.

Taking a breath, I pick up the documents. "Before we begin, have you had these witnessed?" I ask, wondering if the man took my advice and shoved them under his solicitor's nose. I sincerely hope he did, because the outcome of today's meeting is not going to be pretty.

"Yes!" he hisses in frustration.

I randomly flick through and check the execution pages, and satisfaction spreads through me. It's not the type of satisfaction knowing his crazy daughter has finally realised she will never be any part of my life, it's the satisfaction of knowing that every six months I will not be sitting here, speaking words that will never change. Unfortunately, his signature on the pages confirms he is now, technically, an employee, and that is something he will find hard in the long run. And something we are, no doubt, going to have numerous arguments over in the future.

The door opens, and Gloria steps in, carrying the offered beverages. Kindly pouring me a coffee – something I never expect her to do - she bends down.

"Stuart just called. He asked you to call him back ASAP," she whispers. I nod, making a mental note to ring him as soon as this unfortunate meeting is through.

"Right, let's begin," I say, the same moment my mobile rings incessantly. "Sorry," I mutter, plucking it out, ready to silence it when Stuart's name flashes. "Sorry, I need to take this."

"Sloan?"

"Yes, Doc?"

"Why haven't you called me back yet?" he rushes out.

"I'm in with clients."

"Kara's just being admitted. She's gone into labour."

"What? She's not due for another four weeks!" I shout; concern, panic and fear already taking over.

"I guess he'll take after his father then – bloody impatient! Have you left the goddamn building yet?"

Looking around, Mr Spencer rolls his eyes, and I glare at him, while Christy stares down at the table sadly.

The door is thrown open, and Gloria runs in as fast as she can and lobs my bag on the table. "John's outside. Go, now!"

"Sloan, don't panic, she'll be fine," Doc says nonchalantly. Easy for him to say, we'll see how the good doc reacts when he's in my position.

"I'm on my way. Don't let him out until I get there!"

Stuart laughs. "I don't think we have a choice in that respect."

"Just look after my babies until I'm there!"

"Always will. Just get your arse over here!"

I run out of the door and into the first lift. Sprinting through the ground floor reception, John grabs me as soon as the front door is open.

"Calm down!" he says, also looking a little on the stressed side.

I climb into the Range Rover and thank the Lord above that he didn't get his licence revoked. As we speed through the streets, my heart is beating rapidly. I consciously chew my fingers, fearful that I might not be a good dad.

John's hand slaps down on my leg. "It's okay to be scared, kid. She'll be fine. Doc and Marie are with her," he says, as we pull up outside the hospital entrance and Dev runs out.

"She's in the delivery suite. Move!" he says, getting into the driver's seat.

Racing through the corridors, I finally reach the delivery ward. Stuart is already waiting at the nurse's station, holding out a set of scrubs.

"Hurry!"

A piercing cry echoes from a room, and I halt because as always, I would recognise it anywhere. Throwing the door open, Marie is holding Kara's hand and strokes her face as she lets out another.

Shifting around the bed quickly, she smiles and it's heartbreaking and elating at the same time. "I'm here, baby. I love you," I say, as another cry emits her throat.

I toss the scrubs down, shrug out of my jacket, then grip her hand. A sickness churns inside, because the truth is, it physically hurts to have to witness her doing this, and there is nothing I can do to assist. Not to mention, I put it there. The same way I intend to put a few more there in the future. *Hopefully.*

"How are you doing, honey?" Stuart asks.

"Oh, fine!" she answers sarcastically, tired and breathless. Her fingers tighten on mine again, and she grimaces.

Doc takes up his position, which I'm definitely not happy about, but I'll see him later about that. "You're almost fully dilated, Kara. Looks like he's finally ready to meet his parents."

"Oh, God, that hurts!" she whines, squeezing my hand in a death grip, bellowing out a pained cry as another contraction tears through her.

I discreetly grind my teeth as she clenches my fingers harder. Yet in comparison to what she is doing right now, I have no right to complain.

"Oh shit, that hurts! Stuart?" she calls out. "I've changed my mind. I want drugs, lots of them! And I want an epidural! And I want them all now!"

"Too late for that, little man's coming."

She lets out another cry, then turns and glares at me. "And just so you know, I'm getting that coil fitted. I'm not going through this again!"

She continues to tell me what I will and will not be doing while breathing as per Stuart's instruction. Marie sits beside her, wiping her head, soothing her between contractions.

"It's okay, baby, let it out," she encourages her daughter further. She then turns to me with a smile. "Don't you want to watch your son being born, darling?"

I instantly look at my beautiful, yet already exhausted wife, who smiles and nods in agreement. Letting go of her hand, I pull up a stool next to Stuart. I feel conflicted, but Marie's right, I do want to watch him come into the world.

"Right, honey, push whenever you're ready," Stuart says, as Kara cries out.

Fifteen minutes later, it finally happens.

His angry cry penetrates the room, and Stuart holds up a screaming, dirty bundle of blood, placenta, and a shock of dark, spiky hair.

"Sloan? Do you want to cut the umbilical, Dad?" I nod, still in temporary shock that the moment we've waited months for is finally here. And that in the space of a few minutes, our world has just been completed. I carefully snip where indicated and step back, for the first time in my life, I don't know what to do.

Stuart puts my screaming boy on the scales and smiles. "Eight pounds, six ounces. You did amazing, Mum."

Marie looks fit to burst with happiness, as a nurse passes Stuart a clean towel and he wraps up our tiny squirming bundle. He moves around to Kara, who is equal amounts of shattered and ecstatic. I shift beside her as Marie helps her up. Stuart hands over our new arrival and Kara tenderly rocks him inside her arms, as the door closes leaving us alone.

"You did it. I'm so proud of you." I kiss her at length, feeling so full of love.

"We made him," she whispers softly, after a long, comfortable pause. Tears flood my eyes as she starts to brush his cheek with her finger.

"We did, and he's perfect," I confirm, watching the loves of my life bond for the first time. "Have you thought of any names?" I query, wrapping my arms around the two most important things in the world.

She shakes her head. "No, I want you to have that privilege." I tilt her chin and kiss her firmly.

"Oliver John, after my fathers," I confirm.

"I like that." She smiles and gently places him in my arms. "Meet Daddy, Oliver John Foster." I stare at her and smile through my tears.

Holding my son tight to my chest and his mother in my arm, I turn her face around. She wipes her eyes and nestles into me, kissing his chubby little hand. She's about to speak, when Stuart pops his head around the door again.

"Ready for a visitor?" I raise a brow, as my sister runs into the room and squeals in happiness. I huff out annoyed, as she takes the baby. Doc helps her into a seat, and she coos at Oliver, babbling on about how great his aunts and uncles are.

"I love you. Thanking you for giving me him, for completing me," my beloved says, watching Charlie with our son.

"I've got you, my love. Both of you, always."

A few months later…

"Baby?" I call out as I enter.

I undo my tie and lay it on the table in the hallway, next to the dummy and bottle taking pride of place beside one of the many large baby pictures.

I pick them up as I pass, and move down the hallway, making sure I don't fall over the toys that he's far too young to play with scattered around – a result of my mother and sister and their apparent broodiness.

Soft music drifts through the house as I get closer and closer.

Entering the kitchen, I put the baby stuff in the sink and switch off the steriliser.

A soft, beautiful whine leads me to the French doors and I still, observing the loves of my life in an intimate mother and son embrace. Oliver is laying against her chest, and her hand covers his nappy clad bottom. My gorgeous girl is sat in one of the large patio chairs looking out over the lawns and adjacent woodland, while my son is suckling away, his small hand trying to grip the source of his feed to no avail.

I hang back, not wanting to disturb the picture-perfect moment. My heart fills to capacity – not that it isn't ever that way these days – as I watch my family. Instinctually, she turns and gives me a beaming smile.

"Hi, I didn't hear you come in," she says, picking up the remote and pointing it over her shoulder towards the CD player.

Oliver burps against her chest, and she carefully pulls him off her breast. I move towards her, pick up a tissue and wipe her tender nipple, bestowing it with a kiss before covering her up. Leaning down for a kiss, she opens up effortlessly, and I indulge in my favourite pastime that is my wife.

Picking up my boy, I hold him in my arms as I sit on the lounger and Kara curls up against me, toying with his fingers.

"I'll never get enough of him," she says.

"No, me neither. Either of you. Ever." She lifts up and smiles.

I gaze at the sun setting in the distance, aware it's time to be honest again. "I've waited for this moment for over a decade. Yet it still doesn't feel enough." She gives me a look of confusion. "Baby, I want to experience everything with you. I've been thinking when he's a little older, I might step down for a couple of years, hand over to Ken. I don't know, nothing's concrete, just an idea at the moment. I don't want to be one of those father's that only sees his kids when they're asleep because work gets in the way. I want to see the world with you and our boy." I look down at him as he gurgles and shuffles his bum. "I want to lay on a beach with him and build sandcastles. I want to see the expression on your face at every new sight we see. I thought maybe we'll go and spend some time with my mother. I know she's dying to see him again. A month isn't long enough, she says."

"Hmm, sounds wonderful," she murmurs.

"Like I said, it's just an idea at the moment, my love."

"I'd love to see the world with you, too, Mr Foster."

Kissing her forehead, every moment, from the first time I picked her up in that cubbyhole, to holding that broken girl in my arms when she returned, comes back in full force. Every single one from soul destroying to life-changing has defined me.

There are a million things I would do differently if given half the chance. And the first thing I would do is walk straight back into that hospital room. Still, I can't change anything, and life has given us what we have now. It hasn't been smooth or easy, and we've faced more adversity and heartbreak than most, but unfortunately, we both had to go there to come back again.

Finally, we have come full circle, and as painful as that is, we both now have closure.

Holding my wife and son tight to my chest, I close my eyes and remember the day she changed my world.

"I've got you, baby. I've got you."

Author Note

Liberated is the third instalment in the series and concludes Kara and Sloan's story.

Not ready to say goodbye just yet?

Faithless is the fourth instalment of the Fractured series and is Marie and John's story. It is a long, slow burning, all the feels book, set over three decades.... Keep turning to read the preview at the end.

Faithless is available to download now.

Finally, if you enjoyed this novel, please consider sparing a few moments to leave a review.

Follow Elle

If you wish to be notified of future releases, special offers, discounted books, ARC opportunities, and more, please subscribe to Elle's mailing list

Alternatively, you can connect with Elle on the following sites:

Website: www.ellecharles.com

Facebook: www.facebook.com/elle.charles

Twitter: www.twitter.com/@ellecharles

Bookbub: www.bookbub.com/authors/elle-charles

Instagram: www.instagram.com/elle.charlesauthor

Or by email:

elle.charlesauthor@gmail.com

elle@ellecharles.com

About the Author

Elle was born and raised in Yorkshire, England, where she still resides.

A self-confessed daydreamer, she loves to create strong, diverse characters, cocooned in opulent yet realistic settings that draw the reader in with every twist and turn until the very last page.

A voracious reader for as long as she can remember, she is never without her beloved Kindle. When she is not absorbed in the newest release or a trusted classic, she can often be found huddled over her laptop, tapping away new ideas and plots for forthcoming works.

Works by Elle Charles

All titles are available to purchase exclusively through Amazon.

The Fractured Series:

Kara and Sloan
Fractured (Book 1)
Tormented (Book 2)
Aftermath (Book 2.5)
Liberated (Book 3)

Marie and John
Faithless (Book 4)

Printed in Great Britain
by Amazon

54214287R00234